You'll h......................whispered, shivering violently. "I'm here and I can't help myself, you know. At least, hold me so I won't be so cold."

He laughed. "Oh, I'll hold you, okay. You'll get to like it here. Think of it as home, maybe, even. . . ."

Then he seemed to descend upon her like a great slow wave from the black lake. . . .

There were feet on the stairs, several heavy people coming up. Voices outside the door, then in the room with her. *They'll take me home*, Kate thought, *they'll snap me out of this*.

One took her arm to lift it. But it clung to her side, resisting his pull without the least effort on her part.

He said, "My own guess is two, three days since she died."

BAEN BOOKS by Fred Saberhagen

The Dracula Tape
The Vlad Tapes
Pilgrim
Berserkers: The Beginning

THE VLAD TAPES

This is a work of fiction. All the characters and events portrayed in this book are fictional, and any resemblance to real people or incidents is purely coincidental.

A Baen Books Original

Baen Publishing Enterprises
P.O. Box 1403
Riverdale, NY 10471

ISBN: 0-671-57878-2

Cover art by Stephen Hickman

First printing, July 2000

Distributed by Simon & Schuster
1230 Avenue of the Americas
New York, NY 10020

Production by Windhaven Press, Auburn, NH
Printed in the United States of America

THE
VLAD TAPES

FRED SABERHAGEN

CONTENTS

Printed in the United States of America

AN OLD FRIEND
OF THE FAMILY

ONE

It looked like the North Atlantic raging at the Devon coast, Kate told herself, recalling a childhood trip to Europe, and the enduring memory of the ocean pounding at those rough English rocks. Now, under the glare of the close-ranked floodlights along the Outer Drive, she saw the black lake reach a fist in past the wintry void, where summer knew a strip of sunwhite beach. Above the ice-draped slats of snowfence the fist shook spume at city and civilization, then crashed down, dissolving itself in an open-handed splash that washed across six of the eight lanes of forty-mile-per-hour traffic. The traffic wavered, minimally slowing, some of it skidding perilously in the freezing wet. If things kept on this way, the police were going to have to close the Drive.

Twenty or thirty yards inland, on pavement separated from the Drive and the reaching waves by a wide divider strip of frozen parkland, Kate's Lancia purred sedately south. Most of her attention was concentrated upon the task of reading addresses from the endless row of tall apartment buildings fronting on Drive and park and lake. The particular numbers she had been looking for now suddenly appeared, elegantly backlighted against a towering granite wall. She slowed and turned. The righthand curve of driveway went down to a basement garage, but she stayed with the left branch, rolled past two parked Cadillacs and a Porsche, and pulled up under the building's canopy.

Despite the heatlamps fighting down against the wind and cold, the uniformed doorman wore earmuffs above the collar of his winter jacket. His eyeglasses were so thick as to resemble frosted protective goggles of some sort. Taller than he, Kate swept in through the door that he held open for her, meanwhile pulling back the hood of her warm blue jacket from natural blond curls.

"I'd like to see Craig Walworth. Tell him Kate Southerland is here," she told the man when he had followed her into the lobby. A few moments later, after the intercom had brought down Craig's acceptance of her visit, she was alone in a small elevator.

If Joe were with her now, he'd be worrying about what the doorman was going to do with the car—or about something else, about anything, maybe just about dropping in on a party unannounced. But then if Joe were with her tonight, she wouldn't be coming here at all. Which, of course, was really the whole point. She hadn't made any commitment to Joe—not yet. If and when she did, things would be different.

And how they would.

Maybe the real point was the fact that she felt compelled to make the point. If she was so certain of her present freedom, why was she here trying to prove something to herself? She could have gone Christmas shopping instead. And she probably should have. For one thing she still faced the problem of a gift for Joe, who was certain to spend too much of his money buying one for her . . .

The elevator, having gone as high as it could go,

eased almost imperceptibly to a stop and let Kate out into a small marble lobby from which two massive doors of handcarved black wood, one at each end, led to two apartments. A small decorative table, ivory colored to contrast with the doors, stood in the middle of the lobby facing the two elevators. On the wall just above the table there hung a picture, or perhaps it was a mirror, of which only an edge of antique gilt frame was visible. Someone had draped an old, worn-looking raincoat over it, perhaps thinking that the loser of the garment would be sure to see it there if he came back. He'd need something warmer than that if he came back tonight.

The righthand door stood slightly ajar, and through this opening came sounds of subdued partying: music, an alto laugh, a glassy clink, and voices murmuring. Kate pushed the thick door fully open and slowly walked on in. She stood in a brick-floored vestibule, from which two interior hallways led off at right angles to each other. A third wall was taken up by a great guest closet, open now to show a modest miscellany of coats and scarves, some fallen from their hangers. It didn't seem that any very large party was going on.

"Hi." The greeting was conspiratorially low. Simultaneously a black-haired, black-bearded head bobbed into Kate's view from two rooms down the hallway to her right. Craig Walworth was three or four years older than her twenty. No more than an inch taller, but so wide across the chest that he looked larger than he was. Often, as now, his shirt was worn halfway open down the front to display some hair and muscle; and he tended to have his large hands planted on his hips—one of them was there now, the other holding a drink—so that standing near him put you at some risk of jutting elbows. "Glad you could make it, Kate. I was starting to think you were really out of circulation." The drink he had been holding somehow already stashed away, he took her jacket as she slipped it off, and with a toss consigned it to the closet's minor chaos.

"You put out a standing invitation for Friday nights, Craig. I'm just taking you at your word."

"I'm just delighted that you are, sweetie. Our little group here will never be the same—thank God." Craig's voice was still low, uncharacteristically near the whispering level, and now he glanced about, a man checking to see if he might be overheard. "Now listen, Doll, there's a little house rule I've got to mention before you join the group."

"Rules? That's not quite what I would have expected at your parties."

"Well, you see, it's not your basic expectable kind of rule." As they talked, he had started her moving down the hall toward the still rather muffled sounds of partying, with an arm round her waist that she somehow minded more than the expected cheek-kiss following. "The thing is, everyone—except me, of course—takes a new name for the evening, and pretends to be someone other than they are. Sabrina Something, and I'll say that you're an old friend of mine from Canada. How's that?"

"Well, I did think of becoming Sabrina once, believe it or not. When I was about thirteen years old."

They had now come to a room where four or five people were gathered, all standing, as if none of them had been here very long. Kate so rarely remembered names the first time round that sometimes she was tempted to give up trying; and since these were supposedly all aliases anyway, she made no effort to retain anything from the round of introductions.

Beside Kate stood a tall girl wearing an odd shawl who wanted to find out how much Kate knew about Tarot cards. When she heard the answer was nothing at all, she wanted to explain them at great length.

Kate tried for a little while to make sense of it, and then, as the group shifted, took the first opportunity to move away. She was offered a drink, declined, then thought that the next time she would accept. In the background she could hear a heavy door, probably the front door of the apartment, being firmly closed. Craig had excused himself, and was somewhere around a corner, talking on the phone.

"Try a joint?" This from a stocky young man with thick glasses who had not been in the group the first time round—no doubt there might be other people she had not met, in other rooms; it must be a huge apartment. The man making the offer got too close, and stared at Kate intensely. Being given a man's full attention is a thrilling experience for a woman—well, sometimes. Hadn't she seen him somewhere else recently? But she had no intention of asking that aloud.

Kate puffed twice and put the thing down. As expected, she felt nothing from it just at first. The few times that she had tried, in school, nothing at all had happened to her. The few times after that had always resulted in a pleasant high, with slow onset and letdown. She wouldn't be surprised if it was nothing at all again tonight; quite likely she was just too keyed up, too nervous, though why she should be . . .

". . . play games in a little while, you know, identities and such." Craig was back at her side, finishing a statement whose beginning Kate had somehow missed. "And someone else is coming, Sabrina, someone I want you to meet. I've mentioned you to him, and he's very interested."

"Oh? My Canadian background?"

Craig's eyes were sparkling with some inner amusement under their dark brows. But now his attention was forced away by someone else, a blondish boy with a loud mouth, who had some interminable anecdote to tell him, as one insider to another. Craig responded with off-hand but deliberate insults, which the loud one laughed at foolishly.

Kate almost tripped over the tall girl, then sat down beside her on the thick, burgundy-colored carpet. "What sort of games is he talking about?" Kate asked. The girl said something Kate couldn't catch. Very loud music was starting in the next room. The Pointer Sisters?

Upon the wall that Kate was facing there hung an Escher print, the circle of lizards crawling up out of the flat surface of the drawing-within-the-drawing, crawling up and around an improvised ramp of books and geometric solids, to ease themselves at last down into the flat again, where in three shades of gray their bodies formed a tessellated pattern. Kate willed for a moment to lose herself in the intricacies of the plan, but her mind was too restless.

She looked around abruptly, with the feeling that someone, no one she knew, had just called her real name: a loud, rude calling in a strange man's voice. But no one else seemed to have noticed it at all. And the voice seemed to have come, now that she thought about it, directly into her mind, not through her ears. Dear Kate, she warned herself, neither you nor Sabrina had better smoke any more tonight.

Restlessness pulled her to her feet. A bar-on-a-cart offered bottles and glasses and ice. Shouldn't mix with the other stuff, but just a taste was not going to do her any harm. In her hand, a glass half-filled with white wine, she wandered, mocking a slinky tall-model walk, up to a window of very solid, unopenable glass that looked out far above the endless chains of head-lights and taillights of the Drive. Beyond the few additional streetlamps that were scattered through the park, the lake stretched out to the edge of everything, a vast black invisibility like death.

One of the nameless boys she had just met came

to the window too, ice cubes tinkling in his glass like Christmas music. God, the shopping she had yet to do. What was she here for, anyway? Trying to prove a point to Joe, who didn't know where she was, and who, when she told him, would fail to get the—

Her name again, but still unspoken.

Looking down a vista of the apartment's archways, Kate saw a huge, dark-haired man standing gazing toward her. An early Orson Welles, but harder-faced, in a brown coat made of one of those rich fake-furs, like her own blue. Or maybe in his case the fur was real. He was standing there as if he had just arrived, though if her sense of the place was right, he was nowhere near the front entrance.

With a vague feeling that it was important, necessary for her to do so, Kate turned from the window and walked toward the newcomer. No one else seemed to be paying either of them the least attention. The Pointer Sisters grew louder still, then faded abruptly as a door somewhere behind Kate was closed. She was alone with the huge man in the hallway—no, not quite alone. From the corner of her eye Kate saw Craig walk out of another doorway to her left. Craig fell into step beside her as she walked the last few strides toward the big man who stood waiting.

They stopped. Craig put his hands on his hips, then at once let them slide off to hang fidgeting at his sides. "Enoch Winter," he said, almost whispering again, "this is Kathryn Southerland."

The huge man said something (what?) to her in an offhand sort of greeting, and she replied. He was really massive, and Kate was reminded of when she had met an All-American defensive end: perfect proportions, but blown up larger than real life seemed to have the right to be.

Enoch Winter's dark hair was slightly curly, and worn shorter than that of most young men. There were only the beginnings of lines in his face. Still, at second glance Kate would not have called him young if she had had to set down a description. His eye were gray-blue, his broad, pale cheeks a little blue with what would be heavy stubble in a few hours if he let it grow. He was smiling confidently at Kate, and all but ignoring Craig. He spoke to her again; once more she somehow could not grasp what he had said.

There was a brief distraction as the short young man with thick eyeglasses appeared from somewhere to stand at Kate's right, looking on in silence. The four of them in the hallway were closed off now by doors on every side. Beyond the closed doors, the sounds of the party went on.

Enoch Winter spoke, and Kate stared at him, straining to understand. His voice was loud enough. And she thought the pot would not take hold of her tonight. She shouldn't even have tasted the wine.

He chuckled, perhaps at something he had just said himself. He didn't seem to notice that she could not comprehend what he was saying. Or else he did not care. With a faint inward start Kate realized that Craig and Thick-glasses were no longer at her sides. They had gone away somewhere, leaving her standing in the shut-off hall with Enoch Winter, who talked and talked, to her alone. She must not ever let her attention waver from him for a moment, must not . . .

His whitish hand, raised, was so big that the great dark stone that rode one finger in a silver ring seemed not only modest but scarcely adequate. Just past his waving hand Kate's eye caught sight of a phone on a hall table, and it came to her with desperate force that there was something she must do at once.

"Excuse me a moment," she broke in clearly. "I've got to call home right away."

". . . hafta do that for?" His accent was midwestern, vaguely rural. All of a sudden he wasn't happy any more.

"I have to. That's all." Walking to the phone was the most utterly wearying thing that Kate had ever done. She managed to do it, though.

". . . careful whatcha say. All right." Enoch's voice had regained some of its good humor, and now good-humoredly he fell silent.

Kate punched at buttons. She could hear the phone at home start ringing, and then a familiar voice.

"Hello, Gran. I just wanted to tell you . . ." What could she say? What was she able to say? "I didn't do any shopping after all. So I couldn't get those things you wanted."

"Well, goodness, dear. Don't worry about it. You sound upset, are you all right?"

"Fine."

"Well, I expect I'll be going out myself tomorrow, I can do my own shopping. Where are you?"

A leaden pause, in which Kate could feel her own mind groping. Crawling. Trying to get free, but leashed. "Downtown," she got out at last. It was almost the truth, the closest thing to truth that she could manage.

"Take care now, Kate, they say the roads are very nasty."

As she cradled the phone Enoch started talking to her again. In this case it really was flattering to have such concentrated attention from a man, attention of a kind she could not get often enough from Joe.

Somehow or other they now were standing by the guest closet and Enoch was watching while she put on her blue jacket. In some far-off room of the apartment voices were cheering now—probably a game was being played. Craig was here again, though, to see them out in silence. Enoch tossed a—condescending?—wink at Craig, whose own face displayed a vast . . . well, admiration, as though for something Enoch was doing or had done. Kate puzzled over all this while she walked out to the elevator, her hand on Enoch's arm.

Going down with Enoch, she thought for the most part about nothing at all. While he perhaps was thinking of her, for once or twice he put out his huge, pale hand and brushed her cheek with it, rather as if she were something that he had long coveted and had just allowed himself to buy. She wouldn't like it if Joe behaved so possessively. But this was different . . . of course.

The elevator let them out in the subterranean garage, and there was her Lancia, keys and all. Kate slipped into the driver's seat, Enoch waiting till he was invited to get in on the right. There was no doorman to be seen, but gates opened ahead of them and out they went, into the cold and up the curving driveway.

Kate drove, without having to think of where to go. As before, Enoch talked, and it seemed to her that she could not understand a word. White needles filled bright globes of air around the streetlights. In some clear corner of Kate's mind the thought occurred that nothing she had ever smoked before had hit her this way. Once the situation struck her so ridiculous that she began to laugh, and laughed so hard and wildly that it was difficult for her to see where she was steering. Enoch spoke sharply to her and she calmed down. Then it was his turn to laugh, loudly and heartily, evidently at something Kate had just tried to say. The trouble was that something in his laughter hurt Kate's ears, so she wanted to put her fingers into them, but instead she had to go on driving.

They had already turned inland, away from the lake, leaving the Outer Drive and the Gold Coast behind. Was this Diversey she was following now? She wasn't sure. Probably they were farther south. Presently she turned again, going where she had to go. Here the street lamps were fewer, and gave a different

light, wan and wintry. It was surprising how in the
city the neighborhoods could change from one block
to the next.

Now here was where they were to stop. Certainly
no doorman here, in fact not even a break in the row
of dull vehicles parked along the frozen curb. Near
the end of the block a fireplug-space at least was
open, and Kate halted just ahead of it and started
to back in.

A car just behind them turned into the same space
headfirst, jounced to a halt there just as Kate also
hit her brakes. At the moment both vehicles had a
tirehold on the precious space, but neither could
occupy it.

She turned to Enoch helplessly. There was an
abstracted expression on his face; he opened his door
and got out. His head vanished from Kate's view, but
from the attitude of his body it was plain that he was
facing back into the glare of their challenger's headlights. Cold air swirled in through the open door to
paw Kate's legs. An engine gunned behind them; the
other car was backing away. Enoch slid in beside her
again and closed the door, the look on his face
unchanged.

Kate parked the car—must have parked it, though
the next thing she was aware of was walking along
the cracked and narrow sidewalk beside Enoch, whose
arm encircled her but brought no warmth. The footing
was treacherous, half uneven pavement, half blackened ice in old refrozen mounds, all under a pow-
dering of new snow. When had she ever felt cold so
intense before?

They passed beneath an ancient neon sign hum-
ming to itself and sizzling with unplanned flashes. A
man went by them, his face as hard and his clothes
as grimy as the street itself. Suddenly there were two
wooden steps, a narrow door that yielded to Enoch's
shoulder, and now at least the wind was gone.

The cold kept pace, though, as they walked up stairs, bare wood creaking underfoot beneath the gritty crunching of a layer of grime. It would be terrible to have to face a night like this alone, but she would not, no, she would not. She clung hard now to Enoch's arm.

He used a key, then brought her through a door into a room of utter cold, a wretchedly furnished room, dark but for pale streetlight coming in through an undraped window. Kate saw smeared glass, one broken pane with rags stuffed into it.

"You'll have to hold me," she whispered, shivering violently. "I'm here and I can't help myself, you know. At least hold me so I won't be so cold."

He laughed. When he spoke now she could hear him plainly. "Oh, I'll hold you, okay. You'll get to like it here. Think of it as home, maybe, even. Wise little rich-bitch." He had closed the door and was standing right in front of her. "You think you know just what is gonna happen now. But you don't know at all, at all."

Then he seemed to descend upon her like a great slow wave from the black lake.

TWO

In the rather more than thirty years since Clarissa
Southerland had come to live in Glenlake, this was
almost the first time that anyone on the village police
force had spoken to her in line of duty. And it
occurred to her to wonder now, somewhat belatedly
no doubt, whether this aloofness from the cops was
after all not a continent-wide American peculiarity,
but simply the result of living in a wealthy suburb.
In England as a girl and young woman she had chatted with the constables routinely; but England, of
course, was different.

Detective Franzen, a balding, sad-looking young
man, was listening to Clarissa's account of Kate's last
phone call home with every appearance of totally
absorbed, sympathetic attention. His behavior was not
at all like that of the New York detectives, years ago,
that time the jewels were taken at the hotel. Meanwhile Kate's mother Lenore, was standing behind
Franzen and worriedly eyeing her mother-in-law as
if Clarissa were some undependable child who might
not perform creditably for the nice policeman. Behind
Lenore was the closed door to the study, and behind

that in turn was Andrew, busy talking on the phone to his office, where people were sure to be working even on Saturday, working on something vital that demanded some of Andrew's attention, even on the day of a missing daughter.

"Now, Mrs. Southerland, do you remember there being any unusual background noises on the phone? Sometimes there's a typewriter, or . . ."

"Not at parties, there isn't very often." Suddenly Clarissa began to lose confidence in Franzen, nice manners or not. It made her feel fidgety, and she wished she had taken a rocking chair, instead of this plush one, which was too soft.

"Oh, you did hear partying noises then?"

"Yes, I believe I mentioned that before." Hadn't she? She couldn't confirm from Lenore's or Franzen's expressions now whether she had or not. "People laughing, way in the background. Ice, tinkling in a glass? No, I couldn't swear to that."

"And all she said about her location was that she was downtown?"

"Yes."

"Anyone call anyone by name?"

Clarissa took thought. Sometimes one gained impressions of things not exactly by hearing them, and later it was hard to sort out what one had actually heard and what one had not. "Not that I recall."

Franzen, poker-faced, seated on a straight chair opposite, studied his notebook. "Well. You all tell me that this staying out without letting someone know is not something that Kate's ever done—"

"It certainly isn't," put in Lenore.

"—and here it is well after noon. So, I think we'd better take it seriously enough to check it out. The Chicago police, and so on." Franzen stood up, just as the door to the study opened. Andrew, balding too, but athletic and aggressive in his mid-forties, came out to join the conversation.

"What progress have we made?" Andrew demanded with brisk intensity. Here was a man switching his attention from one crisis to another, and someone had better have ready a satisfactory, concise briefing for him if they wanted his advice and help on the problem of locating his daughter, because some new emergency regarding business was surely going to come up soon and keep him from spending a lot of time on this one.

This, at least, was the impression his mother got of him at the moment. Clarissa, feeling a twinge of guilt because there were times when she just didn't like her own son very much, grunted and hand-fought her way up out of the too-soft chair: the knees and hips were not too good today. Muttering a few words of farewell to Detective Franzen, she left the search for her granddaughter in the hands of those who were now in charge of running the world, and took herself off to the library, meaning to have a look at the lake through her favorite window.

In the room lined with shelves of dark wood, with the door closed behind her, it was quiet, the murmur of concerned voices almost left behind. Beyond the double Thermopane a field of virgin snow, fallen mostly in the dark hours of the morning, sloped away to disappear over the top of a thirty-foot bluff some forty yards behind the house. Looking past that brink, Clarissa could see a mile or more south along the gently curving shoreline of Lake Michigan. There were trees, there were the houses of the wealthy. The beach was completely hidden beneath a frigid wilderness of ice-cakes, foot-thick slabs that had been broken by waves, washed in and upended in a crazy jumble, stretching for lifeless kilometers under the lifeless sun of afternoon. Beyond the icefields, dark open water reached victorious, almost calm now, to the horizon.

A voice asked: "Granny?"

In jeans and old shirt Judy leaned against the jamb of the re-opened library door. Three years younger than the missing Kate, somewhat darker of hair and eye, more strongly built, not quite as conventionally pretty—but quite possibly, their grandmother thought, fated to be the more beautiful of the two when both were full-grown women.

Smiling involuntarily, Clarissa turned from the window. "What is it, dear?"

The girl was solemn. "Is there any news yet?"

"No. Except it seems that the police *are* going to start looking for her."

"Has anyone called Joe?"

"I doubt that anyone has. And I think you're right; it's probably time that someone did."

Judy's eyes, as they often did, seemed to be probing for the true thoughts of the person she was speaking to. "Do you want to, Gran? Or I will if you like."

Clarissa hesitated, then answered with a nod. Calling Joe was best not left to Andrew or Lenore. "You have the touch, Judy. He'll take bad news—or alarming news anyway—better coming from you than anyone else. If you don't mind." Helping was what this girl had to do when she was worried, as some people had to mope and others to cry. Blessed is the family, Clarissa thought, that has a Judy in it; and I don't know of any other one than ours.

Judy was gone, considerately closing the door behind her. But Clarissa had hardly turned toward the icefields again when it opened again. "Hey, Gran?" a deeper voice inquired.

This was Johnny, the baby of the house. At sixteen he was a strong-jawed, slightly shorter version of his father, one notable difference being Johnny's teen-length, light brown curls. "They're all still busy in there, Gran. If anyone's looking for me, I'm going over to Clark's. He's got that new computer kit."

"Don't be late, Johnny. I'm sure your mother will want you back before dark today."

"Aw, Gran, c'mon. Kate's all right." No doubts at all were going to be tolerated on that point. "She's a big girl. I mean, I know my sister can take care of herself out there."

"And you're grown up too, or very nearly. Yes. But don't be late?"

She made it a question rather than a hopeless attempt at an order, and Johnny at least smiled and waved before he left, so maybe he would at least consider what his grandmother said. Then he was gone, and there was no longer anything to interfere with Clarissa's looking out the window. It took her only a minute to discover that that was not what she wanted to do after all.

It was good to get away from the tension in the family for a little while, to have time for her own thoughts. But why had she chosen the library? Had it been in the back of her mind to find something particular to read?

Clarissa was staring up at the east end of the highest shelf on the south wall when with a minor inward shock she consciously remembered what was up there. Years, it had been, since she had even thought of that. She shook her head deliberately, and deliberately smiled at herself, and moved away. But her steps slowed as she neared the door, which Johnny had left open. Clarissa closed it slowly. She did not want to rejoin the others just yet, she wanted to stay here.

She had been seated in an armchair for ten minutes, reading lamp on beside her, reading a John O'Hara novel, when she suddenly fully understood that she had stationed herself here on guard, on call. She was on sentry duty, a few paces from the east end of the high south shelves. This time she did not try to smile at all.

THREE

On regaining consciousness, Kate was no longer bothered by the cold, and at first she knew a trace of fear that hers were the sensations of death-by-freezing. But her fingers and toes were perfectly flexible and sensitive, her ears were not at all numb, and she was not shivering. Still cold in the room, certainly, but her body was coping with it now. A sort of second wind, evidently—or a second warmth might be a better way to put it.

It was still night, though now she could see the room and its poor furnishings much more clearly than before. Maybe another electric sign had been turned on outside, or more likely her eyes had simply adjusted to the dark. She thought that not much time had passed, for she seemed still to be feeling the effects of what she had smoked, combined with the white wine. But now she was completely alone.

She could remember Enoch's face above hers in the dark, and his weight, pressing her down on the poor bed, where she still lay on her back, atop whatever bedclothes there might be. A forced intimacy, certainly, but not, as far as she could tell, a conventional rape. She was still fully dressed, lying there with her right arm thrown back above her head, and her left hand resting loosely on her middle.

Kate sat up, easily, not hurting anywhere, groping with her toes automatically for one shoe that had fallen off. With this strange high of hers she was not in the mood to wonder about the why of anything, to worry about whether she had actually been raped or not.

Both shoes on, Kate stood up, a little giddily just at first, and observed that she was still wearing her warm blue jacket. There appeared to be nothing to do in this room, so at once she headed for the door.

She went quickly down the creaky stairs, and out into the shabby, unfamiliar street. At the moment fear and worry were as remote to her as curiosity. Maybe in the morning she would have the world's worst hangover, but right now she simply felt like walking. The sky had cleared, as clear as it ever got above the city itself.

Still feeling immune to cold and wind, Kate set out, marching in a direction she was sure was east, and noting the steady diminution of the address numbers that she passed, numbers that seemed to indicate that she had not too far to go, to reach the shops on North Michigan. These days all the best shopping was up there, not in the Loop.

She passed a man who turned to look at her, perhaps only wondering that she dared to walk Chicago's streets at night and alone. In this neighborhood there were only a few people about. What time was it, anyway? Might the stores be closed? Kate's watch showed 7:48 when she pressed its button—which was odd, considering that it must have been later than that when she left Craig's. But she was not capable of trying to puzzle it all out now. She was going to walk.

She came upon Michigan boulevard from the west,

passing through a region of closed printing shops, closed antique dealers, nearly empty parking lots, ad agencies all but anonymous behind their discreet signs, walls, and shutters. An elegant restaurant was open, so was a fast-food place a block away. She didn't feel at all hungry. Here was a subway entrance. She had ridden the subway and El once with Johnny, from Evanston all the way down through the city to the far South Side and back again, just to see what it was like, and nothing had happened to them at all, though their parents had been angry when they found out . . . and here were the stairs to the upper level of Michigan, where she would find the shops she wanted.

And here on the upper level were the shops at last, open till all hours of the night on these last shopping days before Christmas; here were the well-dressed crowds struggling muffled through the decorated streets against a wind that did not bother Kate. The traffic inched. The buses roared, befouled the air, crept ahead two, three, four of them together sometimes, threatening to crush their way right through the endless herds of walking bodies that bravely disputed every crosswalk with the vehicles.

Kate was on the point of entering a store before she realized that she had with her no money and no credit cards. She couldn't remember now whether or not she had been carrying a handbag when she went up to Craig's. She must have been carrying money and cards for shopping. And so somehow they must have been left at Craig's, or in that strange little room.

She wondered, without any real concern one way or the other, if Enoch might have taken them, and if Enoch had returned to the ugly little room by now. She wondered also, every now and then, if she were dreaming, because this high of hers seemed to be just going on and on; there had to be something more than pot, or even pot and wine, involved in it. If she went back to her car, and it hadn't been stolen or stripped or towed away, she might drive home . . . but first she wanted to do some shopping. With this in mind she walked into a store, and then remembered that she had no money . . .

Around and around went the cycle, like a fever-dream. At one point it stuttered and broke, and she found herself in a phone booth, using small change discovered in her jacket pocket, punching numbers. Joe's voice on the line, saying *hello*, came like a tonic shock, a shock that if it went on very long might threaten to wake her up, and in a moment she had hung up the receiver without speaking. He must never see her like this, he must never know . . . but now she had to find a gift for Joe. She had known him now for more than a year, and had never given him a thing that really mattered . . .

The crowd of shoppers had thinned to a mere scattering of people, the stores on the verge of closing, before the cycle broke finally and she was free. Or was she? First, back to the room, of course. Her valuables must be there, and her car was parked nearby. For some reason her life, her new life, centered there now. *You'll get to like it here. Think of it as home, maybe even.*

Kate did not feel physically tired, and walked back at a brisk pace. Approaching the dingy building, she looked for the Lancia, but the space by the hydrant was empty now. Still, she felt no alarm at the discovery.

Walking up the gritty stairs she met no one, though now a radio was playing somewhere in the building, making it seem not entirely deserted. Now what? She had been through all her pockets several times, and was certain that she didn't have a key. She pressed her body against the room's door, though, and it quite smoothly let her in.

Kate made sure that the door was locked behind

her. Then, feeling a little dizzy though not exactly
tired, she threw herself down on the bed. Her right
arm fell back over her head. One of her shoes fell
off.

She did not sleep, or lose consciousness completely,
but lapsed into a queer, semi-waking state, during
which she was aware of the gradual brightening of
the room into full daylight. Kate's eyes, half-open,
ached in the sunlight reflected from one dingy wall.
But she did not even blink, being afraid that if she
tried to move she would find that she could not.

There were feet on the stairs, several heavy people
coming up. Voices outside the door, then in the room
with her. Three or four men in the room, standing
about, talking in low voices. A couple of them wore
fur-collared blue Chicago police winter jackets, with
badges on their fur-flapped caps. She could see details
very plainly whenever they came into the center of
her field of vision.

They'll take me home, Kate thought, they'll snap
me out of this. Not that she cared, yet, whether they
did or not. But gathering in the back of her mind
was the first inkling of concern, taking form like the
knowledge that the dentist's numbing shot is presently
going to wear off.

Starting to grow curious at last, she harkened to
what the men were saying.

". . . so cold, it could be hard to tell."

"Yeah."

One took her arm to lift it. It clung to her side,
amazingly stiff, resisting his pull without the least
effort on her part.

He said, "My own guess is two, three days since
she died."

FOUR

Clarissa was sitting in the breakfast room, the cup of coffee that Judy had insisted on pouring for her still untouched, when the sound of wheels on the drive announced the return of Andrew and Lenore from the Chicago morgue.

Judy jumped up and hurried on ahead, and was almost in the front hall before the old woman could start moving. By the time Clarissa reached the entry, Lenore was inside the house, winter coat still on, sobbing in her younger daughter's arms as if they were her mother's. Andrew came in much more slowly, forgetting at first to shut the outer door behind him. His cheeks were for once unshaven, displaying sandy stubble, and loose flesh showed at his collar where it seemed that yesterday there had been none. His coat still on too, buttoned and forgotten, he leaned against the wall and muttered as if to himself.

"They're going to do an autopsy on Monday. I asked, why not tomorrow? They said some toxicologist is coming in Sunday night, it would be better if they wait for him."

The last word dissolved into a grating sob. Judy

got an arm free from her mother, and pulled her father's head down on her shoulder to give comfort.

Sometime much later in that dazed day, Andrew became aware that Joe Keogh was in the house, wandering about, looking as bewildered and grief-stricken as anyone else. Poor Irish roughneck cop who had thought he was going to marry into wealth. Never to have to face the prospect of him as a son-in-law now. Never have to. Never . . .

So peaceful Kate had been there on the antiseptic public table. He tried to hold in mind that peaceful, contented look, more like one sleeping than one dead. That look would seem to show she had not suffered. Dying there in that sleazy rooming house. What was she doing there? With whom? Someone must have been there. But Andrew was not ready to face those questions just yet.

So considerate were all the officials, holding down the publicity as well and as long as they could. Though in the long run they wouldn't be able to, he understood that. He couldn't estimate yet the effect on business, good or bad. Just one of those things that could not be planned for . . . time enough for that tomorrow.

. . . Judy of course went to place herself by the young man when he sat down, and held his prizefighter's hand. That was her way.

Meanwhile more police—Andrew lost track of what separate organizations they all represented—were in the house and out again. They talked to Andrew, and ten minutes later he couldn't remember what they had asked or he had answered. You planned and worked, and built up your business, all for your family, and then . . .

Johnny, as red-eyed as the rest of the family and for once subdued, came along in late afternoon with the word that he was going over to Clark's for a while, if his parents didn't mind. The Birches were close friends and it was natural that they would want to share the burden of the tragedy.

Andrew spoke to his son in a painful voice. "I don't think you're in shape right now to be driving." He could not really remember himself driving home from Chicago. "I don't think any of us are."

"I'll walk, Dad." The Birches lived only about two hundred yards away along Sheridan road, where the shoulders, though unpaved, were smooth and plenty wide enough to walk on without having to dodge traffic.

"All right, then. Tell them we'll call them later."

Shortly after Johnny left, darkness fell.

The phone rang, rang. Neighbors and business associates who had just heard the news kept calling in to offer sympathy. There were reporters, who could be brushed off for now. But it was in the papers now anyway, and on TV. In the intervals between incoming calls, Lenore began phoning out, talking to relatives and old friends scattered around the country. As if it helped her, just to have the phone in her hand and talk. Andrew didn't know where to look for something that would help him. There was Judy, of course. Thank God for Judy. She came and sat beside her father, saying little, just being there.

Somewhere along the line Joe Keogh had departed. A time came when all the police were gone. Lenore was on the phone, saying for what sounded like the hundredth time: we don't know yet about the funeral. After tomorrow, sometime.

Then the family made an attempt at gathering for dinner. Andrew took over the phone, and rang the Birches. "This is Andy. I think a son of mine is over there?"

"Andy, good lord. Johnny was telling . . . it's so terrible. What can we say?"

"I guess there's nothing." Andrew hardly knew

any longer what he was saying himself. "Is John there?"

"Why, no, he left some time ago. I think about six. I thought he was going directly home, but he might have stopped in at the Karlsens'.'"

"That's probably it." Andrew said goodbye, hung up, and punched for the Karlsens' home.

But Johnny wasn't there either.

Phone cradled again, Andrew tried to think. The Montoyas? They were in Mexico. Where else might Johnny be? Somewhere in walking distance.

Andrew slipped on a coat and without saying anything left the house and walked down the long, curving drive. He felt there was no rational reason for what he was doing, but he was not going to let that stop him tonight. He noticed that some stars were out. Could Johnny be standing somewhere, gazing at them? The boy would do that, sometimes. The telescope was put away, back in the small guest house near the lake.

As he walked down the drive he could hear distant surf behind him, smashing against the icefield, a different sound from that of its impact on rock and beach in summer. From in front came a murmur of light traffic, and passing headlights dazzled at him through the fir trees flanking his drive.

In the light of the next set of headlights Andrew saw that the flag on his mailbox had been raised. He himself had brought the Saturday mail in earlier in the day, and he had told the family often enough not to put anything out there over the weekend, not after that time when the checks were pilfered . . .

As he brought it back near the lighted house, Andrew's mind registered that the little brown-paper-covered package bore no stamps, and that it was addressed, ballpoint in an unfamiliar, clumsy block printing, to himself.

He carried it inside with him, and as Lenore

approached, wondering out loud where he had been, he opened it. Paper fell away, revealing a box that had probably once held a gift pen. It opened easily.

Looking at the object inside, a freshly amputated finger with a ragged, bloody stump-end that had left blood-smears on the inner lining of the box, Andrew felt something like the beginning of comfort. In a moment he recognized the comfort as of the sort experienced when the nightmare goes too far, and one knows at last that one is dreaming.

Except that even in his dreams he had never before heard Lenore, he had never heard anyone, make noises like the ones that she was making now . . .

An hour before midnight, with the drive again full of police cars, Clarissa found herself rising like a sleepwalker from her sleepless chair, moving away from the other members of her distraught family and letting herself be drawn back to the library.

Inside, she closed the door behind her, at the same time switching on one light. The shelves at the far east end were still in dimness.

In a pocket of her sweater her hand encountered a handkerchief, which, come to think of it, was part of her last year's Christmas gift from Johnny. Dear God, let him still be alive! But it was too long since she had genuinely tried to pray.

At the touch of her foot, the library stool glided along the base of the shelves, then settled beneath her modest weight to grip the carpet and hold itself in place. Handkerchief in hand, she ascended to the second step. The seldom-disturbed books on the top shelf must be dusty, given the succession of part-time maids who had lately been in charge of cleaning.

Clarissa whisked with the handkerchief, and pocketed it again. Then her hand went out to the book she wanted, one she had not opened in more than thirty years.

❖   ❖   ❖

November, 1946. Clarissa, widowed early in the war, had been two years remarried to a Yank, John Southerland, lately a brigadier in the US Eighth Air Force. She was preparing to leave her native England for her husband's home in far-off Illinois; one step in that preparation was to bid farewell, for what had seemed would quite possibly be the last time, to her grandmother Wilhelmina Harker.

The old lady had been in her seventies then, though she looked no more than a well-preserved sixty, and another two decades were to pass before she breathed her last. Eight years widowed herself in 1946, Grandmother Harker was still living then in her turn-of-the-century home in Exeter. The house, like the rest of England, had been left almost servantless by World War II, and was in a gloomy, neglected state, with some of last year's blackout curtains still in place.

Grandmother Harker had begun the interview by looking keenly at little Andrew, who had accompanied his mother. "Will he be changing his name to Southerland?" she demanded of Clarissa.

"I think he will." Clarissa's chin lifted, and her tone balanced between defiance and toleration. She had never spent much time with her grandmother and did not know her very well.

"Just as well," the old lady answered shortly, to Clarissa's surprise. Then Grandmother Harker had given the child his farewell present, a book of adventure stories, had wished him well among all the Red Indians of America, and then had sent him off to play with some neighbor's offspring. It turned out that the old woman had, or thought she had, some very private business with Clarissa.

"When you come right down to it," Grandmother Harker said, waving at the younger woman a fat, dark-bound book that Clarissa had not noticed until that moment, "jewels and money and such things are trivialities. At least they are once one has enough of them to get along in comfort. I understand your new husband is quite well off?"

"Quite."

"Then I hope you won't be disappointed that I'm not giving you anything of that sort."

Clarissa murmured a truthful denial, and at the same time wondered: A book? What in the world? She herself was not much of a reader, and certainly no collector; nor would she have guessed her grandmother, who in her youth had been rather adventuresome in a physical way, to have any particular leaning in that direction.

The book was being extended steadily toward Clarissa, in a slender hand that evidently still retained surprising strength. The old lady said to her: "But this is something valuable, my dear, as such a parting gift ought to be. You know, you were always my favorite among your generation of the family. And now, why shouldn't I say so, and do something to show I mean it? Truthfulness is one of the few luxuries whose enjoyment becomes more practical as we grow older."

"A book." When the sound of her own voice registered in Clarissa's ears she was afraid that she had said it much too flatly. The book hadn't been dusty on that day, though certainly it was already very old. "How lovely!"

"You don't mean that, though you say it well. Listen to me now. On the pages where I've put in the marker, you'll find something much more useful than mere loveliness, should there ever come a day of extraordinary trouble for you and your new family."

Clarissa had accepted the book, and was making some remark appreciative of the old binding, when Grandmother Harker cut her off with a headshake and a sharp sigh. "I do hope I can make you understand me, girl. I've had this from the Continent at

great—well, at great expense, though I don't mean
of money but of effort. It wouldn't do for it to be
forgotten, or ignored, or used with frivolity. No, that
especially wouldn't do at all."

As far back as Clarissa was able to remember, her
grandmother had somehow, from time to time,
obtained impressive things "from the Continent."
Lace, jewelry, at least once a fifteenth-century painting, later attested as a genuine Jan van Eyck by a
surprised appraiser called in by the old lady herself,
who must have had her own reasons to be suspicious
of the acquisition. And Clarissa could recall, as a child,
being introduced by Grandmother to a dark, romantic-
looking Continental gentleman of indeterminate age,
come from that mysterious cross-Channel realm to
visit Grandmother, though Grandmother even then,
as even little Clarissa had been able to see, was rather
ridiculously overage for such . . .

"Are you *attending* me, girl? Now when I speak
of a day of extraordinary trouble, I certainly do not
mean the simple deaths, diseases, cripplings; the
common tragedies. Deserting husbands. Financial
failures. Those God sends to us all."

Grandmother Harker leaned forward in her chair,
and something in her eyes came so to life that
Clarissa, a sensible woman of thirty-four who had
come bravely through the Blitz and her first widow-
hood, involuntarily leaned away. The old woman went
on: "I mean a day when the powers of hell seem well
and truly to have you in their grip . . . use it then,
and not before. And in God's name, I say again, never
in frivolity. I should never dare to give it, if I thought
it might be so abused."

"Use it?"

"Oh, don't be addle-pated! I can't abide that in a
girl with brains, of which you have a few, though
perhaps you don't like to use them. And while I think

of it, mind you go to church when you're in America. There won't be Church of England, I suppose, but go." Then, observing Clarissa's troubled face, Grandmother Harker at last showed pity. "Simply open the book to the marked page, and do what it says. You remember your Latin, don't you? Most of the ninnies who might open it up by accident will not, I'm sure, which is a blessing."

"Thank you, Grandmother." In her own mind, Clarissa lighted suddenly on the explanation—though she was not entirely able to believe it—that the old lady must have developed some senile religious mania.

When she got home from the visit Clarissa opened the old, old book and read the page marked by a ribbon. She looked at the lock of hair secured to the page by an incongruous strip of cellophane tape, and tried to laugh. And then she shut up the book for more than thirty years.

With the momentary feeling that those thirty years had never been, she spread the thick book open now, on a small library table of dark wood. 'You remember your Latin, don't you?' *Candel* at any rate gave no trouble.

Nothing was said about using a particular kind of candle, and Clarissa went out of the library again, past a detective using the telephone in the hall, to extract a cherry-red taper from the Christmas centerpiece in the great empty dining room. Some matches from a holder near the elbow of the man still busy on the phone. Then back into her sanctuary. Candle in hand but still unlighted, she scanned the ancient print with the aid of bifocals and Tensor lamp.

As the door opened softly behind her, Clarissa started as if caught in a kidnapping herself.

It was Judy. Like the rest of the surviving household she was face-swollen and dazed. But she took

one look at her grandmother and shut the door
behind her.

"What are you doing, Granny?" The words were
hushed; despite the open book the question was not,
'what are you reading?'

It crossed Clarissa's own dazed mind that in an
earlier century Judy, in adolescence, would have been
just ripe for witchery and hysteria. Perhaps that
thought was what made Clarissa want her help. Or
perhaps it was only a sudden fear of being left alone
again that made the older woman beckon and put on
a smile. "Come here, Judy. Help me read these words.
I know you've had your schoolroom Latin, just as I
did once."

Judy came to stand beside her. The old head and
the young one, almost blond, bent over the old paper.
A page cracked when it turned.

"What is it, Gran, an old prayer book?"

"About the closest thing to a prayer left in my life."

Each read in silence for a little while.

"It says to use a mirror, Grandmother." Not Gran
or Granny; not just now.

Clarissa did what passed for thinking in her present
state of shock. "Go fetch that small one from the wall,
down the hallway near your room."

Young legs in brown slacks, soft-shoed and silent,
sprang away (something to be *done* at last!), were back
in only seconds.

Another minute or two of cooperation and preparations were complete. Stacks of books held the mirror
propped vertically upon the table, so that the pages
of the old book, opened flat before the mirror, were
reflected. And now the words of what was to be read
aloud, printed in reverse, sprang to legibility in the
glass. The candle burned, stuck clumsily with its own
melted wax to the fine wood of the table, and leaning a trifle over the open book.

Now Clarissa pulled from the page the primitive

tape, which in thirty years had deteriorated more than
the old paper had in three hundred. It came free
easily, and immediately gave up into her fingers the
small lock of hair; mixed gray and black. More resil-
ient than either the paper or the tape, as if it might
have been trimmed off only this morning. Whose? It
did not look or feel at all like Grandmother Harker's
own brown-gray curls, as Clarissa recalled them.

Side by side the candle flame and Tensor lamp
stared at their own reflections in the mirror. Plenty
of light, but the words would not come clear for
Clarissa. She started reading aloud, stumbled, tried
to make sense out of them. All higgledy-piggledy
nonsense, about the falling of the sun, the rising of
the night. More, just as absurd. Not evil-sounding,
no, not the black and evil thing—although right now
she might have risked that too—for there in the text
were the names of God and Jesus set down to be
sworn by with respect. She could see that much,
although the words all swam together now . . .

"Grandmother . . . lean back. Rest, please. Shall I
read it for you?"

"Oh yes, my dear. It's so important. My own dear
grandmother once told me . . ." Clarissa had to pause,
or faint.

Judy put back the brown hair from her forehead,
snapped off the Tensor, and in the candlelight leaned
closer to the page and mirror. She gave a schoolroom
clearing of the throat, and read through the passage
twice: first in halting Latin; again in English translation that picked up speed as it went along.

". . . walker by daylight, walker by night . . . come
to my aid whose need is great . . ."

Remembering just in time, Clarissa leaned forward
to do the other thing the ritual demanded. The candle
flame sizzled, snapped at the dry morsels she fed it.
The stink of burning hair stung at their nostrils.

And now there was nothing more for them to do.

The rest was up to the unknown princely power whose aid they had besought; not God, to judge from the obscure text, but not Satan either. A saint?

Time passed, the girl standing straight now behind the old woman's chair, waiting to see if there was anything else that she could do for Gran. To Clarissa it seemed that a great silence now bound the house. The police must have departed once again, or most of them; some had planned to keep watch on the phones. Somewhere a jet, droning in across the lake, was heading for O'Hare.

"Granny, should I turn on another light?" The candle still burned, and one small bulb in a fixture near the door.

Already the spell that Clarissa in her desperation had tried to weave around herself was dissolving, like lake mist in the morning sun. Would God that it were morning already, instead of half the night still to be endured.

As the old woman raised herself from the chair, the joints of her knees and hips felt older than Grandmother Harker's had ever lived to be. "Judy, can you forgive me for all this nonsense? I'm a very foolish old—"

With a sharp sound the mirror, untouched by anything that either of the women could see or hear, smashed into a hundred pieces and crumpled in a heap of glass upon the table. Clarissa turned in time to see the candle, still half unburned, extinguish itself abruptly.

FIVE

Almost exactly sixteen hours, the traveler thought to himself, looking at his new wrist watch while the cab bore him, as he had directed, east and north from O'Hare Field. Here it was now four in the afternoon, and he should be just in time for tea, if one took tea in Illinois, which he was perfectly certain one did not. Sixteen hours from summons to arrival was not bad at all, considering all that he had had to do. My compliments, he thought, to BOAC. Of course he had long ago made preparations for some journey such as this—as he had for many other eventualities—and advance preparation always paid off when speed was essential.

"Turn east upon the next large road," he ordered, loudly and clearly, wondering exactly how his English sounded to the natives here. Of course he must sound basically British after so many years in London. The driver, a thick-necked black, made a minimal motion of his head as if he was moved to turn and argue with his passenger once more that the best way to get where he was going would be to confide the exact address of his destination to such a professionally knowledgeable guide as the driver himself. But the passenger's reaction to argument last time had not been pleasant.

Actually the passenger did not know the exact address he wanted, though he could feel the location of the place growing nearer. He momentarily tilted his dark glasses aside with a long finger, and squinted into dull sun-glow reflected from a long roadside pile of thawing snow. It was a dreary, soggy day, cloudy for the most part, not really as cold as he had expected. "And now, if you please, turn north again."

In another mile he had the man turn east, and then in a little while, once more to the north. What must be Lake Michigan, surprisingly oceanic at first sight, hove into view upon the traveler's right. He noted the appearance of the Shores Motel, and regretted his lack of experience in judging such establishments. A number of expensive cars were parked in front—of cars he knew a little.

Not far, now. A few minutes later the traveler was leaning forward in his seat, intently watching, thinking, feeling where he was being carried. "Slow down. Slower! Now, take that next private drive, *there*, upon our right!"

The man who answered the door was obviously no servant; nor did the visitor take him for a member of the family.

"Good day. I have come to see some members of the Southerland family."

The well-dressed man in the doorway was very watchful. "Can I ask the nature of your business, sir?"

"It is personal." But having by now recognized the other as some sort of policemen in plain clothes (this was a hopeful sign, suggesting that the difficulty for which he had been summoned was not trivial, or better yet that it had already been solved) the visitor handed over a card. "I am Dr. Emile Corday, an old friend of the family, just arrived from London."

Then he stood there on the doorstep, under polite police inspection, holding in mind just who he was supposed to be. Dr. Corday was an old family physician, retired now or on the verge. Basically a kind and comforting man, though with a crusty facade; could be irascible at times. He added: "I attended Mrs. Clarissa Southerland's grandmother in her last illness." It amused the visitor to be perfectly truthful in his deceptions when he could.

He was, as usual, convincing, and the plainclothesman stepped back. "Please, come in, Doctor."

Having already paid and dismissed the taximan, and being unencumbered by baggage, the visitor had nought to do but enter.

The examination, though, was not yet quite over. "Here, let me take your coat. You flew over from London just to see the family, did you?"

A woman of about forty-five, red-eyed and showing other signs of prolonged tension (another hopeful indication that he had not been forced to travel all this way for absolutely nothing) now appeared from deeper within the house, and exchanged glances with the policeman.

"I'm Lenore Southerland," she then informed the visitor, turning on him a gaze in which faint new hope and old terror were mingled.

Again he introduced himself as Corday, which name obviously meant nothing at all to her. Then, just as the policeman was on the point of interrupting with more questions, there appeared from another room a face that the visitor could recognize, given his developed talent for perceiving a child's features in the ruined mask of age.

And the recognition would perhaps be mutual. As soon as Clarissa's eyes (he had come up with her name a moment after her face clicked into proper

focus in his memory) fell on him, it seemed from a
certain tremor in their puffy lids, in concert with a
preparatory sagging of her body, that she might be
going to faint. He locked his eyes on hers—he had
taken off the dark glasses when he came inside—and
presently she rallied and stood straighter.

Ignoring the younger woman for the moment, he
turned to Clarissa and took her hands in his and let
her see a smile of reassurance. "Clarissa!" he greeted,
in his best old-doctor voice. "It has been many years."

"Oh yes, it has," she breathed in answer, and that
was enough to make the policeman retire for the time
being. She went on: "You know—you've heard about
our awful troubles here?"

"You shall tell me about it right away." And, after
a few minutes of polite and blurred conversation
with the daughter-in-law, he managed to get the
aged woman to himself. Apparently having her own
reasons to want to talk to him alone, she led him
into what looked like a functioning library—and yes,
there was the table the vision had shown him sixteen hours ago, complete with a speck of red candle-
wax adhering to the darkly polished wood. On the
carpet beside one table-leg there lay a minute sliver
of broken glass.

The door closed by Clarissa's hand, they sat facing each other across the little table, he with his back
to the windowful of winter daylight that now hung
on as if it never meant to fade.

Neither of them spoke immediately. Clarissa's eyes,
though she fought to keep them from doing so, flicked
up once, twice, three times, to a high shelf behind
him.

At last she had to say something. "You know, it's
been so long . . . I'm afraid . . . I'm ashamed to have
to ask, but—what *is* your name?"

"Corday," she repeated after him, mystified, when
he had told it yet again. "Corday. Do you know,

Doctor, I have the impression that I met you once when I was a small girl? I know that's . . ."

"In that impression I believe you are correct, Clarissa."

"But . . . no. Do you suppose that could have been your father?"

Now she was threatening to burble and gush. He sat in regal patience. Eventually he would hear more, learn more. Eventually he would confront his actual summoner, who had not yet appeared.

"It seems . . . it seems a strange coincidence that you should decide to visit us just now."

"It is nothing of the kind, my dear Clarissa, as I think you know full well. Where is the girl?"

Almost as if he had suddenly drawn a knife. "What girl?"

"An attractive young girl of seventeen or so dwells in this house. Last night—more precisely, about sixteen and one half hours ago—she sat in this room, at this table, with candle and mirror and a certain old book which is probably now on one of these high shelves behind me. I intend to see this girl and speak with her."

Clarissa's face was crumpling, along with the pretense that she had tried to maintain, that folk usually tried to maintain, that the world was a sane place whose basic rules they understood. She shook her head and moaned like someone choking on a bone. At last she got a few words out: "The mirror broke . . . I thought it might have been the candle's heat."

He waited silently.

"I—I hope I did the right thing." Her voice was very tiny now. Her eyes were those of a frightened bird.

"Indeed, I share your hope. I have affairs of my own, as you must realize, to which I should prefer to be attending." He sighed inwardly, wondering just how much Clarissa knew about him. Enough to scare her, obviously. "So, you instructed this girl—what is her name?"

"Judy." With a gulp.

"You instructed this young Judy in the means of summoning me."

"I was the one responsible. She only read the words."

"Only?"

Somewhere outside the library, male voices were droning, drearily determined.

"Clarissa, while I will do practically anything to please your dear grandmother, give every aid I can to anyone as near and dear to her as you are, I would not be amused to find my time and strength being wasted upon trivialities. So if this is a matter, say, of some stolen jewel, or perhaps some juvenile romantic difficulty—or even, God help us, a prank—let me warn you once and bluntly that this family will be left the unhappier for my visit." He had seen indications already that things were more serious than that, but he wanted to make the point. "And in that depressing event I believe I can explain my actions to your grandmother so that she will understand."

There was a pause in which Clarissa could be seen marshalling reserves of strength. She sat up straight and looked him in the eye, almost for the first time. "Dr. Corday. My grandmother, Wilhelmina Harker? She died in 1967. She was ninety-five then."

Again the visitor fetched an inward sigh. "I am aware that in that year dear Mina ceased to breathe. That she was then consigned to her tomb . . . but we are straying from our business. Pray tell me, just what is the nature of this family difficulty which reddens every eye, and populates the house with such discreet policemen?"

The tale came out in a hurried, exhausted fashion. The granddaughter found mysteriously dead, yesterday morning. The grandson kidnapped last night, and mutilated for the pure hell of it, as it might seem; there was not even a ransom demand as yet.

Then someone exists who does such things to folk whom Mina loves. He nodded, showing little of what he felt. He might have been considering a strange problem in chess. "There is no doubt that the finger in the little package was cut from your grandson's hand?"

"They said it was—"

"What?"

"Not cut. More like—oh God, more like it had been *torn* from his hand. I didn't see it. But they had no doubt that it was Johnny's finger. He—he had a distinctive wart on it."

At least, mused the visitor, he is now free of that.

"And the police say that they believe that it was taken from a living hand. They have their scientific tests."

"To be sure. The finger must be still in their possession?"

"It must be. Yes."

"And the girl's body, too?"

"In the Chicago morgue, the medical examiner's office, whatever they call it. They're supposed to have the best facilities there for tests."

It was now time to be nice, and he startled Clarissa away from the brink of collapse by reaching across the little table and reassuringly pressing her fingers between his own. "It is a good thing that you and Judy called me."

"Good?"

"Yes, yes. I should have been angry if I were *not* called on in such a matter. Evil people have, for whatever reason, launched an assault upon her family. But soon it will be the turn of those wicked folk to be unhappy."

Although he smiled as he whispered those last

words, wanting them to be comforting, she pulled back.

He looked sharply over Clarissa's shoulder in the direction of the door. Two seconds later the door opened.

"Gran? Sorry, I didn't know you had company."

He hardly heard the girl's words, though. He found himself on his feet, with no memory of having risen, and staring at her uncontrollably. The first impression, which struck him like a club, was that Mina herself stood before him, young as when he had first met her, in the first flush of warmblooded, breathing life.

Yesterday's vision of his summoner had been no more than a passport photo, compared to this reality. The girl's clothing and hairstyle were of course of the late nineteen-seventies, not of eighteen ninety-one. But the face and the sturdy body and the bearing were Mina's—although at second glance, of course, not quite.

The girl was staring at him also—small wonder, given his reaction to his entrance. How long had it been since anything had caused him so to lose his self-possession? But thank heaven she did not seem frightened.

Clarissa had also risen to her feet. When she spoke her voice was calmer than the visitor had expected. "Dr. Corday? This is my granddaughter Judy. Judy, Dr. Corday has known the family for some time. He's just flown in from London."

"Your servant, my dear," the visitor murmured, smiling, and took the young girl's hand. He would have felt the slightest pullback in her fingers, as he bent to kiss the air above them in the old European style. But pullback there was none.

Some surprise, though, showed in her voice. "You say that as if you meant it." Her voice was jarringly American. Well, what else?

"I do."

Her brown eyes, Mina's eyes, probed at him delightfully, trying to puzzle him out. "*Doctor* Corday? Did I meet you in England, maybe? We were over there in 1967. I'm sorry if I've forgotten, but I was very young at the time."

"Of course you were. But we did not meet," he said, releasing her hand regretfully. "It is impossible that I should not remember if we had."

Oh, those eyes of hers were, naturally enough, not Mina's after all. So young and brown though, and filled with puzzlement about him, and grief for her mysteriously ravaged family. Intriguingly, he could not find in them the personal fear that marked the older women of the family.

Judy asked him gravely: "Are you staying with us? I hope you can."

Clarissa rather lamely began to second this offer of lodging, which the visitor declined with polite firmness. "I shall be staying for some days in the neighborhood, however, and I look forward very much to visiting with you—with both of you. But right now, child, I have a few minutes more of urgent business with your grandmother . . . and, Judy, dear? If your father is in the house, would you ask him if he can spare a minute or two to talk to me? Tell him his time will not be wasted—thank you, Judy."

Watching the young girl leave, he marveled once more at her likeness to his beloved. Then, with an energetic clapping and rubbing-together of his lean hands, he turned back to Judy's grandmother even as the old lady sank into her chair again.

"Now, my child," he whispered to her, bending closer to her ear. "How have your dear son and his lovely wife managed to acquire such demonic enemies? You can tell me—you must tell me—the truth."

At this Clarissa began to weep. Which, as the visitor

could see, was not something she did easily or frequently. "You must believe me," she told him between gulping sobs. "I have no idea."

He looked at her closely, and patted her hands again. "I do believe you. And now, can you arrange for me to have a word in private with your son? Don't tell him that I want to question him, of course."

"Question him? Question him? Why must you do that?"

"Because I have been brought here to help him. To help all of you. It is all out of your hands now, my dear. Let me go about things in my own way."

Clarissa spent a little in sniffling recovery from her tears, thinking about this. "I never thought that old book . . ."

"Ha. Why then did you use it?"

"What is it that you want me to tell my son?"

"That I would like to speak with him—there must be something in which his interest can innocently be caught. By which he may be distracted a little from his grief and worry. He has perhaps a hobby that fascinates him? Chess, photography . . .?"

"Pottery," said Clarissa in a very low voice. Almost completely recovered from her weeping now, she was looking at the visitor with such a guarded, watchful, poker-playing stare that he really had to smile.

"Clar-iss-a! Was your grandmother such a terrible enemy of yours? Would she have delivered you and your own beautiful grandchild into the devil's hands? No, no, no, you must know better than that."

"Then who are you? Really?"

He emphasized the first words of his smiling answer with little hand-pats, delivered on alternate syllables. "I am Dr. Emile Corday, of London, an old friend of the family, and no one, no one, can prove anything to the contrary. Now, will you choose to help me? Or to help the creatures who have torn off your grandson's finger?"

SIX

"Andrew? Dr. Corday is very interested in pottery. He was wondering if you might have time to show him a little of your collection before dinner."

Clarissa and the visitor had come upon Andrew standing in the hallway, gazing at a phone on a small table as if he knew or hoped that it was about to ring. Introductions had been brief.

"He's really interested. Go along, dear, it'll do you good to think of something else."

"All right, Mother." With a last pensive glance toward the phone, Andrew turned away from it. A minute later, Clarissa having effaced herself, he was guiding the visitor toward the rooms where, as he said, most of the things were currently being kept.

This proved to be in an obviously older wing of the house, a one-story extension running north from what was now the main building. The original style of construction of this old wing had been partially obliterated by extensive remodelling carried on (as near as the visitor could guess) some decades back, and survived mainly in pseudo-Gothic archways separating rooms, gray stone walls still showing here and there, and some tall, narrow windows well suited to the needs of defending bowmen.

"Most of the collection is in this room, Doctor."

And now they were standing in the midst of it. The large chamber held not only pottery of almost every conceivable age and provenance, but a jumble of other old things as well. There were two suits of what looked to the visitor like authentic medieval armor. On side walls were some large, second-rate old Flemish tapestries. But he looked most intently at the wall opposite the door, where there hung a portrait of Mina herself.

"That is intriguing, isn't it, Doctor? My wife's grandmother, on the Harker side of the family. But of course you probably know . . . it was done by Gustav Klimt. Nineteen-oh-one, I think."

The old man could not now recall the date with any certainty either, though he well recalled the sunlit sitting room in Exeter where Mina had posed for this painting, and his own quick exit from that room into the noonday sun, with perilously aching eyes, on a day when Mina's husband and the artist had come home sooner than expected. And sure enough, there was gray stodgy Jonathan, still intruding in the only way that he could manage now, just down the wall from Mina in an inferior portrait done sometime in the 'twenties.

"You see, Doctor, we Southerlands are one of those American families who were involved around the turn of the century in what some people think of as the looting of poor old Europe by vulgar young America. That was when some of us here had a lot of money, and a lot of the old European families didn't. It was possible to buy up . . . but I keep forgetting, you probably know all that better than I do."

"*That* was not looting, dear sir. Not at all."

"This incense burner is Chinese porcelain, of course. Wan Li reign. But it came here through

Europe." Southerland went on, evidently seeking whatever distraction he might be able to find here, for there was a dry eagerness in his voice. "Of course we've added in more recent decades, recent years . . . this terra-cotta sarcophagus here was sent over during the war. There was a lot of space available in ships westbound from England in those days, I understand. I myself no longer work at collecting as I once did . . . and this little black bowl is Santa Clara Pueblo . . . Kate was starting to get interested in the Indian things . . ." Eagerness gone, slumping against a table, Andrew paused, as if suddenly exhausted.

"How easy it is," the visitor observed, "particularly in the world of business, for an innocent man to acquire terrible enemies."

"Enemies?" Southerland did not seem greatly surprised at the suggestion; still he thought about it for a while, as if it had never occurred to him before. "Yes, we all make them, don't we, and without even trying. The police have asked me several times: who are your enemies? Any servants with a grudge? Hell, we haven't had any really regular help in the house in years. Servants come and go. They don't even remember who we are half the time, much less hate us."

"I know how difficult it can be to confide in the police."

"What I just can't understand is this happening to a boy like John. Not like some of these other kids, pot-smoking, getting girls in trouble. A little driving trouble once, last fall, was all I ever had with John." Southerland's countenance convulsed, as if he were trying with all the muscles of his face to squeeze something out of himself. "And Kate," he added brokenly, and put his face down in his hands.

"I am a father too, you know." The visitor's voice

was soft, though without perceptible emotion. "Or I was."

"I didn't know," said Andrew, as if it couldn't matter. He looked up, starting to recover from his spasm.

"Not many do. But you are quite right, my family affairs are neither here nor there. Tell me, have you any dealings with what I believe is locally called the Mafia?"

"What? Never." Southerland's reddened eyes, now shocked anew, probed at the visitor. "Who said a thing like that about me?"

"No one, to my knowledge. But if you cannot guess who the guilty parties may be, then I must try to do so."

"You?" Southerland blinked at him stupidly, but aggressively. "What have you to do with this?" When the visitor stood silent, his host went on, now in a conciliatory tone: "Forgive me, I don't mean to insult any old friend of Mother's. But I've gone through all these same questions with the police. I don't know why my children are being attacked. If I knew, don't you suppose . . . I just don't know."

The visitor found himself beginning to be convinced of this. But he said nothing, only turned to watch the gothic doorway leading to the hall, where two seconds later there appeared the figure of a man.

The newcomer was about thirty, sparely muscular, tough-faced, fair-haired, dressed with classless American informality in boots, jeans, and a plaid jacket over a plaid shirt of different pattern. He favored the old man with a quick but judgemental glance that to the latter once more suggested the police. But when he spoke it was to their host: "Andy? Judy said you were back here. I just wanted to tell you—God, what can anybody say?"

Andy—the European visitor could not really manage to think of him by that name—pressed his lips together and shook his head and looked away. So it was left to the old man to break a slightly awkward pause, which he did by putting out a cordial hand. "I am Dr. Emile Corday, an old friend of Clarissa's grandmother."

"I heard about you from Clarissa. Pleased to meet you." The young man's grip was firm, though probably moderated in consideration of Dr. Corday's age. "I'm Joe Keogh, Kate and I were . . ." Glancing toward Kate's father, he let his words trail off.

"I understand. Well, Andrew?" Trying to fit the American style, he could just about manage Andrew. "Shall we all rejoin the ladies?"

Southerland agreed spiritlessly and came with them, walking now as if he were the aged one of the group. "If you don't mind, gentlemen, I think I'm going to lie down for a while . . . Lenore?" They had just re-entered the newer portion of the house, where his wife met them. "Will you call me at once if anything important comes up?"

"Of course. Lie down if you like." His wife, hardly looking at any of them, seemed as distracted as before. "Dr. Corday? Joe? You're both going to stay to dinner, aren't you?"

Corday bowed neatly. "Much as it would please me, Lenore, I cannot. Tomorrow I should like to drop in again, and talk over old times with Clarissa. And of course to do what I can to lighten the burdens on you all. Meanwhile, messages can reach me at the Shores Motel."

Joe in turn made vague excuses for not staying, and then put forward the offer, quickly accepted, to drop off Dr. Corday at the Shores. Lenore did not press either of them to remain. Judy, rejoining them at the last moment, did, but desisted when she saw that both really preferred to leave.

Outside, walking backwards into a gust of wind that howled across the floodlit gravel drive, Joe Keogh had a considerate eye out for the old man's footing. "Watch out, kind of icy here with these frozen puddles."

The old man wondered for a moment if his arm was going to be taken. But that indignity did not occur, and he followed Joe among the parked cars of family members and the police—some of whom were still in the house, listening for ransom demands at one of the telephones. Joe's vehicle, a small, gray German import, was the most modest of the lot.

They had driven perhaps half a mile south on Sheridan road, here fronted mostly by the driveways, walls, and gates of other set-back mansions before the old man spoke again: "You grieve for her deeply." Probing, he put a kind of challenge into the words.

The driver glanced over at him. "I do." He paused. "Do they get this kind of weather much in your part of Europe?"

"You have noticed my accent, which I fear still betrays my central European origins. And my French name, of course. But I really do now make my home in London, where these days cold this intense and snow this heavy are rare. Now I see that you do grieve, indeed. Even though you were never formally betrothed, I take it?"

Joe let a little time and traffic go by. "There were difficulties about that. Maybe you noticed, Kate's parents aren't exactly crazy about me. I felt like I was engaged to her, though she hadn't actually said she'd marry me. You know?"

"You had, perhaps, a rival?"

"That wasn't it." Pause. "She . . . just hated to give up her freedom." A longer pause. "Some of her wealthy acquaintances must have wanted to marry her too."

"Which ones?"

"I wouldn't know." Again snow was falling, a flurry of stray white blurrings in the slow-moving headlights.

"You are not wealthy, then."

"No, I'm just a Chicago cop." Joe felt his lips quirk in a smile half a second in duration. "Some people in my line have gotten wealthy, but I doubt I ever will."

"I suppose you have not been assigned any official part in Kate's case? Or her brother's?"

"The specialists will do a better job. I'm in the Pawnshop Detail: recovering stolen merchandise, things like that. Right now they've given me a few days off."

The road curved, and its new angle had been blown clean by some trick of the wind. Now the houses flanking it on both sides were less monumental, the driveways shorter.

"See," said Joe, "I don't have much family." He cleared his throat and tried again. "I belong to this kind of Catholic social club for single people. Kate got into it too. Sometimes the people in the club go to hospitals, children's homes, and so on, do a little volunteer work. I met her on one of those deals . . . here we are, Shores Motel."

But when the car had stopped, in a splendor of light from the signs and windows of the ornate office, the old man made no immediate move to get out. He just sat there, looking at Joe so regally that Joe wondered for a moment if the chauffeur was expected to get out and walk around and open the door for the distinguished passenger.

But it turned out that his passenger had only been mulling over another question. "Do you know where poor Kate's body is at present?"

"The Chicago morgue. Why?" Joe was suddenly a little angry at this pointless nosiness. He shifted in his seat to face the other more fully. The lights from the motel showed Corday's chin smooth-shaven, lean and firm despite the lines of age. The mouth was tough in a thin-lipped way, beneath a mildly beaky nose. The eyes above were still in shadow, though lights made motionless spots of bright reflection in them. Joe thought suddenly: I would not want this old man for my enemy.

The thin-lipped mouth said: "Determination of the cause of death has long been something of a specialty of mine. Would you be kind enough to drive me to the Chicago morgue tonight? Or at least give me the address?"

"Tonight?"

The old man nodded, minimally.

"Doctor, I don't know what kind of hours they keep in Europe, but they're not going to let any strangers into that place tonight."

Corday's mouth smiled solidly. "But I should like to see the building, at least, that I may know where it is. And I am eager to discover something of the great city near us, and eager also to continue our so-interesting conversation. Would it be a great inconvenience, for you to drive me there?"

"They're not going to let you in," Joe explained, with what he felt was beautiful patience.

"Or would you prefer to go to your home, and brood alone upon life's sadnesses?"

The morgue was a little south of the Loop, only a couple of blocks from central police headquarters on State. After driving past both buildings, Joe found a vacant parking space about halfway between them, on a street of tall office buildings all locked up and darkened for the night. He needed a parking space because it seemed that he was going to have to do a little more patient explaining still.

"Look, Dr. Corday, you're a real good listener, for which I'm grateful. It's been a help talking to you. But as far as trying to get into that place tonight, it's silly. They won't let us in just because I'm a cop or you're a doctor."

"I ask only that you wait here in the car for a few minutes, Joe, if you would be so kind. I shall walk back to the building myself."

Joe shook his head. "Maybe you can just walk around London alone at night, I wouldn't know. Here it isn't always safe—ah!"

The stubborn old man had started to get out. Joe, determined to use gentle force if necessary to make him behave sensibly, had taken him firmly by the coatsleeve. It wasn't reasonable that the old man's flesh could really have delivered a stinging electric shock to his hand through the thick cloth. But that was what it had felt like. Rubbing his thumb and fingers together now, testing for injury, Joe could feel nothing wrong. He must have somehow twinged a nerve or twanged a tendon.

By now the old man was standing at his ease outside the re-closed door. "I shall be quite safe," he murmured with a smile, and touched his dark hatbrim. He turned away and in a moment long strides had taken him around a corner.

All right, the chances were, of course, that nothing would happen. Winter nights were safer than summer ones on the streets of the core city, and the streetlighting here was excellent. But to a stranger, a perhaps innocent foreigner, there was a special responsibility.

Joe got out of the car on his side, buttoned up his jacket, and walked to the corner, flexing the fingers of his right hand. They felt fine, now. He would catch up with the difficult old man and walk along. How did he get into these things? But at the same time he was relieved not to be home alone in his apartment.

He stood at the corner, squinting thoughtfully down a long, broad sidewalk almost empty of pedestrians. The old man was nowhere in sight.

SEVEN

The visitor stood alone in a dark room, halfway along a broad, terrazo-floored aisle that was lined on both sides with double tiers of massive metal drawers. In the next room, the possessor of a pair of middle-aged lungs was sitting in a slightly squeaky chair, sitting quite still and on the verge of snoring. The light coming under the closed door from the room where the watchman dozed was all that the visitor had to let him see the tags on the drawers, but it was more light than he needed. What handicapped him in his search was not darkness but the impenetrable official jargon on the tags, labels for this foreign city's mysterious dead. Presently, with an almost inaudible hiss of relief, he gave up trying to be methodical—never his strong suit anyway—and slid a long drawer out at random.

The sheet-draped body in it was that of an adolescent black male whose forehead had been grossly damaged, the rest of the face less so, by some violent flat impact. Automobile, pavement, weapon? Touching the dark marble shoulder, the visitor still could not be sure of which. But the physical contact

established for him some rapport. Not only with this
one truncated identity, but, by some dimly perceived
extension of the contiguity, with all the silent company about.

That was a start. The old man slid the young black
statue back out of sight and stood with closed eyes
in the near-dark, concentrating deeply. Now he began
to pace along the aisle, brushing his long fingers on
the cold handles of the drawers. Top row, bottom row,
top again . . . he knew without pulling them open that
in one was a woman, somewhat too old to be the girl
he wanted, in the next, a man, another man, a boy,
a girl . . . .

Even before the chosen drawer flowed out on easy
rollers at his touch, he was quite sure that he had
found Kate Southerland. His hand went out to delicately turn back the rim of coarse white sheet from
the face of Judy's sister.

The revealed face froze him into immobility.

For the second time in as many hours he found
himself taken completely by surprise. All his delicately
forming plans, estimations, guesses, regarding the
Southerland affair, every theory that he had begun
to play with in his mind, all vanished like the rising
mist at dawn.

This was not true death before him.

Oh, the girl was cold and unbreathing certainly,
her heart as quiet as her hands: medical student and
expert pathologist alike would certify her dead. But
the old man was able to perceive the energies of
altered life that still charged all this pretty body's cells.
Again he drew a minimal breath, and uttered that
faint, almost reptilian sound, expressing to himself his
own surprise. Had she enemies so bitter that they
meant her to be autopsied alive?

Or . . .

He passed his flat, extended hand once close above
the girl's face, forehead to chin. Then he made the

same motion in reverse. He needed only the one pass to make Kate's eyes open for him. They were unseeing as yet, but a lovely milk-blue, glass-blue, in the night.

It was important to know whether there had been any attempt at autopsy as yet, and impersonally he drew the sheet down farther. The virginally flat belly was marked by no incision. Good.

With doctorly gentleness he drew the sheet up to just below Kate's chin. Then he pressed with two fingers on her cheek to turn her head. As he did so he murmured tremendously old words, in a language that could find keys of understanding within the inner levels of almost every human mind. The rigor of Kate's muscles eased somewhat. Her head turned, her eyelids drooped again, and simultaneously she smiled. *What did you tell me, old man? Something nice.*

He smiled too, for a moment, seeing a trace of Mina's lineage before him in the smooth generous forehead and lips. Oh, this was Judy's sister, yes, though older, blonder and blander, and by his own standards not so beautiful.

The expert pathologist would almost certainly never have thought of looking for the marks which the old man, knowing just where to look, could now observe upon the throat. A pair of less-than-pinprick wounds, now almost closed. By their spacing he knew that a wide human jaw had bitten there.

Next, with one finger the old man parted Kate's cold lips and explored her teeth. The four cuspids all responded somewhat like erectile tissue to his touch; what had once been inert enamel sharpening visibly.

He pressed her hand. "Look at me, Kate!" No more than a whisper was his voice, and yet a fierce command. And when her milk-blue, innocent eyes turned toward him he bent a little, whispering more intently still: "Who is your secret lover?"

Kate's smile failed, and a tremor ran through her

upper body. To give the required answer meant drawing breath for speech, and breath to her was no more an automatic reflex. After a moment of awkward agony her lungs worked once, and she got out one word: "No—"

No secret vampire lover, it would seem, had left her in this state. Some vampire rapist, then. The old man's whisper lost its gentle undertone, came out between thin lips as though from a machine: "Who forced himself upon you, then?"

A difficult gasping. "Enoch . . . Winter . . ."

The name meant nothing to the old man. "How long have you known him?"

"Just . . . met . . ."

"He bit at your throat; I can see that for myself. Forced you to taste his blood as well, perhaps?" Otherwise it was unlikely that a single mating would have brought about her transformation.

Ugly remembrance dawned in Kate's dull eyes; she answered with a soundless *yes*. Her rib cage labored, but pumped little air. It was not surprising that her strength was low; the newborn vampire could be as weak, though hardly as fragile, as the infant newborn in the breathing phase of life. The visitor squeezed Kate's hand as he had squeezed Clarissa's, and made himself smile reassuringly. "I am an old friend of your grandmother's, Kate. Only one more question now, and you may sleep again. Where is John?"

"John . . ."

Now even the old man needed his best efforts to hear her. "Your brother. Is he with Enoch Winter?"

A faint line of puzzlement creased Kate's otherwise flawless forehead. He got the impression that she knew nothing of her brother's fate.

"All will be well now, Kate. Rest, sleep, until I come for you. Answer no call but mine. No call but mine. We will have much to talk of, later. But for now, rest."

And yet her lungs continued laboring to breathe, to get out one more word. He bent lower, intent on hearing.

"*—Joe—*"

For six minutes Joe Keogh had been back in the driver's seat, with engine and heater running, keeping a sharp eye out for the old man and wondering when he should really begin to be alarmed. Now Joe started, with almost the sensation of electric shock repeated. His companion was standing once more beside the car, where he seemed to have reappeared while in the very act of reaching for the door handle. What good would you be in a stakeout? a part of Joe's mind demanded angrily of himself. And another part answered: I *was* watching. He just—just—

"I told you you wouldn't be able to get in," he said aloud, with irritation, meanwhile reaching across the front seat to flip the doorlatch up.

"You were quite right," replied Corday in a soothing, almost contrite voice, as he slid in and closed the door. "The attendants were not at all inclined to be helpful. One of them was sleeping at a desk. A most ill-run establishment. Were I in charge, things would be different there."

Joe sighed, trying to remember if you could see anyone's desk from outside the front door of the morgue. "I'll take you back to your motel."

"If that is out of your way I can easily take a cab."

Joe shifted into drive and moved out, north on State, then swinging east to get back to the Outer Drive. "No problem, I'm headed back to the north side anyway." He hadn't really been headed that far north, but what the hell. Anyway there was something about the old man, in spite of all his oddities—or maybe because of them—that made Joe reluctant to let go of him. An air of hope; maybe that was it. A feeling of purpose, which was more than Joe had been able to get from anyone else around him since Kate's death. Looking at the ugly situation logically, of course, there wasn't much to be hopeful or purposeful about—except the chance of recovering Johnny alive, and to Joe that chance looked smaller and smaller as the hours passed.

His companion's voice, breaking in upon his thoughts, was welcome. "Tell me one more thing, Joe, if you know it. What are the plans for Kate's burial?"

"As far as I know, no time's been set. Waiting on the autopsy, which is supposed to be tomorrow. I'm sure she'll be buried up in Lockwood Cemetery, in the family mausoleum. It's one of those the really wealthy Chicago families liked to put up around the turn of the century: all marble and as big as a middle-sized house. One of those famous architects designed it, I forget his name."

"Thank you, Joe. You have been very helpful to me tonight." It was said so sincerely that it sounded a little odd.

Joe glanced at the once-more shadowed face. "You'll be coming to the funeral, then."

"At my age," the old man said calmly, "it is difficult to know which funerals one will be able to attend."

EIGHT

When the closet door was closed Johnny never tried to open it, not after that first time, even though sometimes the house grew so silent that he could imagine himself alone in it.

On his first night in the closet all had been silent, for what seemed like an endless time, and at last he had eased the door open with his good hand, thinking maybe they had somehow left him unguarded. The huge man had been right there in the dark empty bedroom, standing right there as if he had been waiting hours for Johnny to do just that. That was when the huge man, without saying a word, had torn off the little finger on Johnny's right hand.

The little finger on his left hand had gone even sooner, while he was still in the kidnap-car and trying to struggle. He had fainted, and when he came out of the faint—he couldn't tell how much later—he found himself already here, shut up naked in the closet.

In the car, the huge man had ridden in the back seat, and the black-bearded man had done the driving. Black-beard was the one who had first beckoned

Johnny over to the car as if to ask directions of him. When you were the fourth best high school wrestler in the state at a hundred and sixty pounds, you didn't fear any more that some maniac could just grab you like a baby and throw you into the back seat of a car.

It had turned out, though, that someone could.

Then there was the man with the thick glasses, a short and muscular and sometimes nervous young man. He had not been in the car at all, but he stayed with Johnny in the house, escorted him from closet to bathroom and back again, and put food and water in the dishes on the closet floor.

Also there was the woman. Johnny was not quite sure, in his state of pain, fever, shock, fear, and confusion, whether he was dreaming her or not. He heard her sometimes; he never saw her clearly. She had not been in the car either. Once she came to the closet door and opened it, in darkness so thick that even his now fully adjusted eyes could see nothing but the vague outline of her body. Then she had bent forward to touch him, with a finger or perhaps a toe, as he lay on the floor. And she had laughed, musically, and had spoken to someone who was over near the door that must lead from the bedroom to a hall. Her language sounded a little like Latin, but mostly like nothing that Johnny had ever heard before. Then she had gone away again.

It was not easy to keep track of time. In the bedroom outside the closet, a modern but abandoned-looking room with no furniture that he traversed on his escorted trips to the bathroom, the drapes were always closed. Still he could just tell whether it was daylight outside or not. The trouble was in sorting out the periods of day and night and keeping track of how many of them had passed. And there was more trouble in trying to believe there was a reason why he should bother to keep track at all.

Thick-glasses sometimes left him plain bread in the

aluminum pie plate placed on the luxuriously carpeted floor. Once there was cheese with the bread, and once it had turned into a peanut butter sandwich. Johnny didn't eat much, whatever it was. He did drink a lot of water, though, out of the other dish. Lapping it up was the best way, because then he didn't have to use his hands at all. They both hurt so much he wasn't going to try to use them except to save his life. Maybe not even then.

It might have been his second night in the closet when he heard the car pull up outside. Immediately Thick-glasses went into a flurry of activity, entering the bedroom from somewhere, momentarily pulling aside the drapes to look out, then opening the closet door to growl: "Make any noise and it'll be your left nut that comes off next." Then he closed the door and went trotting off somewhere, closing the bedroom door too behind him.

Johnny could hear nothing more for several minutes. Then two sets of footsteps entered the bedroom, its ceiling light was switched on, the closet door was opened. Even with his eyes dazzled, Johnny could recognize Black-beard from the kidnap car.

The two men stood there looking at him on the floor. Black-beard was wearing some kind of fancy winter jacket with snow on the collar. Thick-glasses wore his usual khakis, almost a uniform.

"If the plan's going on," said Black-beard, "we don't want him to die yet; we'll want to send some more parcels. He's shivering, better get him a blanket."

"Oh, the plan's going on," Thick-glasses said.

Black-beard: "I'd like to get it straight about this house, who owns it, how secure it really is."

"*She's* taking care of all that."

They closed the closet door. Their voices stayed in the lighted bedroom, though.

"Look, man." It was Black-beard talking again. "You've really known her longer than I have, right?

Her and her big friend. It was really you who arranged for her to meet me, huh?"

The other was quiet for a few moment. "Yeah." As if he didn't want to talk about that.

"I'm going to have to talk to her, get a few things straight. Like who really decides things. Meanwhile I want you to understand that I'm the one who does."

"Sure."

"I'm not gonna hang around here. Do either of them ever come out here?"

"They haven't yet."

"What'd you do with his clothes?"

"I got 'em stashed away. This way he's not gonna go running out. Also I don't have to do his zipper for him."

Black-beard chuckled. "Makes something else a little handier for you too, hey?"

"Hey, you know I don't like to touch no one who's unhealthy." Thick-glasses sounded genuinely hurt. "He's all blood and shit—*yuck*."

"You could give him a bath."

"Come on, get off me, Boss."

"All right, all right." Black-beard quenched his amusement. "Look, Gruner, you're doing a fine job here, a helluva job. I'll get word back to you on what to do next. You sure the phone here's not connected?"

"Sure."

Their voices moved away.

Later that same night—though Johnny could not be sure it really was the same night—he swam up out of sleep or stupor to hear that a party was in progress. Not in the bedroom; somewhere farther off. Voices again speaking that language that was almost Latin—this time maybe half a dozen people, having what sounded like a quiet good time. Eventually he could pick out the voice of the woman who had looked in on him the night before. He didn't hear Black-beard's, though, or Thick-glasses' either.

Some strange man's voice said, impatiently: "Oh, speak English here, why don't you?" Impatience was smeared over with good-humor, to make it sound polite.

And then the lovely voice of the woman who had looked in on Johnny, answering in English: "I have lived on this side of the ocean for two years now. I know the custom. I choose to disregard it, usually. But if the mother tongue is hard for you, I will use English, as a favor."

Another woman said: "If you're doing favors, I take it that you want something; you've called us together to ask our help. You have brought your feuds here from across the sea. That boy in the closet is connected with it somehow, I'm sure."

Several voices murmured agreement. The anonymous woman went on: "Well, we want nothing to do with any of that. Here there is no real knowledge of us among the breathers. No persecution ever, nothing but jokes. We wish things to remain as they are on this side of the water."

"*Au contraire*," replied the woman with the lovely voice, now more silken than ever. "I only offer you my friendship. I do not ask your help. What lies between the old one and myself is our own affair, not yours at all."

"That's fine with us," a second man put in.

"I have claimed no titles or honors here among you, have I?"

"Nor has he—you say he is here now, too."

"He is here. And you may be sure that he will claim honors—and obedience—if he wins. But all I ask is that you leave it to ourselves to settle." The fine voice paused. "No, let me be plainer than that. I insist that you give him no help, and above all no place of sanctuary. Any of you who dare to do so will feel our wrath in days to come. His time is past, and none should look to him for leadership."

"I hope that all of you are listening," said the huge man's voice, rough and elemental, like something from a thundercloud. And Johnny felt the world slip from him into darkness.

NINE

More often than not, Judy slept with the drapes of her bedroom window drawn open, and so it was tonight. Starlight and moonlight from the high sky above the lake were welcome, and dawn too, on the rare occasions that it roused her. There was no reasonable way that any human being could look in, on the second story. So when she awoke, near midnight, she wondered for a moment if it could be some trick of starlight from the new-cleared sky that made it appear that the old man, yesterday's brief visitor, was sitting in her dressing-table chair.

"Have I frightened you, Judy?" The voice of the apparition was quite matter-of-fact.

"No, I don't scare easily." Actually she was beginning to wonder if she was dreaming. Judy turned to face her visitor more directly as she sat up in her bed. Automatically her hands pulled sheet and blanket up close beneath her chin, and she felt her fingers touch her nightgown's throat, to make sure that it was buttoned. "But how did you get in?"

"I was invited, yesterday, into this house. And in

my case one invitation is enough, you see. It has a permanent effect."

"I don't think I do see." But truly she was not afraid of him. She wondered a little, now, and later was to wonder more, about this lack of fear.

"Of course I have not been invited into your room. Shall I apologize for being here?"

"No, I don't mind. That is, I suppose you must have some good reason."

The old man made a little hissing sound not quite a sigh, and shifted in his chair. "I need a little help. I thought of waking Clarissa—but when I remembered your delightful lack of fear yesterday afternoon I came to you instead."

"A good thing you did. Gran's had angina. But what was there yesterday afternoon to be afraid of?"

This time the little hiss was almost a chuckle. "People can be very timid. Sometimes they are even afraid of me. Believe it or not."

"Why?"

"And one might think that these monstrous attacks upon your family would frighten you. Your mother and grandmother are both terrified, and your unhappy father is at the end of his wits, as the saying goes."

"Oh, it's not really that I'm so brave. It's . . ." Judy had to pause. She had never really tried before to put into words the way she dealt with fear. "It's just that when you're *really* scared, the only thing to do is try to go beyond the fear somehow. Accept it, maybe that's what I mean. And then go on your own way regardless." Now that she had found words, they did seem right, or almost right, to her. She would not have expected someone else to understand them, though.

But the old man was leaning forward in his chair, nodding. " 'Go on your own way, regardless.' I think it wonderful that you, at your age, already understand that. It does not, of course, imply a freedom from moral responsibility."

His voice had a marveling intensity that made Judy feel uncomfortable. She asked: "What is it you need help with?"

"Help? Ah, yes." The old man leaned back in his chair, and gave his little sigh. "I want some of Kate's clothing. A complete outfit will be best."

"What for?"

"Questions will not help me in what I am trying to do. The clothing may."

Judy considered for a moment, then swung legs swathed in a long, chaste winter nightgown out of bed. She groped with her toes for slippers. "A complete outfit. Underwear too?"

"Everything, please. As if you were helping her get dressed."

"All right. Wait here." Belting a robe around her, Judy went out of her room and down the familiar upstairs hall to Kate's. There she rummaged mechanically in the drawers and closet. What am I doing here? she thought. I'm definitely awake now. Was I dreaming, after all, a minute ago? Will he still be there when I get back?

Trusting her instincts, she finished gathering the clothes before she hurried back to her own room. The old man waited for her, solid as the chair he sat on, dressed as he had been yesterday in a black topcoat over a dark suit. His soft, dark hat was in his lap.

"Here," said Judy. "I even got a bra, though more often than not Kate doesn't wear one."

"Ah," said the old man. The word was not exactly embarrassed, but perhaps he didn't know just what to say. He got up from his chair and held open a small, dark bag that Judy had not noticed before. Into it she dropped the clothing bundle. "Now," he said, tucking the bag under one arm, "since we are co-operating so well, do you suppose it might be possible to obtain the key to the family mausoleum in Lockwood Cemetery?"

"What for?" Again she asked the question automatically. But this time thinking it over only confirmed her right to ask. Hands jammed in the pockets of her robe, she stood waiting for an answer.

The old man seemed to think his answer over carefully before he gave it. "Your father mentioned to me that some of the larger and, ah, less costly pieces of his pottery collection have been relegated to that mausoleum. Should he ever question you about the key, you might mention that you gave it to me so I could look at those items without intruding any more upon his grief. Of course, if he never notices that the key is gone, we need not bother him about the matter at all. Would you concur?"

"You have a neat way of not answering questions."

"Would you concur?"

"I guess so. Dr. Corday?"

"Yes?"

The question Judy really wanted to ask would not quite come out, even when she tried to tell herself again that she might be dreaming. Instead she said: "I think I know where Father keeps all the keys we don't use much. On a big key ring in his desk in the study. They're all tagged, or most of them are. But I'm pretty sure the desk is locked."

Her visitor smiled at her. He had a nice smile. "In that case we need not worry about it tonight. I shall ask him for the key another time."

"Dr. Corday?"

"Yes."

"Is Kate alive?" Now it was out.

For once it seemed he could not find an answer he was happy with. "Would you believe me, child, if I said she was?"

"Don't call me a child, please. Do you think I am one?"

"No." He bowed, fairly deeply. "I am sorry. No, I do not think that at all. I would not have wasted half an hour from my duties, sitting here, to watch a child sleep."

What he had just said was something that Judy did not want to have heard; and anyway she did not want to be distracted. "Give me an answer. *Is* she?"

He studied her in silence.

Judy pressed on. "I've dreamed about her. Last night, and again tonight, before you came. In the dream I see her alive, but locked up somewhere. She keeps calling for Joe, but he can't hear her. And now you ask me for the mausoleum key, and for her clothes. Why do I trust you? But I do."

"Yes, that is very good, you must trust me, Judy. And you must make up your mind that you are never going to see your sister alive again."

"How can I believe that when you won't swear to me that she's dead?"

"To others I can lie. I am very good at telling lies. But to you . . . I am prevented."

"Then she *is*—"

"Consider her dead, I tell you!" There was a sudden ferocity in the old man's voice. "And say nothing, nothing, of these feelings and these dreams of yours to anyone but me. It would be very bad for family morale."

"I—know that." Suddenly Judy was on the brink of tears.

He stood over her, a strong tower offering safety, of which now she felt very much in need. "Judy, you must go back to sleep. And you must dream again. Since you have the power of dreams that are so— so vivid, it may be that we can use them. Hear me. Dream not of Kate. Leave Kate to me now. Dream of your brother. Dream of John. Dream . . ."

It seemed to Judy that even as the old man's eyes vanished and his voice ceased, that she was waking up. She was alone in her room, in bed, well tucked beneath her covers, still wearing her robe over her nightgown. Outside the undraped window, the lake-sky showed a dull, gray dawn. Her brother's cries, silent but terrible, were ringing in her mind.

TEN

The phone awoke Joe Keogh from some dark nightmare, the sound an overwhelming relief because it meant nightmares were over and it was time to go to work. He had the receiver in his hand before the memory came that this was supposed to be another day off for him. And why it was.

"Hello Joe, this is Judy."

"Judy—what's up?" It was broad day. His watch, still on his wrist, said after ten. Last night he had drunk too much, finishing a bottle of scotch alone. He didn't notice any hangover, though, just a dullness. All life was a hangover, these days.

Judy's phone voice said: "There's something you have to know."

Now sitting naked on the edge of his single bed, Joe was staring at a curl of house-dust on the bare hardwood floor under the small bedside table that held the phone. That curl had been there when Kate was still alive.

"What is it?" But before he finished asking, he was sure he knew the answer. Johnny's body had been found.

"Kate's body," the phone-voice told him, and he had a sudden sensation of re-entering a bad dream that he had been through once before. He did not answer immediately.

Judy went on: "She—her—she's missing from the morgue this morning. The Chicago police called us about half an hour ago."

"Missing." Rubbing his eyes made things no clearer. "Are you sure it was really the police who called?" A kidnapping-mutilation and a mysterious death in the same prominent family were sure to draw warped jokers to the scene.

"Yes, the other police are still tapping our phone. And the Chicago police had Dad call them back. It really happened."

Judy's voice sounded more hopeful than dismayed. Well, she was a little weird sometimes. Joe sighed. "It wasn't just some mixup at the morgue? Someone took the wrong body to be buried?"

"It doesn't sound like it could be anything like that. One doctor remembers seeing her there yesterday afternoon. This morning some other doctor went to look, getting ready for the examination. And she was just gone."

He could make no sense of it. "How are you managing, Judy?"

"Mom and Dad are just numb, I think. Gran seems more upset by this than they are."

"Oh. But I meant you."

"Me? I'm coping okay. You sound like you are, too."

"More or less. Look, did you hear from Dr. Corday this morning?"

There was a pause on the line. "Why do you ask? Did he get back to his motel okay last night?"

"Yeah, I dropped him off. Look, just hang in there, kid. I think I'm going to come over and see you."

As Joe hurried into his clothes, his mind was fixed

on the remembered face of the old man who last night had been so intent on getting into the morgue. He turned the image from fullface to profile and back again, as if Corday were standing before the black-on-white hatched inchmarks of the lineup. Put on your hat, take it off. No, no face that Joe had ever seen before.

Kate—gone. But that wasn't accurate. Kate had really been gone for days. The body on the right slab or the wrong slab had been hers, but it was not her any longer, and he could feel no vital concern for anything that happened to it. This morning's bad dream wasn't a new tragedy, only a new craziness.

Dressed and shaved, he called the Shores Motel. Dr. Corday was registered there, all right, but his room didn't answer.

Joe decided to give himself time for one cup of instant coffee—after all, there was no way in the world that the old guy could have stolen the body last night, in the five or six or seven minutes he had been out of Joe's sight. Joe dropped two slices of bread into the toaster. Of course, he *could* have returned to the morgue again later. . . .

He sat at the small table in the dining alcove of his small apartment, and tried to get his thinking back into a police track. In police work you couldn't very often accept that strange happenings were just coincidence; last night the rather strange old man had prowled around the morgue, and this morning she was gone.

In police work also, on the other hand, you had to start with what was possible. In fact, the old man could not even have got into the building there last night. Someone had, though—or did Judy have the story garbled?

Still chewing toast, Joe picked up his phone, dialed a number in Homicide, and asked for Charley Snider.

"Charley? This is Joe Keogh. What is it, what's the story?"

"Oh yeah, the story. I'll give it to you straight, man. I know what this must be like for you."

"Just tell me."

"The thing is, she was there as of about ten P.M. last night. Everybody swears all was in order then, at least. Then, man, as of six-ten this A.M., when one of the junior pathologists decides he wants a preliminary look, she was just not there. Empty bin's correctly labeled. All the paper work's in order, as near as we can find out. No bodies were officially removed from the morgue in those eight hours. The only other funny thing is the lockers where the clothes and other personal effects of the, uh, customers are kept; somebody had been digging around in there, it looks like. No locks broken, but the stuff's all scrambled, and we don't know yet if Kate's property is missing or not."

"Family hadn't claimed her things?"

"Not yet they hadn't."

"No signs of a break-in?"

"None we've discovered, it's a big place. We got our men still swarming through there. We're checking out everyone who was on duty there last night. So far's we know, no weirdos among them."

"That's something."

"Hey, man, one more thing. Remember, we found Kate's Lancia in the pound? It had been towed away from that hydrant. Anyway someone left a big fat thumbprint right on the rearview mirror, angle seemed to show it was someone reaching from the right seat. It's being checked out in Washington now."

"It's probably some garage man's. No, it's probably mine; I've ridden in that car a lot."

"If you got any ideas we can try, I'd like to hear."

"No, no ideas." His suspicions of the old man, if they really were suspicions, had to settle into some kind of a sane pattern before he threw them out as a tip. An old friend of Clarissa's, after all. "Thanks, Charley. I'm going over to the Southerlands' for a while, in case you want to reach me."

He sat there for a minute staring at the cradled phone, but seeing the old man. Then he took a jacket from the closet and went out the door.

Snow, gentle-falling, soft as white night, dimmed the scorch of day to muted gray for the old man, dulled for him the multicolored windows of stained glass that in bright sun would have been explosions of discomfort. He needed rest and sleep. Not, as yet, to the point where his survival was in question, so he stayed on his feet and active. Tomorrow, though, he was certainly going to have to sleep.

Besides dulling the sun, another eminently satisfactory effect of the snow was that it seemed to discourage visitors to Lockwood Cemetery. Or perhaps Americans were just not as enthusiastic as Europeans about visiting their dead. Anyway, during the whole morning he had heard no more than three or four vehicles whispering around the gravel roads of the cemetery, one of them a pickup truck with snowplow attached, that seemed to make but little progress in getting the drives clear.

Gently, but very insistently, the snow continued to fall. By two o'clock it lay ankle-deep on the broad lawns and weathered stones of the cemetery's old section, and clung to the wrought-iron fences, obscuring the signs that warned about the guard dogs being loosed here after dusk. The snow and the dogs were all fine with the old man who stood looking out from inside the Southerland mausoleum, his eye to a small chink he had broken in one window of stained glass.

He supposed that this mausoleum was old and large, as such things went in this young country. It was a one-room house of marble no warmer and no colder than the snow, or than the bones it sheltered—

or than the living but unbreathing flesh that it concealed today.

At intervals, when he grew weary of looking out,
five or six long paces took the old man from one end
of the cold room to the other. This included a slight
detour around the empty sarcophagus and the decorative urns that had been planted in the middle of
the space. Looking at them, he could see why Andrew
had exiled them here, ugly decorations no one wanted
to behold. The central sarcophagus was unoccupied;
so far all internments had been in the vaults built into
the thick outer walls. Southerlands and their kin who
had died in the past seventy years or so were there,
behind the waist-high doors of green-patinaed bronze.

Kate was lying just above one such door, on a wide
marble ledge set below another stained-glass window.
She had been lying there since just before the wintry dawn, curled up like a sleeper, wrapped in a sheet
that revealed only her head.

Kate lay on her left side, facing the room, but with
eyes closed. One arm tucked beneath her head, she
had scarcely moved for hours. The coarse sheet
wrapping her from toes to neck bore on one corner
the stamped legend, PROPERTY OF COOK COUNTRY MEDI-
CAL EXAMINER'S OFFICE. While she was not fully awake,
she was not fully asleep either; which was one reason why the old man, finding himself thrust into the
role of midwife for her new life, hesitated to leave
her alone, even though other important matters
demanded his attention.

This half-sleeping condition of Kate's had him
somewhat puzzled. No reason, he thought, why she
should not be able to sleep the daylight hours away,
in this her native sepulcher. In fact when he brought
her here he had expected her to slip into a deep sleep
at once.

He came back now from another squint out of the
broken window, to stand motionlessly regarding her.

His black topcoat was open, his dark hat set at a slightly jaunty angle, his dark glasses off, his hands behind his back.

Suddenly Kate's eyes flew open. "I don't know you," she said, in dazed mistrustfulness. Her speech was newly awkward: sometimes she forgot to take a breath before she started talking, for breath was no longer a requirement of her life; sometimes she drew in too much air, and the end of a phrase was punctuated with a sharp puff of the surplus.

She had protested that he was a stranger enough times for him to have lost count. But if patience with her confusion was costing him an effort, he had not let that effort show as yet. "I am an old friend of the family, Kate," he repeated, yet again. "Of your Grandmother Clarissa's in particular. I have brought you here for your own protection."

Kate moved her body substantially now for the first time in hours, rising on one elbow. "*How* did you bring me here?"

This question and answer too, they had been through several times before. "Think back, girl—what do you remember of our journey?"

Kate's blue eyes looked into the distance. This time round she was going to manage to take the conversation at least one step farther than before. "There were doors, somewhere . . . in a couple of different places . . . and you told me that because it was after dark we needed no keys; we could slip through."

"What else?"

"It seems to me that I can remember—flying. Like something in a dream."

"Trust your memory, Kate. It was no dream. Now, what is the last thing that you can recall *before* our journey? Think carefully."

Obediently she retired into her own thoughts, to surface again in a few moments. "I can remember being at a party."

"Excellent! We are making progress. Where was the party?"

"I . . . can't remember."

"Try."

Kate seemed to be trying, but had no success. He pressed on: "After the party, then. You perhaps left with someone?"

"Yes . . ."

"Who was it?" The old man could hear, perhaps half a kilometer away, the snowplow scraping slowly.

"He said . . ." Suddenly Kate sat bolt upright on her shelf, clutching the sheet about her. "He said his name was Enoch Winter."

"You have said that name before." The questioner nodded with satisfaction. "And what does Enoch Winter look like, little one?"

"He's big. Very tall. Very strong." The last word ended with a little shudder, wherein horror and repulsion were mingled with the memory of delight.

"Taller than I am? Look at me."

Obediently Kate looked. "Oh, yes. By several inches."

For a long time, he mused, I was considered very tall myself. Now I am scarcely above the average, I suppose. Shall I someday qualify as a midget?

Aloud, he asked: "His hair? His eyes? His face?"

"Dark curly hair. Sort of a deep voice, but much rougher than yours. His eyes are blue, or maybe gray. I'll know him if I see him again."

"Indeed, I should think you—" He broke off, watching her with great intentness.

Kate's gradual return to full awareness had reached a critical point. Now she was looking with terror at the marble walls, the stained glass, and the tombs surrounding her. "What is this place?" Her breath momentarily forgotten, the question fell into a mere soundless mouthing of the words. Then she drew in a gasp of air. "I know where I am. I know what this is."

"I am your friend," the old man said with iron will, "and you are safe."

Words, even from him, were not enough. Kate screamed and leaped in mad panic from her shelf, a corner of the sheet trailing like a cape. She landed awkwardly, but with catlike new strength supporting unsprained ankles. Without a pause she sprang toward the single door of the mausoleum.

Before she reached it, though, the old man was beside her, and had an arm around her waist. Despite the new strength with which she struggled, he drew her back and soothed her like a child. "No, no. You do not understand the dangers yet."

A moment longer Kate fought for her freedom. Then she slumped in his grip, her eyes crazed. "I want to go home."

His clasp was almost tender. "I think you know," he said, "that you are as close to home right now as you are ever likely to get."

A few seconds passed. This time the movement she made to free herself was deliberate and almost calm, and so he released her. She moved a few steps off and turned to face him, now fully aware—and horrified. "I heard a policeman say that I was dead."

"Very likely you did."

"You can't convince me that I'm dead!"

"My dear girl, I have no intention of trying to convince you of such an absurdity. Neither of us is dead—except to our old, breathing lives."

"Then—what—?"

"You have been through a great change. And understanding it is going to take some time." Acceptance and understanding, the old man knew, did not often come fully on the first day out of the grave.

Kate was frowning down at her swathing sheet. "Where are my clothes?"

The old man walked to one of the crypts and tugged open its bronze door. The interior was empty save for two bags, one a white laundry sack, the other somewhat smaller, and elegant black. He brought both of them back to Kate. "You have some choice of apparel, thought I am not sure the outfit in the white bag is complete."

Wonderingly, Kate reached into the laundry sack and extracted from it first her warm blue jacket, rolled up small; then blue pants and a sweater. She looked at the old man with narrowed eyes, then dug into the other bag. Out first came brown slacks, then a brown sweater, shoes to match, a small mass of soft undergarments. "These are mine." There was more sharpness than fear in her voice now. "But I was wearing the blue. Where did you get these?"

"Ah, memory is firming up. Good. The brown clothing I obtained very early this morning, from your home."

"My home. You've been there. What did you tell them, what—?"

"Gently, Kate, gently. Your family thinks that you are dead."

She shook her head. She backed away from the old man a step, her lips forming another word.

"He thinks so, too. For the time being, at least, it is better so. Later, there will be decisions you must make, regarding those you love. But that must come later, when you know more. Now I am going to look out the window while you dress. Then will we discuss what must be done."

When he turned from squinting at the snow, he found Kate garbed in brown. He took from her the blue clothing, including the warm jacket she no longer needed. These garments he put back into the empty crypt, the only convenient drawer this dwelling-place afforded.

Challengingly, Kate followed him. He smiled to see in her something of her younger sister's bravery. "Now," she demanded, "I want to know who you are, really. And what has really happened to me."

"Very well." He looked steadily into her eyes. "I am a vampire, Kate. Because Enoch Winter exchanged his vampire blood with you, you have become a vampire also. I am sure that there is in your mind much superstitious nonsense regarding our race, which you must now begin to unlearn. We're not all as bad as Enoch Winter."

The girl first tried to laugh at him. Then she tried to look indignant, that he should offer her such nonsense. He could see her wondering what she should try next. He could see also that the energy of terror was fading; a normal daylight trance should overcome her soon.

"But why," the old man mused aloud, "has the infamous Enoch Winter done this? Under other circumstances we might merely ask why any rapist does what he does. But there is also the attack on your brother to be considered. There must surely be a connection."

"What attack?" Kate didn't completely believe, yet, anything he'd said. But already she was swaying on her feet.

"Time to discuss that later." He picked her up, gently; it was almost a matter of catching her as she began to fall. One of her pale hands pushed feebly at his chest in protest, but her eyelids were closing, and she could do no more.

Now she should sleep, until the night at least. But before he put her in a resting place, he stood for a moment, listening intently. A motor vehicle, a small auto whose sound he thought he might just possibly recognize, was drawing near over the cemetery's unplowed drives.

Joe Keogh's Rabbit crunched to a stop in snow unmarked except for a few tracks left by the fur-bearing variety. He supposed the bunnies had a good thing going in a cemetery, except maybe after hours when the guard dogs were let in. Anyway the snowfall had now stopped, though the sky was still almost completely overcast. In the west the clouds were stretched to a thin silver sheet covering a sun already on its way to the horizon. The shortest days of the year were here.

Beside Joe, Judy sat gazing with an unreadable expression at the snow-etched stones of the mausoleum's front. He studied her with concern for a little while, then asked: "Did you want to look at something in particular?"

Still looking at the building, Judy shook her head slowly, disappointedly, almost. What could she have been expecting? She said: "It's just that the dreams were very real."

"But still only dreams," he told her gently. "Right?"

She didn't answer.

"Get a hold of yourself, kid. How could they be anything else? Kate is dead. Whatever else has . . . I admit it's possible that Johnny might be locked up in a closet someplace, the way you describe it in your dream. But—"

"Joe, I could find that place. I know I could, if you would only drive me around and help me look."

"Don't start that again, please." And at that moment, beyond Judy's face, beyond the undisturbed white that covered lawn and walk in front of the Southerland mausoleum, Joe saw the green-aged bronze of the building's door in motion, opening inward into a contrasting blackness. And despite the hardened realism created by eight years on the force, the sight produced a moment when something in his heart began to open into blackness also.

Then it was nothing more frightening than a shadowed doorway in a marble building, with the recognized though unexpected figure of a lean man in dark clothing emerging from it in a quite ordinary way. A penetrating voice called down to them: "Judy? Joe?"

Judy, Joe noticed, seemed not at all surprised. Perhaps she was no longer disappointed, either. Frowning, he shut off the engine. They both got out of the car.

Corday had remained beside the mausoleum's open door, frowning through dark glasses at his watch. "I fear I have lost all track of time," he muttered as Judy and Joe trudged up the virgin walk toward him. "The urns proved more engrossing than I had anticipated."

"My father did give you the key, then," Judy remarked placidly, twirling the end of her scarf. Joe wondered suddenly: could she have been expecting that we'd meet him here?

Corday was smiling at her lightly. "There was no trouble about the key."

Joe asked him: "How did you get out here, Doctor? Take a cab?"

"No, someone kindly offered me a ride from the motel this morning."

"Must've been early. Snow's covered all the tracks completely."

"Indeed, it was."

Judy put in: "If you're ready to leave, we can take you back to the motel. Or wherever you want to go."

"Thank you, my dear, that would be kind."

Corday was in the act of pulling the mausoleum door shut behind him when Joe stepped forward, saying: "As long as we're here, I'd like to take a look at the pottery to . . . Judy, what's wrong?"

"Nothing. I just felt a little dizzy, all of a sudden. I'm all right. You go on in, but I don't want to."

She looked so white-faced that Joe and Corday between them, both peering at her anxiously, walked her down to the car and saw her settled in the rear seat.

"I feel better now. I think it was just a little too much like the dream. Go ahead, Joe, I'm all right."

The two men marched back up to the dark doorway, over the now well-trampled walk.

"You first, Doctor."

With a slight bow, the old man went on in. Joe followed. Once inside, there was really plenty of light, coming in the windows. The doorway had looked so black from outside only by contrast with the snow.

Plenty of light, but not all that much to see. Joe wasn't really sure what he was looking for. The tombs and their decorations, and the big urns, and maybe Corday was really enthusiast enough to want to spend a day here in the cold among them. Joe's breath steamed in the air. To him, the place looked not much different from a fancier-than-usual funeral home, or the inside of one of the older Chicago churches. It reminded him a little of the chapel of Thomas More University, where he had been going to take Kate a couple of days before Christmas, to see *The Play of Daniel* . . . there was plenty of pottery here, all right, and in this large urn someone's crumpled bra, which must have been here since last summer, so evidently the door wasn't always kept carefully locked.

As soon as his eyes met Corday's again, he told the old man bluntly: "Kate's body was missing from the morgue this morning."

Corday's response was controlled surprise, or at least a very good imitation thereof. "Really? Is such a thing a common occurrence there?"

"Very *un*common. I was wondering if you might have any ideas about it."

"Because I wanted to go there last night? No. No, I should not care to venture an opinion. Joe, what brings you and Judy here to the cemetery this afternoon?"

Joe sighed. "The kid had a very vivid dream last night. A couple of dreams, rather. She's upset—of course. Anyway, one dream was that Kate was here, in the family mausoleum, alive, but unable to get out of the place for some reason. And all day today Judy's been saying she thought she'd go crazy if she couldn't get out of the house for a while. Andy's back at the office, being a workaholic as usual. Lenore is— sedated. Clarissa can't decide anything. I finally just took it upon myself to decide that Judy would be better off getting out, and it'd be safe enough if I rode shotgun." He blinked at Corday's blank stare. "Chicago cops always go armed, you know, even off duty. So here we are."

While Joe talked they had been slowly gravitating back to the doorway. Now Corday gestured and Joe stepped out. At the bottom of the little slope, Judy's scarf-wreathed face smiled back from the small car's window.

Joe led the way down to her. Behind him he could hear Corday shutting the metal door of the mausoleum carefully, and the key turning, grating, in the little-used lock.

Judy looked well enough when they rejoined her in the car. "I think it was just the idea of going in there," she said again. "I didn't want to go in after all."

"Natural enough," said Joe, getting the engine and heater started. *Why was the old man here, today?* "Where can we take you, Dr. Corday?"

The old man, in the right front seat, was twisting round to face the back. "Joe tells me you had two vivid dreams last night. What was the second?"

Judy smiled, a quick little flicker, as if to mark the passage of some secret between her and the old man. Then her face turned bleak. "Towards morning I dreamed of Johnny. He was in a closet somewhere. All naked, and bloody, and . . . just awful. God, I hope it isn't true. But I can't stop feeling that it is."

"And can you lead us to this closet?" The old man was intensely serious.

"I'm taking her home," said Joe, and reached to move his selector lever into Drive. The old man's fingers settled gently on his wrist. Joe urged his own hand forward anyway; his hand stayed right where it was, as if he were trying to lift the car with it instead of one thin elderly arm. He felt ridiculous. What was he going to do now, start a wrestling match?

The old man continued to stare at Judy, and Joe followed the direction of his gaze. He was disturbed to see that although Judy still sat up straight, her eyes were closed and the utterly relaxed expression on her face suggested that she was asleep.

In wonder, he asked: "Judy?"

"She is asleep," Corday informed him soothingly, and at the same time let go of Joe's wrist.

"Judy, are you all right?"

"Answer Joe, Judy."

"I'm fine." Her voice was pleasant, but remote. Her eyes stayed closed.

Corday asked her: "Can you now guide us to the building where John is being held?"

"Yes." Her voice held sudden urgency. "Turn west as soon as you leave the cemetery."

Joe looked at her a moment longer, then got the car in motion, this time without interference. "What is she, hypnotized? Whatever you're doing with her, I don't like it. She's going home."

"Joe, don't." Judy's voice was intense but calm. "I'm all right. If you love Kate, you'll help to find her brother."

Joe glanced into the rear-view mirror. Judy's eyes were open again and she looked quite normal.

She said: "Do you think the police are ever going to find him? They don't have a single real clue, do they?"

They had reached the plowed section of the

cemetery roads by now. The gate was only a quarter mile or so ahead. Joe said: "If you want the truth, I don't think they'll ever get him back alive."

"There you are. But we can. He's in a white house, out in the country just a few miles west of here. I think the roof has shingles."

"I think you better go home."

"If you try to take me home I'll jump out of the car before we get there. I'll fight and scream. If you humor me a little I'll be just fine."

Joe slowed, indecisively. Half angry, half pleading for help, he turned to the old man. "Doctor?"

Corday's face was altered by a smile, small, confident, and almost irresistibly comradely. Softly he said: "Turn west."

ELEVEN

"Your hour's almost up," Joe commented. Almost an hour after leaving Lockwood Cemetery, they had at last penetrated the western belt of suburbs and were entering real countryside. The two-lane highway, coated in salted slush, ran northwest. On the left were cornfields, snowy stubble now, and on the right at the moment was a new apartment development, decorated barracks that seemed to have been extruded against the road's shoulder by the congestion to the east.

"Keep going," Judy urged. Again, as happened every time Joe so much as hinted at giving up, there was an underlevel of panic in her reply. "Joe, he's so badly hurt. We've got to get to him right away. There's a man in the house with Johnny, but he's not helping Johnny at all. I can *feel* how close it is. We're almost there."

"Six more minutes," said Joe firmly. "Then we're going to find a phone and call your home and tell 'em you're all right. I agreed to spend an hour at this, and we will, and then you're going home. Right, Doctor?"

No answer came from Corday, who had his hands in his coat pockets, and was gazing fixedly ahead, as if he were lost in his own thoughts.

Joe did not repeat the question. There had been moments during the ride when mentally he swore at himself for being taken in by Judy's hysterics and Corday's strange act, and came very close to turning the car around at once. These moments were followed by others in which he nursed the feeling, hardly suitable for a cop but inextinguishable anyway, that weird things in the field of ESP did sometimes happen. His own mother and father had testified to mutual experiences. And the rational part of his mind suggested that the best way to cure Judy of this dream-idea might be to let her see that there was nothing in it. And, again, to get a kidnapping victim back, any effort at all was worth a try.

They were approaching a highway intersection. "What do I do here?" he asked his guide.

"Turn left," Judy ordered. Give her credit, she was always decisive in giving directions. "We're very close now. Another mile should do it."

"Left it is," Joe agreed. He could just picture himself talking to the sheriff's office on the phone: Yessir, we know where the boy is now. His teenage sister saw it in a dream, and sure enough . . .

The new highway ran ahead of him almost straight, and almost empty. The sun, after almost breaking through the clouds a little earlier, had been smothered again in thick gray masses from which it did not seem likely to emerge again today. Although theoretically it was still daylight, Joe had already flicked his headlights on.

The last housing developments had now fallen behind. To right and left the road was bordered by snowy farm fields, brown hedgerows, patches of woods, wire farm fences. A narrow highway bridge came leaping up to bear the Volkswagen over a still

narrower stream, a country creek that twisted its way
in a frozen course to right and left. For just a moment
the engine stuttered—

"Here!" The word burst out of Judy in a shriek.
Joe looked wildly around for some impending accident. He braked, avoiding a skid in the freezing slush
by fancy footwork on the pedals.

Judy's fingers were biting like claws at his shoulder. "That next drive on our left," she agonized. "Take
that, he's in a house back there."

Joe had brought the small car to a complete stop
on the shoulder of the highway. Now he eased it
forward. Looking ahead on the left, he could now see
that there was a driveway, a small unpaved road, a
something, and he turned into it, between patches
of hedgerow. A rural mailbox planted beside the
highway was capped with snow, making any name that
it might bear invisible.

Trackless snow also covered the narrow lane or
drive. But the surface beneath was evidently solid and
level, for going was not difficult. Almost at the start
the drive turned, taking them out of sight of the
highway among wintry thickets and small trees. It ran
straight for fifty yards or so, then turned again, at the
same time topping a small rise of ground.

Just before reaching this second turn, Joe eased
the Rabbit to a stop. Directly ahead there had just
come into his view the upper portion of one end of
what he would later learn was a sprawling, white
brick, ranch-style house. Now, squinting into the dusk,
he thought he could make out cedar roof-shingles
under a partial covering of snow.

Oddly, Joe felt almost cheated. He looked at the
calm, unreadable face beside him for several seconds
before he spoke. "I don't know what this game is,
mister."

Corday's thin lips parted, this time not in a smile.
"It is a very serious game indeed. And I assure you

that you and I are playing it on the same side."
Peering toward the house, the old man added, as if
to himself: "The sun has not yet set."

"What's that got to do with anything?"

Judy said in a tight voice: "Do something, please,
Joe. You're a policeman. My brother is in there."

Joe looked at them both. Then he put the car in
reverse and backed it up a few yards, getting it
completely out of sight of the house. He turned the
ignition off. He looked at them both again, and shook
his head. "Judy, you know I've got no authority,
outside the city. I'll do this much: walk up to the front
door and see who's home, if anyone. You two stay
here, just sit tight."

Judy started to demand that he do more than that,
but Corday reached back to touch her wrist and she
fell silent. Joe got out of the car and, with a last look
at Corday, took the keys with him. "Be back in a
minute or so."

Readying a story about car trouble and needing to
use a phone, he trudged the last yards toward the
house, following the curve of the drive through completely untracked snow. It was all crazy, of course.
Somehow Judy must have glimpsed from the highway a white house and shingle roof . . .

The only sign of life that Joe could see ahead was
the subtle wavering of heated air above a chimney.
Not a great brick one that would have a fireplace at
its base, but the small metal tube that would vent
the house's furnace to the air. The furnace was turned
on, then. But the garage door and the front door
under its shingled overhang were both sealed along
their bases with unbroken snow. No light showed in
any window. There were no Christmas decorations,
either, if that meant anything, which it probably did
not.

When he reached the front door he alternately
pushed the bell button and knocked, police style,

keeping up a steady barrage in a way that almost always got results, making whoever was inside think that there was some real emergency. The doorbell worked, for he could faintly hear the chime. It wasn't answered, though.

A full minute of such thorough treatment got no results. Joe tried to peer into a large window on the porch beside the door, but the drapes were too tightly shut inside. Not quite ready to give up yet, he started around the house, looking for tracks or other signs of occupancy, and finding nothing that seemed consequential. A couple of imperfectly draped windows let him peek into a couple of rooms, which were empty of furniture. He did see some new-looking paint and shiny floors, as if some remodeling or refinishing project might recently have been completed; but it was too dark inside to be sure of even that much. It might be that the owners had moved out during the remodeling, but had left the heat turned on to protect the water pipes and the new plaster.

His circuit of the house completed, Joe approached the front step again, thinking: one more knock, so I can say I really tried. When we get back to the highway, I'll check the name on that mailbox—just to be thorough.

Fiercely Judy hissed the words, almost in the ear of the old man who sat in the seat ahead: "He *is* in that house!"

"I do not doubt that, Judy." Lean fingers on the door handle beside him, the old man was staring ahead with serpent-like intensity. "But neither do I think that Joe is going to discover him. He is an honorable policeman, who will not dream of exceeding his authority on grounds no stronger than those which we have given him."

"We can't go away and leave Johnny in there!"

"We certainly cannot. Especially since this visit must alarm his captor. You say you see only one man with him, now?"

"Yes."

"I think you are right." And with the movement of a lithe twenty-year-old, Corday was suddenly out of the car. He held the door open, his tall form bending beside it, looking in at her. "I am going to take action. And you . . . but no."

"What is it?" She had never seen eyes like his . . . they were so dark. And they were old no longer.

He said, eyes glittering: "I was about to order you to stay here in safety. But this is not the world for safety, is it? Nor are you and I the people who prize it above all. So, will you enter battle with me? In all the world are very few whom I would sooner ask."

The man who spoke to her seemed to have been transformed, to have grown larger than life. And it seemed to Judy that she was transformed too. The young woman who stepped out of the car was a fit companion for heroic deeds. Yet she was still herself, perhaps more truly herself than ever before.

"What must I do?" she calmly asked.

"Come this way at once. Joe is returning." Her companion's voice had altered too, and there were hints of drums and trumpets even in its softness.

She followed him as quickly as she could, along the edge of the drive back in the direction of the highway.

"Now jump this way," he ordered. "Leave no tracks." The best sprint of her young legs took her sideways from the drive, to an area of matted leaves and brown grass that had been blown free of snow. From one snowless patch to the next she followed her companion, who moved ahead now like an acrobat, reaching back a hand from time to time to steady her. He led her through grass and brush and briefly along the top rail of a split-log fence, in a curving path that brought them into some bushes from which they could just see the car.

Crouching there motionless, with Corday's hand upon her arm, Judy could see the alarm in Joe's face as he came trotting the last yards to the vehicle, shocked by the realization that they were gone. "Corday?" he called out, almost threateningly. Then, louder: "Judy!"

In a moment he had spotted their footprints in the snow, leading back along the drive. Swearing, he started after them on foot, and promptly lost the trail where the snow gave way in spots to leaves and grass. Red-faced and muttering, Joe jumped into the car. Spinning wheels in snow, he got the Volks turned round and headed back to the highway. The sound of it died away.

"Now, my girl." Corday—this youthful stranger she had known as Corday—stood up straight, raising her by both arms to stand beside him. "Before I can enter any house, I must be called, invited, by someone inside. Do not ask me to explain just now, but it is so. So you must get into this house, somehow, and then call to me. If no one answers the door for you, break in a window."

"I will." Around Judy the woods were growing minute by minute dimmer, darkness oozing up into them from the ground. But for the moment she was not at all afraid.

"Only call me, and I shall come. *But you must call.*"

Life sang in Judy's blood, life of an intensity that nothing in her memory could match. It forced her to a knowledge that she had earlier refused. She breathed: "I called you once before. Didn't I?"

The man before her nodded quickly, his timeless eyes joyful that she understood. "But ask no questions now," he said. With a light pressure of his hand he sent her on her way.

Fear did not begin until she was out of the woods and well along the drive toward the house, where all the windows were utterly dark in the swiftly gathering twilight. The snow under Judy's booted feet was marked now with Joe's tracks, going and returning. And now she could see where someone, probably Joe also, had circled the house.

On the raised step under the protective overhang of roof that sheltered the front door, the snow was not as deep as in the open yard. It was much trampled by Joe's feet, but an unbroken white grommet remaining between door and threshold showed that the door had not been opened for him. Judy rang the doorbell at once, heard the faint chime, and only then wondered what she would say if someone came. Her car had broken down, that would be it.

But no one answered.

A quick glance to her rear showed only the darkening gloom of woods and lawn and fields, but she knew Corday was there. Before her, she could still feel the habitation of the house. But there was no sound or light to give corroboration to the feeling.

She knocked, then rang again. Inside, she felt— she knew—that Johnny heard the bell. Johnny, locked up in fear and pain and darkness, unable or afraid to even cry out.

The window beside the front door, Judy soon discovered, could not be opened from the outside. Not by her pulling or pushing at it, at least. She balled a fist inside her mitten, then paused long enough to take off her scarf and warp it round her hand.

Judy's first blow at the glass was not wholehearted enough to break it in, and she gave a little cry of frustration before she punched again. This time there was a satisfactory crash, followed by a tinkle on the floor inside.

As if the crash had been a signal prearranged, the front door was suddenly thrown wide. A young man, thick-necked and muscular but rather small, stood there wearing faded jeans and an old army shirt. One hand was out of sight on each side of the door frame. His neatly trimmed hair was somehow incongruous. His eyes were partially hidden behind the distortion of thick glasses; his mouth, twisted in rage or fear or both, was open on uneven teeth.

"What're you doing?" The man's voice was breathless, almost unintelligible with apparent strain.

Its urgent menace for the moment made Judy forget everything else and she took an involuntary step backward. "I—I need help with my car."

"For that you break the window? Who was that guy who was just here?"

"I . . ." From some inward source, invention came. "I asked a man to help me. Now I don't knew where he's gone."

"No help here. There's a gas station down the highway, east, about half a mile." The man's extreme excitement had perhaps eased just a little. He had not changed his position in the doorway yet.

"I don't think I can walk that far," Judy pleaded. "Please, let me use your phone."

"Get outta here," he muttered, almost as if his thoughts were already on something else. He kept darting glances past her into the snowy dusk.

Judy was mastering her fright. Her nerves still vibrated in sympathy with her brother's unceasing pain. "I won't go away," she said, regaining her lost step toward the door. "I can't."

The young man looked at her with very ugly eyes.

She faced his look. "I'm just going to stand here and scream until you let me in."

Her desperation, though not the reason for it,

evidently impressed itself upon him. Several things, most of them frightening, passed through the young man's face in quick succession. Finally caution in some form prevailed.

"All right, I'll come take a look at your goddamned car," he muttered. "Breaking the goddamned window—" He turned away as if meaning to grab a coat from somewhere close at hand. As he retreated he pushed the door from inside, shutting it almost completely.

Not giving herself time to think, Judy sprang forward, throwing her body against the closing door. It burst open before her rush. "Johnny!" she screamed.

A ceiling light just inside the entry had now been switched on. The rest of the house, as far as she could tell, was all in darkness. The floor of the large entryway was tiled, and on the opposite side of it the young man stood before an open closet door. Not the closet that she wanted, no. He was in the act of pulling on a bulky sheepskin jacket, and in his free hand there dangled a long-barreled, very real-looking revolver. His face was just now turning toward Judy in fresh astonishment.

To Judy's left, a great living room, devoid of furniture but thickly carpeted, stretched to a distant red-brick fireplace wall. Somewhere in that direction, a little farther off, Johnny was cowering in his prison, chained and gagged by fear, radiating pain like heat from glowing metal. Judy's screaming of his name still rang like a distant alarm in his dazed brain, and from there back to her own mind again.

"Johnny!" she cried again. "I'm here!" And she moved toward the living room, to place herself between her helpless brother and this armed maniac.

The young man in the sheepskin stepped across the entry and slammed the front door closed again. His face was evilly contorted now. Without a word he moved toward Judy, the weapon in his hand rising with what seemed like endless slowness.

At last remembering what she was supposed to do, Judy cried out: "Come in, Dr. Corday, help me!" As she cried she ducked away from her attacker, to find herself falling softly down the single step from entryway to sunken living room. Her arms were raised to protect her head from blows or bullets. Her last glimpse of the young man as she turned away showed him reaching toward her with his left hand.

Even as the house spun with her spinning fall, she heard the front door fly open with a violent crash. There was a roaring of cold air in the room, an incomprehensible sudden wind that had blasted open the closed door. The hand that had just brushed Judy's arm fell away. Then the door slammed shut again with a thunderous bang.

The wind gave one last, trailing howl, and disappeared.

The house was quiet.

Judy raised her face from the thick carpet and sat up. Corday was in the act of crouching down beside her, one hand outstretched. His fingers touched her hair. "Judy, it is all right now. You are not hurt?"

She jumped to her feet. "Find Johnny."

Her companion was already in motion, his long strides carrying him off into the darkness engulfing the rear portion of the house.

Before following, Judy looked around. The front door was tightly closed once more, though now a portion of its lock hung in at an angle among splinters of newly broken wood. On the other side of the living room, near the great fireplace, the young man's sheepskin coat lay in a bulky mound, and near it the long-barreled revolver. He must have run outside. . . .

"Judy?" Corday's penetrating voice reached her from some distant room. "He is in here."

She ran down a dark hallway, past dim,

unfurnished bedrooms, and a bathroom where she could make out a dirty towel hung on a rack, soap in a grimy puddle on a lavatory top. Light shone out of another bedroom, where Corday was waiting for her. A small lamp burned on an upended crate that served as bedside table for an unmade cot. Odds and ends of men's clothes were strewn about, along with girly magazines, weightlifting journals, bits of food and garbage, tin cans, paper cups, plates, a small transistor radio.

Corday stood beside the open door of the huge closet, gesturing for Judy to go in ahead of him. "He looks bad," he said with his usual calm. "But I believe he will recover."

No clothes were hanging in the closet. Inside, Judy dropped to her knees beside the horrible, pale figure contracted into one dim corner. The figure stirred, raising a head matted with long, dirt-colored hair. Against its naked chest were folded two mummified Egyptian hands, covered with dried brownish stains, their fingers clenched and twisted.

Startlingly pale eyes appeared, in a face that might once have been her brother's. "Judy," a stranger's voice croaked at her. "They caught you, too."

"No, oh no. Oh, Johnny, your poor hands."

Corday was in and out of the closet now, moving with impersonal gentleness and quite improbable speed. He helped Johnny stand, looked at his throat closely for some reason, then wrapped him in two blankets from the cot. Somehow he found Johnny's own boots and helped Judy get them on his feet. There seemed, for some reason, to be a tremendous hurry.

"You are to drive him directly home, Judy, stopping for nothing, except to avoid a collision."

"The car—"

"There is a car in the garage, and unless I am mistaken these are its keys." He handed her a jingling ring. "Hurry ahead and get the engine started—down the hall to your right. I shall bring John."

In grabbing for the keys Judy accidentally bumped her brother's arm and he cried out in pain. Then she flew down the hall in the direction Corday indicated. She caught a last glimpse of the living room in passing; the bundle of sheepskin coat had legs, she saw from this angle, and it was stirring now, raising a face.

A light was on already in the garage, and its door had been rolled up. She was already behind the wheel of the Cadillac, engine started and headlights on, as Corday arrived to stow her brother in beside her.

"Shouldn't we telephone someone first—"

"Joe will be calling for help. Drive straight home now, stop for nothing. Leave all else to me."

"Judy?" The voice coming from the pale face beside her did sound a little like her brother's now, though terribly weak. "Take me home now?"

Corday had already slammed the Cadillac's door shut and vanished back into the house. Even as Judy gunned the engine and pulled out of the garage, two muffled banging noises from in there reached her ears. She had driven miles toward home before it occurred to her excited mind that they might possibly have been shots.

TWELVE

Of the two uniformed Cook County sheriff's deputies who had met Joe at the country gas station in response to his phone call, and had then followed him back to this lonely house, one was now outside in their official car, busy with its radio. The other deputy was with Joe in the house, and had begun a more or less methodical questioning of the only other person who had been on the scene when they arrived.

"Now, you say he fired twice at you, Dr. Corday? Where were you standing when that happened?"

"I believe—here." And Corday moved decisively to a position in the living room not far from the entry. He seemed to have been not in the least shaken by the peril through which, according to his own story, he had so recently passed.

"Uhuh," the deputy remarked. He was not especially excited either. Following the old man closely he pointed to, without quite touching, a shattery-looking place in the otherwise new-looking plaster wall behind him. "If that is a bullet hole, I guess you weren't standing *exactly* where you are right now, when she hit."

"Approximately," Corday conceded, turning to look with mild interest at the damage.

The deputy made a note. "You say he fired twice . . . one could be in the carpet somewhere, I suppose."

"That seems not improbable. As I recall, his arm was shaking."

"Then he ran out of the house, you say. Did you make any attempt to hold him?"

"I am not as young as I once was, officer."

"Yessir, I don't blame you a bit for that. Don't get me wrong. But first, he did let you load the kidnap victim into a car and drive him out of here? I don't quite understand that."

Corday blinked mildly at the deputy. "Perhaps the young man, even though he had a gun, was frightened when Miss Southerland and I broke in."

"Perhaps. Huh. You say you're the one who broke the door in? How'd you manage that?"

"Construction standards are not what they were in the old days."

"Well, that's for sure." Scratching his head, the deputy gave Joe a wary look: You know this old guy, huh? You didn't warn me he was a little crazy.

Corday added: "And it is not always the brave, is it, who bear weapons?"

"That's for *damn* sure." The deputy sighed. "Now, sir, tell me again—how'd you know the Southerland boy was here, as you say he was?"

"I repeat, I am an accomplished hypnotist—" The old man broke off, turning to watch the front door. A few seconds later it grated open. This time a piece of the smashed lock fell completely free.

Deputy Two, wide-eyed, stopped in the doorway. "Carl! I just got the Glenlake chief on the horn. He confirms what our witness here says. Both the Southerland kids are home, they drove up a few minutes ago in someone's Caddy. The girl says they came from out here. The boy has the little finger missing from each hand. They're taking him to Evanston Hospital. The FBI and everyone else is gonna be out here on our ass in about ten minutes."

"Jesus," said Deputy One, with fervor. He gave the old man a look that showed how little of the old man's story had been believed, up until this moment. "Well, let's not screw up anything until they get here."

"Carl, I'm gonna take a look a round outside. The suspect is supposed to have run out, isn't he?"

Number One considered. "Right. I guess you better. But don't screw up anything. Don't mess up the tracks in the snow, if there are any. I guess there must be, if the guy ran out."

"I'll come along," Joe volunteered. "I can show you which tracks are mine, at least."

"Thanks, that would be a help."

Outside, more snow was now falling, in the form of frigidly dry powder. From the front step, Deputy Two's powerful flashlight swept the yard. "The longer we wait, the harder it's gonna be to find anything."

"Those tracks going all the way around the house are mine," Joe pointed out. "Now there, those are new." From the front step a narrow, fresh trail led in a straight diagonal across the yard, angling away from the drive.

"I'd say *two* people."

"Not side by side, though. One following the other."

"Or chasing the other, maybe."

They started across the yard themselves, keeping parallel with the trail they followed. The deputy led with his flash, Joe stepping into the deputy's tracks.

Joe said: "I think they were both running."

"Jesus, I think you're right. Look, can this be one stride, from here to here? It must be ten feet long."

"I'm no expert at this tracking bit."

"Hell, I'm not either."

At the edge of the yard the makers of the double

trail had somehow negotiated a decorative, split-rail fence. On the other side of the fence the trail went on, still practically in a straight line, through a patch of young woods and down an easy slope.

Following the deputy over the fence and on, Joe muttered: "Couldn't have been running to get to a road this way, could they? Highway's back in the other direction."

"All that's down this way is the creek, I think—hey."

A few yards ahead, the slope flattened into what would be in summer muddy creek-bottom land. The dead stalks of last summer's growth of weeds made a thin, wintry jungle, more than head-high but fragile and offering no real impediment to progress. Along the trail a number of the dried stalks had been broken down in its direction. Not many yards farther on, the flashlight's beam now reached the frozen creek itself, a sunken aisle surfaced with plain snow, twisting between overgrown banks.

On the near bank of the frozen creek the double trail ended in a broad, trampled circle, centered on a mound of something that was not entirely snow.

Hurrying forward, looking over the deputy's shoulder along the brilliant shaft of the flashlight's beam, Joe could see blood. The trampled space was marked with it in little flecks and splashes, fresh, not yet sanitized by falling snow. And there, a pair of thick-lensed eyeglasses had fallen. As they entered the circle Joe also saw a human finger, its stump-end ragged and gory. Had someone carried one of the poor kid's fingers out here, meaning to hide evidence? Or—

The central mound was moving in the light. It was sheepskin under newly fallen white. Joe lifted at it with two hands, the deputy with the hand in which he did not hold the light, and it turned over.

"Jesus."

"He's still alive, anyway."

"Yeah."

Joe lifted some more, the deputy held his light and brushed off snow. One arm in a sheepskin sleeve fell dangling.

"Look at his hand."

"It's both hands. Jesus God."

Struggling to move the inert weight back toward the house, Joe found himself stepping on another loose finger. He saw a third. He didn't look for more. Halfway back to the house, the deputy started blasting on a whistle. In a few seconds his partner came running to them through the snow, gun drawn.

With three to carry they made quick work of getting the hurt man back into the house. Corday watched their entrance without comment, and slowly followed them to the bedroom. There they stretched their burden on the cot, the only feasible place.

Joe was angry. "You're a doctor, right? This is an emergency case we've got here, wouldn't you say?" But there was more to his anger than the fact that Corday was standing by so passively.

The two of them were at the bedroom doorway. One of the deputies squeezed past and ran out, evidently heading for the car radio again.

Corday said gently, imperturbably: "I will examine him if you wish." With Joe and the other deputy hovering watchfully, he approached the cot. He bent and touched the young man's face. The eyes of the supine figure opened, squinting, blinking like a newborn's in the light of the single lamp. It took those eyes a little while to focus on Corday's face.

Then the man on the cot raised what had been a hand. A gurgle came from his throat, and with a terrible effort he moved as if to rise, to scramble backward. Joe caught him under the armpits to keep him from falling to the floor, and in that moment the young man's body ceased to move.

Corday continued to regard the youth intently for

a moment, without touching him again. Then he straightened. "Gentlemen, this man is dead."

"We're calling for an ambulance," the deputy argued, as if in contradiction. Meanwhile he was helping Joe lay the man down flat again. "Isn't there anything you can do? Heart massage . . ."

"It is too late."

The deputy stood indecisively for a moment. Then, mumbling swearwords, he stalked out after his partner.

The body on the cot certainly looked dead. Joe waited to hear the broken, grating sound with which the front door closed. Then he looked at the old man. "Dr. Corday?" His own voice was tighter than he liked. He felt close to some kind of violence himself. His anger was largely at himself, he realized, for being taken in.

"Yes, Joe?"

"I want you to tell me what happened to this man's hands. Don't tell me you should not like to venture an opinion."

The old man looked again at the figure on the cot. He was still cool, too cool. Only the crazies could be that cool. Joe should have seen it before.

Corday said: "It would appear that his fingers have somehow been—"

"Torn off, goddam it. I can see that. *Who did it?*"

"Discovering that would seem to be the job of the police. Though not necessarily, I suppose, of the Chicago Pawn Shop Detail?" Corday's voice was tired, as well as cool. That sounded like a request for a little more comradely co-operation.

No more. "This is the same guy who supposedly fired a gun at you?"

"Oh yes. Yes."

"He must have had his fingers then, right? Right? Then he ran out of here. Trying to get away? If he had the gun like you say, why was he running? And who chased him?"

A glint of something other than coolness came into the old man's eyes. Amusement, it looked like. "I would surmise that he ran to get to running water. A forlorn hope, of course. It would not have saved him. But still he was a more knowledgeable young man than some. About some things, at least."

"Running water, save him? What does that mean?" Joe knew he was losing his own coolness, his own control. The knowledge didn't help.

"Joe, believe it or not, I am extremely tired. I must rest before I undergo any lengthy questioning." Corday turned away to seek out the room's one chair. And pallor, tiredness, age, were indeed all showing in his face at the moment.

"Don't go to sleep just yet. I don't like that trick you pulled on me today, sending me off on a wild goose chase. I don't like a bunch of things about you. I'm not here as a cop tonight, and I can speak my mind." He immediately felt a little better, calmer, for having spoken that much of it at least. All right, he should have seen before that the old man had to be at least a little crazy.

Sitting wearily erect, hands on knees, Corday made the old chair almost a throne. "As for the wild goose chase, as you describe it, I would not have done that had there been time to win you over by argument. But there was no time. The boy had to be saved at once."

"You really knew that he was here. But how?"

"You saw."

Joe, the interrogating officer, stood over the seated suspect. "Let that pass for the moment. Let's go over again what you say happened here after you sent Judy and Johnny home. You were in the living room with this guy, he shot at you and then ran out. You stayed in the house. How do you suppose his fingers got torn off?"

Corday took a moment to ponder. "Perhaps, Joe, it would be more profitable to start with *why*."

"All right, then. If you've got a good reason, try it out on me."

"There is revenge as a motive. You must come across that in your work."

"Not as often as you might think. Not like this. People do turn each other in to the police, there's plenty of that. If this was done for revenge, who did it?"

"Some—ally—of the Southerland family?"

"Who?"

"A second common purpose of torture," said the old man pedantically, "is of course the extortion of information. And a third purpose is to make an example of the victim. Perhaps to warn his associates to desist from a certain course of action—the persecution of a certain family, for instance."

Watching the old man, listening to him, Joe felt his earlier anger coming back, more coldly now. Eight years on the force, brushing now and then against every kind of evil that the city bred, had not prepared him for a close look at anyone like this. It was not what Corday might have done, or what he was saying, so much as what he was. Just what the old man was, Joe did not know; but the closer he got to it, the more his deepest feelings recoiled.

"Historically," the old man was continuing, "such frightful warnings have been more effective than many people currently suppose. Then of course, two or even all three purposes may be served by the same act—the same atrocity, if you will. And now, before you ask me another question Joe, will you answer one for me in turn?"

"I don't know. If I can. Maybe."

"Who is Craig Walworth?"

Joe blinked, trying to shift gears. "I've heard the name. Society. From one of the wealthy families in the city. What's he got to do with any of this? Don't tell me this is him?" He gestured at the still figure on the cot.

Corday shook his head tiredly. "I doubt that very much."

"This guy"—he gestured toward the cot, where blind blue eyes stared up—"ran down the hill to get to running water, huh?"

"Thinking his pursuer could not follow him across the stream. Grasping at a faint hope of that, at least."

"His pursuer, meaning you. The gun in your hand, not in his."

The wicked old eyes looked up at Joe were once more amused.

Joe shivered. Words came from him involuntarily: "I think you're crazy. You're a maniac. I should never have left Judy alone with you for a minute."

At last, at last, some basic feeling had been provoked, deep in those dark and ancient eyes that looked, to Joe, not a bit more human for its presence. Joe was suddenly, comfortingly, aware of the weight that rode his shoulder-holster, underneath his jacket. And it was a relief also to hear more cars arriving now, pulling in round the last turn of the long drive from the highway.

THIRTEEN

Again Judy was not alone in her own warm bedroom, though it was the middle of the night. Her waking was gradual and without fear, but she knew he was there even as she woke.

Judy turned over in bed and looked. This time his dark figure was standing beside the dressing-table chair.

"Have I alarmed you?" Dr. Corday's normal voice inquired softly.

"No." She sat up in bed, and was irritated to find herself involuntarily fingering the top button of her nightgown again. "What is it?"

"The truth is that I feel a need to talk. And I much prefer your company to that of anyone else I can talk with tonight."

"Won't you sit down?"

"Thank you." The chair in his hand moved with ghostly silence. He settled into it without a sound.

"I wanted to thank you," Judy said, "for what you did today."

"It was my pleasure, as well as my duty, to be of service." And her visitor made her a little seated bow.

114

"Can you tell me anything more about Kate?" When her question had gone unanswered for a moment Judy added: "I'm certain now that she's still alive. Don't ask me how I know. But I was right about Johnny, wasn't I? It's the same feeling."

"Indeed, you were right. You have a talent in such matters."

"But you don't want to talk about Kate yet. All right, I trust you."

He was silent for a time, and motionless in his chair. At last he said: "It is long, I think, since anyone has trusted me in such a way. Strange, it had not occurred to me for a long time, that I was never any longer trusted . . . ah, Judy, I am tired tonight."

"Can't you get any rest?"

"That is one thing I wished to discuss with you tonight. In the morning you will hear that I have disappeared from my motel. The police, as they believe, have put me in storage there, so they may check up on me with the authorities in London before they begin to question me intensively."

"Are you in trouble?"

He almost laughed, though not at her, she saw with relief. Perhaps at himself. "My dear! I am never out of trouble, one might say. Tomorrow the police will not find me available for questioning. But tomorrow night I shall be active again, and perhaps you will see me then. The task for which you so justly summoned me will be completed—if I can do it. The truth is, the enemy has proven to be rather more powerful than I at first suspected. Still, I believe I can succeed, if I am given occasional help as effective as your help was today."

"Oh yes! Anything. Of course. Do you have a place where you can rest?"

"Fortunately I long go made preparations for a visit to the New World. You see, real rest is not always easy for me to obtain, particularly when I am this far from home. My enemies no doubt have counted on that fact. Oh, yes, it is *my enemies* that we are here concerned with."

"I don't understand."

"What is it about the Southerland family, I have asked myself, that could provoke such seemingly senseless attacks as those you have endured? The unique thing about the Southerlands, I say in answer to my own question, is their special relationship with a very unusual protector, an old friend no one else in America can claim. Ergo, the purpose of the seemingly purposeless onslaught is to lure this old friend of theirs here from across the sea. In America, his foes calculate, their chances of attacking him successfully will be much improved. Here, it will be hard for him to find a place to rest, and perhaps they can locate it when he does."

"And I called you here. I'm sorry. I never—"

"No! Do not be sorry for calling me. Even if I should be destroyed—which I do not for a moment mean to be."

"If you know who these enemies of yours are, we ought to let the police know too."

"It would not be easy to impress the truth upon the police. Nor would it be wise. This is a private feud, best settled privately. We have made a start, one of our enemies is dead already."

"You mean the young man out at the house where Johnny was. I heard the police talking about all that. They were guessing about some strange kind of cult."

"I tried to explain something of the situation to Joe. He did not understand. But I believe you do. At least in part."

"That guy deserved to be killed!" Judy burst out. "When I think about my brother . . . you know we took Johnny to the hospital, under guard and all, and he still cried when I left him. Didn't want me to go. Was afraid they were going to get their hands on him again. Whatever happened to that fellow with the gun, he had it all coming to him."

Showing a little of his former energy, Corday got up to pace the floor. "We have at least three more foes who must be eliminated. And two of them are infinitely more dangerous than the one now dead, who was only their tool. I warn you, you who will at least begin to understand, that they have powers beyond anything you will expect a human being to possess."

"Not beyond yours."

He stopped in his pacing and they looked at each other silently. She could no longer see him as an old man. She felt torn between an impulse to jump out of bed and run to him, and a deeper urge, an inner warning even, to stay were she was.

He said: "In you I see . . . a fragment of my earlier self. And a young love."

"A young love? Is she still alive?"

"She? . . . ah yes, very much alive. In England." His teeth flashed in a smile, and the starlight or moonlight made it appear for a moment that something had gone wrong with their shape. "Will you know your own great love, when he appears?"

"At first sight, you mean? Oh, I'm not so foolish as to think that."

A little silence fell between them once again. The instinct that had warned Judy earlier now seemed to be signaling that the crisis, whatever it had been, was past. Under the covers she could feel her legs relaxing now, trembling slightly at the knees.

"I beg your pardon, Judy. I should not have spoken so patronizingly."

"I think you're a gentleman, Dr. Corday. You know, what people used to mean when they said someone was a gentleman. I don't know if I'm saying it right."

"I think I understand. I thank you."

"I'm glad I called you here. I don't understand how it worked, but I'm very glad I did."

"I also am glad." The tall figure in the gloom moved just a little closer. "Be brave, and we will win. I do not tell you not to be afraid."

"Are you ever afraid?" Then Judy shook her head. "I suppose that when fear ends, life is over."

In the dimness the expression on the tall man's face showed great tiredness, and now for a moment infinite sadness as well, so that for a moment Judy was frightened after all. And in the next moment, her visitor was gone.

FOURTEEN

The police artist was just packing up his sketch pads and getting ready to leave when Joe shepherded Judy and Clarissa past Johnny's police bodyguard in the hospital corridor and into the private room. The artist was chuckling a little as he packed, having evidently just made some little joke—or maybe Johnny was the joker, for here the kid was, sitting straight up in bed and looking well, or almost well, just as his mother and father had so thankfully described him.

A drift of vased and potted flowers and plants was mounting up at one side of the room, and two bed-side tables were almost covered with cards and notes, along with some half-finished sketches that the art-ist had evidently abandoned. Johnny's hands were both heavily bandaged, and he held them out awkwardly behind first Judy's back and then Clarissa's when the women hurried to hug him.

When they took chairs at last, Joe moved up closer to the bed. "Well, buddy, you look a hell of a lot better than I expected."

"I feel real good, too." John appeared to pause to think about his feelings seriously. "Mom and Dad said

119

I shouldn't have a bunch of visitors, but I hope you guys can stay a while."

"Cops have been bugging you with questions, I suppose."

"Oh, yeah, about the people who kidnapped me. They say the guy who stayed with me in the house is dead. They showed me a Polaroid of a dead man, and it was him, all right."

The kid seemed to be able to talk about it all quite lightly now. Wait, Joe thought, a reaction will hit him later. Nightmares at least. A little craziness of some kind, probably. The family will have to watch for it. He asked Johnny: "Who were the rest of them?"

"There were at least two other men, and one woman. And once, I swear, they had like a party going on. Whole bunch of people, talking in some weird foreign language."

"Huh."

"Yeah, I don't think the police and the FBI believe me either. They probably think I was delirious. But one night all these people were in the house, all talking what sounded like Latin."

"Latin," said Clarissa, as if shocked, as if the use of Latin in such a business would be some kind of special sacrilege. She sat back in her chair and looked at Judy, who only gave an impatient little headshake in reply.

John went on: "And the cops keep asking me if I ever got a message out, anything like that. I didn't. I couldn't. How'd you ever know I was in there?"

Wishing that he hadn't quit smoking quite so permanently the last time, Joe bit at a hangnail. "I don't think I know the answer to that one myself."

Judy said defensively: "I keep telling everyone, I just had a feeling of where you were. First in a dream. And then, when Dr. Corday hypnotized me, I could find the house. I seemed to be able to really see you for a while, in that closet."

Mention of the closet made John give his head a twitchy shake. "Where's Dr. Corday now?" he wondered. "I asked Mom and Dad and they just sort of put me off. I'd like to be able to thank him."

Judy said: "He seems to have disappeared from his motel this morning." She sounded almost casual about it, which made Joe feel vaguely relieved.

Johnny's eyes widened. "I hope those guys didn't . . ."

"The kidnappers?" Joe shook his head. "I don't think so. The cops were watching the motel all night, I'm sure."

"Then how'd he get out?"

"That's a good question." Joe had his own ideas about that. His police instincts, if after eight years in the business you maybe began to have such things, told him that the old man had not looked at all like Dr. Corday when he came out, and furthermore Dr. Corday was not going to be easy to find again. Because Dr. Corday no longer existed. Disguises were generally nonsense, of course. But 'the kindly old family doctor from London' had itself been a disguise, one good enough to work, for a while anyway and among strangers. Except . . . Clarissa, of course. Granny Clare. Joe was going to have to talk to her in private when he got the chance. She hadn't met his eye directly all morning.

"Jeez, I hope he's all right." Johnny was starting to get upset about it."

"I'm sure he is," said Judy impulsively, sounding like there could be no doubt.

"I'm just as glad he's gone, myself," said Joe, and felt astonished at the violence of the glare that Judy turned on him.

She said: "*He* got my brother out of there."

"Yes, he did do that." Joe turned to the window, to study the grayness of middle-class Evanston in midwinter, through black skeletal trees. "Afterwards,

though, Corday and I were talking, alone. The dead
man was there on the cot in the same room. The
deputies were out in their car using the radio. Corday
was talking pretty crazy, then. I'm saying this because
if he pops up again I think you all ought to use care
in dealing with him."

"Crazy how?" Judy challenged.

"Well. Like it might very well have been him who
killed that fellow, that way. Though he didn't confess
it in so many words. To brag about something like
that, whether you really did it or not . . . I've got to
see Charley Snider later today and go over all of this
with him."

Judy was angry. "If he killed a kidnapper, does that
make him crazy?" Her brother was watching numbly.
Clarissa was hiding her face, or maybe just resting
her eyes.

Joe continued: "And then he said some incoherent-
sounding things, like how the man had run down the
hill to get to running water. That man's not
normal . . . Clarissa, you all right?"

"Running water," repeated Granny Clare, through
lips suddenly gone pale. Looking worse than Johnny
in his hospital bed, she started to get up, clutched
at a bedside table, sent papers spilling to the floor.
Then she sank back in her chair.

Judy, her normal self again, hurried to fuss over
her grandmother. Clarissa popped a nitroglycerin pill,
took some water, looked a lot better.

Joe asked: "Does running water mean anything in
particular?"

Judy scowled at him again, and turned to her
brother, changing the subject. "What did the other
people look like?"

"Oh, the only ones I really saw were the two men
in the car, the ones who grabbed me. I got the best
look at the one who was driving but he was sort of
ordinary-looking, I guess. See, I was walking along

the side of Sheridan Road there, after dark, coming home from the Birches', and this car just pulled up slowly, and this guy with a dark beard rolled down his window and asked for some kind of phony directions. Then the back door opened, and this real monster sort of jumped out. I didn't get much of a look at his face, not then anyway, but man was he big. He was the one who . . ."

John's voice trailed off. His eyes fell to his bandaged hands, and for a moment the boy's face showed shock, as if it were just coming through to him now what those bandages really meant. "I'll be able to use my hands almost as good as ever," he added, with the air of doggedly repeating something he had been told.

"You said there was a woman," Judy prodded, probably just trying to snap Johnny out of his dark contemplation.

He looked vacantly at his sister for a moment before answering. "Yeah. There in the house, at night. She looked into the closet at me, but it was too dark for me to see her. I dunno. It's all kind of vague." Suddenly turning into a hospital patient after all, Johnny lay back on his pillows.

"I think we'd better let you rest." Judy bent over her brother to hug him one more time.

When it came Joe's turn to say farewell, he grinned at the boy and shook his own two hands together. "Let us know if we can bring you anything."

"I will."

Judy had paused to restore the papers fallen from the table. Looking at one sketch, she gave a little sniff and almost smiled. "Know who this looks like to me? I met him once, when he was trying to get Kate to go on a skiing weekend with him. Craig Walworth."

FIFTEEN

You didn't just find upper-crust society in the Chicago phone book, of course. But if you were in the police department you knew a number to dial to be told the address of someone with an unlisted phone.

Alone after dropping Judy and Clarissa off in Glenlake, driving on south toward the Loop's sky-notching towers, Joe considered for the dozenth time why he shouldn't just lay Craig Walworth's name on Charley Snider. The main reason, he decided, was his feeling that the evil old man wanted him to do just that. Why else had the old man brought the name up out of nowhere when they were alone? *Who is Craig Walworth?* Damn the old man to hell, anyway, for asking that and then disappearing. So there was no real Walworth-connection to be pointed out to Charley. One question, from someone who was very clever and not to be trusted; and one sketch that might look a little like Craig Walworth but had evidently been discarded because it didn't look too much like the bearded kidnapper.

When they had given Joe his days off to mourn for Kate, they hadn't specifically warned him to keep from muddling up the Southerland investigations by doing any poking around on his own. The captain evidently hadn't thought him dumb enough to need a warning of that kind. Well, he wasn't dumb. And he wasn't getting into the investigation, he told himself now. He was only trying to get it clear in his own mind whether there might be anything that could tie Craig Walworth into it.

While driving Judy home he had questioned her casually—as casually as he could manage—about that skiing weekend invitation. Judy had been very definite that Kate had never accepted any proposition like that from Craig Walworth. But Judy would say that now, anyway, just to spare Joe's feelings.

When he reached the tall apartment building on Lake Shore Drive, Joe had a qualm about using his police ID to get in. He compromised by using it and then telling the doorman he wanted to see Walworth on personal business. The doorman, an old-timer whose badly fitting jacket suggested he might just have been called out of retirement, told him, sure lieutenant, that's okay, I'll watch your car, just leave it in the drive. I'll just give him a buzz to let him know you're coming. Oh, yes, the ID helped.

Joe went up alone in the small elevator, up to a small marbled foyer where someone's old raincoat hung covering a mirror or picture. He touched a bell button beside a dark door of massive wood, that reminded him of yesterday's broken-in front door. A lean old fellow like Corday, wiry-strong or not, could hardly have done that without a sledge . . .

Walworth himself came to answer the door. And Judy had been right about the sketch, it hadn't been far off at all in depicting this man's face. The dark hair and even the short beard were messed up now. Walworth was wearing a loose, short, very fancy robe of some kind, his hairy, muscular arms and legs protruding. He had the look of someone just out of bed, even to the puffiness around the eyes. He also looked a little jumpy. But a great many perfectly innocent people looked jumpy when you came on as the police.

"If you're a cop," said Walworth in a voice whose loudness sounded habitual, "come in and get it the hell over with, whatever it is."

"Thanks." Joe came in, let Walworth close the door behind him. The palatial apartment was a littered mess, evidently from last night's party. "But like I said, it's not police business. I just wondered if I could have a word with you about Kate. Sorry I got you up."

"Kate?" The dumb look might be genuine.

"Kate Southerland."

"Oh. Oh, yeah. Sure. Terrible. What can I tell you? I hardly knew her." Walworth picked up a half-empty bottle, frowned at it, put it down. No doubt the maid, or a battalion of maids, would soon be along to see that it was disposed of.

Joe said: "You see, I had asked her to marry me."

"Oh," said Walworth, and his face went through several changes of expression, the first of which looked like genuine surprise. None of the expressions seemed likely to be helpful. "I'm very sorry," he thought of saying finally.

"Yeah. Well, I just wondered if you could tell me about what happened the last night she was here." Joe had designed this question, or statement, with great care, and had rehearsed it on the long drive down from Glenlake.

"Here?" For a moment, consternation. "But she was never *here*."

Joe had also rehearsed his next step, to be taken after this anticipated denial; but before he could put his plans for further probing into effect, he heard a door opening and closing somewhere down a hallway.

"Craig?" The one tentative word in a softly feminine voice preceded the girl around a corner and into the room. She came wearing a cloud of red hair almost the color of fresh copper wire, and a large green towel wrapped around her body from armpits to hips. She had a green-eyed pixie face, with an upturned, freckle-sprinkled nose that made her look so young that *statutory jailbait* was the first thought— or anyway the second—that sprang into Joe's police-trained mind. But she could have been six months or a year past eighteen.

"Craig?" Her voice was still soft but Joe could tell now, watching her sober face, that there was intense anger driving it. "Where did you put my clothes?"

Walworth gave Joe a look that seemed to be meant as an appeal for man-to-man solidarity in this situation. Then, shaking his head, the host walked out of the room in the direction the girl had come from.

Now looking at Joe, the girl in the green towel announced, in a different though still distant voice: "My name is Carol."

"I'm Joe."

"Joe, could I ask you to give me a lift? It won't be very far."

"Sure. I've got a car."

Carol continued to look at him, as if daring him to try to say something about the towel. He had nothing funny available, even if he had wanted to try. He walked over to one floor-to-ceiling window and looked out through the thick protective glass at the Drive twenty stories below, a strip of snowbound park beyond, and then the winter-blackened lake, a rim of white snow and broken ice extending outward from the shore a hundred yards or so. A very dull December day. What day was it, Wednesday?

He would try to pump the girl a bit before he decided whether to come back to Walworth, or to give Walworth's name to Charley Snider, or just what to do.

In about one minute Walworth was back in the room, carrying an armful of assorted garments.

Wordlessly Carol accepted these, meanwhile maintaining her towel's position carefully. The she went out the way that she had come, silent pink feet sinking into carpet. Her legs were very nice.

Walworth paced the floor, showing no inclination to say anything more to Joe. Once he stopped to pick up a stray bottle, take a drink from it and grimace. All right, Joe told him silently, you've answered my question. You'll find out about it if I decide your answer doesn't stick.

Before Joe had begun to expect her, Carol was back in the living room with them, wearing boots and jeans and a carefully faded, expensive-looking shirt: what the wealthy wear when they want to look like they don't care. She went straight to the guest closet, took out a hip-length ski jacket, went through its pockets, came up empty.

"My money?" she demanded then, of Walworth's back.

He turned right around, not having to pause for an instant. "What d'you charge?"

That stung enough to show for just a moment in her face. "I mean the money that was in my pockets when I came in here last night."

"I don't know." He glared at her brutally. "Look around for it, if you want. Or if you don't want to miss your ride, come back later and maybe it'll have turned up."

"For eight dollars I'm not going to stay here long enough to look around." She pulled her jacket on, turned to Joe. "Not for eight hundred. Can I have that ride now?"

Wishing he could think of comebacks that quickly, Joe just managed to have the door open as she reached it. A last glance back as they went out showed Walworth picking up a bottle again.

"Don't like him, do you?" Joe remarked, when they had ridden the elevator halfway down.

"Not at a second look." Carol's manner had relaxed a little as soon as they got out of the apartment. "Met him last Friday for the first time. Oh, he can come on very strong and decent when he tries. Then last night—that was something else. I'd rather not talk about it."

"Sure." The elevator delivered them. The gray-haired doorman smiled and nodded. Joe led her out to the Rabbit in the drive.

She said: "I don't know what your business with him was, but I got definite vibrations that you don't like him either. Which is why I took a chance on asking for a ride."

"You're right, I don't like him. So, where shall the ride be to?"

"The Art Institute, if it's not out of your way. I hear a girl can pick up a better class of man there than in the bars."

"I suppose they might be better educated, anyway." He pulled out of the drive and melded into traffic gently, heading south.

After two blocks Carol said: "No, I don't want to pick up men. One stab at that was plenty. I'm going to have to think of something, though, being entirely out of money."

"I'm not trying to be funny when I say, how about Travelers Aid? Really. You do have the look of someone who's some distance from home, and they'll help you wire someplace for money. Or I'll advance you a loan myself. But it'll have to be small."

"I'm afraid—" Carol's voice cracked suddenly in the middle, and she had to start it over. "I'm afraid sending out wires isn't going to do me any good. Thanks for the offer of the small loan. I may just accept. Could we start out with a coffee someplace?"

"Joe's Coffee Shop and Breakfast Bar is open. That's my place, which is not terribly far. Or we can go public if you like."

"Joe's place sounds fine. It's got to be a lot nicer than the one I just got out of."

He turned west for two blocks, then back north. "I'm a little out of the high rent district, as they say."

There was a legitimate parking spot open only half a block from his front door, so he didn't have to drive through the alley to his rented garage. While they were climbing the stairs to the second floor of his building, he could hear the muffled sound of his phone ringing, and ran ahead to answer.

"Joe? This's Charley Snider."

"What's up, Charley?"

"Just wanted to bring you up to date. Nothing new on the mystery at the morgue. But, we finally did get a make on the thumbprint on the mirror in Kate's car. Now don't get your hopes up. You said you wanted to know anything that happens, and so I'm calling to tell you."

Joe didn't feel in any danger of getting too much hope up about anything. "What about the print?"

"Well, the name the FBI files come up with is Leroy Poach. Pee-oh-ay-cee-aitch, as in egg. And now, get this man, I'm not makin' this up. Murder, armed robbery, kidnapping." Charley paused, as before a climax.

"Yeah?"

"The thing is, this Poach was hanged in Oklahoma in 1934."

"Oh, Jesus. Are they crazy in Washington?" By now Carol had come into the apartment, and was standing by in the next room, politely not listening. Joe caught her eye and made gestures toward the kitchen alcove. She brightened a little, and moved in that direction.

"Well," said Charley's phone-voice, "there obviously some mistake. If it turned out somehow that he wasn't hanged, he'd still be about eighty-five by now."

"Well. I did ask you to tell me everything."

"Hey, now, don't quit on us. We're tryin'."

"I know. I'm sorry." Sounds from outside the bedroom indicated Carol was filling the coffeepot. "Charley? What does running water mean?"

"Huh?"

"Why was that fellow out at the house running down there into the woods along the creek?"

"I dunno. Oh, by the way, we got his name now. Max Gruner. Has a minor record, sex offenses, larceny. We don't know what he's been up to the last six months or so, but it looks like it wasn't anything good. And the house, you know, where the kid was being held? It belongs to some people who moved away last fall. They're down south now, and they've been paying a couple to come round and look at the place every day. Only the caretakers have just up and disappeared. Sweet setup for a kidnapping hideout."

Joe asked: "Anything on Corday yet?"

"Seems to have left his things in the motel room and just departed. His bill was paid in advance. We've checked with London, and they don't know him. Hasn't been practicing medicine in London, not under that name anyway, not legitimately. Might have been living there, of course. His name was listed on a BOAC flight into O'Hare from London a few days back."

"I bet you don't find him, Charley."

"Any ideas where he might be, Joe?"

"I don't have any sane ideas about any of this right now. If any come to me I'll pass them along."

They said goodbye and he hung up and went out into the dining alcove. Carol had set out a couple of paper plates and was scrambling some eggs.

She looked at him. "I couldn't help hearing. The name Corday and all, that's been in the news. I think I just had a lot of the air let out of my own troubles, because it just hit me, who this girl is, that you told Walworth you were going to marry. God. Craig knew her too?"

He went to pour boiling water in to the two cups where she had spooned in instant coffee. "Slightly, anyway. Tell me about last Friday night up there at Walworth's."

"Oh. That's when I met him. I was there most of the evening, but I don't recall any girl who fits my picture of Kate Southerland. Describe her to me?"

When he had done so, Carol shook her head. "No. Unless she could have been there earlier, six o'clock or so."

"She was still home then."

The eggs and some toast were ready, and they were just sitting down when the phone sounded again. He went to the bedroom, sat down heavily on the bed, picked it up. "Joe Keogh."

"Joe?" It was Granny Clare's voice, sounding tremulous. "Are you—is everything all right?"

"Yeah. Why not? No new disasters, anyway. Why? Is everything all right there?"

There was a small delay before Clarissa answered, but when she did she sounded definite. "Yes. I . . . oh, I shouldn't have bothered you. I'm sorry. Goodbye." And she hung up.

Some of the modest portion of food on Carol's plate was gone when he came back. She had already set down her fork. "I think what I mainly am is tired. I've just been through a night you wouldn't believe."

"I might." Joe sat down opposite, took a bite of toast, discovered he was mildly hungry. "I've recently been through an unreal thing or two myself."

She sat with arms folded, looking over his shoulder. "I'm sorry if you don't want to hear this, but I don't think I can keep from talking about it after all."

"Go ahead." He tried to sound no more than willing.

"I was up there at Walworth's for a long time Friday night. There was some sex going on, okay? Too kinky to interest me. Somehow Craig gave me the impression then that it wasn't really his thing either. Then, last night, I went up with him, thinking we were going to be alone. All right, I was planning to spend the night. But what he had in mind was ... well, nothing I'd consider ordinary, and I don't think my life has been especially sheltered."

"How old are you, Carol?" he asked her, almost without meaning to.

"Old enough, in the legal sense." But he had brought her story-telling to a halt.

"All right, go on, sorry I interrupted."

"Well. He turned out to be kinkier than I had thought, that's all. And if wasn't until after my clothes were off and had been misplaced somewhere that this was fully explained to me. Hell, why am I telling you all this?"

"Because it bothers you."

"That's for sure. Then there were arguments. There were some other people around, by that time ... not Kate, no one as nice as Kate, I'm sure. Oh, I'm dead. I don't know if I'm going to fall asleep first or start to cry."

"You can do either one. Or both. But eventually I think you ought to tell me where you live, really live, so I can see that you get home."

"I don't think so. Oh, damn. Every time I shut my eyes some tears come squeezing out."

"I *do* think so. Really. Is home that bad?"

"No," she said, surprising him a bit. "My parents live right in Chicago, actually. All right, let me give them a call."

"Help yourself to the phone."

She went into the bedroom, and he could hear her dialing. Now soon she would be gone. He didn't quite know exactly what he thought of that. He drank some coffee. He thought he heard her once say *Daddy* on the phone—he couldn't make out what else she might be saying, but at least it didn't sound like a fight.

In a couple of minutes she hung up and came out again, looking more relaxed than he had seen her yet. "Joe, can you give me one more ride? It's only about ten minutes away."

"Okay. Were your parents glad to hear from you?"

"Oh, you know how it is. But that's a silly thing to say, isn't it? Maybe you don't know how it is at all."

He smiled at her. "No, I guess I don't."

Back in the car, she directed him toward the Near North Side. It was actually the same general area as the half-abandoned building where Kate had been found dead, an area in which a few blocks one way or the other made a big difference in what the city was like.

ENCHANTRESS COSMETICS, said the sign, discreet but expensive bronze. It was on a modern gray concrete building, two stories high, that occupied almost half a square block.

"You live here?"

"It's the family business, or the office and laboratory ends of it anyway, with living quarters attached. My folks think it's a lot neater than commuting, or living in one of those high-rise apartments."

He had heard of a few other wealthy people in the area, advertising agency owners and such, who had made similar arrangements. "It sounds neat."

A private automobile entrance was blocked by a great openwork gate of what looked like blackened steel and ebony. This rose up out of the way when Carol worked some kind of miniaturized electronic device she brought out of a pocket. Good thing, Joe remarked to himself, she hadn't lost that in her recent adventurings.

Inside, below street level, were private parking spaces, one or two out of a dozen of them occupied. From the sunken garage a large but fancy elevator very silently raised them to the floor above.

At the far end of a small, carpeted hall, another

doorway was fitted with a wood-and-metal gate. This one stood open, and beyond it a luxurious though badly lighted apartment was visible. Silhouetted in the doorway was a man, very large, well-dressed, smiling at them both.

"Goodbye," Joe said to Carol, taking her hand just briefly.

"Don't say goodbye." Her smile was warm.

"So long for a while, then. How about that?"

"Not even that," she said. "You must come in for a visit." She turned to flash the well-dressed man a merry wink.

Joe looked from one of them to the other. He wanted to smile at them but couldn't quite. "Your father?" he asked, then realized that the man who was strolling toward them looked too young for that.

"Oh, goodness, not at all." Carol's green eyes danced, as if with some joke soon to be revealed. "Does the name Enoch Winter mean anything to you, Joe?"

"Enoch Winter. No." The huge man was looming beside him now. A joke was coming. Or *something* was—

"Then how about—Leroy Poach?" And she giggled brightly, watching the slow progress of his reaction.

On the threshold of the luxurious apartment Carol and the giant man had laughed at him. Still laughing, the giant had reached for Joe in a leisurely, careless way. There had been nothing at all funny in the power of the grip that closed on Joe's right arm. He had let go at once with a left hook that landed square on the other's jaw. The only effect was a shock of pain through Joe's fist, as if he had hit a wall. With that Carol stepped in and caught Joe by the left arm. She was still amused. Between them the two of them carried his kicking figure into the apartment as if he were an obstreperous two-year-old.

Inside, a vista of elegant though poorly lighted rooms seemed to stretch away for half a block. Carol closed a solid wood-and-metal door behind them, while the man held Joe by both arms. The man stood in front of him, grinning, daring him silently. When the girl left them, walking unhurriedly into another room, Joe tried again. Wrenching free was hopeless, clumsy though the other's grip appeared to be. When Joe tried for a kick, the man with overwhelming power simply forced him lower. Joe's knees buckled.

"Yeah, I know you're a cop, sonny," the man said, in answer to a choked-out, embarrassingly feeble protest. "I like the idea of you being one. I really do."

He then let go of Joe's arms so suddenly that his victim was left off balance and did a pratfall on the thick carpet. "All right, pull out the gun." The huge man's voice was perilously soft. "Go on."

In eight years he'd never drawn it, except on the firing range. He was ready to use it now, except the big guy was just too willing. Some fighter's instinct warned Joe to choose another tactic. There was a small end-table within arm's reach, and as Joe crouched to get up he seized it by one leg. Whipping it ahead of him as he rose, he jabbed it into the giant's face as hard as he could. He got the surprise he wanted, and felt the table connect with what ought to have been a knockout impact.

But his opponent came at him right through the blow. Again Joe scrambled backward; the table was knocked from his grasp. Now he tried in earnest to draw his gun, but the quickness of his enemy was as incredible as his strength, and again Joe's arm was caught before his fingers could reach the holster.

This time, it seemed, the arm might in fact be twisted off—

"Stop!" the sharp command in the woman's voice

brought the torture to a halt. Joe was dropped to the floor, where he rolled helplessly for a moment, trying to verify that nothing in his arm was broken or seriously torn.

Somewhere above him, Carol lectured. "The object is to learn something from him, remember?"

"Whatta you want to learn? He'll tell us."

"I want him to speak to us freely, Poach. Giving little details that will be clues, though he may not realize it. And I want to waste none of his sweet blood, if we can help it." Her voice, that had begun normally, ended in a ghastly whisper, and long before she had finished speaking, Poach had moved away. Joe, getting shakily to his feet, could see the other man's forehead marked with an almost straight horizontal line, oozing red. Poach dabbed at his hurt with a finger, looked back at Joe with the eyes of a wounded predator.

But Carol was standing between them now, a hypodermic in her hand. "I have a little something here for you, Joe. It will only make you sleepy. Are you going to be a sensible young man and let me do it? Or are you going to try again to—"

He tried again. Ten seconds later he had a few more minor bruises, had discovered that a heavy metal ashtray made no more impression on either of his foes than knuckles did, and was being held down like an infant atop a great wooden table, a drafting or designing table of some kind, one place in the room where lights were bright. He could feel his shirt and jacket being peeled back partially from one shoulder. About all he could see from under an elbow that held his head immobilized, face down, was part of the nearest wall. What appeared to be a pair of harpoons were mounted there, crossed diagonally like fencing foils. Crude, early harpoons perhaps; even their heads were wood, or looked like wood, with pointy wooden barbs. . . .

The needle stung him in the shoulder and almost at once the world dissolved into a fog, a haze through which two pale faces hovered over Joe. One was haloed by red hair, the other blued with gun-metal stubble and blooded with a forehead crease. Both of them were made gigantic by his own helpless terror.

"Where is the old man, Joe? You know who I mean."

He knew who she meant, all right, but nothing more. If he had, he would have told her. He had been relieved of all choice in what he said.

Carol was gentle and understanding. "If you don't know where he is now, Joe, tell us where you saw him last."

"That house . . . out in the country . . . the night we. . . ."

"The night Gruner was killed. Yes. And where before that?"

His mouth worked by itself. All he had to do was lie there on the table and observe the process. He mentioned the Southerland house, the parking lot of the Shores Motel, the Loop, the mausoleum in Lockwood Cemetery. . . .

"Enough," said Carol when he started to repeat himself, and his mouth shut up at once. She turned to Poach. "That mausoleum ought to be worth a try. First, do you know where Lockwood Cemetery is? And, second, can you check it out before sunset? Do not try to meet him alone at night."

"You tell me that about twice a day."

"Because I don't think you believe me, Poach. Look up the cemetery on the city map."

"Okay, okay. Then what about the house? We got to try to get in there sometime."

"Yes, the house too, today. If—"

"Before sunset. I know. I'm on my way."

SIXTEEN

Sitting up in bed, Craig Walworth could feel on one side of his throat the paired coolnesses of two fresh drops of painless blood. No mirror at hand to see them in, but he knew from past experience they were so small that touching them would mark his finger with red specks barely visible.

"A couple of months ago," he remarked, "you couldn't have convinced me it was possible for people to really get their kicks doing this. I mean relatively normal people."

Carol had just rolled away from him and now her naked body lay curved in a far quadrant of the huge circular bed, her flame of hair almost covering an outsize pillow. Beyond her the unshaded window, twenty stories above observation, looked out upon great clouds above the lake, clouds painted now with the reflection of a sunset developing in the opposite direction.

Carol gave one of her little laughs. She had them in several styles, and this particular style, Walworth was slowly coming to realize, was derisive. She said: "You consider yourself relatively normal, darling?"

I guess I do, though I'm not proud of it."

"Anyway, two months ago is just about when we first met. And it didn't take me long at all to convince you that vampirism really works."

"I mean, no one could have convinced me by argument. Demonstration was what did the trick." The sensations accompanying her sipping from his veins were more diffuse than those of any other sex act he had ever performed, but nonetheless orgasmic. "And one of the points I like best is that we can alternate this vampire act with going at it in the more traditional ways. You never seem to take enough blood to leave me weak, or anything. One of these days, my love, we're going to try both at once, and what a hit that'll be."

"I think it's time we got up," said Carol, ignoring everything he had said.

"I still don't get just how you do it. I mean, make tiny punctures like this with just your teeth. I can see you'd have to have teeth like needles. It never hurts a bit and the holes are so small. But your teeth don't look the least bit odd. I've had my tongue in there between 'em too, not to mention—"

"Don't be gross." Her voice cutting him off was cold, but then she winked. "I really do think it's time we jumped up and got dressed."

"What's the hurry?"

"There are things to do tonight. Things are going to be happening."

"What things? Goddam it, you can answer me. How do you do the biting?"

"Just like in the movies," she said, and rolled out of bed on her side and started to pull on her dress. Nothing under it, of course; cold never seemed to bother Carol.

"Movies?"

"Vampire movies. Craig dear, don't be dense. Now *will* you dress?"

"If it's that easy I ought to be able to do it to you too."

From the top of the green dress emerged green eyes, looking at him coldly. "I do not enjoy having my throat bitten," Carol stated. "Anyway, tasting my blood would change you too fast. You are perfect just the way you are. I wish to enjoy you and use you just a little longer yet."

He stretched out with hands behind his head, thinking to himself how nicely his big biceps showed in this position. "You're using me, huh? When are you going to get over your hangups about my mirrors?" The large glass on the nearest wall had been sprayed opaque, like a store window at Halloween; there were only a few scars in the ceiling to show where his overhead mirror had been taken down completely, at Carol's insistence, before she would mount the round bed with him.

"Sometime soon, I think," she answered, seriously enough to surprise him a little. She was sitting in a chair now, gracefully putting on a shoe. "I think you're ready."

"You do a good act about the mirrors," he said. "Never explicitly explaining why. Just putting these out of action, and covering up the one in the lobby with that raincoat. Leaving it to me to make the connection with the fairy-tale vampires who won't show up in a mirror."

Shoes on, Carol had stood and turned away to watch the sunset-reflecting clouds. "Big storm's coming," she remarked, as if to herself. Then she turned back. "Tell me more about the fairy-tale vampires."

"Well, you know. You do it well."

"I think I'd better be blunt," Carol said. "When have you ever actually seen my reflection in a mirror? I really do want to have you around a while longer, and you're not going to last unless you start to understand some things. In fact, you may not last out the night."

"What's all this," Walworth demanded, starting to get angry, "about how I'm going to be used?" She had never talked like this to him before; he realized now that some kind of crisis in their relationship was at hand. "If you've got any ideas about turning me over to that dumb Irishman as a kidnapper, forget them. You and King Kong are in this just as deep as I am, remember. If that kid ever identifies me as driving the car, your ass has had it too."

"Craig, don't ever let Winter hear you call him that." Carol issued the warning calmly but seriously, a stewardess telling you to put on the belt. "As for the dumb Irishman, as you call him, he won't be coming around again. That was well played, darling. You do have talents outside of bed."

Walworth was still lying in the same position. "So, what'd you do? Pay him off? Kill him? I'd like to know about it. I mean, I'd really like to know, dearie, if you're killing people and it might someday involve me. An hour later you were back here. Did you take him home and bite his neck?"

Carol seemed to be considering her answer seriously. Meanwhile she was straightening her dress around her, fluffing out her hair. She did, now that he thought about it, have the habit of doing such things without mirrors. At last she said: "No, I haven't bitten his neck. Not yet. Anyway, it's not really the police you have to worry about."

"It's not? That's a pretty good one."

"No it isn't, dear. It wasn't the police who pulled off Gruner's fingers."

"Obviously. I know who that was. Your psychopathic playmate Winter or whatever the hell you think I ought to call him. Who else does things like that? But if he ever comes after me, baby, he's not going to get within arm's length of me alive."

"It was not M'sieu Winter who did it, either. *Please* get up and dress."

"Why should I?" But there was a certain psychological disadvantage in nakedness when she stood there like a nurse, so before it could become a real issue Walworth got out of bed and started rooting for some clothes. He said: "You're too smart to stick with a crazy like him. So why try to cover up for him with me, of all people?"

"I am not covering up. It is just that I still need Winter for a while, or at least I would like to be able to use him."

"Just like me," he mocked.

"Exactly. So please, Craig, can you take seriously the warning I am about to give you? Whether or not you are arrested is almost of no consequence any more—"

"Don't pretend *you're* crazy, baby! I know better." He jiggled himself into his pants, pulled up the zipper.

"—but there is a certain old man you must look out for, Craig. Of course he may not look like an old man when you see him ..." Carol sighed prettily, a concerned nurse whose patient just will not co-operate. "I'm really not getting through, am I? I was considering sending Winter over to be your bodyguard for a while, but now I don't think I'd better."

Walworth snorted, tucked his shirt into his pants. He decided to leave the shirt open halfway down the front. "Damn right you hadn't better. What is all this shit, all of a sudden? 'Don't bother to worry about the cops, Craig.' 'You may not last out the night anyway, Craig.' *I'll* last out the night, baby. 'Be nice to Winter, Craig.' You're setting up something. Hey, is this where you try at last to stick it to me for some money? Enchantress Cosmetics not making a profit after all?"

There was an edge in Carol's voice now. "Don't give me any money, please. I probably have more than you."

"Hah."

"But do watch out for the old man. He is the one who pulled off Gruner's fingers. He may well be coming after you tonight. I'm sure Gruner must have told him your name."

"And yours too, huh?" Walworth smiled, unable to concentrate enough to decide which shoes he ought to wear; this was really getting entertaining.

"He knows my name already. He's mentioned in the news stories, by the way, as a Dr. Corday of London. He's called himself that before."

"Oh? So, who is he really, Al Capone?"

"I see now you would only laugh like an idiot if I tried to tell you his real name, so never mind. Among other things he is an old friend of the Southerland family. And a very old enemy of mine."

Sitting on the bed with one sock half on, Walworth paused. "You're telling me, in this newly devious way of yours, that it's not an accident after all that we picked the Southerlands."

"Not a bit of an accident." Carol folded her arms. She was not a nurse any more; maybe the president of a company.

"Now wait a minute. The object was, we were going to look for some new kicks, right? Pick out a family and just utterly destroy them. An ultimate kick, better than just a simple killing. Right?"

"So it was presented to you at the time. So you thought you were presenting the idea to me."

"All right, say the idea was something you conned me into. Picking the Southerlands as the target must have been at random. Winter tore a page out of the Glenlake phone book—"

"A selected page."

"All right, say you fixed that too. Then I pinned

the page up on the wall myself, and you stood clear across the room and tossed the dart. Don't tell me you could have hit a name on purpose from that distance. Hell, you couldn't even have seen it. You were lucky to hit the page, even."

"I can do many things, Craig, that you would not credit as being possible. So can the old man. I think I may send Winter over, after all, when he gets back."

"I may not let him in."

Carol stared at him a long moment, different emotions contending in her face. Then it was as if she gave up. Fought to keep herself from dissolving in laughter, but had to yield at last. "Oh, Craig, Craig, but you are such an innocent! Haven't you yet understood the first simple truth about me? And the man you know as Winter? We are *vampires*, dear. You've asked us both in here already. Do you think that you can now simply tell us to stay out, and we will?"

Walworth stood up in his socks. He had a growing feeling of unreality, and if he thought about it, he would have to admit that fright was growing too. "I've got a gun. I tell you, I'll blow that bastard Winter's head off, right on my own doorstep if I have to." The police would then come down on him for sure. His connection with the kidnapping would almost certainly come out, and he would be fighting in a courtroom for his life. Somehow he had always felt sure that, sooner or later, things would come to that.

She was calm and almost pleasant again. "Go get your gun, Craig dear. Right now. I want to show you something."

He looked his uncertainty at her.

"Oh, all right, never mind the pistol. It would probably only complicate things anyway. You'd think we had loaded it with blanks, or something. Just watch this."

And saying that, Carol disappeared, green dress and
red hair and pink skin just swirling away to nothing.
Not from a position where there was anything at all
to hide behind: from right in the middle of his bedroom floor.

PCP, Walworth thought at once. He'd seen the
elephant tranquilizer hit like this before, with heavy
hallucinations. Not on himself, of course. He'd never
used it on himself. But now Carol or someone had
sneaked it into his food or drink. Intending to get
rid of him ... no, not in his food, an injection, that
was it. A mainliner right into the jugular, managed
somehow by Carol when she was supposed to be
drinking his blood. No wonder she hadn't wanted mirrors around the bed ...

A spring-loaded panel in the wall near the head
of his bed, a movieish gadget that no one would
expect to come across in real life, delivered his .38
into his hand as he reached out and pressed the wood.
He was reasonably sure that neither Carol nor Winter
nor the maids nor anyone else who had been in the
apartment recently knew it was there; it had been
installed a year ago, and he hadn't spoken of it to
any of them—not even of the gun until just now.
Nevertheless he suspiciously broke the revolver's
action open, slid the faintly oily cartridges one be one
out of the cylinder and weighed them in his fingers,
looked at them and tamped them gently back. Firing pin was in place too. He snapped the weapon
shut, ready for business. The thing looked and felt
awfully functional.

From behind him, in the direction of the huge
bedroom window, there sounded a brisk, light tapping, as of something very hard striking on glass. Even
as Walworth turned it seemed to him that he knew
already, in some nightmare-hatching inner corner of
his mind, just what it was that he was going to see.

Carol's face hovered close outside the almost

unbreakable glass, twenty stories in the air. Her feet were extended toward the lake. With lightly moving arms she swam, a great smiling fish in an immense aquarium . . . then she was gone again.

"How was that?" her voice asked, once more from behind him, this time from in the room. Before turning again, he noticed that the night-backed glass showed him a half-reflection of the lighted bedroom— but not of Carol.

He spun around again then, to face her across the wide, round bed. "Bitch." His voice was low and murderous. "You stuck me with a good one, didn't you?"

"Stuck you?" She pretended not to understand. "I see you found your pistol. If you think it will protect you against Winter, or the old man, then fire it at me. Right now."

She sounded too eager. Whatever her game was, he wasn't going to play it. He shook his head. But in his anger he moved toward her. He was expecting that when he got close enough she would try to kick him where it would hurt the most. He was expecting that and ready for it. But only when he swung his arm to club her with the pistol barrel did she move, and then only to lift her arm. Her little palm caught his forearm, and it felt like he had swung at a cast-iron statue.

And almost before the pain of the impact had time to register, Carol had grabbed him by both elbows, picked him up, and spun him in mid-air like some casually victimized infant. She spun him once more, in reverse, and ended the mad ballet by throwing him contemptuously into a chair, which nearly tipped over as he landed. He sat there blinking at her stupidly, for the moment unable to do anything more.

"You utter goddamned fool," she said, and added something in the same withering tone, but in a language he did not know. She finished up in English: "I wash my hands of you."

His rage had reached the point where his body acted of itself. His arm came up and fired the gun point-blank. The sound reverberated, the smell of burn explosive stung his nose, the fruitwood table behind Carol leaped up against the wall and came down on its side. She stood there, icily contemptuous.

At his elbow the phone was ringing.

He debated whether to fire at her again. She waited, perhaps also debating something in her mind.

Five rings, six.

He reached out his left hand and picked it up.

Winter's voice, rough, excited, incoherent.

Carol came near him and snatched the phone away. Walworth spun away out of his chair, not wanting her to touch him now, and afraid of what she might do if she did touch him.

"Are you sure?" she said into the phone. What she heard from it then transformed her into a goddess of victory, standing tall with head flung back. "Are—you—sure—that—it—was—him?" Her lips looked rigid, driving the words like nails into the phone.

The answer this time brought from Carol an outcry that sounded as if she had been hurt. But Walworth could see in her face that it was triumph. He backed away a little farther, sat down on the bed.

"No!" she was saying into the phone now. He had never seen anyone so beautiful. In that case he should be kept alive—yes, yes, yes, *alive*, until later, when I can get to him. Later tonight. No, the gathering is at my place, within the hour. Leave him where he is, and come to my place. Yes, right away."

Very carefully she replaced the receiver in its cradle on the little table, near the bed. Walworth sat very still. A Carol he had never seen before looked down at him.

"Maybe, darling, just maybe—you will survive the evening after all. And I suppose you had better, after all, watch out for the police. Until later, dear."

With that, Carol was gone again.

As she disappeared, Walworth had been staring with fascination at a spot near the center front of the green dress. A small hole the size a bullet might make was there, showing a glimpse of pink, undamaged skin.

After a while, when he could begin to believe that he was really alone, he got up and looked at the fruitwood table where it lay on one side against the wall. A great splintered gouge had entered its top from underneath and emerged through the upper surface of the wooden top, where something had passed with tremendous force. Plaster had trickled from a small crater in the wall just behind where the table had been standing.

Walworth, gun still in hand, walked to the front door of the apartment, where he made sure that the door was securely locked, chained, and bolted. The only other way in, unless you counted the sealed windows, was the service door in the kitchen. That was his next stop.

Then he went into a bathroom, and in the mirror over the sink examined the small wounds on his throat. They looked no different from the marks Carol had left him with the other times. They could be needle punctures. They were needle punctures, and he was a fool not to have realized that fact the first time round, or anyway the second.

Syringes capable of injecting drugs hidden in her teeth? It sounded like something from a crazy spy adventure. He had set down the revolver on the broad ledge beside the bathroom basin, and now he suddenly grabbed it up and spun around again, in expectation of hearing her contemptuous voice once more. But there was nothing. Now he hurried through the apartment shutting the drapes on all the windows. At times he ran from room to room, wanting to get them shut before he could be made to see her swimming out there once again.

When he had closed the place up as much as he was able he went through it again, this time turning on all the lights. Why having more lights on should make him feel any better he didn't know, but so it was.

That accomplished, he still didn't want to sit down, stand still, or close his eyes—he might hallucinate himself being grabbed up and tossed around again before he could get them open. After a few moments of dull mental vacuum there occurred to him the idea of calling one or two people he knew, bad-trip specialists, whose help he had enlisted in the past. Never before for himself, of course: he enjoyed watching people take drugs much more than he did taking them himself.

Could he keep his head on tight enough, talking on the phone, to keep the helpers from suspecting that this time he was the one who needed help? He had damn well better be able to. He wasn't at all sure what they would do once they learned that this time, for a change, he was the one climbing the walls.

At the first number he tried a woman answered, with the information that the man he wanted to talk with was out. Walworth left his number with her, asking that the man call him back, trying to sound as calm as possible. He punched out his second number, and the woman he wanted had just answered when there came the sound of the buzzer at the service door, back in the kitchen.

"Hang on a minute," he said into the mouth-piece, and set the receiver down and tiptoed in his socks back toward the kitchen. On the way he observed that the gun was still, or once more, in his hand. Maybe the gun wasn't real right now, either. But he held on to it anyway. Silently he put his eye to the see-through on the back door, choking back his fear. Nothing, but nothing, was going to surprise him this time.

Or so he thought until he looked.

SEVENTEEN

A sudden pounding on the front door jerked Clarissa into wakefulness. She had dozed off on the sofa, as it seemed to her only a moment before, despite the television set playing on the other side of the room, the book in her lap that she had been trying to start to read, and even her own unsettled thoughts.

She was alone in the house. About an hour ago, before the early December darkness fell, her angina had come on again. Not bad enough, she thought, to warrant calling the doctor. But still her last nitroglycerin tablet had been needed to ease the pain; with so many other matters to distract her lately, she had neglected to replenish her supply. So Judy, bless her, had volunteered to get more, and had gone off in her little car. There was no trusting the drug store these days to deliver anything, particularly in weather like this.

The pounding on the door came again before she had got herself up from the sofa, and was echoed by a chiming of the doorbell. Clarissa, straightening slowly, muttered something, belting up her robe. Her heart was beating faster with the surprise awakening, but for the moment at least there were no pains in her chest. That at least, she told herself, was something. She was now on the brink of real old age, no doubt about it, and shortly she was going to have to hire a companion, or else persuade Lenore and Andrew to try to make a go of it again with live-in servants. It wasn't fair to Judy to depend upon her so much for the care of an old woman . . .

Most likely the knocking at the door was that of Judy herself; the girl had uncharacteristically forgotten her key for once. In her slow progress toward the front hall, Clarissa paused to switch on some lights. A quarter to five, and the sun should not be down yet, but the day outside the windows was as dark as night, and there was a heavy snowfall in the air, a regular blizzard in fact. Andrew was probably going to be stuck in the city again tonight, for once not on account of business reasons.

She flicked the outside lights on before looking out through the small viewer built into the front door at eye level. Just outside stood a man that Clarissa had never seen before, a rough-looking individual in workman's clothing, heavy jacket and wool cap. He was big and heavy, dancing a little in the cold, rubbing one exposed, blue-stubbled cheek with the back of a work-gloved hand. In his other hand he bore a long, wood-shafted tool of some kind, resting the butt end of it on the ground like an operatic spear. The upper end had been wrapped in plastic and Clarissa could not make out what it was. Across the man's face the falling snow made a multiple streaking blur, like a white beard.

He's come to tell me of an accident. Judy has been hurt. That was the first thought that came into Clarissa's mind. Simultaneously she knew there was no logical basis for this sudden fear; it was one of those chronic, baseless ones that seemed to intensify as one got older. But her knowledge did not ease the sharpness of it much.

Pain twinged now in Clarissa's chest. Gripping her robe tightly about her with one hand, she turned the bolt back in the lock and opened the door a crack, leaving the heavy chain fastened at eye level.

Seen without the mild distortion of the viewer's lens, the man outside impressed her at once as bluff and hearty. He was really enormous, and his blue shadow of beard reminded Clarissa somehow of her husband's.

He smiled at her in reassurance. "Hi, missus." His voice was deep and she found it confidence-inspiring. "My truck's stuck out here on the highway. Okay if I come in and use your phone?"

"Oh." Relief that there had been no accident washed through Clarissa, fluttering the pain. She smiled back, squinting into the narrow blast of frigid air that came in through the open door. "Of course," she said, and reached to move the chain. "Come in."

The drugstore Judy was bound for stood just across Sheridan Road from the Shores Motel, in a small shopping center that seemed to have sprung up as unplanned as a patch of weeds amid the elegance of wealthy suburban housing surrounding it to north, west and south. As usual for the time of day, northbound traffic on Sheridan was heavy and the southbound, Judy's lane, was light as she turned off the highway into the shopping center's parking lot. The snow was very thick, but it had not yet completely reconquered even the edges of the road since the last fall had been plowed away. A lot of places would probably have closed down early today, so that people could get started for home. Daddy wouldn't have started home early, though; he never did.

Getting out of her car, Judy squinted through

driving snow toward the bright lights of the motel across the road. She wondered if Dr. Corday's room had been in the back or the front, upstairs or down. She had never known its number.

Last night in her bedroom he had warned her, not to be careful, but to be brave. The police now seemed to think that the danger to the family was over, and they had withdrawn their listening post. But he hadn't talked like that at all. Anyway, Gran needed the medicine, and who else was going to get it for her?

The man ahead of Judy was buying cigarettes. Another woman was already waiting for a prescription to be filled. When Judy had handed in her scribbled paper, and it was her turn to wait, she wandered back to the front window. There she looked past magazine racks and jugs of colored water, through steamed glass that made the motel lights gigantic blurs.

A thought that had been coming and going in her mind all day returned now with sudden force. What if he came to her room again tonight? He might very well. They certainly had plenty of things in common, problems at least, that they needed to talk about.

He was old, very old, she had no doubt of that. But his age had a different quality than that of any oldster Judy had ever met. It carried no weakness. Was he older than Granny Clare or not? The question seemed meaningless, like asking whether Chinese jade was more important than baseball. It was unimaginable that *he* should ever have to send someone out for a prescription.

Next to the drugstore was a specialty dress shop with a wedding gown in its front window. On her way back to her car with Gran's medicine in her pocket, Judy saw this, and the thought of buying a long white nightgown crossed her mind. Her sleepwear now was all girls' things, teen-aged cuteness, plaids and animal designs. It was time for—something different.

As she unlocked her car door, the electric signs across the highway glared an intense loneliness at her through the blizzard. Where was he now, this moment? For just a moment she thought she was about to discover him waiting for her inside the car.

She didn't realize just how bad visibility had become until she got behind the wheel and tried the headlights, and found they didn't help very much. It took skill and a measure of luck to pull out of the parking lot and cross the southbound two lanes into northbound traffic, slow though all the traffic had now become. Snowdrifts seemed to be growing up right under the wheels; most of the pavement had completely disappeared.

It was odd, she thought, but the storm itself gave her no concern for him. From the first she had made it a habit not to think much about his strangenesses. But even without thinking she understood that his dangers and most of his problems were not the same ones that ordinary mortals had to contend with on most days of their lives.

Being herself a member of a family of ordinary mortals, Judy was still concerned to find out what she could about the storm and its effects, and turned on the car radio. "The Little Drummer Boy" was playing. She changed stations, to a jock babbling about a repeat of the great Chicago blizzard of '67. He managed to make it sound, as he managed to make everything in his world sound, like a prospect of nothing but infinite fun. But he conveyed no solid information.

For a little while she forgot the radio, having to concentrate on steering and adjusting speed so as not to ram the red tail lights just ahead. The highway, when she could see it at all through the blinded air, did not look at all like the same thoroughfare she had traversed only a few minutes ago coming south. Here a drift, though still a shallow one, had established itself all the way across, resisting the continuous work of wheels to cut a sideways segment of it into slush. At this point Judy passed her first genuinely stalled car of the night, which blocked part of what was rapidly becoming a single northbound traffic lane. She eased around it and kept going, at about ten miles per hour. Now she could once more spare a hand to switch the radio.

After three more tries she found a station giving some substantive weather information. Travelers' advisories had been changed to warnings . . . twelve or more inches expected tonight and tomorrow . . . wind from the east, the lake effect . . . again, the great blizzard of '67. Judy's memory held one vivid record of that event, a picture of a shoveled walk with walls of snow almost like those of a tunnel on either side, their tops level with her childish head.

As long as she could keep her car going at all, it didn't seem that maintaining a more or less steady five-to-fifteen miles per hour was going to be a problem. The lights ahead were not trying to go any faster than that, and those in her rearview mirror held their distance cautiously. She counted a few more stalled cars and then stopped counting. They were already everywhere, sometimes up to their fenders in drifts, angled onto the shoulder of the road, or, in one case, right athwart an intersection and surrounded by futile pushing men. Yet still the single northbound lane kept moving, winding right and left among the fallen.

Daddy would certainly be spending the night in town . . . he did that fairly often, usually, of course, because of business . . . and Mother would be stuck in Evanston tonight, Judy supposed, camping at some friend's house if she could reach one, at worst settling into a chair in the hospital lobby. They would be phoning home by now, most likely, giving explanations.

Luckily she reached the next intersection on a

green light, so she was able to creep through without stopping. Once stopped in this, anyone without four-wheel drive might very well not get moving again. Now only half a mile more. Things wouldn't be to bad now, even if she did get stuck. She would simply tuck her pants into her boots and make it home on foot.

But minute after minute Judy's luck held and her skill prevailed. She reached the home driveway in falling snow so thick that she almost missed the familiar turnoff when it came. Then she spun the wheel, gunned the engine, and her car lurched into the untracked drifts of the drive. Snow caught and held it, with a great feeling of finality.

Let it stay stuck until spring; she was home. With a sigh of relief Judy turned off the engine, pocketed the keys, tightened her scarf, and got out into the blizzard.

Looking toward the house, she saw at once that the front porch light had been turned on; Gran must be up, and would of course be worried about her, about all the family scattered in the storm. Struggling toward the light, squinting at it into the teeth of the storm, Judy was halfway across the drifted lawn before it struck her that something must be wrong. To begin with, there were huge tracks in the snow just in front of the door, and more of them than she could possibly have left on her departure. Worse than the tracks, a line of interior light shone out now at the door's edge. Gran had a thing about drafts, about keeping the cold sealed out . . .

Hurrying forward, gasping in the frozen wind, Judy tried to tell herself that what she saw were only signs that her father or mother had somehow managed to get home after all. The fantastic disasters of recent days were making her see perils and imagine monsters everywhere . . . it didn't help at all that this scene reminded her inescapably of that other house she had so recently approached, walking alone through almost untracked snow.

She reached the door and hurried in, gasping with sheer animal relief at the cessation of cold and wind. Automatically she made sure at once that the door was snugly shut behind her.

"Gran?" In the quiet of the house Judy could hear the television still softly playing in the living room. "I'm back." In her own ears her voice sounded louder than it ought to have, yet still it went unanswered.

The door of the closet in the front hall was standing open now, though Judy thought she could remember closing it after getting out her jacket and boots for the trip to the drugstore. Without removing any of her outdoor gear she walked on into the living room. The sofa where Gran had been was empty now, the television played for no one.

Judy walked on into the formal dining room, and stopped. Granny Clare lay on the carpet at the far end. Her old-woman's legs were crossed, one arm pinned beneath her body and the other one outflung. It was a pose suggesting not a simple fall, but the come-to-rest position of a body that had been thrown. Even before she hurried closer and bent to look at the still face, Judy knew that her grandmother was dead.

Pulling from her jacket pocket the medicine that would not be needed now, Judy carefully set the small bottle in its paper bag on the dining room table. Then she moved dazedly for the extension phone that stood on a small table in the hall. Picking up the receiver, she realized that she had no clear idea of whom she ought to call first—and then realized that it did not matter, because the line was dead. Ice on the lines, the storm . . .

But the act of careful listening had discovered another sound, an unfamiliar one, in the still house. Judy went back to the living room—glancing involuntarily into the dining room again as she passed—but could not hear it there, even when she had switched the television off. Further exploration showed that it was coming from somewhere down the cross hall in the direction of the old wing.

At the entrance to that connecting hallway, Judy paused to listen. It was a scraping or a scratching, very soft. It fit into no niche at all in her memory. It got no louder, came no nearer. But neither did it go away. It was repetitious, but not quite rhythmical.

For the first time it dawned on Judy that whoever had attacked Granny Clare—she did not doubt for a moment that someone had—could still be in the house. Conceivably the intruder had missed hearing Judy's return. Therefore she could now flee out into the storm again, and try to get help at a neighbor's. Police could be called—if all the phones in the neighborhood weren't out. Police would come—whenever the blizzard let them.

But even as she thought with part of her mind about running out of the house, Judy had taken the first steps toward her father's study. She knew he kept a gun there in his desk . . . and now, from down the hallway, there came a new sound that stopped her dead in her tracks.

"Judy . . ." The voice was ghastly, barely louder or more distinct than the scraping that had preceded it. It brought to Judy's mind an image of dried snake-skin, being drawn tautly over jagged bone. But despite the horror of it, the terrible change, she knew at once whose voice it was.

She ran toward it, flicking on a hallway light. To rooms on her right and left the doors stood open, and closet doors stood open inside the rooms.

In the doorway to the room that housed the pot-tery collection she stopped. Enormous ruin was before her. Display cases and tables had been overturned as though in some giants' struggle, glass and pottery alike smashed into a million pieces. Almost nothing seemed to have been left intact. The great terracotta sarcophagus that had stood in the middle of the room had been cast down from its base, and then broken, pulverized, as by madmen with sledgehammers. The lid of it was still almost intact, but it lay on its edge now yards away, beneath a window where one small pane was broken out. In through the hole a tortured tendril of the snowstorm groped, a dancing ghost in the near-darkness.

"Judy . . ."

She touched the light switch near the door. Destruction sprang out at her in all its horrible detail. A leather traveling bag, as unknown and out of place as something in a dream, lay half open in the middle of it all, and from the bag there spilled a man's dark suit, clean shirts and ties.

Only after she took a step into the room did she see him, lying in the middle of the one large open space left on the floor.

Him? It was a scarecrow figure. It seemed to be hardly more than a suit of dark clothing that lay there, transfixed against the polished hardwood by a wooden shaft as thick as a hoe handle and a man's height long. This incredible spear had somehow been driven down into that floor, like a gigantic nail. Where the shaft of it entered the dark coat near the right shoulder, upwelling red was already congealing and drying into brownish jelly. And everywhere around the figure, the floor and walls and wrecked furniture were marked with red-brown gouts and splashes.

Of course the bloody clothing was not really empty, no more than that sheepskin coat had been. Dark cloth moved and swelled. What turned toward Judy was more skull than face, a loved face horribly transformed. Bared teeth grinned starkly white, the cheekbones bulged sharply beside a shrunken nose. But deep in the darkened caverns of the eyes, fierce life still burned.

Between those lipless teeth the snakeskin voice scratched out a question: "He . . . is . . . gone?"

Falling on her knees beside him, Judy spread helpless arms. "There's no one here but me. Gran's dead. Oh love, who did this to you? How did you get here?"

A dark sleeve tried to gesture. "Pull . . . out . . ."

"Are you sure?"

"Yes . . . I am not . . . as other men. Pull it out."

Straddling the shrunken scarecrow, Judy laid hands on the shaft. It felt unyielding, like something fixed to the floor as part of the solid house. Hard as she pulled, it would not move. She bent to get a better grip and tried again. Eyes shut, she twisted and heaved with all her strength.

The old man made a sound that Judy interpreted as pain. But when she let go of the stake his voice lashed up at her, more terrible for its very weakness: "Pull!"

Eyes still closed, she straightened for a moment and tried to pray, then gripped the wood again. His fingers, whisper-feeble at first touch, came creeping up the shaft to settle on it beside hers. Now Judy threw her weight sideways, first this way then that, like trying to loosen a nail before you pulled it out. She felt the spasms of quivering in the spear as his arms joined their efforts to her own. She thought of wrenching at a nail with a claw hammer . . . suddenly the stake pulled free, with a cracking as of a barbed head breaking off, down in the solid floor.

The abrupt release of strain sent Judy staggering back. She threw the horrible, broken-ended thing away from her, and swiftly crouched at Corday's side again. Fresh blood, dark red, was welling up now from the great wound between his shoulder and his chest. His body shuddered, then lay so still that for a moment Judy was sure that she had killed him.

But once more feeble movement returned. "Better, better," rasped his voice, though it sounded as lifeless as before. There was a pause. Then one of his hands, its fingers hardly distinguishable from bones, brushed feebly at the floor, re-creating the sound that had first drawn Judy's attention to this part of the house.

He said: "Bring here all you can of the dust . . . earth of my homeland, you see. Fragments of my bed."

"Dust?" she wondered aloud. "Bed?" The only dust in sight was that from the crumbling fragments of the shattered sarcophagus. Obedient without really understanding, she began to scrape the pieces and their powder toward him with her hands. "So you rested . . . inside this," she murmured as she worked.

"He came upon me sleeping. Otherwise . . . but never mind. He will come back, or another even deadlier than he will come. So you must flee now, love. Run to some house nearby. Tell them to allow no strangers through their door tonight, no matter—"

"Here, I've got a bunch of this dust scraped into a pile. What do I do with it now?"

The sparks in his eye-caverns glittered at her thoughtfully. He said: "Push the dust under my body, along my side—no, do not try to lift me! I die quickly if you move me now. Else he would have taken me away with him—to her."

As though tucking a dry blanket beneath the fragile-feeling body, Judy performed the foolishness with the dust. As if playing a game that had to be won, however childish and ridiculous it seemed on its face.

She sat back. It was hard for her to look at his terrible face, his wasted form. She fought for control over her face and voice, and asked: "What now?"

His horrible voice said: "You must flee."

"I can run out somewhere, to one of the other houses here, and get them to call for the police. Then I'm coming back to be with you."

He shook his head feebly. "Police will be of no help to me. Any doctor they bring will order me moved. That must mean my death. Neither of us will be able to prevent it."

"Then I'm not leaving you at all," Judy decided. "What's the next thing I can do?"

"Oh, my dear," he whispered. And again: "My love." Then just when she thought her tears were going to break out at last, he ordered: "Gather more of the earth. Crumble the larger pieces to powder. You will find them brittle. It is the earth of my homeland, and very special to me. Mix the dust with my blood, and use it to stanch my wound."

Again Judy did as she had been bidden. She pulled back his ruined clothing to get at his parchment flesh, and fought to stem the flow of blood that still oozed richly from God knew where inside his mummified body. In all this nothing now struck her as horrible, except only the chance that she might fail.

At last the bleeding stopped. Judy had lost track of time, but her neck and back ached as if she had been crouching in the same position for hours. Her patient let out a sigh, and moved his whole body for the first time since she had found him, stretching out to what must be an easier position for him on the floor. Suddenly mindful of her first-aid training, Judy wanted to bring him a blanket, but he insisted that it would do no good. He also refused her offer to fetch an ordinary pillow, preferring that she slide a fragment of the broken sarcophagus underneath his head.

That done, he took her hand and pressed it in his twig-like fingers. "Thank you. Now, for the last time, Judy, again, I warn you—go."

"No."

"Listen to me. He who made your sister a vampire—yes, that is the truth—he will soon be back. I am still too weak to fight him, or even to get away."

She pushed back brown hair from her eyes. Her voice was hoarse. "I'll fight him, then. You'll tell me how."

"Oh. My dear love."

Her tears were threatening to brim again. "You do look stronger than you were. You can move, now, at least a little. Maybe if you rest a while . . . then I'll help you get away. Can I lift you now, and hold you?"

He nodded, feebly. Judy shifted her position, sitting on the hardwood floor. His head weighed almost nothing when she laid it in her lap. Gray hair and paper skin on bone. She stroked his forehead, too fleshless to have wrinkles. She told herself his face did actually look a little fuller now than when she had first found him. Though she had to admit that the improvement was pitifully small.

The deep sparks in his eyes burned up at her. "You will not leave," he said, stating a fact.

"No, I will not."

"Then you will be here when he comes."

"If he is coming. But yes, I'll be here till someone comes." With infinite tenderness she smoothed his hair.

His mouth emitted a ghost of its old hiss. "Then there is only one thing we can do. For your own sake as well as mine."

"What? Tell me."

"You know that I am not as other men."

"I know."

"Even wounded—so—it is possible for me to regain my full strength, or very nearly so, in no more than hours, or perhaps only minutes."

"Love, tell me how."

"The sun has set now and that helps me—of course it will help *them* also. Pulling out the spear and stanching the wound have helped me greatly. Yet one thing more is needed."

Judy raised her head. Had she heard a footstep, somewhere in the house? No, she thought, only the storm. Just inside the broken window, the narrow wraith of snowflakes danced and melted. "What is it, my love? Anything."

"My darling Judy, have I not told you again and again to go, to leave me here?"

"Stop wasting time and tell me—oh."

Her lover's hand had risen to the back of her neck, caressingly. First feebly now, then with strength surprising in a limb so thin, his arm urged her to bend lower over him.

Judy rearranged her own limbs, her body, to bend down in the way he seemed to want.

"Oh," she said again. His lips, that had appeared so dry and wasted, felt soft and warm upon her throat.

EIGHTEEN

Before the immobilizing drug wore off, Carol bound Joe's arms and legs with strong cord and tape. She worked so cunningly that the bonds were almost comfortable, and yet when he was able to try to move again he soon discovered that he could barely twitch a muscle.

A preoccupied expert, Carol smiled at him absently as she worked. "Joe, my little dear, are you awake? Yes. Too bad, in a way. You might just have slept from here on. Don't worry, though. You're going to rather enjoy things at the end, I promise you that. It really does work that way. Now, all nicely packaged." She gave him a pat, then picked him up, dandling a baby effortlessly. "You must be packaged safely, because Mommy is going out for a while. I have to go and play with little Craig once more—to try to salvage him. Because at the moment he's the only breather I have left who'll work with me. And you breathers are so useful for some things. Yes, you are."

Carol carried Joe into an unfinished side-room, about eight feet by ten, hardly more than a large storage closet. Barrels and crates and boxes almost filled the place. A second door, the upper half of it glass-paneled, led to another, much larger, darkened room or area, where streetlight entering by distant windows showed bare concrete walls and floor, saw-horses, scraps of lumber, a can of paint or two.

He got only one glance out through the glass panel, for Carol promptly lowered him to the floor, left him sitting there leaning against something solid at his back.

Before she straightened up, she kissed his forehead briskly, as people who kissed their dogs might do. "I'd like to give you a real kiss, Joey, of a kind you've never had. But there just isn't time. Not right now."

Her feet in high heels tapped back into the finished rooms of the apartment. The door closed solidly behind her, so only the street lighting, very distant and indirect, reached him now. He could hear vague sounds of movement from the apartment for a little while, then there was silence.

They hadn't bothered to gag him, so it seemed he was free to yell for help as much as he liked—Johnny hadn't been gagged either. Well, maybe later he would try.

They hadn't even bothered to take away his gun.

The viewer built into Craig Walworth's back door showed him that Kate Southerland was standing just outside. She looked just about as she had when he had seen her last, blue jacket and all. Without consciously intending to do so, he spoke her name aloud.

His voice was low, but Kate evidently heard him through the door, for at once she rattled its handle.

"Craig?" Her voice coming through the thick wood sounded dazed and empty. "Craig? Let me in, please." Her image in the viewer appeared dazed too, staring glassily forward as if she could see him through the door.

Taking his eye from the viewer, Walworth turned himself around in a full circle, looking at his brightly lighted kitchen. He did not really see anything of the cheerful colors. His mind was devoid of plans, and he felt that he was waiting for something to be explained to him. When he had turned to face the door once more he tried looking through the viewer again. She was still there, and once more the handle of the door rattled.

"Hell, why not?" he said aloud. "Come in. If you're a phantom I won't be able to keep you out anyway, will I?"

It took him a full ten seconds to undo all the alarms and fastenings armoring the door, and then he swung it wide. Kate walked in at once. Before he did anything else he locked the door completely up again. Then he turned to look at her.

She certainly looked real and solid enough, and her confused state was even plainer than it had been through the viewer. Her face was paler than he remembered it, her hands kept rubbing each other nervously, her eyes jumped erratically about the kitchen, looking everywhere but straight at him.

Abruptly she began to speak in a staccato voice. "This place where I've been staying—you see, he broke in there today, while it was still daylight. Cloudy, but still so bright when I ran outside that I thought I was going to die."

"Huh." He studied Kate's face desperately, trying to make sure that it was real. If he fired his pistol at it, what would happen? "Somebody broke in on you somewhere, huh?"

"Enoch Winter." Her empty blue eyes flicked at Walworth, then past him at the stove. "He was looking for the old man, I know. He said—he said Joe told him where the old man might be sleeping. He looked in all the vaults, I think."

"Joe," said Walworth, just to be saying something.

"Yes." Kate's eyes fixed on him suddenly. "Do you know where Joe is?"

"I don't know any Joe, lady," he said, suddenly remembering who Joe must be.

"I have the feeling that Joe has been here recently."

"Why in hell should Joe be here?"

"Joe shouldn't be in hell," Kate answered instantly—making as much sense, Walworth thought, as anything else she had said so far. She appeared to stop to think. "I don't know why he should be in this place, then," she went on. "But he was here."

"My God." Walworth was speaking to himself again. "I think it really is Kate. Then there must have been someone who looked just like her in the morgue— someone they found in that rooming house—I don't know. God, what a day and evening this is turning out to be."

Kate nodded at him, a wise-old-woman sort of nod that made her look crazier than ever. "You speak of God a lot, don't you? They can, too, you know. It's not really like it is in the stories. They can handle holy things. They're no worse than we are, really."

"Sure, whatever you say." Suddenly Walworth remembered leaving the phone off its cradle, back in the other room. Immediately he felt pleased with himself for having his head on so straight now that he remembered that. "Excuse me one second," he said, and left the kitchen.

Sure enough, there was the loose phone; score one for the consistency of the world and dependability of his brain. He hung it up, not bothering to find out if there was someone on the other end of the line now or not. He could call back later for help if it was necessary, but right now it looked like maybe he was going to fly home from this trip on his own.

On his way back to the kitchen he hoped fiercely that his visitor was still going to be there. She was, he saw with considerable relief, and she still looked like Kate. But a Kate still really out of it, staring now with great apparent interest at the icemaker on his refrigerator door—

Why couldn't he see her reflection in the chrome?

Some trick of angles—

Going up to the girl, Walworth quietly touched her on the elbow. She started, not at all the way a phantom ought to behave, and turned her quietly wild gaze on him.

Those eyes of hers made him shaky. "Kate, d'you know what? Everyone thinks you're dead. Hey, now, don't start flying around outside the window, or do anything silly like that, hey?" He could hear the real pleading in his own voice, and it disgusted him.

She looked at him with a total lack of intelligence. "What?"

"I'm just telling you, don't do anything silly until I have the chance to show the world that you're still alive and in one piece. That's going to get me off one hook, anyway. Now you *are* here, right?" He squeezed her jacketed elbow. "Sure you are."

"I'm here. Of course I am."

"Great. What brings you to my place tonight, anyway? Not that I mind." His hand, falling back to his side, brushed the butt of the gun still stuck in his belt, and he wondered if it would be smarter now to put the weapon away. He decided to carry it with him a little longer, just in case . . . in case of what, he didn't exactly know.

"I must find Joe." Kate's fine forehead creased in puzzlement. "I went to his apartment tonight, right after sunset, but he's not there. He's been *here*, I can feel it."

She raised both hands to her head. "Oh, those people drugged me, that night when I was here . . . maybe you . . . but you're not one of them."

"No, no I'm not."

Kate let her hands drop to her sides, and her

speech fell back into its earlier lifeless tone. "I think I left something here . . . I didn't have any money with me when I wanted to go shopping."

"Shopping. Sure." Walworth stared at her for a little while. "My God, they really dosed you good, didn't they? Well, welcome to the club. I knew they were giving you something good that night . . . how many days ago was that? Almost a week, I bet, and you're still wandering. I hope it's not the same thing they gave me. God."

She looked at him as if she were trying hard to understand.

"So, what do I do with you now, Katie? Just call up the cops, I suppose. No, my lawyer first. Then the cops. Tell 'em you're here. Say you just wandered in. I know you slightly."

He decided to take a look around the apartment first, because there were probably a few things he'd rather the cops didn't see. He had better put the gun away, to begin with—suddenly recalling something else, Walworth turned his back on Kate and walked out of the kitchen again. When he reached his bedroom, the little shot-to-splinters table was lying just as he remembered it, on its side against the wall, dusted with a little plaster from the cratered wall above.

So, the shooting incident had been real enough—except of course he must have been shooting at a drug-induced hallucination. Carol herself had doubtless been long gone before things started to get dangerous. Her idea in drugging him must have been that he would eliminate himself with his own crazed violence—an unreliable method, it would seem, of getting someone out of the way. And why should she want him out of the way anyhow? Maybe this was only her idea fun. He himself, he knew, had some ideas on how to have a good time that would seem far out, to put it mildly, to most people.

But Carol and her pal the ape-man must be completely crazy. . . .

He righted the little table. Still, there was no way that the damage wouldn't be noticed if anyone came into the bedroom. I was cleaning my gun this afternoon, officer, and it just . . . they must hear that pretty often. But still the gun had nothing to do with Kate, or with her brother's kidnapping. So that would be all right. What he had to do now was show the world that Kate Southerland was still alive. After that, there ought to be lawyers around sharp enough to demonstrate to the world that whatever had been happening to Kate lately was not Craig Walworth's fault.

But this time, when he got back to the cheerful kitchen, his chronic fear was realized. Kate was gone. No trace of her. And the back door was still locked and bolted from the inside.

Partial relief came with the realization that she must have wandered off somewhere, and still be in the apartment. He found his front door still chained up, too, when his hopeful search for Kate took him that far. He stood in the living room and called her name a few times, tentatively. He was completely certain that that image of Carol, with a hole shot in her dress but not the pink skin of her belly, had been a picture projected out of his own doped mind. That had to be. Tonight's Kate, though, had looked worn and almost sick, and despite that—or maybe because of it—she had been very real.

Of course Carol, now that he thought about it, never looked all that real anyway. Beautiful, God yes, but . . .

So he went through the whole place once more, calling Kate's name softly, peering into closets as he went and even under the beds. Doing this made him feel no sillier than anything else he could think of doing.

Once the gun in his belt pinched his belly when

he bent over to look under a bed, and he had a sudden almost overpowering impulse to draw it out and put the muzzle to his head and pull the trigger. Would death be a drug-delusion too, an unreal sleep? Was Kate really dead and was he sharing the ultimate bad trip with her? When people got up from the morgue and walked . . .

His doorchime sounded distantly. Someone at the front. The lobby desk should have called up—or had he missed hearing the intercom?

This time he didn't even bother looking through the viewer first. He just undid the fastenings of the door and opened up, ready to take whatever came.

It was Kate again, standing there dumbly, looking just as she had before.

"How do you do that?" Irritably he reached out and grabbed her by the solid, real jacket sleeve and pulled her into the apartment. "Now stay put, will you, and let me think? I got a head full of shit and I got to try to think. Baby, I've got to be sure you're real before I call the cops to try to show you off."

"He's coming after me," said Kate, in her dazed voice that assigned nothing any gradations of importance.

"He? Who?"

"I went downstairs just now, and there he was, coming along the walk. He wants me to go back with him. Give me orders, put me out of the way somewhere, that's what he wants. But I've got to keep looking for Joe—"

Reality was suddenly as unmistakable as an onrushing truck. "Winter's coming? Up here?"

"—and he won't let me go on looking."

It was quiet enough now that Walworth could hear one of the front elevators running.

He ought to show the world one Enoch Winter, dead, along with one Kate Southerland alive. Winter had forced his way in, trying to attack her. Tell that story, and then let the good lawyers guide him through.

Quickly he closed his front door again, leaving it unlocked. His last look out into the lobby showed him the mirror with its draping raincoat. Show business, he thought.

Waving Kate to stand back, he retreated just a few steps from the door and drew the gun and thumbed the hammer back very silently. He raised it in a two-handed aim, keeping his gaze squarely on the door.

"What are you doing?" Kate's voice was suddenly changed radically toward the normal, as if the sight of the drawn gun had acted as a tonic shock. "Craig!"

The doorbell chimed. Somehow, with the distraction from Kate, he had missed hearing the sounds of the elevator stopping and opening.

"Who?" he called out sharply. His hands, center-aiming at the door, were very steady.

"Winter," the deep voice answered.

"No," Kate whispered, somewhere behind him. "It isn't. Be careful, don't shoot."

"Come in," Walworth called, his trigger finger very slowly taking up slack. "It's unlocked."

The knob turned and the door swung in. Not Winter at all. Almost as tall, but lean. Under an open black topcoat, what looked like a new suit of expensive black. A somehow Christmasy red tie, a fine white shirt. Smiling, jaunty, vigorous, but obviously old.

The old man.

I see now that you would only laugh like an idiot if I tried to tell you his real name.

Walworth fired. Even though he knew, before the gun went off, exactly how much good the bullet was going to do him.

NINETEEN

Kate saw the old man step in through the front door, and in the same instant she heard the pistol fire. Only with that shock did her mind grow fully clear. If the old man had really needed help, she would have been too late to help him. As it was, she sprang forward with a speed and strength that she had not known she possessed, reaching past Craig's shoulder to knock down his joined hands with the weapon still clasped in them. The force of the movement knocked Craig to his knees.

The old man smiled reassuringly at Kate. Then calmly bending with his own fluid and unhurried speed, he caught Craig by the shirt front and lifted him erect again, letting the gun stay somewhere on the floor. Reaching back with his free hand, Corday pushed the door shut behind him. Then he gently questioned both of the people with him: "Where is Joe?"

"He's been here," said Kate. "He's not here now."

Craig said: "I'm not gonna take any heat to protect her. Go over to Enchantress Cosmetics. As for Carol."

"And what does Carol look like?" The question was in a tone of mild interest. Walworth's strong, young body was swaying, and he seemed to be trying without success to avoid the old man's eyes. The old man seemed to be keeping the young one propped up with one finger.

"Real good shape," Walworth muttered. "Sharp dresser. Young. Red hair—"

"Ah? And where is the place you mentioned?"

Walworth named an intersection. "About eight blocks from here, west and south. I gotta warn you about her. She's really got it in for you."

"Indeed."

"And for me too," Walworth added hastily. "She wants me dead. Just today she drugged me—bad, man, bad. You wouldn't believe the things I've seen. I thought you were a friend of hers just now, coming to finish me off. That's why I . . ."

"Kate has told me," the old man softly interrupted, "how and where she came to meet them. Johnny has spoken to me of a bearded man driving a car, who asked him for directions."

Walworth's hands that had aimed the gun so steadily were shaking now. He couldn't seem to find anything to say.

Kate could only think of one thing clearly. "Please," she broke in, talking to the old man. "I can help you now. I'm all right. Let's go find Joe. He's in real trouble."

Still holding Walworth almost tenderly with one thin hand, the old man turned thoughtful eyes to Kate. "Go to the location this man has just given us," he ordered. "I shall follow presently." When Kate hesitated, he repeated firmly: "Go."

Kate nodded, turned, and fled toward the kitchen. There was no sound of the back door being opened, but Walworth knew that she was gone.

He asked: "You gonna call in the cops on me?"

"No," the old man assured him gently.

"You're not really here anyway, are you?" Walworth asked him, shivering. "I could almost wish you were."

At the mausoleum the old man had shown Kate something of how to use her recently acquired powers. How the night change in her body would enable her to pass like smoke through locked and bolted doors. The kitchen door went past her like some vague and insubstantial curtain, but this time she had hardly thought about the process. As she started down the back stairs of the apartment building, all her mental energies were concentrated on the job of finding Joe.

The back stairs were concrete and steel, designed as an interior fire escape as well as a service passage. Not until Kate had descended past two landings did she come to a small window. At once she used her marvelous new agility to leap up upon its narrow inside sill. Once she had located the knife-edge crevice where reinforced glass met metal frame, the closed window was no obstacle to her passage.

In the passing she willed an alteration in the cells of her body, the fabric of her clothes, the very air that filled her lungs and all the spaces in her bones. Outside, her altered body was at one with the wind. Her altered senses blurred. A creature of the air now, and no more solid than the air, she sank through clouds of falling snowflakes. Like blowing snow she skimmed above rooftops, down and up and down again.

Propelling herself by her will, she moved south, and west.

Joe was near.

His danger was terrible, but at least the threat did not seem to be immediate. And fortunately he had not yet been greatly hurt. Kate's inner senses were keener now than before, but at the same time sight and hearing had grown blurred and dull and indirect with her physical body dispersed to hardly more than mist. She felt rather than saw the glowing streetlights and the bulking buildings of the city below, and anything dimmer or smaller could hardly be perceived at all. In order to reach Joe she was going to have to take on solid form again.

In theory, she knew, the forms of animals were available now for her to put on. But she had as yet tried nothing like that, and at the moment she had no mental energy or time to spare for experimentation. So when she came down with a crunch in roof-top snow, her shape was her own, as human as before. And as her senses grew keen again Kate was at once aware not only of the details of the buildings and the storm around her, but of two other forms that were passing as she had just passed in the air. They were the diffuse bodies of a man and a woman that Kate was almost sure she had never seen before.

Joe was very near, now, but not in the building where Kate had come down. She moved to crouch motionless beside a chimney, while the couple she had just detected materialized in a slow descent out of the beflaked air to another roof only half a block away. The building they came down on was no more than two or three stories high, of concrete gray.

In the little storeroom there were a couple of fifty-five-gallon steel drums, with clamped-on lids. There were wooden crates and cardboard boxes. It was too dark to see how any of them were labeled. Joe thought that if he could get to his feet he could make an effort to spill one or more of these containers on the chance that they might hold something helpful. A box of knives would seem to be unlikely. Maybe glass to break, to try to get an edge with which to cut his bonds—if he could move his hands enough to pick up anything. Something to start a fire with, to attract help? He hadn't yet reached the stage where burning himself to death looked like a desirable option.

But it didn't take long to convince himself that trying to work free of the ropes without some kind of tool was going to be futile. Maybe if they left him here two days unwatched he'd manage it. But by then he would have died of hypothermia, or whatever they called it now. The storeroom wasn't as cold as the outdoors tonight, but even with his jacket still on he was no longer warm.

The ropes were fixed so he couldn't stand. He might be able to spill boxes, though. If one of them contained glass, and if the glass broke, that might help—more likely, though, they would just be irritated by his noisiness and come in and twist one of his fingers off.

There was one box on the floor, about as high as a piano bench and as long as a piano, whose lid was slight askew, so that it ought to be possible to see or maybe reach inside. A place to start, something to try. Crabbing his way along the cold concrete as best he could, almost silently, Joe got beside the large crate. Here his face was in reflected streetlight, while the interior of the box remained in heavy shadow; looking in, he could distinguish only vaguely mounded white, about halfway down.

He had to find something to cut his ropes with, the way people were always doing it in stories. Anything.

At once end, the whitish surface inside the box was marked with a dark ring a couple of inches across. Just above that were two glassy spots. . . .

He froze, even the cold-trembling in his limbs suspended for the moment, and in that moment he was afraid that he was going to faint. A dead woman lay there, her staring eyes hardly a foot beneath his own. A young woman dressed in white.

Jesus. Jesus. His back against another crate, Joe slid away from his discovery, trying to keep from blacking out. His arms and legs were throbbing, and at the same time trying to go numb. If he fainted now . . . they hadn't even taken away his gun. . . .

. . . there were two voices again, somewhere out in the apartment. Joe understood that he was coming out of some kind of blackout. Probably a brief one, for he hadn't frozen yet, or wet his pants either. Something else to think about . . .

A Chicago cop shouldn't pass out at the sight of one more dead woman. It made his enemies no worse than before, he'd known what they were like ever since Kate's body had been found. . . .

Oh, God.

But it wasn't Kate. Blondish hair, perhaps, but—

In a moment Joe had pushed himself back in position to peer again into the crate, or coffin. Of course it wasn't her, he would have known at first glance if it had been. He forced himself to gaze into the box, trying to make out details that he had earlier avoided. It wasn't Kate, even allowing for death's changes. This woman was smaller, sharper-featured. And something was wrong about her mouth.

Out in the apartment, the two people talking had moved closer to the storeroom door. "You simply left him there," Carol was saying now. Whoever had been left where, she wasn't sure whether she liked the idea of it or not.

"He woulda died," answered the rough voice of Leroy Poach, who had been hanged in Oklahoma in 1934. "No way he would've lasted if I'd tried to bring him here. As it is he's prob'ly finished by now. I think I got him right through one lung. You shoulda seen the blood."

"Oh, I'd love to fly out there now . . . if I thought I could be there for the end." Carol's voice suddenly became a whisper of concentrated hate. "So much effort, so much time. Even you can't begin to realize . . . and now, to miss the end at last."

"Take off, then. Enjoy. I'll talk to the people till you get back. Explain to Lady Wanda when she gets up."

"No." Carol was regretfully decisive. "This conference is too important. I must be here for all of it, if I can. I must be unhurried, in control of everything. There must be no doubt in any of their minds that I am now in control. That the future is going to be what I say . . . Poach, what about the Southerland family?"

"They were all out somewhere, except the old woman. I put her out. It don't look to me like any of the others will get home tonight, the way it's snowing. If they do, well, they'll move the old bastard one way or the other, and that'll be it. Cops'll buzz around for a while, but the body'll be gone to nothing before they get a good look at it."

"Tell me again about the fight. I want to hear it all."

"Well. I looked in all the closets and everywhere as I went through the house, see? Then I got to this room in back, and I knew right away. There it was, a big stone coffin like the one I found out in the cemetery."

"It must have been earthenware of some kind, to provide the home earth. Clever. We must remember that for future use ourselves. Go on."

"Anyway, I just knocked it over and he rolled out on the floor. I got the stake in before he even got his eyes open. *That* opened his eyes for him! He managed to stand up, and we thrashed around a lot, but it wasn't really a fight. He didn't have a chance—right through the chest. Nailed 'im there like a bug."

When Carol spoke again her voice was low. "I suppose it was for the best."

"Suppose?" Poach's voice did not really show anger; rather it was as if he would have shown anger if he dared. "In the two years since I met you, you been drummin' it into me, how I gotta kill him quick if I ever get the chance. How dangerous he is. Also how much you hate him. So I thought it worked out just perfect. I got 'im but I didn't finish 'im. I give you the chance."

"Yes, you did the right thing. You have done very well."

"You don't act too happy."

"Ah, dear Poach, don't sulk. It is just—can you imagine what it is like, to hate someone for four hundred years? You cannot, you are not yet a century old. After such a length of time, there is something like love in it."

"Love?" The tone was crude, incredulous. What had been near-anger was near-laughter now.

Carol's voice lashed at him. "Remember your place, my man. What you were when I found you. What you are and will be still depends on me."

Poach mumbled something.

"What?"

"Yes, my lady. I didn't mean. . . ."

"See that you don't."

The door to the storeroom opened without warning, and Carol was looking in at him. She was wearing a kind of green jumpsuit now, a fancy party coverall, and she smiled at Joe enchantingly. Then her eyes moved beyond him, just as a faint noise came from that direction.

The dead woman had got out of her box and was standing beside it in her white gown, plainly visible in the brighter light from the apartment. She stretched luxuriously. There were traces of something dried around her lips, and she licked them with a perfectly pink tongue. . . .

❖   ❖   ❖

. . . when he could hear the distant voices chattering again, and knew again where he was, he refrained for a long time from opening his eyes. He didn't want to see the walking dead. He thought about the sensations of numbness in his feet and hands. That he could assess them so carefully meant that he was awake now, didn't it? Before, he had been drugged. The woman in the box must have been only a drugged dream.

Joe opened his eyes, though, when he heard the door again. It was a smiling Leroy Poach, hanged in 1934, attired now in black evening dress, come to take Joe to the toilet. This prophylactic attention was actually just about in the nick of time.

"Wouldn't want you to be messy when we bring you out, cop." Poach was quite jovial now, despite his crusted forehead crease. It looked like a days-old wound, cared for and then forgotten. "Nice and clean and fresh is the idea. You're gonna be the piece de resis-*tahnce* at the party tonight. Know what I mean? Not yet you don't. Wouldn't believe me if I told you, either."

While being carried to the bathroom and back he could hear Carol and the other people chatting, off somewhere in other rooms. He could see no one but Poach. The apartment was still mostly in darkness. There were lamps but no one had bothered to turn on more than a very few of them. Rusty water ran into the toilet when it was flushed, as if the fixture hadn't been used in a long time.

Back alone in his chill room, bound as securely as before, Joe thought he could hear more people arriving. There were more voices, and the voices were getting somewhat louder, as they tended to do at any party. And now Joe imagined that he could hear them talking in Latin. At least he might have called it Latin, if he had been forced to take a guess.

Latin was bad, because it made him remember

Johnny. Johnny in his closet, losing f
reporting the Latin conversations which
believed. . . .

Somewhere in the outer air, between
distant streetlight, moved something th
and thicker than a snowflake but just as silent as the
snow. There was no way that he could see what it
had been.

The box that the dead woman had climbed out of
was completely open now, lid beside it on the floor.
He had been hallucinating. If he looked into that box
now, he would see something ordinary. But he wasn't
going to try.

"But, why do we not speak English now?" said
Carol's voice, not far outside the storeroom door.
"Some of you in the past have chided me for using
the old tongue too much. Poach, I think there are
more guests on the roof, go up and ask them in."

"Thank you," said a man, not Poach. "English will
certainly be more convenient for most of us. I suppose half of us at least have been born on this side
of the Atlantic."

"And many of the rest," a woman put in, "have
been here a hundred years or more. Long enough
to forget a great deal of the Old World." Other voices
murmured polite agreement. There was a nervous
little female laugh.

Poach was back, saying something. With him came
a man and a woman, new arrivals, for various greetings were exchanged. When that was over, Carol
talked. She had become a public speaker now, addressing a gathering.

"I trust you have all had a tolerable journey,
weather notwithstanding. Let me assure everyone that
this storm is perfectly natural, at least as far as I and
Poach are concerned. Our whole energies have been
directed elsewhere."

Someone commented: "It's a great night not to be

...ather." It had the sound of a quoted proverb. ...ain there was a scattering of nervous laughter.

When this had died, the hostess resumed: "As you know, this meeting was originally called that I might solicit your support in a struggle for our freedom." She paused. "That, I say, was the *original* purpose."

Another pause. The room they were all gathered in was suddenly extremely quiet.

And the shadow in front of Joe's streetlight was back again. Its presence was continuous now, but it was not still—there was a shapeless outline, shifting with some kind of movement. It was only the snow. What else could it be?

Abruptly Carol's voice rang out: "Your support in that struggle is no longer necessary, for victory is ours. This afternoon our enemy overreached himself. He attempted to attack Poach in his earth." This last was delivered as an indictment, made with disgust, as of an offense that was not only criminal but represented some ultimate breach of decency. "That ancient, evil . . . I scarcely know what to call him. That tyrant had evidently been taking his own publicity too seriously. He overestimated his own powers, and underestimated those of Poach."

A few moments of silence intervened. Then Carol, in a harder voice, continued: "Surely no one here regrets this turn of events?"

Another woman eventually answered. "It is only that we are—surprised."

Someone else murmured a faint question.

"No, he is not yet dead," Carol replied. "But he is firmly in my hands, awaiting judgement."

A man's voice, stammering a little but with more boldness than any of the others had yet shown, asked: "And who is to sit in judgement on him then? Of what is he accused?"

"Of—what—accused?" Carol whispered back the question as if incapable of believing that it had been asked. "Of what? To begin the catalogue, of attempting to murder Poach—but I can't believe that you are really serious."

Another man's voice put in: "I am older than any here, I think, except yourself, lady. If judgement is to be rendered on a *nosferatu*, a tribunal of seven is called for by the law. At least five are necessary, if seven cannot be found who—"

Now Carol's young voice snapped like a whip. "I warn you, I warn you all, things are going to go hard on his secret sympathizers. His crimes are legion. Even the breathers' histories document them. Do you think he is milder now, less murderous, less oppressive, than he was in the fifteenth century?" She paused. "Some of you, I think, do not yet appreciate the positive aspects of today's victory. What it is going to mean in terms of freedom for all of us. No more are we to be a powerless minority on the face of the earth, always hunted and in hiding."

A woman replied tremulously: "I think—I think we will all come to understand it better, in time. Can you explain it to us more fully, Morgan?"

"If necessary." Carol's—or Morgan's—voice went on. "That foul old man has had some of you completely brainwashed for centuries. That must be changed. When I call him old you know I am not speaking of mere spins of the Earth. He has been selfish and unchanging in his thought, blind to all our needs. Insisting that all of us be fettered by what he calls his honor. Not to use the breathers who swarm about us, not to taste their blood unless they give consent. Not to remove those who give us offense or stand in our way. Not to enjoy the treasures of the earth, that by rights belong to us as superior beings . . . but today a new world has been born. All that is changed."

There was a little silence. The speaker's voice was bright and confident when it continued. "Have any of you any more questions? Yes. Dickon?"

The pause dragged on before one of the men's voices dared: "I was only . . . I still think it would be better if we . . ."

"Poach, it seems we have an agent of the old man's here among us. Place him—"

"No, Morgan! I did not mean to dispute your authority in this. It's nothing to me, really. He—he whom you call the old man is nothing."

When Morgan spoke again, her voice had grown even more light and cheerful. "Then enough of business, I think, for the time being. Would any of you care for some refreshment?"

Maybe if a man had to, if there were nothing else, he could break ropes with his arms. Even if his arms were numb. If he really gave it *all*. . . .

TWENTY

As soon as the couple that Kate had seen descending through the air were out of sight, she flew again. This time she landed on the roof of the building into which they had somehow vanished. There she crouched in woman-form again, straining all her senses to locate Joe.

She knew he was very near now, somewhere below her, somewhere inside. His presence felt strongest when she approached a certain window. When she hung her head and upper body downward from the edge of the roof this window let her see into a large, unfinished room or area of some kind in which workmen's tools and building materials lay scattered. Joe was still not visible. But, as Kate looked into this window, her attention gradually became centered on a door at the far side of the unfinished space. It was a plain door, with a glass upper panel, leading to some kind of small, dark room beyond. Gradually she understood that Joe was there.

The window she was looking through was barred with heavy metal-and-wood grillwork, and wired with electrical alarms. But these gave Kate no trouble.

Once inside, she moved straight across the empty, unfinished space, solidifying her body again as she came to the glass-paneled door. Joe, doubled over and bound, lay on the floor inside it, amid a confusion of stored boxes. His eyes were closed and he was motionless. But she was certain he was not dead.

Wanting to keep her senses at maximum alertness if she could, Kate did not pass through the closed door but retained her solid form and gently tried its knob. It was not locked, and swung smoothly outward. She rushed in silently to Joe's side—

She willed to rush to him—

The threshold, or something in the air above it, caught her like an invisible, impalpable steel net. She could feel no solid barrier opposing her, yet she was unable to reach even a finger into the room.

Kate shifted forms. The solidity of her body gone, she tried again. The doorway was as impervious as before.

In woman-form again, she stood just outside the open doorway, biting her nails and trying to think. The old man had said something about this. The room that she was trying to enter was living quarters, part of someone's dwelling. He had said it would be impossible now for her to enter any such space uninvited. Listening to the old man, back in the mausoleum, she hadn't really understood or believed what he was trying to tell her. Now—

She must rouse Joe, get him to call to her, invite her in. But she could hear other voices now, including the voice of Poach, just beyond the storeroom's inner door. They would certainly hear her if she called to Joe.

Again and again she pressed her body, in alternate forms, against the barrier. But it was like a breather trying to go through a wall. She tried urgently to force her thoughts into Joe's mind. But his stupor was too deep.

If only the old man were here. But even he would not be able to drive his way in uninvited.

Six feet away from her, she could feel Joe's life gently ebbing.

There were tears on Kate's face. She would have sobbed or screamed, but those in the apartment must not hear her.

The old man had told her something else. That whatever powers any human being could seize beyond nature came from the will, not through diabolism or magic. That if the will were strong enough, very little in this world need be impossible. That if—

Kate closed her eyes. She stood on the threshold, leaning forward. But she was not pushing any longer. That had proven useless. This was something else.

Is this what it means to pray? she wondered briefly. And then she ceased to think at all about what she was trying to do, or what was happening to her. Her self was entirely forgotten. There was only Joe, and his need, and the help that had to reach him, somehow.

Prayer, or giving birth. Or could they sometimes be the same—

—and something, some agony, was over. Kate came to herself lying face down on the concrete floor. Air, cold and unaccustomed, was filling her lungs with repeated pain, and it took a great effort to manage this labored, almost sobbing breath in silence. The birth, some kind of birth, was over, and the thin cry floating in Kate's mind was not a baby's but her own, unvoiced. She saw that she was lying halfway across the threshold. She crawled forward, arms trembling with a sudden weakness, the weakness of the new-born. With fingers that suddenly seemed almost powerless she began to work to remove the cords holding Joe's hands. He was still alive. His breath and hers were mingling in the air.

She whispered his name. That, or the tugging at

his arms, made his eyes open presently. His eyes saw her, and yet they did not see; his mind had not reacted to her presence yet.

In her new relative weakness she was not going to be able to carry or drag him very far. So he was going to have to walk, and perhaps climb, and so she was going to have to free his legs. His hands were now free at last; numbly he moved them in front of him, trying to get the fingers working.

"Kate?" His voice was weak, yet loud enough to present a danger.

"Shh! Yes, I'm here. It's going to be—"

"Kate?"

"Oh, love, be quiet!" She pinched his lips together with her fingers, then closed them with a kiss. And now the last bindings on his legs were coming loose. And now—

The inner door of the room swung open suddenly. Enoch Winter stood there in dark evening dress. The difference between his face as Kate now saw it and as it was in her memory lay less in the new scar on his forehead than in the dumbfounded surprise with which he looked at her.

Kate leaped to her feet, but would not flee alone. Winter's loud voice burst out with some exclamation; in another moment his massive fist had somehow collected both of her wrists within its grip. Other people came flooding around, gabbling their astonishment. A young-looking, red-haired woman barked orders. Kate was dragged stumbling out of the storeroom, into luxurious though badly lighted living quarters. At the moment it seemed that the last of her strength had been used up. Joe, looking worse off than she, his wrists gripped in Poach's other hand, was pulled along staggering at her side.

Joe didn't really begin to come out of his faint or stupor or whatever the hell it was until he was already on his feet. At that point Poach had him, was drawing him along to what Joe thought must be some kind of final confrontation with his enemies. Joe understood at once that Kate was now with him again, and in a way it seemed quite natural that she was. They were both of them now dwelling in the domain of ultimate things, of life and death. The trivialities making up what was usually called ordinary life had all been left behind—by Kate some days ago, by Joe himself only during the last few hours. Now they were in the land of life and death together.

Together they were pushed up against the edge of the massive worktable, on whose top Joe had earlier been drugged and then bound. The bonds were gone now, and he could stand. His arms were still so numb that he could barely move them.

"Bring her closer to the light." That was Carol—no, Morgan was probably the right name, Joe remembered.

Now Morgan was inspecting Kate's face closely. "She's certainly breathing steadily enough," Morgan pronounced a moment later. "I really don't think she's faking it." A murmur went up from the people gathered in the circle of shadow just beyond the table's light. Now Morgan was pushing back Kate's upper lip, as if inspecting a horse, then tilting back her head to examine the smooth skin of her throat. "This is Kate Southerland?" she snapped at Poach.

"Yeah, sure." Poach blinked. "Hey, at least it's the one that Walworth introduced me to."

"You assured me that when you were through with her, she had been changed."

In the silence, all of them seemed to be watching Kate's breath, steaming faintly in the room's chill air. Joe's breath steamed too. But he noticed now that no one else's did, except for the briefest momentary puffs with speech.

Besides Joe and Kate and the woman called

Morgan, there were about a dozen other people present. Looking at their shadowed faces now, Joe could see that they were divided about evenly between men and women. Judged by surface appearances, the gathering might have represented a cross-section of middle-class America. A couple of people were black, one Oriental. Most were dressed in clothing that might have been worn to the office, a few outfitted as for a casual party. One sturdy, young-looking couple wore denim jeans and jackets that had the look of real work clothes. One of the older-looking women, rather beefy, almost motherly, was already gazing at Joe when his glance fell on her. She gave him a sharp-toothed smile, and in the middle of it her tongue came out and licked her lips.

Before he could start to think about that, his attention was caught by the girl who stood next to the beefy woman. She had been dead in the box in the storeroom when Joe first saw her. A blond girl, thin and nervous, as well dressed—he saw now—as a fashion model. Her eyes were resting on Joe too, and she was smiling.

"I have heard of this, but never seen it before." The speaker was a gray-haired man, the oldest-looking of the group. "A girl, or a young man, changed unwillingly. Then a few days later a spontaneous relapse to the breathing state. What the breathers, I suppose, would call a spontaneous cure. It happens under intense emotional stress."

"I have seen it, Dickon," Morgan mused. "But only once before . . . this is a genuine reconversion, it would appear. Her blood will again be good to drink."

There was a silence, while each from his or her own viewpoint considered this. Looking past Morgan, who stood on the opposite side of the large table, Joe could see a vista of semi-darkened rooms and halls, ending at a large, draped window, through which some exterior light sent in a filtered glow. If he could tear free, run on his half-numbed legs, leap, cry for help as he crashed outside . . . on Morgan's left as Joe faced her, a great fireplace held cheery embers. There was a tang of aromatic woodsmoke in the air. Above the fireplace was mounted a lone diagonal spear.

As if struck by a sudden thought, Morgan bent across the table to look keenly at Kate once again. "Did any *send* you here, child?" Then she appeared to think better of the question. "Never mind. It does not matter."

"Who would have sent her?" asked the gray-haired man, Dickon. He looked round at all of them, then back at Morgan. "What did you mean?"

Morgan returned his gaze through narrowed eyes. "It was in my mind that there may be others who still cling to the old man's faction. A remnant who have not accepted the fact of his destruction."

"Destruction?" Kate's voice was as clear and loud as it was unexpected by them all. "She's told you that the old man's dead? She lies!"

Poach did something to Kate's arms behind her back, so she cried out and bent forward over the table. Joe tried to struggle; in a moment he was face down on the table too.

"What does the girl mean?" asked Dickon in a shaky voice, looking round at all of them again.

"Mean? To prolong her life, if she can manage it," Morgan answered calmly. "What else?"

A woman spoke up now, with timid reluctance, but speaking up to Morgan all the same. "Where is your prisoner being held?"

"Very well! If you still doubt me. He is miles from here, nailed like an insect to a specimen board. If any of you still doubt that, I'll fly with you to show—"

"Dr. Corday!" Kate screamed out suddenly. "Come in and help us!"

As if by a magic blow Kate's outcry cut across all other voices, even Morgan's, and wiped them into silence. Looking round him, Joe could see that no one was moving. The pressure of the silence was such that it felt like a growing weight. The grip pinioning his arms, though, did not slacken.

Someone's voice began a Latin whisper. It seemed to have no purpose other than to relieve the silence.

Morgan was looking over Joe's shoulder. The faintest of smiles was on her lips and her adolescent eyes had an expression that he could not read. Never again, though, would he be able to think of her as young in any sense.

The whisper had trailed away. The stillness in the room was more intense and ominous than before.

Poach was perhaps the first to move, letting his grip on Joe's wrists slacken and fall away. Joe saw Kate raise her head. He followed her gaze, in the same direction to which other silent faces were turning now. All were looking down the long vista of the rooms.

At the end the drapes were now drawn back slightly from the widow. And someone was standing there, a man's form outlined against an icy city night now cleared of falling snow. The form was motionless as some effigy of wax.

"I knew," Morgan murmured. "I think I knew it all along." Now moving slowly, unsurprised, she turned her back on Joe. She took two steps toward that distant apparition, and her voice rang out boldly: "Come in then, Vlad Tepes! I say it now of my own free will. Enter my house, and we will settle all that lies between us, here and now!"

TWENTY-ONE

Silently, with deliberate strides, the distant figure was pacing toward them.

Poach moved then, with such quickness that for a moment his great bulk seemed an illusion. Before Joe could react, the giant had reached the fireplace, and in an instant the eight-foot wooden spear mounted above it had come down into his hands. Morgan meanwhile backed up slowly, until one hand extended behind her rested on the table's edge.

For a long moment no one else stirred. Then, with a broken cry, gray-haired Dickon broke out of the group and stumbled into the next room. There he threw himself at the feet of the one approaching, who halted rather than step on him.

"Master!" Dickon cried out. "Master, I have never betrayed you. I would not believe that you were dead."

"Stand up, fool." For Joe's eyes, the face of the speaker was still in darkness. The voice, resonant and commanding, was like Corday's, and yet unlike. It went on: "This is the new world now, Dickon, have you not heard? Such sniveling ill becomes one who

is ready to take his rightful place as a member of the
superior race of beings."

Dickon's collapse became total. With his face down
on the thick carpet, his words fell into muffled howls.
The man whose path he had blocked stepped round
him, and continued his advance.

The fashion model was next to fall upon her knees.
"Vlad Tepes," she choked out, "we did not
know . . . we never believed that you were . . ."

"When have I ever asked for groveling?" the newcomer interrupted. "From any of you?" He took one
more step, and Joe could see that he wore Corday's
face—and yet he did not. Like the voice, the face
had been transformed. He who was not that old man
Joe had known—and yet was—took yet another step.
He stopped there, in a position from which he could
see Poach and Morgan both.

In Morgan's left hand, held behind her back as if
for support against the table, there had somehow
appeared a long knife. In the table lights it looked
to Joe as if it had been fashioned blade and all from
one piece of some dark and oily wood. Near the
fireplace, Poach stood poised like a harpooner with
his wooden spear. The bloody mark on his forehead
was throbbing now, looking almost raw.

For the moment, the two breathing people in the
room were being ignored by everyone else. Joe saw
that Kate's eyes were fixed, calculatingly, on the knife
in Morgan's hand; all right, let Kate do something
about that. Joe's left hand moved out stealthily over
the surface of the table in front of him. His fingers
touched and picked up a stub of pencil. If only it
were not too big around—

"Watch out!" he yelled, and heard Kate's voice ring
out in chorus with his own.

Had their warning been needed, it would have
come too late, for Morgan's swift strike had taken
them both by surprise. The old man had been ready,

though. He was out of the path of the knife-blow when it arrived, and with a whiplash of his arm he slapped Morgan staggering back. Joe saw him vanish then. Poach's lunge with the spear found only air.

An explosion of frightened voices filled the room. All around, solid bodies were going out like candle flames. There was a howling exodus in the air. Joe had drawn his gun at last, and now he got himself in front of Poach. The giant was looking past Joe, holding the spear ready, seeking for Corday. Joe slid the pencil stub eraser-first down the snub barrel of the .38, felt it check in place, rubber against chambered load.

Poach's eyes widened, discovering something behind Joe. Keeping the spear for bigger game, Poach lifted a free hand to sweep the irritation of a mere armed policeman from his path.

The revolver blasted once, and Joe's mind registered that at least it had not blown up in his hand with a jammed barrel. The hammerblow of the wooden impact slammed Poach's head backward, one side of his forehead disappearing in a great smear of jellied blood. The spear fell from the giant's hands, and the roar he uttered drowned out other shouting voices.

Though staggered, Poach somehow kept his feet. A second later, one eye showing clear and horrible in a face half masked in gore, he was coming after Joe.

Joe stumbled backward. With eyes and mind and hands he scrambled to locate some possible weapon made of wood. The table was too big for him to lift. He crawled beneath it, but a moment later it was knocked away. Lights went smash. In the deeper darkness, screaming and rushing seemed to go on without end. Joe, on his back, despairing of reaching useful wood, raised his pistol toward the huge form that bent toward him with hands outstretched to grab.

A different kind of rush went past him in the air, as of a grazing blow. Something struck Poach with disembodied but elemental power, lifting him to his feet. Joe could feel the floor vibrate when the big body struck the wall.

Automatically holstering his gun, Joe got to hands and knees and crawled toward the fireplace. Sparks were visible there, and there were streaks of luminosity in the air, screaming, fluttering gigantic shapes and shadows. One went right up the chimney with a shriek. A panic, as of whipped animals unable to break out of a pen, filled the place like fog. Joe groped his way amid crazy smashings, outcries, smells unlike anything he had encountered in his life before. What was he doing? Yes, looking for the spear. But he couldn't find it.

Turning away from the fireplace, he saw Kate. She was halfway across the room, trying to hold on to Morgan.

Joe charged, in mid-stride grabbing up a wooden chair.

He swung the chair with all his strength. It cut through empty air as Morgan's figure disappeared.

The chair landed on the floor, as Kate almost fell into his arms. Both of them were swaying with exhaustion. The darkened apartment was quiet now. They were alone.

Joe gripped Kate, looked hard at her while she looked back. He started twice to try to speak.

"We'll talk later," Kate said at last.

He nodded. "Let's get out of here."

Now, with a moment in which to look for it clear-headedly, he found the spear without difficulty. Kate, thinking along with him, had already picked up Morgan's wooden knife from where it lay on the floor.

They went out the front door of the apartment, at the bottom of a carpeted stair going down beside

the elevator. Joe led the way, spear ready. It was a
simple door that opened to the sidewalk—

Or to where the sidewalk was supposed to be. Joe
had to push the door hard to make it open, and at
first the knee-deep snow that had blocked it from
outside seemed to him only one more artifact of the
evil nightmare from which he and Kate were trying
to fight free.

The night air was clear, the snowfall stopped at last.
A keen wind was busy drifting whiteness over buried streets, impassable to cars. The old man, standing where the curb should be with his hands in his
topcoat pockets, was gazing over a half-buried auto
toward the other end of the street. There, almost
directly under a bright streetlamp, a pair of figures
waited, looking back at him. Morgan in her torn party
suit, her cloud of red hair blowing free, looked tiny
beside the giant man in evening dress, with the half-
ruined face.

The old man did not turn to look at Joe or Kate
when they came out of the building behind him. But
he said to them calmly: "They will not fly now, or
change their form. My hand is on them." He raised
his voice. "Morgan, you see that my allies have not
deserted me. Where are yours?"

Whether in answer to him or not, the woman
across the street tilted back her beautiful face to the
invisible sky above the electric lights. Then from her
throat there burst a long, keen, eerie cry. It echoed away among the dark and lifeless buildings,
above the brilliant snow, and was followed by deep
silence. Joe, listening, could not recall such quiet
in the city at any time of day or night. Far away
somewhere, diesels were laboring, doubtless either
plowing snow or dragging emergency loads through
it. Poach was listening too, turning his raised face
this way and that. Already his fresh wound was
healing. Both of Poach's eyes were open again, and

the blood that covered one side of his forehead was
congealed in the frigid air.

At last Morgan lowered her gaze again to the old
man. She shrugged. "If you can gather them in, from
the four winds, they will doubtless be your allies
now—for as long as you seem to be winning. Much
good may they do you. Cowards, one and all. Gods,
is it long life itself that makes so many of us cowards?"

Corday said: "The one who stands beside you has
not yet lived a century. Yet he was cowardly enough
to attack me in my earth."

"Oh, now we are to have considerations of honor."
Morgan shook her windblown hair. "But then with
you it is always honor, is it not?" She waited a
moment, then added quietly: "We are going to walk
away now, Vlad. You have won."

The old man made no reply. Morgan looked at him
a few seconds longer, then turned away and began
to walk. Poach, after a last wary glance, followed.
Trudging through the deep snow to the nearest street
corner, Morgan looked weary as some laboring woman
struggling to get home. She turned there, with difficulty heading east into the wind. Poach lurched
along beside her.

The old man took his hands out of his pockets and
with each hand motioned one of his companions
forward. He still had not taken his eyes off his foe.
He walked ahead of Joe and Kate, keeping the distance between himself and his enemies nearly constant. The deep snow made hard walking. Joe
wondered how long he and Kate were going to be
able to keep up. The going was a little easier when
they got to where Morgan and Poach had broken trail.

After leading them east through untrodden drifts
for half a block, Morgan stopped and turned under
another streetlight. "Drive us into a corner," she called
back, "and it will be at your own peril."

Corday had stopped also, and once more waited with hands in topcoat pockets. "Alas," he called back cheerfully, "to our greater peril if we do not."

"Yours, perhaps," Morgan answered. "I speak now to the others. Joe? Kate? He is as cunning as the Evil One himself. Don't you understand that if he is the survivor, he must kill you at the end? You know too much about him now, for him to let you live. Kate, he has already killed your grandmother tonight."

"And you?" Kate called back. "Liar. What will you do with us—refresh yourselves?"

"You do not matter to us, fools. We only meant to frighten you—you will be left in peace forever, but only if you turn around and go home now."

"This is the way I'm going," Joe told her. He took a step forward, his grip tightening on the spear.

Morgan looked at them all again, one after another, then once more turned and walked away. Poach kept at her side, walking unsteadily. At once the old man followed them, and Joe and Kate kept pace. Presently, under a blaze of neon from the windows of an otherwise lifeless tavern, Joe noticed occasional red-brown drops spattering the snow.

At the next cross street, Joe could see other people struggling along on foot a block and a half away— perhaps trying to get home, or to get away from home, or to find a doctor or an open liquor store. With sunrise the city, still crippled but aroused, would begin to live again and painfully try to move. Then how would the chase go?

Morgan turned north. Holy Name Cathedral appeared ahead, slowly fell behind as they walked past it. Would there be an early Mass this morning? Involuntarily Joe glanced at Corday's profile, then up at the stone cross. The old man's attention was not distracted from his enemies. He did not even appear to blink.

Suddenly the going was easy. They had come to

a long stretch of sidewalk blown almost clean of snow. Joe and Kate moved up to walk closer at the old man's sides.

Joe said: "It goes back a long way, doesn't it? Between you and her."

"It does, Joe. But all things must end."

"I heard Poach saying something tonight . . . that he killed Granny Clare."

"He did." The old man paced on for several yards before he added: "Judy was at the house also. But she is going to be all right—if we win. Now we must concentrate on the hunt. Our enemies are still deadly dangerous. But dawn is not far off, and it will weaken them."

"And you too," said Kate.

"But not my brave allies." Corday turned a sudden grin to left and right, including both of them. Joe wished to himself that the old man's face hadn't looked something like a skull when he did that. Still it had more life in it by far than many faces that were fat with flesh.

Corday went on: "If I should be destroyed in sunlight, and they survive, still they will be weakened. And forced to remain in human form until night falls again. So if I fall, you must kill both of them today at any cost. But I have survived many such wintry northern mornings, and afternoons as well—ah, they turn east again."

The distant diesels, or another squadron of them, could be heard again, a trifle louder now. Among tall buildings Joe could not be sure from which direction the sound came. Nearer at hand another noise was growing rapidly; a helicopter's rotors beat the invisible sky. Only a set of red and green running lights were visible as the machine darted past almost directly overhead.

The streets through which Morgan led them were still empty of other people; superb lighting shone on untracked snow. Another block east, thought Joe, and they'd be on Michigan Boulevard. Joe wondered if Morgan had a goal in mind or was simply fleeing. "They're sticking close together," he commented.

"As long as they do," said the old man, "I have no wish to encounter them without your stout support. Though they are perhaps gaining a little on us now, I think they will run out of gas, as I believe the saying goes, before we do."

Joe tried to speed it up a little. Police officer needs assistance. It would be a busy day in Communications. All furloughs canceled. Sorry, captain, I just couldn't make it in, there were these vampires I had to hunt . . .

Kate appeared to be doing fine. She walked with the long wood knife swinging in her hand.

"Corday, I said some things about you before. I'm sorry. What do your friends call you, if it's any of my business?"

The old man shot him a glance. "Your apology is thankfully accepted. I am comfortable with the name you know me by."

"Good enough." Morgan had certainly called the old man something else, something that Joe could not now recall. Well, he certainly wasn't going to push the question. If any reason other than gratitude were needed, he could well believe that there had been a grain of truth in Morgan's warning.

They were now gaining slightly on the enemy.

"You are doing excellently," the old man complimented Joe. He turned to Kate. "And you."

"I feel fine," Kate answered. "I wonder a little myself at how good I feel."

"This fortunate reserve of strength is doubtless a residual benefit of your recent life as a, shall we say, non-breathing human. When the life of your attacker who walks ahead of us is ended, weakness may come upon you temporarily. But then it should be about time for all of us to rest, hey?"

"Is it certain that I'm going to—to stay—this way?"

"It has been my experience that miracles do not reverse themselves. You will remain a breather. As long as that is what you truly want."

The pursuit emerged abruptly from between buildings onto Michigan Boulevard, as wide as some city blocks were long. Joe had never counted its traffic lanes, but all of them were completely buried now. Here and there cars, trucks, buses were entombed too. There was as yet no sign of snowplow resurrection. On every lamppost were festoons promoting Christmas commerce. The Boulevard was kept free by law from projecting signs of any kind, and the lines of its varied buildings stretched dreamlike to right and left, framing a cathedral aisle of clear snow.

There came a raucous buzz from somewhere, on ground level, nearby, getting closer fast.

Joe was first to identify the sound, and the first to react. Spear ready, he floundered out into the deep snow near the middle of the boulevard, prepared to defend his position there. He called out for help, and Kate and the old man were right behind him.

The snowmobile snarled round a corner behind Joe, and turned speedily in his general direction. Facing Poach and Morgan with his spear leveled, he heard it pass a few yards behind him, going north. Morgan snarled at Joe, but her chance of intercepting and seizing a conveyance had been blocked. There were two people on the vehicle, and one called out something cheery on seeing folk in evening dress out for an early morning romp. The words were lost in the engine noise, and shortly the engine itself was fading in the distance.

After a long pause, Morgan turned silently toward the east side of the street, and once there headed north. Poach kept with her, stumbling more noticeably now. Joe wondered if he might be faking greater injury than he felt.

Above the city's lights the sky was changing subtly and at intersections Joe could see the sky to the east, above the lake; there it was no longer dark so much as blank. He looked at his wrist watch, but what he saw conveyed no meaning to his worn mind.

Stoplights blinked out an elaborate ritual, timing nothing.

"Do you think they'll go into a building?" Kate suddenly wondered aloud.

The old man shrugged. "We could follow. They do not really want to seek a general involvement of the breathing world, any more than I do. That would be ultimately bad for all of us. Our branch of the human race has the habit and tradition of settling its own affairs."

"I just thought," said Kate, "If they keep going east much farther—"

"Yes?"

"They'll wind up out on the ice. On the lake. That's considered very dangerous. When people do that the police sometimes bring out a helicopter and pick them up, right Joe?"

"Ah."

"Fortunately," said Joe, puffing steam, "all the copters in the city are going to be very busy today doing other jobs."

And still Morgan led them north. Going north would also, in time, bring them to the curving shore. Ahead, the gray canyon of buildings in which they moved came to an abrupt end. There, at Oak Street, the Boulevard melded with the Outer Drive and with a delta of lesser arteries. There the park began, and the beach. And, inland, the rank of tall apartment buildings in one of which Craig Walworth lived. "It's just hit me," Joe announced. "They're trying to get to Walworth's place."

Corday nodded. "That seems quite probable."

"You won't be able to get in there to get at them. If I'm beginning to understand how these things work?"

"Your new understanding is in general correct, I think." The thin lips smiled faintly. "But I was asked into that apartment a few hours ago."

"Oh."

And now they were at Oak Street. The white-shrouded curve of the Drive, for once as silent as a country lane, stretched away to the north under the streetlamps and the altering sky, strewn with abandoned vehicles. The wind off the lake, now dying, had ridged the Drive with snowdrifts. But unlike the Boulevard it was already scrawled with rutted tracks where something had managed to crawl through. The sound of diesels was again a little louder now, and Joe thought he could see a yellow snow-mover laboring far to the north.

Morgan and Poach still headed north, now crossing blank white that had been parkway. East of them lay snow-covered beach, and then a fantasy of ice. Beyond that, more than a hundred yards away, the almost invincibly open water of the lake was leadenly visible under the changing eastern sky.

When she had gone another block north, Morgan came to an abrupt stop. She stood there looked ahead and inland, to where apartment buildings rose above barren trees. Joe realized that Walworth's building had just come into full view. One window of it, about twenty stories up, was leaking interior light of a different tone than the light from other windows near it. In a moment he realized that the glass of that window must be gone—those windows were not made for ordinary opening. Looking at the ground below it now, Joe could make out human figures, beaming flashlights at one another and on an object lying in the snow. Some of the tiny figures were wearing caps and jackets of police blue. A black face showed between an orange ski cap and a brown civilian coat. Joe had seen that cap before; at this distance Charley Snider's features were unrecognizable, but fortunately distance worked both ways. An olive-drab halftrack with a red cross on its side, something borrowed from the armory, stood by with its headlights helping to illuminate the scene.

Morgan and Poach were standing still in conference. Now the giant raised an arm to point eastward at the approaching dawn. The desert of water and ice in that direction was becoming gradually more visible. The pale, still sunless sky above it was generally clear. Now the two turned and walked in that direction, not looking back.

At once the old man moved to follow, almost at a trot. Joe and Kate were gasping with the effort of staying at his heels. Joe foundered across a snow fence, only the top two inches of its ineffectual slats showing above curved powder.

Beyond the snow fence, forty yards of unbroken white ended in a jumble of foot-thick ice slabs, broken up and cast ashore by yesterday's or last night's powerful east winds. As Joe drew near the wilderness of ice its jagged horizon reached higher than his head. Above the ice beautiful streaks of pink were being born in the southeast sky.

First Morgan and then Poach vanished, this time in something like a normal human way, climbing into the cold maze of broken ice. Corday paused for an instant in his pursuit to ask: "Will it be possible for them to find a boat of any kind?"

"Not here. Not in the winter." Legs laboring, lungs pumping on frozen air, Joe labored after Corday's effortless, snow-plowing sprint, holding his spear at the ready, like a slow pole-vaulter, thanking God he had at least found gloves in his jacket pockets.

Following Corday's gestures, his allies spread out

to his left and right, then followed his advance into the ice field. Joe had the worst of it, handicapped with the spear when two hands as well as two feet seemed hardly enough for clambering among the jumbled, slippery slabs.

Trying to keep Corday's head at least intermittently in sight, Joe advanced as best he could. The sky was light enough now to let him see what he was doing, but still the going was very awkward and treacherous. Moving silently was impossible, at least for Joe.

In a minute or so the whole city behind him was out of sight. Here it was as silent as Alaska, except for the sounds of his own progress. And, somewhere that could not be very far away, a gentle lapping of water against ice or rock or sand.

Joe lost Corday for a little while. Then, dragging himself up into a saddle between two cakes, he was relieved to see the old man's head and shoulders against a third, still and silent as the ice he rested on. He's probably letting me draw the first attack, Joe suddenly realized. The clumsy, noisy one . . . well, if that's the way we have to do it, it still has to be done. He gripped his spear and went ahead.

In a moment he had slipped on impossible footing, skinning a knee painfully inside his trousers and wrenching an ankle, fortunately not hard enough to cut down on his mobility any further. Joe cursed silently and gripped his spear and went ahead. When he got close to the place where he had last seen Corday, the chuckle of water was much closer too. It sounded like it might be eating at the ice right beneath his feet. If a man were to fall into one of these deep, dark blue holes . . .

Here was where Corday had been. But the old man was gone now. He and Kate must be nearby, following, listening even as the enemy were to Joe's clumsy progress. On the other hand he could imagine the whole chase gradually progressing away from him, and he, the dull-sensed one, falling and freeze-drowning here and never knowing its result. Someone would find him in the spring . . .

Ahead, around the corner of another tilted green-gray slab, an object of a different nature came into view. It took Joe a moment to recognize the tilt-topped mass of a concrete breakwater, draped as it was with smooth curves of ice. A few hours ago, great roaring breakers must have beaten on it. Deep water was nearby, then, underneath the ice-jam.

There was a small sound like a sigh, and from the top of an almost level lintel of ice at Joe's right the enormous form of Poach came leaping down at him from ambush. Joe got the spear around barely in time. The needle point of it made wooden contact, hooking Poach's dinner jacket and perhaps his ribs beneath. At the same moment, a woman screamed nearby and Corday shouted something.

The butt of the spear was jammed down against ice by Poach's weight on top. It rotated then, deflecting him in his leap to land with what ought to have been deadly impact, on concrete sheathed in ice. A sound like a drumbeat was driven from his open mouth. The barbs of the spearpoint tore free. Poach slid from the breakwater into black open water just beneath.

For a moment he was gone. Then he surfaced at Joe's feet, mouth roaring water and air mixed, his eyes fixed on Joe. His huge hands scrabbled for a grip on ice or spear or enemy.

Groaning as if with his own death, Joe forced the barbed spear home once more. This time it went straight into the giant's throat. But Poach's long arm shot forward. His hand locked on Joe's arm farthest forward on the spear shaft. They were going to go down together. Joe's feet were slipping on the ice.

Someone seized him from behind, just as he was being dragged to watery death. A thin arm round his waist supported him. He could not turn his head. A wave washed at Poach, and suddenly most of the exposed flesh of Poach's hands and face was gone. The next wave seemed to knock apart the bones of skull and fingers—Joe could hear them hissing, see them dissolving, as if the water were purest acid.

It was over. Even the clothing had gone down. The spear was bobbing in the water. Joe found his footing and shakily stood up straight. Turning, he met Kate's eyes. He started to ask: "Where's—"

Kate uttered a horrible little cry and struck at something on his arm. Poach's skeletal right hand dropped off, bones shattering when it hit the ice. The first direct rays of sun were on the still-moving bones now. Joe watched them crumble into dust, and then to nothingness.

"Where's Corday, Kate?"

"This way. He sent me to help you."

Scrambling after Kate around a monolith of ice, he came upon the old man and Morgan in its shadow. The two of them looked almost like lovers seeking privacy. But Corday had the long wooden knife in one hand now, and his other hand held both of Morgan's wrists tightly behind her.

She was looking into the distant sky. Her eyes and face might have been carved from the slab she leaned against. Corday turned to the two breathing people. "It is over. You may leave us now." When they did not go he added: "What would you have me do? Do you want to sentence her to one of your prisons for her crimes? Leave us."

But when they had turned away he called: "Wait. Tell—tell those who know me, that I shall be all right. That I am going home."

Joe took Kate's arm. Suddenly she was leaning

against him weakly. It would be a struggle to get back to where they could call for help, but they would make it.

Behind them a woman screamed loudly, once. That name, again.

TWENTY-TWO

After the first preliminary session with Charley Snider and Franzen of the Glenlake force, Joe's head was spinning with exhaustion. But he still held to his determination not to collapse, and not to let Kate out of his sight, until she was ready to collapse too. As for Kate, she swore that she was holding out until she'd seen her little sister.

Snider obligingly drove them from Glenlake to the hospital, over freshly plowed thoroughfares. On the way he told them about Walworth's plunge through a broken window. Nobody knew yet whether it was suicide or not. But this time, the Homicide man made it plain, the authorities mean to get to the bottom of the whole business, once and for all—

Judy had been found at home, unconscious amid the ruins of the pottery collection. A pillow had been tucked neatly beneath her head and there were two blankets wrapped around her. *Someone* had called police about her and fortunately they had been able to get a four-wheel-drive vehicle to get her to the hospital. On regaining her senses, in a room near her brother's, Judy had been unable to give any coherent account of how she had come to be where she was found. Examination disclosed that she had suffered a moderately serious loss of blood. Internal bleeding of some kind was diagnosed, because no wounds were visible that might account for the loss. When the news came that her older sister was after all alive, Judy accepted the happy shock with no apparent surprise at all.

"Tell me once more now," Charley Snider asked, going up on the short hospital elevator ride with Joe and Kate. "Try to think. *Where* did you two first run into each other last night?"

"I told you, I've been drugged." Kate looked happily giddy. There was a Band-aid on her arm where blood samples had already been taken for the police. "Somewhere on the Near North, I think it was."

"I can't remember," Joe chimed in. "I can't think very straight just now." He felt horrible, out on his feet, and he knew he must look the same, quite bad enough to lend some credence to his story, or lack thereof.

Snider gave him a look that said: We're going to have a long talk soon. Right now Joe did not care in the least.

"We got your grandmother dead," said Charley, thinking aloud while he looked at Kate. "But so far all the other Southerlands are still alive, though some are damaged. We got Gruner dead. And now we got Walworth dead, right out of the building where Gruner was the doorman. This Corday is still missing. This Winter that you and Johnny describe is nowhere."

"Try finding Leroy Poach," said Joe, and giggled. The giggle had a strange sound.

"I think you better check in here yourself," Charley told him.

"No." Kate pressed his hand. "He's going to come home with me and sack out there."

"Thanks," said Joe. "I will."

The elevator stopped at Judy's floor and they got out. Two rooms down, the hall had police bodyguards.

"Daddy still glowers at you," Kate said. "He'll glower worse when I bring you back home. And then I'll punch him in the nose." Now first she and then Joe were laughing uncontrollably. Snider shook his head and walked off somewhere. A nurse came to stand looking at them doubtfully. When they had done their best to try to look like decent visitors, the nurse said: "You can go in now, if you're quiet. She's been asking and asking for you."

Snider reappeared from somewhere to follow them in silently. There was only one bed in the room, with a pale Judy lying in it. In a chair nearby Johnny sat in his bathrobe. Judy sat up with a jerk as they came in.

"We're all right," Kate got out. Johnny sprang up to give her his handless hug. She looked over his robed shoulder at Joe, appealing for some way to communicate the rest.

Joe tossed Judy a wink. "I have the feeling that the good guys are going to be all right now."

The pale girl couldn't help herself. "Dr. Corday too?"

Joe could feel eyes boring into the back of his neck. The ears of Homicide would be tuned in like dish antennas. What did he care? He was going to marry into quite a wad of money soon. "Him especially," Joe said, and winked again. "He can take care of himself. If I was him I'd be going back to Europe as soon as I could."

"The airports will be watched," Judy worried weakly.

"There are night flights, aren't there?" Kate commented. Let Homicide try to make something out of *that*. And Joe could hear Charley Snider's shoeleather creaking quietly out of the room.

"Oh, Kate," said pale Judy from her bed, "are you really all right now?"

"I think so. Listen, Jude. You and I are going to have a lot of things to compare notes on, when we get the chance."

"Oh, yes. Yes, we are."

"And then," said Kate, "I think we'd all benefit from a winter vacation somewhere."

"Great weather to go south," Joe put in.

Judy took thought. "Yes, going somewhere to rest up sounds like fun. Only . . ."

"What?"

"Maybe not south . . . they say the off-season is a great time to visit Europe." Judy's eyes had begun to glow, to dance a little. With one finger she picked at a spot, a tiny pimple maybe, on her throat.

THORN

PROLOGUE

The runaway fled gracefully through the smooth white tunnel, her small bare feet moving with quick darting strides. Her slight, girlish body, completely naked, was splashed by a quickly shifting disco spectrum of fantastic light that followed her from the room she fled. Music, loud rock music, followed too, throbbing with the light. Like the light, it lost its violence only partially and slowly as it increased its distance from its origin.

As if the music had caught up with her in midstride, the girl's graceful run changed abruptly, halfway through the tunnel, into a dance, but a dance that still carried her rapidly forward into the large, white room at the tunnel's end.

It was a long room, like something out of a museum almost, and the windowless white walls were angled and rectangular. The white carpet was immaculate and thick. On the walls hung many paintings, drawings, prints, and all of them were hard to see in the bewildering, reflected disco rainbow that came through the tunnel to provide the only illumination. There were carvings hanging on the walls too, and statues large and small stood everywhere. The girl's dance moved her in and out among them, as if she might be looking for another way out. But the tunnel was the only entrance, and the only exit visible.

The girl's dance was a performance meant for no one but herself. Her face was a lovely mask, utterly unlined, looking very young, and looking too calm to be a dancer's face. Around it, long brown hair swung wild and dark, dirty and uncared for. Her dark eyelids were half closed, the full lips parted levelly over white, slightly uneven teeth. The skin of her body was childishly smooth, and gleamed lightly in the strange changing light, as if she might be sweating despite the coolness of the air. Her feet were tiny and arched, grained here and there with dirt, and she set them precisely and silently down in the thick whiteness of the floor.

The driving music had less and less to do with the dance as it continued. Its movement shifted to a slower rhythm, becoming almost courtly. Then halfway through a pirouette the girl's eyes opened wide. Her balance, perfect through all the movements before this one, abruptly broke, and she went down on one knee on the rich ivory carpet, stunned into awkwardness by something she had seen.

She stared with wide eyes for a long moment into the dimness straight ahead. Then, bare shoulders heaving with a great sighing breath, she slowly turned her head. Hardly did she dare to try to see again what she had seen a moment earlier.

It hung there on the wall, amid the hundred other paintings. Conflicting emotions struggled in the girl's face; and then presently her face became tranquil again, but on a different level. She was gazing outward now, away from self. She stayed crouching there on one knee, almost exactly as she had fallen, becoming almost as motionless as one of the surrounding statues. Now even her breathing appeared to stop.

"There you are." The voice of the approaching man was slurred and gleeful, and it contained hostility. The light coming through the curious white tunnel was modulated by his approaching shadow. He moved into the girl's range of vision now, but she ignored him completely. He was as naked as she was, and looked to be a few years older. Perhaps he was twenty-two or twenty-three. Reddish hair with a tendency to curl fell damply to his muscular and freckled shoulders. He was only a few inches taller than the girl. And he was breathing heavily, as if he too might just have finished a dance or some other physical exertion.

The girl was still down on one knee. She had regained grace in her pose, but otherwise had not moved since turning her head to look back over one shoulder. She had not yet taken her eyes from the sight that had made her fall.

The young man followed her gaze for a moment. Nothing but a row of old paintings, mostly in wood frames, hanging on the white wall and, like everything else in the room, hard to see in the odd pulsing light. He was not really interested; he was used to being around people who stared at nothing. He walked toward the girl until he was standing close beside her, but still she gave no sign of being aware of him at all. Not even when he buried the fingers of one strong hand in her wild hair and tugged.

"Hey," he said, trying to turn her face toward his body. As he spoke the music in the other room cut off abruptly. Still the mad light continued to pulsate through the tunnel.

Abruptly the girl thrust out one slender arm in a graceful shove. The young man, who had no dancer's balance, went staggering back. He reeled helplessly into a towering marble statue, which rocked on its base and settled back. Mumbling something, the man tried to recover, clawed at a wall, then sat down on the white carpet with a soft thud.

Again the multicolored light wavered with approaching shadows. Another naked man was coming from the far room. The legs that bore him round the white curve of tunnel were moving trunks of bone and muscle, well designed for his great weight. The torso above the legs had once been heroic, but now sagged grossly with advancing age. Still the clean-shaven face, its chin held high, was alert, controlled, imperious. Only a fringe of hair, all white, remained around the massive head; and gray hair grew matted thickly on the chest and belly and on the heavy, still-powerful arms.

This man advanced a little way into the room and halted, looking with displeasure at the scene. "There are some very valuable things in here," he announced in a bass voice, "and both of you are evidently crazy, or completely freaked out, or whatever the word for it is this year. Therefore I am not going to let you make this your playground. Got that?"

The last words trailed off just a little. The aging man had at last taken some notice of the extreme rigidity of the girl's gaze and the strangeness of her frozen posture. The arm she had used to shove the youth away was still extended. Her head was still turned, eyes looking back over her left shoulder.

The only sound in the room, besides the violent music, was the labored breathing of the young man. He still sat on the floor, and now he was glowering angrily at the girl.

The old man said, in his bass voice: "If that on the wall really strikes your fancy, little girl, then you have good taste. Better than some people who have entered this room fully clothed and supposedly in their right minds. Well, I have good taste too, and you doubtless don't know what you're staring at anyway, and I appreciate your round little ass. In fact, out of all the orifices available tonight, I may just choose to end my evening there. But I want to do it back in the other room. So get up."

Now through the tunnel behind the old man three more naked figures were approaching, pushing before them an extensive interplay of shadows. Slightly in the lead there walked a leanly muscular man of about thirty-five. His suntanned body was marked with the pale outline of absent swimming briefs. Just after the man came a boy who appeared to be in his mid-teens, small and slightly built, pale-haired, blinking lost eyes at the world. The boy supported himself every few steps by leaning a frail arm against the white curve of the tunnel wall. When he emerged from the tunnel into the room and the wall flattened, he stopped, leaning his back against it for support. A step behind the boy, another dark-haired girl strolled in casually. In size, and build, and coloring, she fairly closely resembled the girl who had been dancing. The brown eyes of this newly-arrived girl were keen with interest—but they were focused on the empty air an arm's length before her face. She paid no attention to anyone else. Her full lips mumbled soundlessly, then smiled.

The red-haired man who sat on the floor ignored them all, all except the girl who had danced. Now in his throat a low murmuring of rage and humiliation had begun, and grew in loudness. On the second try he struggled back to his feet. His right hand went out to a small white cube, and from its flat surface he grabbed up a small but heavy artifact of silvery metal. Raising this, he lunged straight for the crouching dancer as his right arm swung the lethally compact weight straight for her skull.

The old man's was the only voice to cry a warning, and his yell did no one any good. It sounded simultaneously with a sharp, dying scream.

The thin young boy still leaned back tiredly against the flat white wall. His blinking eyes, completely lost, were looking somewhere on the far side of the dim room. The dark-haired girl who had come with him through the tunnel stood quietly beside him now. She was thoughtfully probing with one finger inside her own mouth, as if intent on making sure her teeth were all still there. She took no account of what had happened to the white carpet just a few feet away.

The athletic man, who was alert and could move very fast, was already a step in front of the huge old one. But there he halted his swift advance, warily astonished; his move had obviously come too late, and he had no wish to step into the fresh blood.

The huge, gray old man was astonished too. Then, because he was no stranger to sudden violence and it did not particularly upset him, and because he possessed a quickly penetrating mind, he was immediately struck by circumstances even more amazing than the mere fact of abrupt murder. Inspiration of a magnitude extremely rare grew swiftly behind his clear blue eyes. Slowly he put out a massive hand, to take his wiry companion by the shoulder.

"Gliddon," the old man said. He used the careful tone of one who wishes to wake a sleeper gently, not to startle.

"What?" The attention of the wiry man was still warily absorbed in the scene before him. Hell of a mess to be cleaned up, at best, he was thinking. The killer was now standing, swaying, as if dazed. The silver artifact lay on the floor, near something else.

"Gliddon. These two kids behind me. I want you to get them out of here. They're both stoned blind, and I don't think this has made any impression on them at all. I doubt that they'll remember seeing a thing—but anyway we'll cross that bridge when we come to it. Right now get 'em out of here and put 'em down to sleep somewhere. I want to deal with this." He nodded at the red spectacle before them.

"But."

"Oh, you can take charge of the cleanup later. But right now just get those two put away." The old man, an expression in his eyes befitting the discoverer of a new continent, was moving forward slowly, his gaze shifting from the dazed, spattered killer to the demolished victim, and back again. "I want to handle this, alone. I have my reasons."

ONE

In my opinion I owe the breathing legions of humanity no explanations of any of my affairs, no apologies for any chapter of my life. And I consider this judgement to apply with particular force to my role in the events surrounding the recent and much-publicized disappearance of one of the world's noblest works of art. Let those breathing folk who in financial anguish claim rights to the painting recover it if they are able, or get along without it if they are not. Nor do I consider that it is up to me to interpret for them those strange and violent events, mystifying to so many, which like red parentheses enclose the painting's vanishment. By the standard of objective justice it is rather I who deserve an accounting from the breathing world, I who am entitled to some reparations ...

Bah. At my age I should know better. And in fact I do. I press no formal claim.

Only this much do I insist upon: you will understand that almost my sole purpose in setting down this history is to please myself. *Almost*, be it noted. Mina, my true great love, my delight now for almost a century, accept these pages from me as my humble

228

effort to explain some things you must have wondered
at; and be assured, my dear, that none of the breathing women mentioned here could ever begin to mean
as much to me as one look from your eyes, one touch
from your sweet hand. In addition, I would like to
think there are a few other readers who will be able
to appreciate the story, as a story, as I tell it on my
own terms, in my own way. And part of my pleasure
shall be to use my informed imagination to create for
those discerning readers some scenes at which I was
not present and could play no role. I warn you—if
it is not already too late—that in these scenes it
amuses me sometimes to be accurate and deceptive
at the same time. You may accept those portions of
the story or not, just as you choose. Indeed—do I
need to say it?—you may think what you like about
the whole business.

It is my decision to begin upon a certain warm
spring night, not long ago. It was a night through
which the smell of orange blossoms spread, to bless
the Arizona air. More than five hundred years had
passed between that night, and the last time I had
seen my treasure. Time had marked my long-sought
masterpiece, and I too was changed . . . very much
changed. And yet, merely seeing it again awoke in
me such things . . . one look and I was back in the
City of Flowers, where winters are too cold to tolerate orange trees and palms but where nevertheless
the pungent summer atmosphere bore and still bears
the blended fragrance of a thousand blooms . . .

*This is she, Signore Ladislao. An excellent likeness,
if that is what you wish. From this you may know
her. Pray Jesus and San Lorenzo that you may bring
her safely out . . .*

An excellent likeness; oh yes indeed. When at last
I stood before that panel of polychromed wood again
in Arizona, I could feel its craquelure of centuries
like a net of painful scars on my own skin. I thought

for a moment that my eyes were going to fill with
tears. And who will believe that of me, now, no matter
how solemnly I write it down?

But this history is so far getting off to a very
rambling start.

Consider Phoenix, Arizona. Consider wealthy suburban Scottsdale, to be precise, as it was upon that
recent warm spring night. Palm trees of all sizes and
several varieties mingled everywhere with the ubiq-
uitous orange. At dusk the streets were busy, in part
because of the natives' habit, bred into them by their
summer temperatures, of putting off, as much as
possible, business and pleasure both till after sun-
down. One tourist who was present on the evening
we are talking about found himself in particularly
hearty agreement with this practice. He was registered at his downtown Phoenix hotel as Mr. Jonathan
Thorn, permanent address listed as Oak Tree, Illinois.

At sunset a taxi took Mr. Thorn from Phoenix to
Scottsdale. The street where he debarked from his
taxi was wide, not too busy, and lined on both sides
with expensive shops. The shops' signs were all small,
discreet. Rows of expensive vehicles were parked
diagonally in front of the low buildings. The plank
sidewalks, partially blocked from the street by imitation hitching posts made of real, weathered wood,
were roofed with more planks against the summer
sun. Beyond these wooden cloisters, the low-built
expensive shops were modern, though constructed in
part of real adobe brick.

The building that Mr. Thorn approached was typi-
cal, being grilled on all its doors and windows with
thick bars of black wrought iron. The front door was
intermittently open to the plank sidewalk, admitting
a trickle of people in elegant but open-throated warm
weather attire. As he passed the hitching post in front,
Mr. Thorn took note of an incongruous old Ford
sedan, inscrutably battered and unrepaired, waiting

there between a Mercedes and a new luxury model Jeep. He took note, I say, but only barely; at that moment he had other things to think about.

Just inside the door, a security guard in business suit and tie took note of Mr. Thorn, classified him as acceptable, and offered him a light smile and a nod. Thorn found himself in a moderately large, efficiently cooled room where a dozen or so folk, mostly middle-aged and prosperous, to judge by appearances, milled slowly about or sat in folding chairs. Under bright lights at the front of the room, high wooden tables already held some of the lesser items from the Delaunay Seabright collection on display. The overall decor was determinedly Southwestern, with the massive, rough-hewn ceiling beams exposed and Navajo rugs hung on the white, rough-plastered walls. Set up to face the front of the room were many more folding chairs than seemed likely to be necessary. In theory this pre-auction viewing was open to the public, but it appeared that few of the public were going to intrude upon what was in fact a pasttime of the rich. A month earlier, and the notoriety attendant upon the killings of Delaunay Seabright and his stepdaughter would probably still have drawn something of a crowd. But the auction had been well timed. By that spring night, the spectacular murder-kidnapping was already fading from the popular memory.

There were only two people present, a couple, who looked as if they might be thrill-seekers. Quite proletarian in appearance, they were being watched with vague, discreet apprehension by the auctioneers, smooth men in business suits who looked as if they might just have flown in from New York. Mr. Thorn, catching a little of that watchfulness, observed the couple too.

At one end of the rear rank of folding chairs sat Mary Rogers. (Thorn was not to learn her name until a little later.) Mary's long hair was sand-colored, somewhat curly, and usually disheveled. Her age was twenty-one, her face freckled and attractive, her disposition choleric. Her body was all shapely strength, superbly suitable for work and childbearing, and would have made an ideal model for some artist's healthy peasant—though Mary would not have made a very good peasant, or peasant's wife, or, for that matter, a very good artist's model either. She planned to use her strength in different ways, in a dedicated lifelong selfless service of humanity. She always visualized humanity as young, I am quite sure, and as eternally oppressed. Well, there are billions of youth in the world, after all, more or less oppressed. Probably cases exist even in Scottsdale. But in that auction room, alas, were none at all; Mary had to have some other reason to be there.

The auctioneers, as I have said, were a bit uneasy about this young, comparatively poorly dressed couple. What bothered them was not the fact that Mary wore blue jeans—so did a couple of other women in that small crowd. But Mary's jeans were probably of the wrong brand, and their fadedness suggested not some manufacturer's process, but utilitarian wear. Successful experts in the world of fine art can be amazingly sensitive to subtle differences in color and texture, not only in the merchandise but in the customers.

But mainly I think it was that the faces of Mary and her escort stood out in that little gathering. Their countenances were not filled with thinly veiled greed for the treasures (so far only quite minor ones) displayed, nor with calculation as to how to bid on them. Oh, it was evident enough from Mary's face that she had *some* keen purpose in that room—but what could it be? That she might try to buy anything seemed highly unlikely, considering the prices that were certain to be asked and bid. If she and her companion were really wealthy eccentrics who simply enjoyed dressing in the style of the non-wealthy, then who belonged to that old Ford out front? Anyone who drove *that* car out of eccentricity would probably be staying at home anyway, in rooms filled with piled garbage and a thousand cats.

Whatever apprehensions the auctioneers may have developed regarding Mary—that she might be contemplating some mad attempt at robbery, or an even more hopeless effort at social protest—these doubts must have been at least somewhat allayed by the face and attitude of the young man seated at her side. He was a bearded young man, with his arms folded in his not very expensive checked sports shirt. His look was not one of fanaticism, but of uncomfortable loyalty. He was bracing himself, perhaps—but not for bullets, only for boredom or embarrassment.

Also present, to define the opposite end of the auctioneers' spectrum of respect, was Ellison Seabright. When Seabright entered the front door, a few minutes after Mr. Thorn, the salesmen gave him the warmest welcome they could manage without seeming to be effusive about it, without drawing possibly unwelcome attention to his presence: the greeting for a celebrity, but one who temporarily has more attention than he wants.

Seabright was about fifty years old. In general appearance, he reminded Mr. Thorn strongly of Rodrigo Borgia. Mr. Seabright weighed about three hundred pounds, Thorn judged, and if the tales of the family wealth were anywhere near accurate he might have balanced himself in gold and had enough left over to purchase any painting or sculpture that he might desire. According to the publicity that had begun to appear since his brother's kidnapping and strange death, it was a family trait to desire a good many.

Ellison Seabright, from where he stood in quiet conversation with the auctioneers, once or twice shot a hurried, grim glance in the direction of Mary

Rogers—as if he knew her, which was interesting. Mr. Thorn, from his chair in the front row, could not tell how the young woman in the rear reacted to these glances, if at all.

The other potential bidders in the room all glowed in their not very distinctive auras of material wealth. The auctioneers, when they conferred privately (as they thought) among themselves in the next room, had voiced hopes that a local record was going to be set. They were daring to compare themselves tonight with Christie's, with Sotheby Parke Bernet. This time, even leaving aside such relatively minor treasures as Mimbres bowls and Chinese jade, this time they had a probably genuine Verrocchio to put on the block.

Mr. Thorn was doubtless among those they were counting on to run the bidding up when it officially began tomorrow night. Although they had never seen or heard of him before, it was surely apparent to such artistically expert eyes that Thorn's dark suit had been tailored at one of the best London shops, and that his shoes were a good match for the suit. He wore, on the third finger of his right hand, a worn-thin ring of ancient gold. His general appearance was at least as elegant as that of Mr. Seabright.

The height of the two men was about the same, somewhat above the average. Thorn's weight was considerably less—though not so very much less as it appeared to be. He looked to be Seabright's junior by ten or fifteen years, but that comparison was deceptive too. Their faces were both striking, in different ways: Seabright's for massive arrogance, Thorn's—in a way not nearly so massive. As for their relative wealth—but Mr. Thorn had not really come to Scottsdale to bid and buy.

"No, I'm sure it's going to go to Ellison," Mary Rogers was whispering to her dour young companion with the sandy beard. "The old bastard probably has more money than all these others put together.

And he wants it, I know how he wants it. After what he's done already he's not going to let mere money stop him."

There were several rows of chairs between Mary and Mr. Thorn. The room was abuzz with the noise of other conversations. And her whisper was really more discreet—that was the key word of the evening, up to now—than her misfit appearance promised. So Mary's words could be heard only by her friend seated beside her, and by Mr. Thorn, whose ears were wonderfully keen. Also it is a fact that Thorn was constitutionally unable to ignore either of the two women in the room he found genuinely attractive.

The second genuinely attractive woman was dark and slender, somewhere in her mid-thirties, and sheathed in a gown that you might think had been designed expressly to wear while inspecting expensive art. She was physically young for her years, but not as young as she wanted to be or tried to be. Probably to no one's surprise, she was clinging to Ellison Seabright's right arm. Certain subtleties of body language in her pose suggested to Thorn that she was clinging there in order to avoid having to swim elsewhere. At the moment her massive escort was standing at the right end of the front row of chairs, in conversation with the head auctioneer, and with one who must be a fellow collector, a bearded elderly gentleman wearing another New York suit. Seabright was turning his massive head, looking round him in irritation. "Where's Gliddon?" he was inquiring of the world in general, though his voice was hardly more than whisper-loud. A voice not in the least Borgia, but thoroughly American. "Got as far as the front door with me, and then . . ."

A bodyguard even taller than Seabright, and almost as wide, stood nearby teetering on his toes. He was not very obtrusive, handling at least the passive aspects of his job quite well. The dark woman clung to

Seabright's arm, smiled brightly, and seemed to attend closely to his every word, meanwhile wistfully wishing that she were somewhere else. Mr. Thorn could tell. He had hopes of soon discovering her name.

"Then you might as well give up, hadn't you?" the young man at Mary Rogers' side was whispering into her ear. His tone was quietly despairing, that of one who knows full well that argument is folly, but feels compelled to argue anyway. "You think he's going to listen to any kind of an appeal now?"

"No." Mary's monosyllable was quietly ominous.

"Then why the hell did we come here? I thought . . ."

At that point every conversation in the room trailed into silence.

Through a curtained doorway at the front of the room, between the two large tables, two armed and uniformed men came into view, rolling a mobile stand between them. The stand was draped with a white cloth, completely covering the upright rectangle that was its cargo. The rectangle was about the size of the top of a card table, somewhat larger than Mr. Thorn had been expecting. Then he remembered the frame. According to the news stories and the sale catalogue, a frame had been added to the painting, probably sometime during the eighteenth century.

With the stand positioned on the dais between the tables, the two armed men stood still, alert, on either side of it. An auctioneer came to join them, placing his pale hand on the white cloth. He let his showman's hand stay there, motionlessly holding the cloth, while in a low voice he made a brief and scrupulously correct announcement.

"Ladies and gentlemen, as most of you know, Verrocchio has signed this piece. But in the time and place in which he worked, such a signature often signified no more than a master's approval of work done by an apprentice. What we can say with absolute certainty is that this painting is from Verrocchio's workshop, and that it is in his mature style. The minimum bid tomorrow night will be two hundred thousand dollars."

With one firm twitch, the showman's hand removed the cloth.

Mr. Thorn forgot even the live and lovely flesh of the two genuinely attractive breathing women in the room. He rose from his folding chair and like a man in a trance stepped forward, closer to the painting. It of course shows Magdalen, not as she came to Christ, but as she must have looked when rising from His feet with sins forgiven. Yes, of course, painted in the mature style of Verrocchio. But by an imitator—though transfiguration would be a better word than imitation for what the creator of this painting had accomplished. How could they all fail to see the truth?

And of course at the same time the face is that of the model who posed for it, that young runaway girl of more than half a thousand years ago. *An excellent likeness, if that is what you wish . . .*

Incipient tears in the eyes of Mr. Thorn were stopped by harsh cries of alarm. Another sort of liquid, flung from behind, struck him on the shoulder, and scarlet droplets spattered past his ear to mar the cheek and hair of Magdalen.

He turned with a snarl. The girl in unfashionable blue jeans was on her feet, holding in one hand a small plastic bag almost emptied but still drooling red on the expensive carpet. Vindictive triumph ruled her face. Closer at hand, Ellison Seabright had been incarnadined from head to foot, Rodrigo Borgia skinned alive, standing in stunned disbelief. His bodyguard, galvanized too late, came pushing forward in a fury. Men and women in uniform, springing from the walls and woodwork, were all around the triumphant girl, about to seize her. You are under arrest, they cried, and in a moment they would manacle her wrists . . .

TWO

Quite early in the game, long before our long marching column approached Buda, the chains of hand-wrought iron were unlocked and taken from my wrists. At the same time, my ankles were untied, and I was given a better horse to ride. To my thinking all this served as an early confirmation of my own good judgement in deciding to throw myself upon the mercy of King Matthias. Of course with the Turks close at my heels and the remnants of my own outnumbered army fast dissolving, there had been little real choice.

The king, when he accepted my surrender, had been angry with me—mainly as a result of certain false accusations, lying letters planted by my enemies for him to intercept, a whole devious chain of circumstances that I do not mean to go into here. But evidently His Majesty soon realized the truth. I did not have another chance to talk to him during the march to Buda, but his officers must have been given orders to treat me well. When we reached Buda they put me into a cell high up in the fortress, a stone chamber better ventilated and cleaner than many of the free houses of the time.

My food also was good, by the standards of the time and place, and plentiful enough. This was, you understand, more than twelve years before I fell under the treacherous swords of would-be murderers, stopped breathing, and acquired my present idiosyncrasies of diet. And when cold weather arrived I was allowed a fire. Guards took me out each day for exercise in a courtyard. There I sometimes walked under the noses of papal legates—I recognized Nicholas of Modrusa once—ambassadors from here and there, some other important men and curious ladies whom I could not identify. None of these ever spoke to me, but observed silently, from balconies where they usually chose to remain half concealed. Even then, you will understand, my reputation was under construction, by German enemies who employed Goebbelsian thoroughness in their attempted destruction of the truth. Now, for important folk visiting His Majesty at Buda, the in thing to do was evidently to ask to see the monster caged. Well, at the time I enjoyed my walks despite observers, and perhaps I should now think more kindly of them. Some were doubtless sympathetic to my cause, and they may have expressed their feelings to Matthias. Still, I spent a year in that first cell.

From time to time I was given brief audience by the king, who limited himself for the most part to looking at me keenly and inquiring how I was. Matthias was then only twenty years of age, but had already spent four years on the throne of Hungary. He had come to power by what amounted to popular acclamation; and time had already begun to vindicate the confidence thus shown him by his people.

At the end of a year I was suddenly moved about fifty kilometers up the Danube to Visegrad Palace, where Matthias was currently spending a good deal of his time. A good deal of money, also, which he extracted mercilessly from the wealthy landowners of his realm, and not all of it was going to feed and equip his formidable army. Scholars and artists from across Europe were beginning to assemble there at his invitation. Already they had started to put together the magnificent library that would be known as the Corvina, and only a few years later the palace would house the first printing press in all that region of Europe . . . but I am beginning to stray from my story.

At the Palace of Visegrad I was again incarcerated. Just as the history books of the twentieth century will tell you—they do now and then get something right, at least—I was put into a cell in what was called the Tower of Solomon. My cell, or perhaps I should even call it a room, was even more comfortable than before, and the conditions of my confinement still more lenient. The thought of attempting to escape from Matthias had never struck me as a very good idea, and now even the faintest tendencies in that direction quite vanished from my mind. All signs tended to reassure me that my instinct to trust the king had been correct. Escape, even if it succeeded, could hardly get me anywhere, for I had literally nowhere to go. But patience would reveal what plans that wise, just prince was formulating, in which he meant me to play a role.

I felt increasingly certain that the king's plans, whatever they might be, must offer me something better than mere confinement, however mild its terms. I had never been more than technically Matthias's foe; his anger at me was due more to the conniving of my enemies than to anything that I had really done. And, if I may say so myself, I was too good to be wasted. Sooner or later the king would determine the right place in which to use me, and when that happened I could not fail to be restored to a position of power and official honor.

As you will see, my thinking in all this was basically correct. Even if never, in my highest flights of fancy, did I guess correctly just what the king would ultimately decide my right place was to be . . .

What you will find set down in today's history books is that the Tower of Solomon remained my prison for the next eleven years. The historical experts, who in other respects often behave as if they are perfectly sober, relate that during that time I was often granted the special boon of having small animals brought living to my cell, that I might entertain myself by torturing them and impaling them on miniature stakes. This quaint behavior must have so impressed the humanist Matthias that it was during this very period that he decided to arrange my marriage to his sister. At the same time, to punish her for consorting with such a beast as Drakulya, he had her name obliterated from all the family records. (And it is true, that historians can now find out hardly anything about her, save the mere fact of her existence, and our marriage.) When eleven years of this idyll had passed, Matthias decided for unknown reasons that it was time for a change, abruptly brought me out of my cell—whether my bride had meanwhile been locked up with me is left to the imagination of the reader—and in due course restored me to my former eminence as Prince of Wallachia.

Now, I ask you. Does it require prolonged reflection, penetrating intelligence of the first order, to infer that the above scenario lacks something, that it might perhaps profit by correction?

Truth is hard to attain. But let me at least try to restore to the record a little sanity. After the move to Visegrad, the king saw me more frequently. At each audience he probed me deeply with searching young eyes, eyes rapidly growing wise beyond their years with the experience of statecraft. At each meeting now he asked me many questions. What did I think about this particular military problem? Supposing I were the king's chief adviser, what course would I recommend in that political difficulty? What was George of Podebrady up to, and how about the Germans? Should women be encouraged to read and write? He interrogated me in areas philosophical and moral, he sought to know my mind on matters of theology and art. Always I strove to answer truthfully, weak though my knowledge was in many fields. I wanted to appear to His Majesty as neither more nor less than what I truly was: loyal and capable, yet prone, as all men are, to human imperfection.

The key conversation between us took place one sunny day in the early spring of 1464, when I had been about six months at Visegrad. My guards, whose gradually improving courtesy had fed my hopes, on that day positively bowed as they came to escort me from my now well-furnished cell. I was led into a part of the palace that I had not previously visited, through rooms where some of Matthias's growing legion of painters and bookworms were at work. The king himself was waiting for me in a large chamber, magnificently furnished. Its broad shelves contained more books, all hand-copied of course, than I had ever seen before in my entire non-bookish life.

At this meeting the king for the first time dismissed his soldiers completely. We were for all intents and purposes alone, there remaining in our sight only a couple of gray-bearded researchers at the end of a long gallery, doddering the remainder of their lives away over manuscripts.

The young king's smile lay thinly across his prominent jaw. "Drakulya, we have heard it said that you are a completely fearless man. Nor have we ever seen evidence of dread in you, not even on that first day when you stood before us in chains."

To my surprise, His Majesty had spoken not in Hungarian or Rumanian, our usual vehicles of

discourse, but in Italian. His slow, mechanical pro-
nunciation gave me the impression that he might have
learned the little speech by rote.

Puzzled, I bowed to him, and made shift to answer
in the same tongue. "My life's ration of fear was used
up, Majesty, before I had a beard to shave."

Smiling, evidently pleased by my reply, the king
relaxed the conversation into Hungarian. "The Turkish
prison, yes. Well, it is the Turks who fear you now,
Kaziklu Bey. I remember well the bags you used to
send me, Lord Impaler, stinking to high heaven by
the time I got them, filled with Turkish noses,
ears . . . but never mind that now." He paused. "There
are certain Christians who dread you also."

"A few may have good reason, Majesty. Most
certainly do not."

"And, by the way, we have sometimes wondered
why it is that you have never presumed during these
talks to remind us of our father's friendship for you.
It might be expected that a man in the position of
a prisoner could hardly fail to do that."

I bowed again. "It had never occurred to me that
such a friendship could possibly have been forgotten by Your Majesty."

"Ha. And some say you are no diplomat. Well."
And Matthias stared at me, thoughtfully, as only kings
in the age of kings could stare, his eyes a regal gray
above his still almost beardless cheeks. "Of diplomats
we have enough at present. Of army officers too, it
seems. Although rumor has it that the Sultan himself intends to lead his armies this year, in Bosnia,
as I mean to lead my own against him . . . you see,
I trust you with a military secret. Though I suppose
it can hardly be a secret any longer. Oh, you are an
excellent field commander, Drakulya. But if I gave
you a command old jealousies would come to life
again, old enmities would be rekindled. I have a lot
of Germans in the Black Army, you know. In adding

one fine leader, yourself, I would be bound to lose others, in one way or another . . . no, our army is not for you. Not right now. Yet we are loath to see you wasted in a cell."

I spoke impulsively. "Sire, I hear from my guards that the Holy Father is still preaching a Crusade, and still means to lead it in person. That the Emperor and Philip the Good have both pledged their support. If Your Majesty were to release me, secretly perhaps—"

"You would follow the Pope?" Matthias immediately seemed interested, and my hopes leaped up.

"I am a Christian, if no Catholic. The Pope has my respect. I will follow him if he will have me. Any attack upon the Turk should work at least indirectly to Your Majesty's benefit."

But I had misinterpreted the king's interest, which at the moment was not centered on the Turks. "Is it then not beyond the bounds of possibility, Drakulya, that for sufficient reason you might abjure your Orthodox faith and accept Catholicism?"

I had no idea why the king should put such a question to me, but I could see that he was very serious. And of course it was not a question to be answered lightly. But after giving it some thought, I nodded my assent. "If that were how I might best serve my king—it would not be impossible."

Matthias gripped my arm. "Drakulya, it rejoices our heart to see your loyalty! Those intercepted messages, that sowed such enmity between us, and caused your imprisonment—I can see now that they were, as you said, a vile trick of your enemies. And now we will unfold to you our wishes, regarding your own immediate future."

Here the king paused, eyes fixed on mine. With my own heart rejoicing perhaps even more than his, I waited to hear his plan.

When he went on, he was obviously choosing his

words with great deliberation. "The service we have in mind requires a man well born, utterly loyal, and of the most solid judgement. He must be able to—how shall we put it?—inspire respect. He must also be able to follow orders. And to hold his tongue. To be utterly ruthless when the need arises. And he should have skill in arms—yes, that may prove to be of importance."

"I am honored that Your Majesty thinks I—"

"But not in this so-called Crusade. That is a great folly. You hear garbled rumors about it from your guards. But we are informed by shrewd observers everywhere. No one is going to follow the Pope. What we have in mind for you, Drakulya, is something altogether different. It is not only an important matter of state, it also concerns our own family very closely."

The king, gesturing for me to keep up with him, began to walk, as he was wont to do when weighty matters were to be decided. I remained in close attendance. His voice fell to a whisper now, so that I had to bend my head to hear.

"Drakulya, do you know how many sisters I have?" Of course everyone knows such things, and more, about his reigning monarch. But before I could fall to naming siblings, Matthias silenced me with a raised finger. Suddenly he was not so much a ruler as simply the young, worried head of a family.

"I have a younger sister, Helen, whose name has not been mentioned in my family for two years. Her age is now seventeen. At fifteen she was betrothed to a Sforza. That would have made a valuable alliance. But she behaved with great folly, so that the engagement had to be broken off. She ran away with an artisan, if you can believe it, rather than marry into one of the great houses of Italy. When she was found, we had her put into an Italian convent, until we could decide what to do next. But it was the wrong convent, as it proved, so gentle a place that

she had no trouble getting out of it and running away
again.

"A few months ago some Medici traders brought
me the latest news of her. Quite unpleasant news, and
they were too diplomatic to tell it to me directly,
realizing that I must not be put in the position of
having to take notice publicly of her scandalous affairs.
But their report placed her in Venice . . . you can and
must hear the sordid details later, and I will give them
to you myself, if you agree that you are the man I
need. As I think you are. I need one who will restore
the honor of my crown and of my family—in one way
or another—"

THREE

"Because he's a bloody murderer, and I want the world to know him for what he is. That's why I did it. I waited till they brought the painting out so all the guards would be concentrating on it. I knew he wouldn't press charges against me, he doesn't want any more publicity."

Outrage and enjoyment made a heady mixture in Mary Rogers's voice, and she talked as if she were familiar with their blended taste. At the moment she was seated in an awkward armchair in Mr. Thorn's expensive Phoenix hotel suite, sipping from time to time at a can of beer. Her sturdy legs were crossed in their tight blue jeans.

It was evening again, almost exactly twenty-four hours after Mary's dye-throwing outrage. Over in Scottsdale, just a few miles away, the auction should be getting started just about now, doubtless under a heavily reinforced guard. Mr. Thorn was going to miss the bidding, which was all right with him. He had seen the painting, and he was virtually certain who was going to buy it. And even if by some chance the Magdalen should be bought by someone else, he could easily find out whom. It was not going to get away from him again.

So he felt that he could afford the time to indulge his curiosity regarding Mary and her motives. He had the habit of thinking, whenever anything bizarre happened nearby, that it was somehow meant for him. Quite often he was right.

Lounging near the window now, he glanced out through his new polarizing sunglasses at the last fading tinges of a gory sunset. Clouds were hung theatrically above a distant reach of desert, studded with a few Hollywood mountains. From the twentieth floor, a lot of distant scenery was visible beyond the smoky metropolitan sprawl.

"You can bet *I* didn't know what she was going to do." This was the voice of Robinson Miller, Mary's young man from the auction room, who had turned out to be her lawyer also. He and Mary, Thorn understood, had encountered each other on some pathway of the legal jungle into which she had been parachuted by her accidental connection with the infamous Seabright murder-kidnapping; and they had been getting better acquainted ever since.

"Completely irrational behavior," Miller added now, drilling Mary with a stern look that she did not seem to feel at all. From what Thorn had seen of her lifestyle so far, it was hard to estimate whether she needed friend or lawyer most.

Last night as Mary was giving the police her name, address, and phone number, Thorn had been nearby, although she had not seen him. Today Thorn had called her up—Miller answering the phone—and had invited her up to his suite for this evening chat, saying there were matters of mutual advantage to be discussed. Yes, certainly, she was welcome to bring a friend along to the hotel lair of the mysterious stranger; and so it was that her legal adviser and probable lover sat beside her now in another chair constructed like hers at disabling angles, sipping a glass of ginger ale and ice and puffing at a large-bowled pipe.

"What I *really* wanted," Mary announced now, "was to get hold of some blood."

Mr. Thorn, who had been paying only desultory attention, forgot about the scenery and took off his glasses long enough to give her an intense look. It took him a moment to realize what she had meant.

"At first I thought maybe I'd use beef blood. But then I realized that it wouldn't be appropriate to throw anything real on *him*. Except maybe some real acid." Mary gave a bright giggle. "So it was just that stuff they use in movies, harmless. A friend of mine who works in a studio got hold of some for me."

"The dry cleaner found it interesting," commented Mr. Thorn. "A type of stain with which he had never had to deal before. But it came out of my suit quite easily."

"Your—?" In a second Mary's mood changed to regret and horror. "Oh, I'm sorry! I hadn't realized that any of the glop hit you. Is that why you wanted me to come up here? No, of course not. Look, I really am sorry."

"Your apology is accepted. Think no more of the matter, I was not harmed. And it is fortunate that the painting sustained no damage either."

"Yes, fortunate," concurred the lawyer. Taking his pipe from his mouth, he made fencing motions in the air with the curved stem. "Ah, you mentioned some matters of mutual advantage?"

"I did." Thorn smiled at them both, then addressed himself mainly to Mary. "It is to my advantage to learn more about Mr. Ellison Seabright. It may be to your advantage to help me do so."

"Whom do you represent?" Miller asked quickly, before Mary could respond.

Thorn turned to him. "Only myself. Therefore any

information you may give me will go no farther." After a pause he added: "You may be confident also that none of it is likely to be used to Mr. Seabright's advantage."

His visitors exchanged a cautious glance, and slight shrugs. Then Mary asked: "What sort of things do you want to know?"

Mr. Thorn moved a little closer to his guests, taking a seat on a sofa opposite their chairs, his lean hands clasped before him. "To begin with, whom do you accuse Mr. Seabright of having murdered?"

"Mary," Robinson Miller cautioned, shaking his beard at her.

Mary took another sip of Coors and ignored legal counsel. "He killed his half-brother, Delaunay Seabright. And Helen, his own step-daughter. You must have heard and read about those killings, they made news all over the country. Oh, I don't mean he did it with his own hands. But you can bet he was involved."

Thorn allowed himself a pained frown, and objected gently: "Were not the police of the opinion that Helen was killed by men trying to abduct Delaunay for ransom? And that Delaunay himself died almost accidentally, though while he was in the unknown kidnappers' hands?"

Mary brushed back her wayward hair. "I bet they weren't unknown to Ellison. I was there that night, when Del and Helen were killed—was I ever there. And I know what I saw. And I know that Ellison's no good."

"Kid," warned Miller, hopelessly.

Thorn nodded to Mary. "When I learned your name, I of course could place you as the escaped hostage of the news stories. But your claim that Ellison was implicated comes as a surprise to me. Have you any evidence that will support it?"

"No, if you mean legal evidence," said Mary,

dismissing the idea. "Do you know the family at all?"

"Only through the news accounts."

"Well." Mary looked at her lawyer at last, then back to Thorn. "Excuse me, but just what good is all this going to do you?"

Thorn was not at all sure of that himself, but he was interested. He said: "I find myself in the position of being Mr. Ellison Seabright's rival. Therefore I wish to learn everything of importance that I can learn about him. If, as you say, he is really involved in murder, that is certainly an important fact."

"You're his rival as an art collector?"

"Exactly. Now can you explain to me just what he stood to gain from his brother's death? Or from the girl's?"

"His half-brother," Mary corrected, as if she thought the difference had significance. "What did he gain? The chance to buy up Delaunay's collection, at least the part of it that he really wanted. That's what he's doing over in Scottsdale right this minute. Look, poor old Del hated Ellison. He wouldn't have given him the sweat off . . . so according to Del's will, Helen was to get it all. She was the closest family he had, that he cared anything about. Del's own wife died years ago, and they were childless."

"You say he left all to Helen. His half-brother's stepdaughter."

"Yes. I don't suppose she ever knew about the will. He was always nice to her but I don't think she appreciated him very much. In some ways, I have to admit, Helen could be a snotty little bitch." It was said much more in affection than in anger. Mary gulped beer audibly. "She was still a minor, only seventeen. So everything was to be held in trust. Right, Robby? And if Helen predeceased Del, or died at about the same time, which was the way things turned out, then everything in the collection was to be sold at auction, proceeds going to a charitable foundation Delaunay was setting up. Except—"

Here Mary broke off with a sigh, an unexpected, hopeless sound. Miller was shaking his head again.

"What?" Thorn prompted.

Mary said: "The Verrocchio, that's what. It's really mine."

Miller said quickly: "I think Mary is quite right, I mean I believe what she tells me. But of course legally, again—"

Mary interrupted him. "You see, Mr. Thorn, I lived there in the Seabright house for a couple of months before the night of the killings. And two weeks to the day before he died, Delaunay Seabright stood there with me in the midst of his collection, and told me that Verrocchio was mine. I didn't know what to say, how to react. Then he got sick, and that meant there was a delay in making the gift official, and evidently he never mentioned it to anyone else before he died. Or if he did, no one is going to admit it now."

Thorn made no attempt to hide his doubts. "You say he simply gave you the Verrocchio."

"I know it isn't the easiest thing in the world to believe, that anyone could be so generous. 'This is yours now, Mary, I want you to have it.' Those were his words."

"You told this to the police?"

She glanced at Robinson Miller once more. "Yes. Or I tried. For all good it did me. We've never tried to file any kind of legal claim, since I have nothing to support it."

Thorn could not tell whether she was fantasizing or not. He felt sure she was not simply lying. He asked, in curiosity: "What would you have done with the painting, Mary? If it had actually come to you?"

Her laugh was surprisingly gentle. "Why, hung it over Robby's Salvation Army sofa. No, I'd have sold it, of course. I would have hoped to be able to sell it to some museum, where everybody would be able to see it for a change . . . Del didn't care for museums, you know, he thought they were more arrogant and greedy than anybody else. The people who run them . . . did you get a chance to look at the painting closely? It's really so beautiful."

"I agree."

"I certainly wouldn't have sold it to that creep who's got it now. I'd have made sure he never got his hands on it, and I'm sure he knew I felt that way."

There was a little silence. "May I refresh your drinks?" Thorn offered.

"You see," Mary explained suddenly, "I got to know Del because I helped out his niece when she was a runaway. I met Helen in Chicago, when she was ready to give up being on the road. I was a kind of official social worker then."

"You were a nun," her lawyer interjected.

Mary gave him a glance. "I hadn't taken my final vows. Anyway, I was able to help Helen get her head together somewhat. Delaunay appreciated that, and at his request I wound up living with them here in Phoenix for a couple of months. Helen's parents came along too, at his urging. The old man was grateful to me for helping Helen, that's all there ever was between us."

"I see." Mr. Thorn considered Mary's lush figure, the full veins in her throat. He was unsure whether he ought to envy the young lawyer with whom she was apparently living now, and/or feel regret on behalf of the dead old man who had been only grateful. There wandered into his mind the image, thin and dark, of the other attractive woman who had been at the auction room. Stephanie Seabright, mother and sister-in-law respectively of the two victims. A woman desperately wanting to be young, to start over, perhaps, somehow . . .

Mary had paused for a full breath. "Excuse me, Mr. Thorn, but you're not an American, are you?"

"I am not. Though I have made my home in America for the past year. I like your—"

"You see, we have in this country a very serious and tragic problem, of teenagers, some kids even younger, who find their homes, if you can call some of them homes, just completely unendurable. So the kids take off, hitchhiking or what have you, and quite a number of them, more than you'd think, wind up as murder victims. Nobody's done a really good study yet to demonstrate how many." Mary smiled eagerly, giving the impression she enjoyed either the lack of that crucial study or the prospect of reading what it would someday reveal. "The others, the relatively lucky ones, are sexually abused, robbed, molested. They wind up in jail, on dope, in prostitution." Mary continued to smile. No doubt it was unconscious.

Mr. Thorn said: "I see the problem. It is not a new one." Several floors below his suite, a radio was softly playing a lament that concerned, if his old ears were to be trusted, the fate of a limestone cowboy. Very little surprised him any more.

"There are official means of attempting to deal with the problem, of course. Courts, agencies, juvenile homes. They all can do some good but it's not enough. I intended to sell that painting and use the money to show what can be done. I intended to set up a halfway house for runaways."

"Ah." Mr. Thorn appeared to be giving the suggestion his most thoughtful consideration. Then he nodded. "That sounds like a most worthy plan."

Mary, who had perhaps not expected such quick and unqualified agreement, blinked at him and slowed down. "I really can't think of anything that's needed more."

"Amen," said Robinson Miller.

Thorn asked: "This plan of yours, I hope, has not been abandoned?"

"No. Not at all. We've had to postpone things, of course, but—"

"Then you would be willing to accept a contribution?"

The sudden, innocent joy in Mary's eyes realized some of the potential beauty that her habitual fierce smiling tended to obscure. She looked at Miller. "We could at least start an account, Robby . . . I'm very grateful, Mr. Thorn."

Only grateful. "I was wondering," asked Mr. Thorn, meanwhile slowly drawing out a checkbook, "if you intended to return to the Seabright house for any reason? I assume you have moved out."

"I haven't been back since that night. Except once for a police re-enactment. But I do still have a few things there, if Ellison hasn't had them burned. They'll have to be picked up sooner or later, I suppose."

"Might I come with you when you do that?"

"Why?" asked Miller bluntly.

Thorn opened the checkbook on his bony knee and drew a pen from his breast pocket. "I have been trying to arrange a meeting with Mr. Seabright, in his late brother's house. I have phoned several times and have been told that he will see no one. He has not returned my calls. I hope to arrange, somehow, a simple invitation to cross the threshold of that dwelling. No more than that."

Miller opened his mouth, glanced at Mary, closed it again. His eyes came back to the open checkbook on Thorn's knee, the pen poised over the blank check. At last he repeated Mary's earlier question. "You're his rival in the sense of—collecting?"

"Yes. Precisely. I should like very much to get a look at his collection."

"He's not very likely to give any friend of mine the grand tour, you know," said Mary doubtfully. "In fact

I don't think he'd let either of us in the house. More likely he'd just have my things thrown out the front gate, and us with them."

"I ask only that you do what you can to help me cross the threshold. After that I shall manage for myself. Agreed?"

"Agreed." She was still doubtful.

"As for your projected charitable home—" Thorn wrote, tore out a check with a crisp noise, handed it across. "Something on account, shall we say? I hope to be able to continue my support of the project once it has begun."

Mary's eyes widened, looking at the small piece of paper. "Thank you! Jeez, what can I say? Oh, Rob, this is a start, a real start."

Miller looked, made as if to whistle, then raised puzzled eyes to Thorn. "I'll say. Thanks. You must have a real affinity for lost causes."

FOUR

The Vicar of Christ lay dying in a tent on the lonely, rain-sogged beach at Ancona, where he had had himself brought that he might keep a personal watch for ships. Inside his fevered brain, phantasmagorical armies of Crusaders had been embarked, and he did not want to miss the first sight of their rendezvous here, at the place he had ordained—the hosts of the Emperor, the massed cavalry squadrons of Philip the Good.

I arrived overland, to find the coastal town swarming with churchmen. But as I had expected, there was no sign of any military or naval force of consequence. A Swiss mercenary escorted me to the Pope's tent, and waited by my side till word came out that His Holiness would see me. Inside, a pair of gray-robed monks were in absentminded attendance upon the old man propped up with pillows.

The Holy Father, looking clearheaded enough at the moment, beckoned me close to him. "You are welcome," he murmured in Italian as I knelt to kiss his ring. "And your companions? Men at arms? How many have you brought?"

I was sure he recognized my name, but it did not seem to have alarmed him. "I am alone, Holiness," I answered, standing as he motioned for me to rise. Actually of course my presence had nothing to do with Pius's call for swords about the cross. The trail of King Matthias's wayward sister had led me to Venice, and in that city I had been told she had come here. According to my Venetian informant, she had embarked—in what capacity was uncertain—on one of the two galleys of Venetian volunteers that city had actually dispatched to take part in the Papal fiasco. The ships were now anchored in Ancona's harbor, and my first move on arriving at the port had been to locate and question some of their sailors. These told me that no woman, high-born or low, who answered Helen's description had been aboard either ship. Having offered the seamen gold for confirmation of her presence, I was compelled to believe their regretful denials.

"Holy Father, I have come alone. But I bring you greetings from King Matthias. He regrets that vital affairs of state prevent his joining this most sacred enterprise, but he is praying most earnestly for its success." That seemed a safe-enough message to put into the king's mouth. Certainly Matthias would have welcomed a successful Papal foray against the Turk. But already the true Crusades were centuries in the past. Matthias fought the Turks because they were on his own doorstep, but no Christian prince in the late fifteenth century was going to spend years in a military campaign far from his own domain, exhausting his treasury and army in the process, while schemers at home worked to relieve him of his throne. Eleven years of relative stability had dulled the shock of terror sent across the continent by the fall of Constantinople. The Turk was for the time being more or less contained, even though the Ottoman Empire pressed up into Europe to the Danube and beyond.

As I spoke, the Pope gradually let himself sink lower among his cushions. He was greatly disappointed by my words, and his lips moved in silent prayer. It was hard to tell, now, what this man had looked like in his youth; I had heard that he had spent it largely in debauchery and riotous living, that only in middle life had he turned to God. But what he had once been like no longer seemed to matter. The aged, wasted, dying tend to look all the same. I could see that he was holding one hand lightly clenched, in order that the Fisherman's Ring might not slide off his diminished finger.

His weary gaze moved out through the open doorway of the tent, vainly questioning the sea-horizon once again. Then it returned to me.

"Yet you are here. It must have taken great courage for you to come alone, my son. I have heard of you."

And had written about me, too, the damned compulsive old scribbler, repeating for posterity all the vile gossip transmitted from Buda by his loquacious legate Nicholas. But at the time I did not know that Pius was a writer, and I pitied him. I said: "You have probably heard little to my credit, Holiness."

He sighed. "Yet you are here, when Catholic kings have turned their backs. Your sins will be forgiven you. I would like to give you my blessing."

Lacking the heart to explain to that sad old man the truth about my presence, down I went on my knees again and bowed my head. He yearned to lead an army, to see the banners fly, to smite the unbeliever, to retake Constantinople. But he had trouble getting the attention of one of the monks to bring him a pan to piss in. That old man, though, bestowed a blessing on me which I remember still. I suppose it must have been the last he ever gave.

Together we watched darkness slowly cover the horizon. Neither of us had the least idea how wide the oceans were, or that America lay undiscovered somewhere in their midst. Side by side in the harbor rode the two Venetian galleys, twin lanterns burning, their captains probably already in private conference deciding how soon they might be able to give up the farce and sail for home. The Pope's breathing was growing louder and more labored. I remained in the tent, unchallenged and almost unnoticed, as physicians and prelates, recalled from God knows where in that small town, began to gather.

A final time Pius beckoned me to his side. "You will be going far, my son. To a strange, long life, in distant lands. You will be going farther than . . ."

I bent over him, trying to hear more. But the rest was lost in the struggle of his old lungs to breathe, in a chanted dirge the monks chose that moment to begin. Pius died near midnight, and the ranking churchmen on his staff scrambled away in an excited effort to be first back to Rome.

FIVE

Travel by automobile was not something that Mr.
Thorn enjoyed. In fact—except for flying machines
of all types, which he liked immensely—complex
machinery of any kind had always impressed him as
perverse and unreliable. He detested, for example,
firearms. But he could get along in an uneasy coex-
istence with mechanism when he had to; and recently
he had been brought to the reluctant conclusion that
the advantages of being able to drive oneself about
in one's own automobile outweighed the attendant
irritations. Thus it was that two evenings after Mary
Rogers had splashed her Hollywood blood on Ellison
Seabright, and one evening after her visit to Thorn's
hotel, Thorn was alone in a rented vehicle, on his
way to see the Magdalen again. Or so he hoped.

Persistence on the telephone had finally paid off,
and he had wangled for himself an invitation to the
Seabright mansion. Persistence, and a ploy of passing along for Mr. Seabright's ears some hints of information that Thorn guessed the most recent purchaser
of the supposed Verrocchio would be unable to resist.
The guess was evidently right.

The house lay in what was probably the wealthiest suburb of the metropolis. The high wall enclosing its several hectares of grounds was constructed in large part of real adobe; looking at this wall, Mr. Thorn thought that some segments of it, near the house, were possibly old enough to have seen forays by hostile Indians. He knew little of the history of this part of the world, but meant someday to study it, an effort he suspected would not be easy. History, unlike machinery, he always found interesting; but he had seen too much of history to have any faith in the official account of anything.

As soon as the drive leading to the house parted company with the curving public road, it passed under an iron gate, now closed, in the old wall. Just outside the gate, Thorn stopped his Blazer—having seen what a high proportion of the natives elected to use four-wheel-drive vehicles, he suspected they had some good reason and had followed their example. A gatekeeper, a Spanish-looking man, appeared now inside the ironwork, which opened itself on electric tracks as soon as Thorn rolled down his window and announced his name.

Inside the gates the graveled drive curved to and fro through spacious lawns now enjoying their evening sprinkling from an automatic system. Citrus blossoms blessed the air. From behind a mass of greenery the house came into view—for its time and place, quite an impressive villa, though it was not like some that Mr. Thorn had visited. Like its surrounding wall it was eclectic, with some good old sections that looked especially venerable. Additions over a number of decades, some quite recent, had made it very large.

As Mr. Thorn parked his Blazer and approached the sizable front portico, there sounded from somewhere on the other side of the building the thrum of a diving board, followed by the trim splash of a

lithe body entering a pool. It was, somehow, a
definitely female splash; and Thorn, with no more
than that to go on, immediately visualized the dark
and slender woman who had been with Seabright two
evenings ago. Stephanie Seabright, bereft of her only
child just two months past. Stephanie who did not
seem to mourn, but yearned. And swam, too, evidently; though Thorn could not really be sure from
a mere splash that it was she.

At the front door Thorn was met by a butler, who
resembled physically the bodyguard who had attended
Seabright at the auction room. This man was a little
slimmer and younger, though, and therefore presum-
ably a little faster on his feet.

"Come in, sir, you're expected. Right this way,
please."

"Thank you." To Mr. Thorn, the simple crossing
of any house's threshold for the first time was always
something of an event; and in this house he had a
special interest. Once inside, enveloped by air conditioning, he was led across a wide entry floored with
Mexican tile into a sort of manorial hall that made
the house seem even larger than it had looked from
outside. The ceiling of this hall, at about third-story
level, was supported by wooden beams so gigantic that
the whole effect reminded Thorn of nothing so much
as the passenger concourse of the Albuquerque air-
port, where not long ago he had spent part of a long
bright afternoon between planes, beseiged by sunlight,
squinting through sunglasses and changing his place
in search of deeper shadow. He had in his time been
inside private homes that had rooms bigger than this
hall. But not many such homes, and not much bigger.

Pushing open a massive door of carven wood, his
guide stood deferentially aside. Halfway down the
length of the booklined study thus revealed, Rodrigo
Borgia rose up from behind a desk, all red smears
cleaned away, and dressed as for a leisurely safari.

"Mr. Thorn, glad to see you again," Ellison
Seabright boomed. "That's all, Brandreth," he added
in an aside to the butler, and then came forward as
to some old friend, extending one great arm for a
handshake. "Too bad we didn't have more of a chance
to talk the other night." In fact they had never talked
at all. "That damned woman . . . you'd like a look at
the collection, right? Of course you would. So let's
go downstairs and do our talking there." Seabright
had a light, homey, completely American voice. Mr.
Thorn could easily imagine him reading the ten
o'clock news, getting high ratings on the job.

Thorn murmured something in the way of a
response. The easy voice of his host chatted on, while
a massive hand on Mr. Thorn's bony shoulder guided
him out of the study again and back across the
baronial hall. At the far end of the hall a small elevator opened its bronze door and without a groan
accepted the combined weight of the two men.

Of the several levels indicated on the elevator's
control panel, two appeared to be below ground, and
Seabright pressed the button for the lowest. During
the brief descent he chatted with Thorn about the
Arizona climate, and the importance of always maintaining the proper atmospheric conditions in rooms
housing a collection. As he talked Mr. Seabright kept
eyeing his guest steadily. It was a gaze not quite
offensive, but still it would have been found intimi-
dating by almost any visitor. The elevator eased itself
to a stop meanwhile, surrounded by deep silence.
Scream down here, thought Mr. Thorn, amusing
himself privately, and no one will hear you.

"Ah, Stephanie!" Seabright exclaimed, taken by
surprise as the door opened. The lift had delivered
them to a perfectly cooled lounge or game room, of
a size and elaborateness appropriate to the house. At
one end of the room was a bar, and on one of the
bar's six chrome stools perched the dark lady of the

auction room, the lately bereaved mother. In a few more years she would have to give up brief bikinis such as she was wearing now—but not for a few more years, and she was making the most of the time left. Over the shreds of cloth she wore as symbolic cover-up a translucent short cape, some hybrid perhaps of cloth and plastic. Behind the bar, Thorn noticed at once, there was no mirror, but a mural of youths and maidens, pseudo-Greek and semi-porn, and Stephanie had to turn her head to see the men. Her dark hair as she looked round at Thorn was almost wet enough to drip, and her face bore the practiced smile that he remembered from the auction room. At Stephanie's fingertips on the bar, a tall glass held a little dark liquid and some ice.

"Mr. Thorn, my wife. Steff, you probably remember seeing Mr. Thorn, of Chicago, at the auction room night before last? That damned woman."

Thorn took the lady's tanned hand when it was offered as if he meant to bow and kiss it, but did not go that far. Stephanie's eyes rested perturbedly on his. On the skin her hand was cool, but there was a faint, heated trembling underneath. "My heartfelt sympathy, madam, on your dear daughter's passing."

"Thank you. Everyone who knew Helen says what a remarkable girl she was." It sounded like a rehearsed line. Probably it had been used very often in the past weeks and months. Stephanie's eyes would not hold Thorn's directly for very long. Common enough. But he knew she was still wishing that she was somewhere else. Somewhere, perhaps, that did not exist outside of her own imagination.

"Anything to drink, Thorn? Then let's go take a look at a few things. Right through here."

Just as he was leaving the lounge, Thorn was granted a last unexpected glimpse of the swim-damp lady, in a mirror that had been almost concealed, for some reason, in a niche. She was still on her stool, eyes gazing back with vague puzzlement at the same area of reflective glass. Perhaps she noticed that the mirror bore no image of the lean man who had just pressed her fingers in a way that could be taken to mean something if she wanted to think about it.

More likely, Thorn considered, the oddity of what was lacking in the glass escaped her.

Experience had long ago proved to him that people usually accepted such accidental nonperceptions without thought, or sometimes rejected them completely as being caused by momentary aberrations of their own senses. Of course there was a chance that the mirror had been placed there deliberately, and Seabright might have looked into it to check out his guest. Thorn himself, of course, could tell a vampire without any such subterfuges; but even the wisest breathing folk might have difficulties sometimes in doing so.

Fortunately for him.

Meanwhile the two men had walked through an odd little curving tunnel, with white curving walls, and had entered what looked like a miniature museum. All white walls and new brown carpet. As far as Thorn could tell, Seabright's mind was still firmly on things other than vampirism.

"Some of the things in this room are mine," the big man intoned, sounding quite satisfied. "*Were* mine, I mean, even before last night's auction. Never seem to have room in my own house in Santa Fe for all my stuff. What do you think of this?"

It was a graceful silver ship, intricately modeled, standing alone on a low cube of furniture. Thorn chose not to see his host's generous gesture inviting him to pick it up. If he touched it the nonreflectable quality of his fingers would be very plain in the curve of argent hull. Instead he bent his head and walked around the object on its low stand, looking at it carefully.

"German . . . almost certainly sixteenth century. It is some time since I have seen a nef of this quality in private hands." Well, the piece was not really all *that* impressive; but it did not seem likely that a little judicious flattery would do any harm.

It seemed that he had passed the examination, or its first question anyway. Seabright, a little more relaxed now, chatted some more. Still probing, doing what seemed his best to probe cleverly. Finding out, as he must have thought, a fair number of things about Thorn without giving away much about himself. Thorn inclined more and more to the opinion that the mirror in the game room-lounge had been completely accidental. He doubted more and more Mary Rogers's estimation of this man as a Machiavellian murderer. Seabright simply did not seem bright enough to carry off any such scheme successfully.

The portion of the Seabright collection here visible contained a couple of really respectable things, not to mention the one in which Thorn was really interested and which they had not come to yet. Also it contained some that verged—no, more than verged—upon the pornographic. Those two young ladies under the oddly rumpled coverlet had their eyes closed but were enjoying more than sleep; the sculptured monk standing close behind the choirboy was, on second glance, not really intent on music. These examples and others more explicit appeared to be for the most part underground Victorian imitations of earlier masters. Maybe the porn things were all Ellison Seabright's to start with, for he discussed them roundly and seemed to take an extra pride in their display. They were not really to Mr. Thorn's taste, but he could be polite.

The walls of these underground rooms were thick, Mr. Thorn knew, inside their earthen envelope. Even with only interior surfaces visible he could sense the thickness all round him, virtually impenetrable, like the walls of a bomb shelter or a bank vault. Fault-less air conditioning, that even Thorn could barely hear, maintained a good museum's silence, coolness, balanced humidity.

Yet there were soundless echoes of murder and violence in the air down here. Death not all that old. The much-publicized Seabright murder-kidnapping, of course. But Thorn had got the impression from the news accounts that all those scenes had been in the upper levels of the house.

Trading opinions, some of which may have made sense, about the Renaissance, the two men presently moved farther into the gallery. Mr. Thorn came to a halt. He saw with a pang the well-lighted, centrally located space on a wall where the Magdalen should obviously be. She was not here, though she must have been. The empty place of honor was marked by the very faint outline of her frame.

He hoped, but did not immediately ask for, a quick explanation of where she was right now. Feeling more disappointment than was entirely reasonable, he continued his expected admiring commentary on the lesser works surrounding him. A few of these he could recognize as having been at the auction room. They had been brought back here afterwards, but *she* had not.

At last he stopped talking, to stand gazing point-edly at that central gap.

His huge host gestured, with selfconscious drama. "That's where the Verrocchio was, of course. Natu-rally I'm curious as to just what you meant when you mentioned the question of its origins to my secretary on the phone. I hope you're not going to try to cast any doubts on its authenticity? I'd hate to think that my confidence in that painting as an investment has been misplaced."

Thorn smiled. "Oh, by no means. It is extremely valuable."

"I'm glad you agree. I *will* take your opinions on art fairly seriously, you know, now that we've had this little talk. Though frankly some of the ideas you have on the Renaissance seem pretty far-fetched, no offense, I'm willing to concede there may be areas where you know what you're talking about." Seabright emitted a calculated chuckle. "You mentioned the painting's origins. I've already heard one crackpot theory on that subject, which I hope you're not going to endorse. But there, I'm sure I do you an injustice, Thorn. You must have something sensible to say on the subject. Possibly with evidence to back it up?" The big man paused, in an attitude of hopeful inquiry, of generous expectation that he was going to be told something that made sense.

Thorn hesitated. "I do have some ideas on the subject, as I told your secretary. As for evidence . . . before I begin, Mr. Seabright, would you mind telling me how long the painting has been here?"

"In this room? Why not? Since 1953. That's when my brother brought it home from Argentina. Some Nazi who evidently saw the end coming sent it there from Europe in 1944. During the war one of the collecting teams working for Goering had evidently liberated it, shall we say, from a chateau in Normandy. How long it had been at that particular chateau, or where it had been before that, we were never able to discover. Only a tantalizing hint or two . . . these things, the great ones, tend to have remarkable histories, don't they?" Seabright ran a hand back over his suntanned brow.

Thorn glanced at him, then back at the blank wall. "Indeed they do. They also have a habit of being stolen."

"Had you ever laid eyes on it, yourself, before two nights ago? I don't suppose you had the chance."

"On the contrary. I saw it several times. Some years ago."

That had not been the answer Seabright was prepared for. The big man swung his heavy arms, like a furniture salesman getting bored on floor duty. "You saw it here? Ah, I see, you were acquainted with my brother, then."

"No, I regret, I did not know him. Or that he had the painting here . . . it was in Europe."

Obviously calculating years, moving his lips very slightly as he counted, Seabright gave a little shake of his head, whose thickness seemed to be becoming more and more apparent. "You must have been only a child."

Thorn had turned, was leaning with his arms folded against the blank space on the wall, staring at things on the far side of the room. "Yes . . . yes, I suppose I was. An ill-tempered child. Though at the time I was quite sure of my own power and wisdom, and there was no lack of people willing to humor me. But then—this painting—"

He came to a halt, not knowing how much he ought to say in the presence of this fool. Talking to Seabright was helpful, in a way, as talking to a child might be. But who else might be listening?

"The painting," Thorn went on, "acquired for me some special associations. Special meanings, that even now I find it difficult to explain. Yes, even difficult to explain to myself." He looked closely into Seabright's uncomprehending face, and for the first time the big man drew back a little. Thorn added: "For a long time I have wondered where it was." Then, more mildly, with a smile: "My own collection runs heavily to the Renaissance."

"Oh." Seabright blinked. "Then our tastes are alike in that, at least. Forgive me, Mr. Thorn, but I continue to find it somewhat odd that your name has never come to my attention before now. I had thought

that all the world's important collections in my field
were known to me."

"Almost all of them are, I'm sure."

"Almost. Yes, I see. My brother and I never cared
for a lot of publicity either. And I am sure your
collection must be important."

"Thank you, yes, I believe it is. And you are right,
very little known. And also, regrettably, incomplete."

Seabright let out another chuckle, this one gross
and uncontrolled, the laughter of a man who cares
nothing for what he sounds like. "What real collector is ever satisfied? Tell me, are your things in this
country?"

"Very few of them."

"I see. Well, I have no wish to pry. But I am always
on the lookout for genuinely valuable articles. As
investments, even if they do not match my own tastes
perfectly. I prefer to deal confidentially whenever
possible. I needn't talk to you about taxes and so on,
you understand those matters, I am sure. There are
possibilities of barter and exchange as well as purchase. I even, sometimes, have things that I wish to
sell. Well, Stephanie. Join us?"

She had entered the gallery on bare and silent feet,
still wearing her tiny swimsuit and her beach cape.
Her dark hair was uncurling quickly in the dry air.
Almost without looking at the two men she came to
stand, in a model's pose so practiced as to be second nature, before the dim scar on the wall showing where the large painting had been removed. Her
liquor glass had been left back at the bar.

"I miss that picture," she announced. "Isn't it
foolish, with everything else . . . but I do miss it."

"You have good taste, then, in painting," said Mr.
Thorn, pausing ever so slightly before the last two
words. Stephanie's eyes turned from the wall to him.

"I myself," said Seabright, "prefer something more
sensual than Verrocchio."

"A matter of taste," said Thorn. "So, you have paid a fortune for a supposed Verrocchio that does not really suit your preference?" He was still looking at the lady. *Help me,* her eyes seemed to be broadcasting. *I would like very much to get out of this. Sometimes it seems that I can wait no longer.*

What is it that are you waiting for? Thorn would have liked to ask. But there was no way to put the question now. He could be patient.

Seabright was answering him: "An investment, my friend, remember? But 'a supposed Verrocchio'? Aha, you are going to have some supposed revelation concerning the painting to offer me after all."

Thorn turned back to his host and asked him bluntly: "Is it being brought here today? I look forward to seeing it again."

"Here?" Seabright tried to sound surprised. "Why no, it isn't being brought back here at all. I'm taking it to Santa Fe, to my own house." He consulted his wrist watch. "In fact it's en route right now, on my own plane. Most of this other stuff is going to follow in due course. I'm having another room built on. But I wanted the Verrocchio there right away."

Thorn stood up straight, no longer leaning on the wall. "Ah," he said slowly. "Then I must hope to be able to see it there someday. In Santa Fe." He had the feeling of just having been checkmated. But not by this great fool, surely, nor this preoccupied woman. He felt a certain bewilderment. His real opponent, it seemed, had not yet even come in sight.

"Why not?" said Seabright, jovial and insincere. "If you're ever there, give me a call. It's been a real pleasure to converse with someone who knows what he's talking about. Now what was this idea you had about the painting's origin?"

Mr. Thorn had nothing to say on that subject now. Anyway he would not have had much chance to talk. He could hear the sound of the elevator door opening, back in the lounge, followed by the agitated approach of one person, a young man, and worried, to judge by the sound of his busy feet.

A figure to match the calculated image appeared, almost dancing through the white curve of the tunnel, garbed in white shirt and necktie, topped with a neat haircut. His face, that Thorn had never seen before, bore an expression eloquent of disaster. Thorn was conscious of calamity, like a compact cloud of darkness, hanging somewhere just above.

"Mr. Seabright, sir? Santa Fe just called."

Seabright rounded on the perturbed aide, turning his broad back on Thorn. "Well, what? Spit it out."

For a moment the young man sputtered, as if trying to take the order literally. Then he managed speech. "The plane is almost three hours overdue now, sir. And they can't contact Mr. Gliddon on radio."

SIX

During the fifteenth century, for good and sufficient reasons, travel across most of Europe was considered hazardous. In one or two geographical areas this rule had happy exceptions, about which more presently. But in general one did not set out alone on a journey of any length, not if trustworthy or only moderately dubious traveling companions could be found. So before leaving Ancona, I attached myself to some Medici traders who were on their way home to Florence after successfully completing a mission in the south of Italy. Helen had last been reliably reported in the northern portion of the boot, and I could think of no better place than the City of Flowers, that nerve center of every type of communication, in which to try to pick up further news of her. As for the merchants, when they had looked at the letters of identification and introduction that had been given me by my king, they were glad to have my sword added to their escort. One crime of which I have never even been accused is brigandage. If my reputation had reached my fellow travelers' ears, and if they recognized me despite the letters' ambiguous treatment of my name, the recognition must have made them more rather than less eager to have me in their company.

On the second day of our journey north from Ancona we encountered another party of honest merchants. They were southward bound, their wagons freighted with rolls of Florentine cloth. These men had from us their first word of the Pope's death, and we received from them in turn some news that my companions considered at least equally momentous. It made the good merchants of my own party look at one another grimly, and issue orders to their servants to prepare for a forced march. Cosimo de' Medici, head of the great mercantile family and the de facto ruler of the city-state of Florence, had gone to his own reward, in the manner of a stoic Christian by all reports, and just thirteen days before the passing of Pius in his lonely tent.

My traveling companions were not really surprised by the death of their master Cosimo, who had been ailing for a long time. Their concern, as we remounted and pushed on, was over what might be happening now. What was the effect going to be on business? The southbound travelers had told us that in Florence it was considered certain that Cosimo's middle-aged and eldest son Piero, called the Gouty, was going to take over his father's position as head of the family. This meant that Piero would probably also become the untitled but practically unchallenged ruler of Florence. What effect this change of leadership was going to have on the city and on the world it was difficult to say, and at the same time imperative to find out as soon as possible.

Being myself anxious to waste no time, I willingly went along with the forced march, and in a few days more had my first look at Florence. The city burst upon us as a splendid, nearby spectacle as we topped a hill. It was then one of the largest metropolises in Europe, enclosed by three miles of defensive wall, the high stonework of which was reinforced by sixty square towers. When seen as we saw it from the nearby hills, the city was truly impressive, its interior dotted thickly with church spires, with here and there the palaces of the wealthy rising amid acres of lesser construction. The Arno made a lopsided bisection of the city, and its waters, half mud, half rainbow, flowed out of it bearing all the colors of the Clothmakers' Guild, as well as the sewage of seventy thousand people. As we passed inside the walls I saw that the Guild artisans with their dyes and fabrics seemed to occupy all the banks and bridges of the river. The streets of Florence stank, like those of any city of the time; but there was also splendor in the air. The population was still much reduced from the pre-plague days of more than a century before, and considerable tracts within the walls had been denuded of buildings by fire and decay, had become gardens in which a million flowers grew along with plots of vegetables and fruit.

Just as foulness and beauty were mixed in the city's water, and stench and perfume in its air, so its mansions and hovels stood cheek by jowl in what appeared to me at first as a total confusion of society. Actually there was a logic. By tradition each Florentine family, however wealthy or poor it might become, still dwelt in its ancestral quarter. There was no enclave of the rich, no slum to confine the poor. The larger and finer houses contained within their walls their own storerooms, stables, and sometimes shops—none of this city's upper class disdained the touch of money or the business of buying and selling. These facilities would be of course on the ground floor, with gardens, halls, and courtyards added when there was room. The preferred living quarters were on the level just above. A floor or two above that dwelt poor relations, guests of secondary importance, and servants, in cramped apartments more exposed than those on the first floor to summer's heat and winter's cold. On the day of our arrival in the city the weather was still quite warm, and my companions had been wondering aloud whether the chief men of the Medici clan might not be found in one of the family villas that were scattered through the surrounding Tuscan hills, rather than in town. But as matters turned out we found them in the city palace, still working to master the turmoil of business matters brought on by the death of Cosimo.

The Medici palace was, as it is today, a massive stone building near the church of San Lorenzo, rectangular as a modern apartment block on the outside, and decorated with great art to which I at the time was almost indifferent. The outer walls of the ground floor were of simple, roughly dressed blocks of stone; the masonry of the second level followed the Doric pattern, and that of the third, the Corinthian. But as I say, such niceties were at the time quite lost on me, a rude barbarian soldier. Once inside the first courtyard, my fellow travelers dismounted and hurried at once into a private room to make a confidential business report to some official of the family bank. After I had goggled at the statuary for a while I too got off my horse and was courteously conducted to another room, where I presented to another officer my letters of introduction and credit from King Matthias. I realized that if my project was to thrive in Florence, I had best get off on the right foot with the Medici.

The preparations at Visegrad for my mission had been as thorough as they were secret, and the letters were in several languages, including of course Italian. In those of that language I was named rather ambiguously as Signore Ladislao—a fair translation of my Christian name—and all the letters promised royal gratitude for any assistance given me.

The merchants who had traveled with me had

doubtless speculated among themselves about my unspecified mission for Matthias, but had accepted the letters with little open comment. Now the Medici official, after a first reading, borrowed the documents from me, politely enough, and gave orders that I should be provided with suitable refreshment after my long journey. The weather being quite warm, I was led to a shaded table set in an open courtyard.

At any given time in that house it was more likely than not that some group of folk were banqueting. And though my interest in most kinds of food has long since waned, I can still remember . . . to gorge oneself whenever it was possible to do so was then the European standard of behavior. But not in mannered Florence. It was in Florence that I, the rough soldier, first saw a table fork, though that was on a later day. On that first day I dealt forkless with sausages, slices of melon, boiled capon, and pastries of whose elegant existence I had never before dreamt. I fell to with a will.

Presently some of the men who had shared the road with me appeared, smiling, to join me at table. While they were busy answering some of my questions concerning the city's history and customs, a young man I did not know came into the courtyard. He was dressed in new, rather simple clothing, cut of the best cloth. In a grating voice, and with a sad-faced courtesy and gravity beyond his years, he addressed me as Signore Ladislao and made me welcome to the house of his family. He was introduced to me, between mouthfuls and without ceremony, by one of my former fellow travelers. This youth was of course Piero's eldest son, Lorenzo, later to be called the Magnificent; and when his own hour came for subtle rule in Florence, he would wield more power than many an anointed king, and his patronage of art would markedly surpass even that of King Matthias. On that day in the late summer of 1464, however,

Lorenzo de' Medici was only fifteen years of age—
though there were moments when his swarthy face,
with its grim eyes, shave-resistant stubble, and the
natural beginning of a furrow in his brow, looked
thirty-five. Already the elders of his family had begun
to trust him with minor diplomatic work. Beside him
at my table now stood his little brother Giuliano, only
ten, but already an apprentice Medici and at the
moment sober as a German count. In those days
childhood was a rare thing, for people of any class.

Lorenzo, however precocious, had not recognized
my name. He had seen my letters, though, and could
identify importance. He sat down at table and
munched a piece of fruit while like a seasoned diplomat he killed time and sounded me out with a
discussion of relatively neutral topics: the death of
the Pope, the sad state of Italian roads. Then presently Lorenzo's father hobbled into the courtyard to
join us. Here was the ruler, certainly, and I rose to
my feet; but Piero's gnarled hand waved me to sit
down again. Leaning on the table for support, he
handed me back my letters, and bade me stay as a
guest in his house for as long as I might choose.

Lorenzo too had sprung up with alacrity, that his
father might have the seat at my side. And Piero knew
who I was; I could see it in his eyes as at last, he
settled himself on the bench beside me with a groan.

"Is it possible, Signore Ladislao, that we have met
before? Have you lived in Targoviste, perhaps?"

My old Wallachian capital. I doubted, though of
course I could not be sure, that Piero himself had
ever dragged his gouty frame that far from home.
Medici merchants had certainly been there, though.
Where in the known world had they not been? I
admitted cautiously that I had once lived in that city.

"Then perhaps," continued Piero, "you were there
some eight years or so past when an incident occurred
that caused one of my family's most dependable

trading representatives to bring back a strange report. Despite the man's good reputation, some found his story difficult to believe.

"It seems that this merchant, through a chain of the most unlucky circumstances, found himself alone and unescorted on the road, and carrying a great amount of gold coin, so that the first robber's eye to light upon him must have meant at the very least the total ruin of his life's work.

"He had just entered the domain of the young warlord Drakulya, said by some to be a prince of unparalleled ruthlessness and ferocity—I do not know the truth of those stories myself. But at any rate our exceedingly fearful merchant, perhaps never having heard the worst of the stories, dared to approach Drakulya himself, pleading that the prince assign guards to protect the traveler's property whilst he was passing through Wallachia.

"The prince only stared at him coldly. 'You say, then, that my good people are thieves?' 'Great prince, there must be some thieves in any land.' 'Not here, I do not tolerate them.'

"The merchant, having seen the skeletons of impaled brigands at roadside—or at least skeletons labeled as guilty of that crime, among others—was not going to argue. The upshot was that the prince commanded him to pick out a dark street corner at random within the capital and to leave all his goods, unguarded, piled there for a whole night. The merchant of course had no choice but to do as he was ordered. Then, resigning himself to ruin, he spent a sleepless night in a room of the prince's palace. In the morning, expecting nothing but the worst, he returned to where he had left his gold. In the daylight the bags looked like just what they were, bags of coin, unguarded by any visible presence. But not one had been touched. People of every degree, rich and poor, going about their morning business, were

walking round them, giving them a wide berth as they
passed." Here Piero paused, looking at me with
inquiring eyes.

"I have heard the same story," I replied, "when I
lived in that city . . . of course it is possible, Signore
Piero, that you have seen me before and do recognize me, but on the other hand I am sometimes
confused with a great rogue who is presently imprisoned in His Majesty's palace at Visegrad. It is of
course not to be expected that such a man would be
sent on a confidential mission for His Majesty; yet
so strong is the resemblance that it sometimes causes
me embarrassment."

Piero smiled his understanding. "Say no more, good
Signore Ladislao; the farthest thing from my intention is that you should ever be embarrassed in my
house. Say no more." And he stood up, and bowed
to me; and with that the offer of hospitality and
friendship was sealed.

When I had satisfied my appetite for food—which
I moderated somewhat in conformity with what
seemed to be the local custom—I was shown to what
was to be my room, a sizable chamber on the first
floor above the ground. Left alone in it, I blinked
about me, wondering by what witchcraft these folk
of common blood had managed to commandeer a
royal palace. By comparison, my former palace in
Targoviste was a savage barracks. Here, the bed was
of inlaid wood, its covers and canopy and cushions
all green velvet. A Byzantine mirror, its gilt frame
wrought with cherubs, hung on one wall, reflecting
a fresco of great beauty painted on the opposite. I
stared at my lean, dark soldier's visage in the glass—
incompatibility with mirrors was some years in the
future still—wondering how many similar or even
richer rooms were in the vast house, and wondering
also at how little I seemed, after all, to know about
the world.

How can I, even now, describe what the house of Medici was then? I cannot. Still, I will relate a thing or two. In a sense the place was like a luxurious, or I should say aristocratic, private hotel. There were merchants of other companies lodging there during my stay, along with religious men of several ranks, agents, bankers, soldiers, travelers of every respectable kind coming and going daily. Of course Cosimo's recent death must have done something to augment this traffic, so that I probably saw it at its peak. But though I was a welcome and even pampered guest, I was only one of I know not how many.

Yet I was given what seemed to be special consideration by my hosts. Among the local people invited for dinner that evening was a man whose name I recognized as that of King Matthias's official ambassador to the official government of Florence, which was a council whose deliberations passed for the most part without great public attention. Shortly after Morsino and I were introduced, we were politely given a chance to converse alone. And as soon as he had the chance, the ambassador began to question me delicately about my mission. It seemed that he, as well as his fellow Hungarian envoys to the several Italian states, had received secret instructions from the king to the effect that a secret agent of his would soon be in Italy on urgent business. The ambassadors were not told what the business was, though some of them may have guessed; but they were strongly enjoined to give me all the aid they could.

There is a time for tight secrecy, and another time when full candor is required. I judged that the latter epoch had now arrived, and told Morsino plainly that I had been sent to find Helen Hunyadi, the runaway younger sister of our king. I did not discuss what I meant to do with Helen when I had found her, and Morsino did not ask. But he at once expressed his relief that I had arrived. Four days earlier a rumor had reached him, from two independent sources, of the presence in Florence of a woman who spoke Italian with a heavy accent that might well be Hungarian, and who had supposedly told someone that she belonged to the high Hungarian nobility. And if the stories regarding this woman's disreputable behavior were even approximately true, and if her family in fact had even a clerk's pretensions to respectability, then that family whoever they might be were in for trouble.

What disreputable behavior? I naturally asked. Morsino glanced around to make sure that we were quite alone. As he had heard the tale, a young and attractive girl of diminutive stature had recently arrived overland from Ravenna, in the company either of a troop of strolling players, or an itinerant artist, or some low company of that kind. (As Morsino admitted, he had been somewhat infected by the notorious Florentine free-thinking attitude in matters of social standing. Still, even in Florence, there were limits.) On arrival in the city, the woman had reportedly engaged in business as a prostitute. And before Ravenna, so one version of her story went, she had been aboard a Venetian galley, traveling mistress of some adventuring scoundrel or other, perhaps one of the foreign mercenary soldiers who in the fifteenth century lived on the body of Italy, as numerous as fleas on a dog. Whoever he was, this man had grown nervous and rid himself of her when he had happened to learn her true identity.

"And in your opinion, Signore Morsino, does she belong to the Hungarian nobility?"

"I have not seen her. And I do not know how much truth is in all these stories . . . but the truth is, Signore Ladislao, in the form in which the story came to me, what scared off the adventurer was the woman's claim to be none other than the legitimate sister of our blessed King Matthias himself."

"He must have found that claim convincing."

"Evidently so."

"And where is this young woman now?"

Morsino shrugged. "That I cannot say. But I suppose it likely that she is still in Florence. Of course as soon as I heard these rumors I asked my local agents to quietly find out all about her. But they have not been able to pick up her trail."

I then asked the ambassador how far he thought we should take the Medici into our confidence. He considered, then gave his opinion that I ought to tell them as much as I felt I possibly could; the woman might be able to hide from Morsino and myself in Florence, but if she were anywhere in the city there was no way that she could hide from them. Even if she were here no longer, they might well be able to learn where she had gone. The goodwill of King Matthias would certainly be important to such far-traveling traders and bankers, and there was no reason to think our hosts were anything but well disposed toward our cause.

Later that evening I had a chance to talk privately with Piero and Lorenzo, and took them almost completely into my confidence, telling them that the woman I sought was a relative of the Hungarian royal house, and that I had been sent to locate her with as little publicity as possible. Piero nodded thoughtfully and agreed to help. But when he asked me what the young woman looked like, I found myself at something of a loss. Matthias's elder relatives, in the process of reading Helen angrily out of the family, had somewhat overshot the mark, unwisely burning the few existing portraits of her as well as effacing her name from all the written records they could reach.

"She is short of stature, Signore Piero, and of a slender figure. Her face is said to be beautiful, her coloring moderately dark." Piero looked at me, perhaps revising downward his estimate of my intelligence. But beyond that I had been given no real description, and could offer none.

That very night, searchers were sent discreetly out. And in the middle of the next morning the report came in of what would now be called a solid lead. A young woman speaking a language that was very possibly Hungarian had been seen three days ago, modeling in the workshop of a rising young artist named Verrocchio—a man who could be expected to co-operate fully with me in my search; his career was blooming chiefly as a result of Medici patronage.

I held a quick conference with Morsino, in which we decided it would be better if he did not accompany me to Verrocchio's workshop. If we were able to avoid giving notice of official Hungarian interest in the woman, so much the better. But Lorenzo volunteered to come along and it was perfectly natural that he should do so. He was already known as a budding patron of the arts; he had visited the place before, and was well acquainted with its master. As far as anyone but Verrocchio himself might know, Lorenzo and I would be visiting only to inspect and possibly purchase some of the shop's output. The subject of the Hungarian woman, whether she was still there or not, could arise for discussion as if by accident.

We went through the streets on foot and without escort, which seemed to be the ordinary way for the Medici to get about in town, though Piero with his gout frequently used a litter. Every few paces, or so it seemed to me, Lorenzo was greeted by someone high or low, and as often as not he paused to exchange good wishes and bits of gossip.

"Do you think the woman we want is this artist's mistress?" I asked him when we seemed to have a moment clear for private conversation.

Lorenzo paused in the middle of a narrow way,

smiling and gesturing with an exaggerated flourish for
an elderly woman carrying a market basket of vegetables to go ahead of him. I had been told again
and again that this family of wealthy merchants who
were my hosts were also the virtual dictators of
Florence; never before had I seen dictators who
behaved in such a fashion.

"I do not think so," he answered me when we were
alone again. "I know Andrea's tastes . . . no, I think
not."

The workshop was a smaller, poorer place than I
had been expecting. One large room, well lit by
skylights and windows, took up most of the interior
space in a building rudely constructed of planks and
timbers. Off this large room a few doors led to smaller
chambers in the rear, and to a yard. All was primitive as a stable, or very nearly so. Verrocchio its
master was rough-looking too, a stocky man of about
thirty with a gross face, dressed in workman's clothing covered with various kinds of stains. He greeted
Lorenzo with warmth, and told us that his poor house
was ours—then grew nervous when Lorenzo whispered in his ear something of the true purpose of our
visit.

In the middle of the big room, under a roof
panel open to the clear Florentine sky, an old man
with rheumy eyes was posing in loose Biblical-
looking garb while a single unshaven apprentice
sketched him in charcoal on a prepared panel. After
stammering some shy greetings to us, they both went
on with the job. The door to one of the rear rooms
stood open, revealing an elderly female domestic
scrubbing at a pot.

Lorenzo and I sat at one side of the studio for a
while, playing the role of customers while its master spoke with us about current projects. Or, rather,
the tough-looking artist spoke with his young patron
who rather resembled a Mafia don of a later century,

while I listened and tried to look as if I understood them or at least was interested in what they talked about. Then, with a hint from Lorenzo to guide my taste, I purchased a small, newly-wrought gold chain.

Lorenzo then said that he had an important commission in mind; for the supposed heavy business discussion Verrocchio conducted us into the privacy of what must have been his own bedroom. The chamber was small, its walls heavily decorated with paper sketches. As the elder guest I was granted the single chair; Lorenzo perched on a chest, and Verrocchio sat on the rumpled bed, the only other article of substantial furniture available.

Yes, *signori,* about that girl, of course. She had been gone for the last two days, and Verrocchio did not know where, any more than he knew from where she had come. Some weeks ago one of the apprentices had brought her in, saying that he wanted to use her as a model and that she was willing to pose for others also. So she had been, even posing naked without protest, which had convinced Verrocchio that she was a whore. A good model, though. He had given her food, a place to sleep with the female servants, and a little money once or twice. She had spoken Italian badly and with an odd accent— certainly not the Greek accent so common in Florence since the refugees from fallen Constantinople had swarmed in; but outside of that, and a certain odd beauty in her face, he had thought her no different from any of a hundred other vagrants and runaways who could be picked up in the streets and taverns. Yes, somewhat better looking than most of them, that was all. Here on the wall were a couple of sketches of her made by his apprentices, if we would like to see.

I naturally looked with interest, but only one sketch showed the model's face at all clearly, and it had distorted her features into such an artificial expression of heavensent rapture that I thought it would be useless for identification. I made no comment.

Verrocchio talked on, nervously. He had had vague plans of posing the girl himself—yes, there was something truly lovely about her, *signori*—but the next thing he knew, she was gone, no one knew where.

I asked: "Which apprentice was it who brought her round? That stubbly fellow out there?"

"Yes. Would you gentlemen like to talk to him?"

We went out into the large room again, where Lorenzo with his usual good humor approached the dark-cheeked youth. Would he settle a small bet? That young woman who was here until a few days ago, what language did she really speak, besides her bad Italian?

The pseudo-prophet with the rheumy eyes got a chance to rest from posing. The apprentice put down his tools. He dropped things and was upset at being questioned. He stuttered that he really didn't know, he didn't think that he could tell us much.

I demonstrated what Hungarian sounded like. Yes, said the nervous youth, that might have been it. But he wasn't really sure. He had never talked to the girl much and didn't know her name. True, he had picked her up in a tavern, and brought her here for some modeling, but you gentlemen know how that goes— excuse me, perhaps you don't—but a man doesn't always learn their names. No, he didn't know where she was now. She had seemed unhappy—she had gone off—

It seemed to me that there was more to be learned from this man, but he was not mine to question as I willed. He was probably a valuable worker here. Perhaps later, I thought.

"Let us talk to the servants, then," said Lorenzo, still effortlessly maintaining the pose of a small bet to be settled. "And to the other apprentices."

The few servants were soon casually processed. I allowed them to get away with knowing nothing whatsoever, at least for the time being. As for apprentices, Verrocchio informed us that he presently had only three. The second, a somewhat younger and handsomer lad than the one we had already spoken to, was called in from the yard where he had been mixing pigments. This one, acting not too bright, only giggled slightly and glanced nervously at his master when I asked him how well he had known the woman; he did confirm, though, that my Hungarian sounded like the language the young woman had muttered to herself in when she was upset.

"What was she upset about?"

The youth made an eloquent gesture with both arms, that seemed to take in all of life.

"I have only one more apprentice, gentlemen. He lives at home, but is due to arrive here at any time now. Will you honor me by waiting?"

"It is we who are honored by your company, maestro," said Lorenzo, and sat down again for some more leisured conversation about Art. The staff went back to work. Presently the lad we were waiting for appeared. He looked to me no more than about twelve years of age, though quite tall and strong for his years. He was better dressed than either of his older colleagues.

Lorenzo, beginning to put a question to him, paused in mid-sentence. "Say, I think I know you. Your father is Ser Piero the notary, is he not? Yes, of course, and how is he?"

"Father is well, *signore.*"

Again we went through our list of questions. This time Lorenzo, as an acquaintance, did most of the talking.

"The girl perhaps talked to you about herself? Your good master here says that you spent more time drawing and painting her than any of the others did."

"Yes, she modeled for me many days. But we did not talk very much."

"Perhaps," I put in, "you have a drawing, at least a sketch, some good likeness of her that you can show me?" I realized that our fiction about the bet was by now too tattered to be of any other further use. "Since you say you put in so many hours at it. Can you draw well?"

The boy looked at me. There was something intrinsically cold, withdrawn, about him. "I can draw. I threw some of my sketches away, but I think there is something. I will see what I can find." He turned away.

"Stay," commanded Lorenzo. "The important thing is, do you know where she is now?"

"Yes, *signore*, I think I may know." We all stared at him. "In the *palazzo* Boccalini."

This obviously meant something to Lorenzo and Verrocchio, who exchanged looks. Then the master of the studio demanded of his young apprentice: "How do you know this?"

"I saw her on the street, two days ago, arguing with two young men of that family. They were starting to pull on her arms, and laughing. She was not laughing. And she has not been back here since."

Verrocchio looked all about him, as if calling on witnesses to this strange behavior. "Yet you said nothing to anyone here about this? Why?"

"No one asked me about it, until now."

Verrocchio glanced at us, then waved the youth away. When he was gone, Lorenzo said to me: "The Boccalini are no friends of my family. And what the boy said may be true, for they have a bad reputation of taking advantage of undefended young women. If she went with them, it may well have been unwillingly. I believe the older men of their family are still at their summer villa, leaving the young gallants unsupervised in town. We will do what we can to find out for certain whether she is there."

Verrocchio, chewing on his lip, had moved a pace or two away; he was not anxious to take part in these intrigues. At this point the young boy came back, lugging a fairly large wooden panel. "The little sketches are all gone," he said laconically.

His master took the painting from him and held it upright on a table, in good light. A twelve-year-old has done *that*? was my own first reaction, even untutored as I was in the difficulties of the art. For once, I think, Lorenzo's judgement was the same as mine; he scowled intensely and murmured something. Verrocchio, who must have seen the panel before, still sighed faintly with what sounded very much like envy. He snatched up a small brush from the table, and hastily flicked in his signature across a lower corner where part of the background had been finished.

He sighed again. "Yes, this is she, Signore Ladislao, an excellent likeness. From this you may know her. If she is where the boy says she is, I pray Jesus and San Lorenzo that you may bring her safely out. If that is what Your Honor really wants to do."

Lorenzo was still marveling at the painting in silence. Then he asked: "The boy really did this?"

The master nodded. "Indeed he did, Signore Lorenzo. I watched with my own eyes."

What impressed me most, at my then primitive level of artistic judgement, was of course the marvelously lifelike character of the face, which like most of the figure was completely finished; parts of the background, as I think I have mentioned, were still not done. With this face before me, I felt I must know the model at once if ever I saw her in the flesh. And this suggested to me another point: such a perfect, breathing likeness, if allowed to remain here, might someday serve as evidence in the hands of King Matthias's enemies, proof that his sister had indeed once been here and posing.

"I would like to take this painting with me," I said, reaching for my purse once more. "What is its price?"

But this time the master of the shop would have none of my gold. "Please, *signore*, you will honor me by accepting this trifle as a gift." Verrocchio made the offer quickly and easily; I am sure he calculated that in the long run he would not lose by such a gesture, which ought to bind him closer to the Medici in friendship; and, anyway, the gift was not all *that* expensive. Not in 1464, though within only a few decades the value of ready-made art from Florentine studios would increase tremendously.

"It is only the work of a novice, *signore*, though he is gifted beyond—" Verrocchio broke off, catching sight of the boy still standing nearby, silently attentive. "Back to your work now, Leonardo."

SEVEN

So.

It may be that some of my readers, equipped with good memories or else forearmed by a fortuitously recent reading of some art history, anticipated the little revelation at the previous chapter's end. But before these readers congratulate themselves too heartily, let them consider why none of those supposedly expert folk involved in the art auction uttered that most potent name. Why, barring one hint by Ellison Seabright, there has not been even the most tentative suggestion along that line. Two points awarded for the correct answer, and more on the subject later. For the moment let it suffice that the reader has now caught up with Mr. Thorn in this much at least: that Magdalen was definitely not a Verrocchio, worth perhaps the quarter of a million dollars or so that Ellison Seabright paid for it; it was instead a genuine Leonardo da Vinci, heretofore unknown to the experts as such, but if its origin could be verified worth easily twenty times that much.

The announcement of the missing aircraft caused Mr. Thorn to cut short his visit to the Seabright mansion as soon as he politely could—which, under the circumstances of confusion prevailing there, was not long. He took his leave without offering his host any further revelations of his own about the painting. He had not been about to provide that gross, half-clever criminal with any very truthful revelations anyway. The two of them vaguely agreed that they would talk to each other again sometime and with that matters between them were left hanging.

Driving his rented Blazer back into the more plebian regions of the city, Mr. Thorn felt unhappy for several reasons. First, the painting was once more out of his reach, gone again, somewhere, where he could not even look at it. Second—or perhaps really first—it is always a painful experience, that dawning realization that one has underestimated an opponent. That first moment when the placidly grazing prey turns suddenly, baring its own fangs, unsheathing its own sharp claws . . . and, perhaps thirdly, perhaps worst of all, is the suspicion that one has finally grown old, become ineffectual through overconfidence.

Mr. Thorn, still determined of course to have his painting, but denied it, and realizing now that he did not even know who his true adversary was, would have liked to go back in time two days, and start over again in the auction room. That being impossible even for him, he decided to do the next best thing, which was to come as close to starting over as he could.

Sighting a public phone booth, he stopped and made a call. Twenty minutes later he was ringing the front doorbell of a modest house on an anonymously modest Phoenix side street.

Robinson Miller, eyes full of subtle suspicions, appeared inside and let Thorn in. At Miller's feet a small dog, on getting his first whiff of the visitor, yapped once in extreme surprise, and then was still. Behind Miller in the living room was the sofa that Mary once had mentioned, looking indeed as if it might have spent part of a long and adventurous career inside a Salvation Army store. Mary herself was just rising from its sagging cushions. Tonight her jeans had been replaced by shorts, revealing legs quite as attractive as Thorn had expected them to be. She wore a blue vinyl vest, doubtless because there was no bra beneath her blue T-shirt. With her usual eagerness for any new development, she greeted the visitor more freely than Miller had. "This is a surprise, Mr. Thorn. Glad to see you. Something's happened, hasn't it?"

"Yes. Though I am not sure exactly what." Thorn took the offered armchair, a place of honor that got the main benefit of the laboring window air conditioner. He declined well-intentioned offers of coffee and beer, and looked calmingly at the small dog who was edging close to offer worship. To the humans he related the essentials of his visit to the Seabright house.

Mary was quite as upset as Thorn had been to hear about the missing plane, though her disquiet had a nobler basis. "Then the plane is really down? That's bad. How many people were on it?"

"Oh, I am sure that by this time it is down, somewhere. I gather that it carried only the pilot, a man named Gliddon. A search is to be started in the morning."

"Gliddon," said Mary, and made a face. "I didn't like him." Still her dislike hardly seemed to make any difference in her concern over the pilot's fate. "When I lived at the house he was always in and out, though I never knew what he did. It must have been some kind of work for Ellison."

Robinson Miller said to Thorn: "Do I understand you to mean that you think the plane didn't really crash?"

"Correct me if I am wrong," said Thorn, "but I believe that the land between here and Santa Fe is somewhat sparsely populated?"

Miller nodded. "Five hundred miles of nothing."

"Mountains, deserts, some forests," Mary amended. "Late last spring two Air Force planes from the missile range at Alamogordo were lost. They crashed right out in the open and in spite of a big search it was months before the wreckage was found. At least it's not winter now. I suppose if Gliddon survived a crash in the mountains he's got a chance."

"Somehow," said Thorn, "I have little doubt that he survived."

Mary looked puzzled; she didn't get it yet. Miller said: "I suppose Seabright was having a fit. Though not over the missing man, of course."

Thorn nodded. "He was going through the motions of one who is, as you say, having a fit over some lost property. Barking orders, phoning hither and yon, demanding explanations, demanding action. But I . . . have had some opportunity of observing humanity under various kinds of stress. And I am sometimes able to see through efforts at deception. And—this is why I have come to talk to you tonight—I think Mr. Seabright was not truly surprised by the news that his masterpiece and his aircraft and its pilot were missing. Indeed, I suspect that one reason I was invited to his house tonight was to provide him with a neutral witness, able to testify to his surprise and his dismay."

Some of Mary's old fierce delight quickly returned. She thumped the arm of the battered sofa. "I believe you!" she cried. "He's pulled another trick! He's getting away with it again!"

But Miller was frowning, shaking his head. "The suggestion being, I suppose, that Seabright is somehow spiriting the painting away into hiding by faking a plane crash. But he's just bought it and paid for it. Why the hell should he steal it from himself?"

Thorn had his ideas on that subject. But he said nothing for the moment.

"Insurance money!" Mary pounced.

Her lawyer was still shaking his head. "No, I don't think so. That kind of thing isn't easy to get away with—"

"Neither is murder, but he got away with killing Helen and Del."

"—and *anyway*, since the painting was being carried on his private aircraft I doubt that any insurance coverage on it would be in force." Miller's gaze focused suddenly on Thorn. "You're not from some insurance company, are you?"

"No," Thorn said patiently. "I am a collector, as is Seabright."

A few feet away, in the kitchen, the telephone began to ring. Miller got up to answer it.

"Mary." Thorn looked at her intently. "Why did Delaunay give you that painting?"

His gaze did not bother her. "Why? I told you. Out of gratitude, for my helping Helen. He was that kind of a guy, I guess. He knew I'd sell the painting, I'm sure. He just wanted me to have some money to use, helping other kids."

"You say you think Ellison knew about this gift? How can you be sure?"

But Mary was looking toward the kitchen doorway. Miller was standing there, rather like some interviewer with a microphone, holding out toward Mary the yellow telephone receiver on its helixed cord. But the look on his face was that of a man in shock, and Thorn got to his feet.

"Who? What?" asked Mary vaguely, standing also.

Miller licked his bearded lips. "She says . . . she's Helen."

There was a pause in which no one did anything. Then Mary sprang forward. In a moment she was holding the phone pressed against her disheveled hair. "Who is this? If this is supposed to be some kind of a joke, it isn't . . ."

A feminine voice at the other end of the connection had begun to answer. It was a quiet voice, and its tones were mottled and distorted by an imperfect connection somewhere, and at first Mr. Thorn could not make out the words. But Mary could, and they had an immediate effect. Her face lost color, and her hand holding the receiver slumped a little. "What?" she asked weakly.

The voice at the other end made itself louder. Now both men standing by in the kitchen could hear it well enough to distinguish words. "Mary, this isn't any joke. It's me. I can't come back now, it's too dangerous. Anyway, I don't really want to. Everything's fine for me the way things are. But I wanted to talk to you. You're my best friend, Mary." Mr. Thorn, listening hard, thought there was a certain dazed quality in the voice; a disconnection from present reality, as if it might be reciting lines learned for a play.

"Helen? What do you mean, dangerous?" Mary's own voice now sounded no less dazed. "Why? Where are you?"

"You know why, Mary, if I come back *he's* going to try to kill me again. Look, I wanted to tell you, Mary, I'm sorry about running away again, after all your work with me and all. But there was nothing else for me to do. Please don't try to look for me again, this time I'm gone for good."

"Baby, if this is really you . . . you tell me not to look for you? How can you call me up like this and say a thing like that?"

"You always said you wanted me to have a happy life someday. So now I'm going to be able to have a happy life. So let me alone."

Miller stood beside Mary where she sat in a kitchen chair. He was slowly bending over her, getting his ear closer and closer to the phone in her hand; and meanwhile his eyes squinted, as if he strained to see something in the far distance. Thorn waited motionless in the kitchen doorway, and he also was listening very carefully.

Mary was starting to recover from her first shock. "Listen, if this *is* Helen speaking . . . if this is Helen, tell me who was killed? Whose body did I stumble over in the dark?"

"There was a girl you didn't know about in the house that night. A girl named Annie, just a runaway from somewhere, she didn't count. Only Uncle Del knew that she was there, and he was killed too . . . but Mary, I don't want to talk about all that any more. I've found someone who I thought was lost to me forever. We're going to do real things, and it's all going to be okay. He's going to put me in real movies. Someday."

"Real movies? What do you mean, you've found someone? Who? Where are you? Helen, this can't be you."

"It's me, Mary. Remember what you once told me, about something you said you'd never told another soul? About you and your boyfriend in Idaho? Want me to play that back to you now?"

"Oh my God." Mary turned still more pale. "My God, it is you, baby."

"Not your goddam *baby*." The distant voice turned petulant. Still a poor contact somewhere in the wires distorted it. "Just let me alone, please. Oh, Mary, I'm going to be so happy."

Mr. Thorn, listening, had doubts.

"Helen? Tell me where you are?"

"Goodbye, Mary." It was a lament, a ghost's farewell.

"No, Helen. Wait. Where are you? Helen?"

A click; what connection there had been was gone. Mary talked into nothingness for a few seconds, and jiggled the switch at her end of the line. After that she could only hang up too.

Then she lifted a dreamer's face to the two men. "You heard her. It was her. What do we do now?"

Miller appeared unconvinced. "It did sort of sound like her voice," he admitted. "Not that I ever talked to her that much, but . . ." He had to pause to clear his throat. "If that really was her, if Helen's really still alive, do you know what that means? That masterpiece that Ellison Seabright just paid for is really still her property. In the legal sense, I mean," he hastened to add when Mary looked at him.

"Even if Seabright has paid for it?" Thorn asked.

"Absolutely. No question about it. There'd be a devil of a legal and financial mess to untangle. But the painting would have to be held in trust for Helen, as per Delaunay's will. Assuming *he's* really dead. Wow," added the lawyer, looking at Thorn. "And the painting was on that plane."

"The matter of the missing plane," said Thorn, "is now perhaps explained."

Miller nodded slowly. "If Helen is still alive, and Seabright somehow found out about it, he'd then have a good motive to get the painting out of the way. Maybe sell it secretly; there are collectors who would buy."

Mary for once was not delighted to discuss villainy. She slumped in the kitchen chair, not looking like her usual self. "Rob, shall we call in the police and tell them about the call? How are we even going to start looking for her if we don't do that?"

"Indeed," put in Thorn, "how are we to start looking in any case, whether the police are notified or not?"

"Then you advise against calling them?" Miller was fumbling nervously for his pipe.

"My advice is that we first take thought: What exactly can we tell the authorities, and what will they believe? All three of us heard someone on the phone, but which of us can swear convincingly that it was

Helen? Certainly not I, who never heard Miss Seabright's voice."

Miller, having found his pipe, held it in his hand forgotten. "I did—a few times. But I couldn't honestly say. Mary?"

Mary had her face down in her hands now. "Maybe . . . I don't know. Maybe it could have been someone else. I saw Helen lying on the floor in the Seabright house, dead. All shot to pieces."

Thorn asked: "You recognized the victim's face?"

"Her mouth was almost gone, her lower jaw. I never realized till then that guns did things like that. Her hair . . . it looked like Helen's hair. I assumed it was Helen. Everybody did. It never entered my mind that it might not be her, because I never had any idea that there could have been another girl in the house. 'Annie.' Whoever it was on the phone just now said 'Annie.' Did you hear?"

Thorn and Miller both signed agreement. Mary went on: "It's crazy. I don't know any Annie, and I don't believe there could have been another girl. Dressed in Helen's robe?"

Thorn prodded: "But is it not possible? Some runaway, perhaps, being given shelter? That only Helen and her uncle knew about?"

Mary hesitated. "Delaunay would've *told* me, if he'd been doing that. Let me think about it. It's not absolutely impossible, I suppose."

Miller was now inspecting his pipe as if it were some interesting alien artifact. "Assume we went to the authorities with this phone call, and could get them to halfway believe us. Then ordinarily, you know, a court order could possibly be obtained, the body in question could be exhumed, a certain identification made. Fingerprints, dental records, and so on. But Helen—if she was the girl who was short—was cremated."

"That's right," murmured Mary. "It was the family

tradition." Rotating her head as if to ease weary neck muscles, she looked at the men. She seemed now to have pulled herself essentially together. "But—oh, this is awful—the more I think about it, the more I feel sure that it must have been Helen on the phone just now. That dead girl in the house . . . she *could* have been someone else, although I don't know who. But the girl on the phone mentioned something, a thing that happened to me in Idaho." Mary sighed and looked at Miller as if asking to be forgiven. "Something that I know I've never talked about to anyone but Helen."

"But that Helen might have talked about," said Thorn.

"Well . . ."

Thorn went on: "The girl on the phone said 'he' would try to kill her again if she came back."

Neither of the others wanted to comment. There was a short pause. Then Miller said: "She—whoever it was—said something else that I thought was strange. About being put into 'real movies,' if I heard it right."

"You did," said Thorn. "And mentioned reunion with someone she had thought 'lost forever.' Who had Helen lost forever, Mary?"

Mary did not reply at once. Miller had put away his pipe and was massaging the back of her neck, her shoulders. She leaned back in the chair, yielding to the motion. "I don't know," she murmured at last. "She's run off . . . it'll be a rerun of last time, I'm afraid."

Thorn asked patiently: "What happened last time?"

She looked up at him, her head bobbing with the rhythm of the continuing massage. "Helen ran away and got as far as Chicago. Some jerk there had her acting in porn movies. She wasn't basically like that at all."

"I see. And do you think that this jerk, as you

call him, is the long-lost lover she has now rejoined?"

"Oh no. Not him, never. She doesn't hate herself that much. But she did talk to me about someone else she met on the road, a boy who meant something to her. She told me his name was Pat. I don't know if he was involved in the porn factory thing or not, but she must have known him at about the same time."

"Pat was a runaway too?"

Mary thought. "I got the impression from Helen that he was older, a little older anyway. Not a runaway any more, an independent adult. No, independent is not the right word for what adults are like when they've grown up that way, on the road. I've seen a bunch of them. Lost, usually. Isolated. That's what they tend to be like when they manage to grow up at all."

Miller said: "Come to think of it, I do seem to remember hearing Helen once mention someone called Pat. With a kind of wistful look in her eye."

"O'Grandison, that was his last name!" Mary had suddenly come up with it. "Oh, Rob, that must have been Helen on the phone. Oh, my poor baby. I remember now. She used to say Pat had talked to her about making good films, wishing he could help make them, something like that."

And here, unexpected by either man, came tears. Miller, still rubbing Mary's neck tenderly, tried to react lightly. "Mother Mary," he joked.

"Don't laugh at me."

"I'm not." He squeezed her neck muscles firmly again and looked at Thorn. "What do you think?"

"I think," said Thorn, "that in the matter of making vile films in Chicago, and in the matter of this Mr. O'Grandison, I may be able to learn something. I repeat that I am not an official investigator of any kind, but in the course of an active life one forms connections."

EIGHT

My Medici connection was going to be of no direct
help in learning whether the woman I sought was in
fact within the walls of the *palazzo* Boccalini. In fact
if the alliance became known to the Boccalini it would
have the opposite effect, for the two families were
rivals, at odds in all sorts of Florentine affairs. My
friends the Medici were of course the stronger, but
I could not expect them to use their power too
nakedly. Their rule in the city was a subtle thing,
based on the maintenance of harmony among factions;
and although King Matthias's gratitude would mean
much to them as traders, it would not be worth
upsetting a Florentine political balance already teetering with the impact of Cosimo's recent death.
Lorenzo assured me of his family's continued help,
but also made sure that I understood its limits. If I
was willing to be patient, in a few days a Boccalini
servant could doubtless be bribed, a spy perhaps
planted in their household.

But my nature was impatient to begin with, and
anyway it did not seem to me that I had time to
spare. If Helen was not after all with the Boccalini,

I was wasting time; on the other hand, if she was, not only might her life be in peril but her identity could be exposed at any time. In view of this I told Lorenzo that speed was necessary; and, within a few hours of leaving Verrocchio's workshop, my young benefactor and I had agreed upon another scheme.

At that time there was in Florence—I think the building may be still standing, near the Mercato Vecchio—an inn known as the Tavern of the Snail. This snail was much frequented by the adventurous young bloods of the leading families, the Boccalini in particular. Therefore we felt safe in gambling that one or two Boccalini youth would approach the place that very night, or at worst within the next few evenings. As events turned out, our most optimistic hopes were justified.

Lorenzo had three or four reliable men stationed in ambush, along the route our game would most probably take. The scion of the Medici did not, of course, place himself among the ambushers. He could not afford to have his involvement in the affair discovered, and in any case his skills were not those of physical violence. My own part was to wait as patiently as possible in concealment nearby. As soon as the pretended robbers had sprung their trap I was to bound out, crying for the watch, and rush upon them with drawn sword.

As I have said, we were lucky on the first night, and carried it off well enough. One of the paid ruffians, playing his part with cheeky skill—there is nothing easier than to ruin a plan of this kind by a lack of convincing effort by all concerned—offered me resistance, whereupon I ran him through the arm, a touch of authenticity he had perhaps not been expecting. After I had drawn blood, there was nothing more to be seen in the dark street of the attackers, and nothing heard of them but their fast-flying footsteps in retreat.

My eyes had had a long time to grow accustomed to the poor light, and I could get a fairly good look at the two Boccalini. They had managed to get their backs against a wall, side by side, and were now slumped down somewhat in that position. Both had weapons drawn, both were panting and cursing, and one was bleeding in a minor way. Besides ourselves the street was now deserted, the hour of curfew long since past. As a rule curfew received little attention from young hell-raisers like these, of good political connections. Nearby dogs were ravening bravely at our recent dueling noises, their canine courage fortified by stone walls.

Warily I moved a little closer to the two dim figures. "Are you hurt, gentlemen? The pigs have taken to their heels."

The Boccalini snarled, grumbled, groaned, at Fate, at the world in general, at their attackers, at me. Then the smaller of the pair stood up straight and offered me at last some words of gratitude. From Lorenzo's briefing I thought I could recognize him as the eldest brother of the younger generation, Sandro.

We all three sheathed our blades, and introductions were informally exchanged. It was apparent that Sandro's younger brother Guilio was bleeding from his wrist rather more than could cheerfully be disregarded. An attempt at bandaging the wound with a strip of clothing failed to stanch the flow sufficiently, and the two young men decided that the tavern could wait, and that a retreat to their home was in order. It may have been in the minds of both brothers that assassination rather than robbery could have been the motive for the attack. Their family was certainly not without enemies, and assassins would be more likely than footpads to have a second try. At any rate, I was invited to go with them, and accepted with inner jubilation that I had not had to spend hours with them in the Tavern of the Snail before the invitation came.

Their house, no great distance away, was as
Lorenzo had described it to me, a smaller, older, less
well-built version of the Medici palace. A great barred
door was opened to our shouts and pounding, and
at once there came a rush of startled servants to care
for Guilio. I followed the excitement through halls
and a small open courtyard to a room where there
was a soft couch for him to lie upon. On the way I
kept my eyes open and took note of several girls and
young women, dressed differently than the regular
servants, in a gaudy style suggestive of the bordello.
Though I looked sharply at each face, I could not
recognize my Magdalen.

No sooner had we laid Guilio on this couch than
with another rush we were surrounded by three more
young men of the family, the brother and two cousins of my street companions. For the next hour things
were operatic. Mighty oaths of outrage and revenge
rang in the stone rooms. Shouts and gestures
expressed extravagant grief and rage. Sword-wavings
were directed at the unknown dastards who had done
this deed; but they were absent and the naked blades
imperilled only the help. It was unanimously agreed,
a number of times over, that a punitive expedition
must be launched into the night as soon as Guilio
had been properly bandaged—a purported physician
who lived nearby had now been sent for, and spider-
webs were being gathered as a coagulant. The correct target for this retaliatory raid could not be agreed
upon, however, and all the talk came to nothing, as
I had surmised it must. In the morning the young
men of the family were going to have to take the
practical step of informing their elders at their suburban villa; at present, though, there was really
nothing to be done but to make sure that all doors
and windows were secure, and then get on with the
nightly debauch. Guilio, once the doctor had tied his
arm up properly, was not so badly off that he would

be forced to abstain from this. And of course I, as their heaven-sent ally and savior, was hospitably invited to take part.

Looking back, I see that perhaps I have not made it clear enough that from my first entry into the house, even with all the other things they had to shout about, my young hosts made me welcome with thanks and praise and every courtesy, extravagantly expressed. Like their greater Medici rivals in the Bankers' Guild, the Boccalini were often dependent for success on foreign men who lived by the sword, and the family habit of politeness to such had been ingrained in all its members.

"Have some more wine, Cousin Ladislao—you don't mind if I call you that? You have shown yourself more than a cousin tonight. Wine, and how about a woman or two? There are plenty here to choose from."

Indeed, I could see there were, all of them young and well-formed if not all pretty. Drawn by the excitement, ten or a dozen of these girls were nearby, a couple petting Guilio, others lounging about, chatting idly among themselves in a manner that showed they could not be ordinary servants. Some of them had managed to acquire rich clothing, and their confinement here, if such it was, appeared to be on quite lenient terms. Doubtless for all of them life here in the *palazzo* was a definite improvement over what it had been on the streets outside. I saw no one who looked like an unwilling kidnap victim. But neither had I yet seen one who wore the face of Magdalen.

"By the beard of St. Peter," I commented, "there are more women here than in the tavern, I would guess." I reached out a hand to squeeze a passing buttock, whose owner paused briefly to give me back a nervous smile. I drank some wine—not much. "But I am a hard man to please, gentlemen. Without meaning the least disrespect to your hospitality, I must admit that these wenches look to me like so many cows filled with milk. To a man like myself these are as nothing. I want fire." At this point I emitted a loud, completely unFlorentine belch; and I must confess that it was a deliberate attempt to express bold worldliness.

My hosts averaged about fifteen years younger than myself, and I was still far from an old man. They were duly impressed, and exchanged glances.

"It is something more fiery than these that you require," mused Sandro.

"Something different, at least." I waved a haughty hand.

A fat genuine cousin, Allessandro, raised his brows, hiccuped, and offered a suggestion. "There is a stableboy here, I am told, who plays the part of a girl quite—"

"Bah!"

Sandro was coming visibly to a decision. "Nay, old cousin Ladislao, come along with me. If it is fire you want, real female fire, then I think that I can promise you a treat."

The others, understanding what he meant after delays corresponding to their several states of drunkenness, hiccuped, shouted, and belched their approval. Sandro rose, and with a flourish took up one of the candles from the table, signing me to do likewise. Then with another great gesture he bade me follow him.

We went up one flight of stairs after another, to a cramped top floor where some of the heat of the past day still lingered in the roof whose beams forced me to duck at almost every step. I counseled myself as we climbed that if this rare treat proved not to be the one I sought, I had better enjoy it anyway, or appear to do so. If I stayed on good terms with the Boccalini, sooner or later I would find out what had happened to Helen. If they had really taken her.

With my luck, I thought, she was probably at that
very moment on her way to Naples, or to England,
or the Sultan's court.

But my luck was not that bad. We came to a
heavy, crude door, from which Sandro took down
a bar. Then, having to duck his own head at this
point, he went in ahead of me with his candle. The
room was small and windowless, meaner than my
own cell back in the Tower of Solomon, and ovenish
with heat. A girl lay on the floor. Her face was in
shadow and she appeared so small my first thought
was that they were offering me a kidnapped child.
But as she sat up on the strawed floor I saw the
soft proportions of a grown woman's body under the
rough shift that appeared to be her only garment.
I noticed now that one of her ankles was secured
with a fine, bright, elegant pet's chain to a verti-
cal beam supporting the low roof.

My guide held up his candle, that I might see the
captive better. "She has been here two days, continu-
ally insulting us," he explained, rather like a physician detailing the symptoms of a mysterious illness
to a visiting specialist. "She will have nothing to do
with us willingly, gentle though we are."

The girl's face, when at last I could see it under
her fall of darkly matted hair, was bruised as well as
grimy. Yet I was certain of it at first glance. "Why
then did you bring her here?" I asked.

Either Sandro did not hear the question, or he
preferred to let it pass. "Two nights ago she was
scratching and biting like a wildcat, my brothers and
I can all testify to that. All the fire anyone might want,
my friend. Myself, I haven't been up here since
then—maybe she is a little weaker now, I don't think
she has been fed much."

The girl's eyes, that at first had blinked and
squinted even in the weak candlelight, were steadily
open now. She had the self-numbed, withdrawn look

of a brave prisoner. With gentle caution I put a hand under her chin and raised her face more fully into the candles' glow. "She'll nip you," Sandro warned. But she did not.

Yes, beyond doubt my first impression had been correct. This was precocious Leonardo's model—but a Magdalen who now looked as if she had lapsed from divine forgiveness. She would indeed have liked to bite me, or to spit at me at least, but she no longer quite dared to do so. The Boccalini, not trying very hard, had taught her that much in two days.

I set down my own candlestick on the floor. "I thank you, cousin. This is what I wanted. I will see you in the morning."

"I wish you a sound night's sleep," laughed Sandro. And with a bow my benefactor left, taking his own candle with him and leaving the door ajar.

I could hear him starting down the stairs. As far as I could tell the girl and I were now the only people on the whole upper floor of the great house. With a tired sigh I sat down on the dusty boards beside my candle, and then in the afterthought turned and bawled after Sandro: "Send up some water and wine! And food!" There came some unclear words in reply.

Waiting, I sat looking at the girl and thinking about her in silence. She was holding her torn shift together with both hands, and leaning against the wooden post to which her chain was fastened. She was looking back at me rather as if I were some inanimate tool with which she was going to be hurt.

A small padlock held a loop of the chain around the wooden post. Another similar lock bound another loop round her tiny ankle, which was certainly smaller than my wrist. The little room stank. In one far corner was a crude clay chamber pot. A dish and cup for food and water, both empty now, waited on the floor closer to the door, through which a little air had now begun to circulate.

In a few minutes a slave girl, one of the working servants, came up with the provisions I had called for. As soon as this servant had left the two of us alone again, I pushed the silver utensils within Helen's reach and sat back. After a quick glance at me she grabbed up the bright cup and drank thirstily, then began to eat the biscuits and sausage. She kept what must have been a half-starved appetite under careful control, like one who has had experience of what a sudden load of food might do to a shrunken stomach. Between measured bites, she cast at me more calculating looks than before.

The pauses in her eating began to grow longer, and I helped myself to a portion of the remaining food. Helen sat back on her haunches and looked at me steadily. "And now?"

She had spoken in her bad Italian; I answered in her native Hungarian: "Now you are going to come away from here. With me."

It was a shock. Until that moment I do not think that she had seen me as anything but another rapist to be endured somehow. But now she started. Her expression changed rapidly, as surprise was followed by the beginning of understanding, and that in turn by relief—a relief mixed with bitterness, but still a great liberation for all that.

She said in Hungarian: "Our Lady be thanked, for she has heard my prayers. I will certainly go to my brother, even, to get myself out of this."

"I should think you would." I did not tell Helen that returning her to Hungary was not one of the two options allowed me by her brother's royal command.

I moved close to Helen now, and drew my dagger. The bright links of the chain had scraped her slender ankle sorely where she must have tried to force it off. Holding her ankle and the chain against the floorboards, I could feel a delicate trembling in her leg, in her whole body. My dagger, a crude northern weapon, bit silently through the links when I leaned my weight upon it. It took me another moment to cut the other end of the chain free of the lock that held it round the post.

The blade went back into its sheath. Helen was still trembling, with the relief of the strain of fear. She told me later that she had been utterly convinced that the Boccalini were never going to let her go alive after what they had done to her against her will. Probably she was right. No one would take very much notice, or remember it for long, if a street waif simply disappeared. On the other hand a survivor telling stories would have been at least somewhat detrimental to the family's standing in the eyes of business associates and of the church.

"He is not really a savage man," Helen told me, rubbing her freed ankle, and at first I thought that she meant Sandro. "But he is king." Her eyes lifted, and for a moment I saw a spark of her own royalty in them. "And your name?"

"Here I am called Ladislao. But at His Majesty's court, Wladislaus." I could see at once that the name suggested nothing in particular to her. All to the good, I thought. Had the lady known me by reputation, my task might well have been still further complicated.

As it stood, it was quite demanding enough.

One of the options allowed me by the king was to report back to him that with my own eyes I had seen his sister safely and anonymously dead. For me to take that course would mean at least that the family name was guarded from any further damage. And it would be possible to hope that in time the scandals already generated might be forgotten.

The only other alternative I had been given by Matthias was to try to civilize the girl—which would of course require that first I take her to wife.

Startled though I had been when the king first broached this plan to me, I had now been able to

mull it over long enough to appreciate the reason-
ing behind it. I had been forced to conclude that from
the king's viewpoint it had merit, the advantage of
making some positive good at least a possibility.

Consider. For Matthias to *somehow* put an end to
Helen's escapades was imperative. They put him in
danger of becoming an international laughingstock,
and a king who has that happen to him is lucky if
he retains his crown, let alone such a position of
world leadership as the ruler of Hungary was grasping
for. So he had to either kill the girl, tame her, or send
her to a convent—and having had one bad experience with such an establishment already, His Majesty was not disposed to favor them as instruments
of policy. To tame the wench into a public asset was
a much more attractive idea—Matthias was never one
for wasting people who could still be used. Helen as
my wife would bind me to his service, and might even
produce strong nephews to aid the royal cause in later
years. And, again, Helen's re-emergence into public
life as a lady of importance would tend to give the
lie to the extravagant stories that must be already in
circulation regarding her behavior. Whereas her
permanent disappearance would tend, if anything, to
confirm them.

For my part, I had wit enough to see that such a
marriage must be a mixed blessing for me at best,
despite the royal alliance that it entailed. Like an
awkward military position, it might have to be
defended constantly, not to mention the time and
effort that would probably be required to manage the
woman herself.

"Should you choose to wed her, Drakulya, then I
will not have you put her away again, do you understand? For as long as she lives, once you are married, she must appear in public, as your devoted wife,
honored by all and worthy of honor. Any more scandal
I will not tolerate. In time I mean to have you both

back at court—when time has proven that the arrangement works."

On the other hand, killing the girl quietly and quickly here in Florence would present me with no serious problems—no immediate ones at least. If the Boccalini came up to the attic in the morning and found her dead, they might disapprove—but not very loudly or strongly. They would certainly see to it that any killing in their household was effectively hushed up. In time the Medici would doubtless learn about it; but as long as King Matthias sent them no anguished inquiries about his sister, they would keep the matter quiet too.

So what held me back from instant murder? Was it only my own daring ambition, my wish to get ahead by presenting my lord king with the best possible solution? Was there no pity in me for Helen's helplessness? Looking back through the centuries at myself I believe there was, though I was not known for pity, and it was in general a hard and ruthless age.

And was I not attracted to Helen's beauty, which hard usage had not yet destroyed? Again, yes, I was—and, yet again, I think there was still more.

I had a feeling for what Matthias in his heart of hearts must really want, however firmly he had empowered me to kill his sister on the spot as soon as I could find her. Oh, he really meant it when he told me I could do that. Doubtless, if I reported to him that I had seen her dead, he would reward me for the favor. But then, afterwards . . . aye, forever afterwards. What would such a monarch always feel for the loyal servant who had carried such an order out? I had been a brother myself, and a prince too, and I could guess. Sooner or later a good use could be found for such a loyal man right in the forefront of a battle. And if the Black Army did not actually retire from him, and he survived—well then, later there would doubtless be something else again.

And still, besides all these reasons to spare Helen, I think there was yet more. My mercy in that little attic room had purpose yet unfathomed.

I had spoken earlier to Lorenzo about the possibility of a wedding. Seasoned intriguer that he already was, he had offered no comments and asked no questions but had obligingly set in motion some necessary arrangements. All I need do now was to get Helen out of the Boccalini house and to some place of safety, without overt Medici help.

While my unknowing bride-to-be prudently consumed the last crumbs of food from the silver plate, I wondered silently what would be the reactions of my adopted cousins if I simply strolled downstairs with her and asked to have the front door unlocked. Opening that door would not be something that we could do casually for ourselves; I had seen how they barred and chained the place up like a fortress for the night. And if Sandro should decide that he did not want me to take the woman away . . . well, I would not be able to manage either violence or bribery on the scale required to gain my way.

I stood up and stretched as well as I could under that low roof, then looked out into the corridor. All was dark and I thought there were no listeners nearby. Doubtless none who could speak Hungarian, anyway.

"Can you still walk, Helen?"

"Yes." She got to her feet, stretching too, but not as I had. Her movements were furtive and sinuous.

"Can you run?"

Still holding the wretched shift together with one hand, she tried walking for a few limping steps, then paused to look at me. "If I must, I can. Then all has not been neatly arranged? I am willing to try anything to get out of here, but I must know."

"Arrangements have been made. Perhaps not neatly, however, and not with the people of this house.

These people we are going to have to surprise. Bend your knees, swing your legs, loosen them up."

She did as I bade her, exercising as well as the tiny space allowed. "I can run."

"Excellent. Now, I am going to chain your hands together—that is, I will wrap the chain around your wrists, but so you can shed it at will. After that we will go down-stairs, and, I hope, out into the street. If there is any argument about our going out, pretend you are reluctant to do so. And move slowly, as if you can hardly walk—yes, that's fine. Then when we are outside, as soon as I tug twice on the chain, slip it and run hard. Right into the darkness, in the direction I will have you facing. Helpers should be waiting for us." So I hoped it would be; so it had been tentatively planned. "Run, run till you are caught, and pray Jesus it will be a friend who has you then."

NINE

The bored male midwestern voice at the other end of the long-distance line informed Mr. Thorn that Lieutenant Keogh was busy right now on another phone, and would he like to hang on? When Thorn submitted that he would, he was left to do so with a minimum of courtesy and a mutter of subdued office noise to keep him entertained. During this lengthy interval it crossed Thorn's mind that he might have made this call last night, and caught the good lieutenant at home instead of during business hours; but then, last night Thorn had himself been quite busy.

At last the receiver in Chicago was picked up again. "Lieutenant Keogh." The voice was familiar to Thorn, but at the moment it carried a load of official boredom he had not heard in it before.

"Yes, Lieutenant. This is Jonathan Thorn, calling from Phoenix, Arizona. Regarding that merchandise you were trying to trace, I believe I will have the information you need very soon now. If you could call me back, at your convenience, here at my hotel?"

At the other end there was a silent pause,

concluding in a sigh and followed by a muttered vulgarity. After this a footstep, and then the shutting of a door which effectively cut off the office background.

When the lieutenant's voice returned it sounded no happier than before, but at least all traces of boredom had been effectively expunged. "We can talk now. This is something really important, I take it?"

"Of course, Joe, of course." Thorn smiled and lay back on the bed, letting his lean frame relax. A white plastic bag as long as a mattress and as narrow as a cot had been unfolded on the rich green spread. This bag was thin enough to be folded into a suitcase, and it was sparsely stuffed with something that crunched faintly as Thorn's weight came onto it, sounding for all the world like dried earth.

"Of course," he repeated into the phone. "Neither of us would call upon the other in a merely trivial matter, is it not so? Your wife's family did not summon Dr. Corday from London, after all, until the situation warranted. By the way, how is the lovely Kate? And how are her fine parents?"

"Fine, fine," The distant voice remained wary. "Her brother and sister are okay, too. By the way, if you're looking for Judy, she's away at school. But I guess you must know that." The comment was tinged with a certain fatalistic disapproval.

Thorn made his own voice soothing. "Say hello to Kate for me. No, Joe, I am not looking for Judy. Nor do I want anything from you that might be embarrassing to you officially. My dearest Mina would be unhappy if I did anything like that with anyone in the family. By the way, I am somewhat surprised—pleasantly, of course—that you continue on the force."

"I like to work, and I'm too young to retire." Joe's voice showed no sign of relaxing yet. "Anyway, Kate's busy a lot with volunteer work, and her old man respects me more for being self-supporting . . . so, tell me what you want."

"I would like whatever information you can give me about two people. The first is Mary Rogers." Thorn recited a brief description. "Mary tells me that she was a nun, or at least a postulant, in the Chicago area, where she did charitable work with runaway youth. She—"

"Wait a minute, wait a minute. Mary Rogers rings a bell. Wasn't she a kidnap victim, a hostage, in the double Seabright killing out there in Phoenix?"

"Yes. I was about to add that."

"Ho. Wait a minute. Ho, ho, ho. You're mixed up in that?"

"My present concern is not with that sordid crime directly. Of course if I should come upon anything that might aid in its solution, then you in turn shall hear it from me. As from an anonymous and confidential source. Is that to your liking?"

"Well, yeah, of course I'd appreciate any kind of a tip. If you'd rather send it my way than tell it to the locals, and it worked out, it wouldn't do my career any harm. Who's your second person?"

"A young man. Patrick O'Grandison." Thorn gave the spelling that seemed to him most likely. "As I understand it, this youth is somehow involved in making films, quite possibly pornographic ones. Probably in Chicago during the last few months. I should like to find and talk to him."

"What about?"

"A personal matter."

"I know what some of your personal talks can be like. Listen, I wouldn't want to help you find this guy, assuming that I can, and then hear later that he's missing some parts or something."

"Joe." Thorn sounded reproachful, almost hurt, a wounded uncle. "I have said that I mean only to talk to him. Of course what he tells me may conceivably change my attitude. But at the moment I bear him no ill-will."

"On your honor?"

The question had sounded grimly serious. And it was taken seriously, as Joe Keogh must have known it would be. Lithely but slowly Thorn arose from his crackling bed of rest, to stand with squinted eyes fixed on some point in the burning sky outside his tinted window. "Yes, on my honor, Joseph."

"All right." The distant voice reluctantly gave in. The scratch of some writing implement told that Lieutenant Keogh was making notes. "I'll see what I can find out. Give me your number and when I have something I'll call you back."

"I shall be waiting for your call. Oh, Joe, one more thing. You might try to learn whether the young lady has ever been in Idaho."

Thorn put down the phone, then picked it up again and dialed the front desk. "Have there been any calls for me?"

"Yes sir, there was one, as I recall. About half an hour ago. A lady, but she didn't leave her name."

"Thank you." Half an hour ago he had been asleep; more than sleep. Waiting now, in no hurry, Thorn strolled to stand at the high windows and confront the daylight world through slotted blinds and tinted glass. An inferno of sun out there; he peered at it as into a blast furnace. Later in the afternoon he would rest more, and then go out again at sunset. Right now the high view made him think of flying. It helped to take his mind off certain things in the far past, things about which nothing could now be done. Nevertheless they were lately coming back, for some reason, to bother him. Most likely because he had again seen the painting at long last. He watched the smoggy landscape until even the filtered light began to make a dull pain behind his eyes. Then he drew the drapes shut and turned away.

Why should it bother him, irritate him so much, that the identical Christian name had been borne by two runaway girls half a millennium apart? A million other runaways down through the centuries must have borne it also, in aimless flight, great unsung migration, across Europe and America and God alone knew where.

Apparently there had even been a certain physical resemblance between the two . . also shared with more other girls than even God could count. No, he told himself sharply, stop this now. Helen, your second wife, is dead, has been for five hundred years in some unknown grave, and only on the Last Day, if then, will you see her again. Or hear her voice. Leonardo had not known how to record *that*.

The voice on the phone had certainly not been one that he, Thorn, had ever heard before. He could be sure of that, at least. As sure as one in this sad, mad world could ever be of anything . . .

God and damnation. He had walked into an auction room, and had simply stood there, surrounded by strangers, and looked at an old picture. And there had been *tears* in his eyes. In *his* eyes. What next?

A reminder, anyway, that not even he was immune to change. Though he had known for some time that he was not.

It could not have happened to Helen as it had to him. It could not. He would have known, must have known, centuries ago. After all that had been between them in his breathing days, he must, he must have been aware centuries ago of her altered but continued life. He had no reason to think that anything of the sort had happened to her. Only to one in ten million or a hundred million did such change come.

But he was changing. Doors were opening around him, and he was trying to read the symbols on them.

Last night he had spent hours prowling secretly inside the Seabright house. There he had slid past

real doors and tried to discover real things. He had
watched the occupants while unseen himself, and had
listened to them while remaining unheard. In most
of their private actions they were as banal as everybody else. Despite all his alertness and his new readi-
ness to discover subtle meanings, he had been able
to find out surprisingly little.

The people had been asleep most of the time he
watched them, servants and masters alike, and he had
listened to their incoherent mutterings as they slept.
Listened and watched carefully, though he had known
for ages now that the secrets of the bedroom were
for the most part very dull, like those films made by
scientific researchers whose excruciatingly patient
cameras dutifully record the writhings of pajamaed
volunteers in semipublic sleep, the sleepers now and
then twitching and generating brain waves with the
onset of dreams.

He still had dreams himself. Not many who knew
his true name would have guessed that he himself,
here this very afternoon in this very hotel bed, at
about the time when some unknown woman was
trying to reach him by telephone, had seen an infant
nursing at the breast of Mary Rogers, an infant girl
who had turned to look at Thorn with Helen
Hunyadi's five-hundred-year-dead eyes. And then he
had seen Guilio Boccalini, suffering with sword
wounds and calling himself Gliddon, had helped Mary
Magdalen to carry a small wrecked aircraft down a
steep and pine-grown mountainside . . .

Dreams could sometimes be of real help. But
Thorn had no reason to think that this afternoon's had
included anything at all veridical.

He sat down near the phone again, waiting
patiently for Joe's call. Age taught patience. In his
solitude Thorn made no effort to look like anything
but what he was. His chest performed no breathing motions. His eyes stared, blank and unblinking,

staring perhaps at nothing. No part of his body moved, except for the fingers of his left hand, which played gently with the worn gold ring on the third finger of his right.

Last night, prowling alone through the Seabright mansion, Thorn had come upon a locked, plain, heavy door adjoining the subterranean art gallery. Naturally he had investigated, and had discovered beyond the door a rather extensive laboratory facility. He was no scientist, or technologist either, but had been able to identify in a general way a mass of photographic and video recording equipment. There were concealed see-throughs leading to the lounge-game room, so whatever went on there could be secretly recorded. The lab held other scientific equipment also, the purpose of which Thorn could not immediately fathom. It looked vaguely medical to him. There was a small, almost cell-like anteroom to the concealed laboratory. This anteroom contained a metal cot, folded now as if for storage, a simple table and a chair. A toilet and shower were in an adjoining cubicle; neither had been used for some days.

A large wall safe in the laboratory, concealed under a large but very minor painting, had room enough inside to contain Thorn's whole body once he had altered form enough to let him flow in through the almost perfect sealing of its door. There was no real light inside, but enough infrared radiation to let him see essentials. The safe stored mostly cassettes of video tape, and canisters of film. He opened one of the latter and examined, as well as possible under the circumstances, the reel that it contained. He could see enough frames of film, all showing nude figures in full color grappling orgiastically, to be sure what kind of film it was.

Well, a Seabright porn factory. That was no real surprise, after he had met Ellison. A private operation, no doubt; this family would hardly be in it for the money.

Thorn stood outside the safe again, leaning a newly resolidified hand upon the wood frame of its concealing painting. The precautions seemed somewhat exaggerated, in this day and age, to hide mere porn. Was there some other angle, purpose, to the concealed records? Blackmail? But that too now seemed rather outmoded. There was something here that deserved thinking about. He could come back later, if he decided it was important, and look again.

Right now he closed his eyes. Like the rest of the house, these laboratory rooms had had many people in them at various times in the past. He could not be specific about a number but he had the feeling that the number was surprisingly high. People had been paraded through here, he sensed suddenly, one at a time, several days or weeks or months apart, for a period of years. Most of them had been young, he thought. A certain flavor of the house of the Boccalini . . .

Upstairs in the mansion again, he prowled the silent hallway, which was lit by a backwash of outdoor security lights coming in through curtained windows on one side. He stopped at one closed bedroom door after another, trying to get a feeling for which room had been Helen Seabright's. He thought he could detect the aura of Mary Rogers's past occupancy in one bedroom. Ellison Seabright's gross snore obviated any need for subtlety in telling where he slept.

Here . . . in this room some young female, but not Mary, had spent a good deal of time a few months past. Thorn went in, through the crack of the closed door. The room had been stripped of almost all furnishings, but some things remained. Traces of young merriment, and fear . . . and considerable unhappiness . . . and just a touch of old perfume.

The occupant was certainly no one Thorn had ever known before. And she certainly had not been a vampire, either.

He found another room, one that had certainly been Delaunay Seabright's before the night of kidnapping and murder. This room too was now unused. Thorn stood in solid form in the center of its floor, mulling over in his mind the few photographs of the former occupant that had appeared at the time of the kidnapping and murder, when word of the painting's existence in the private Delaunay Seabright collection had first reached public print. Those pictures had shown Delaunay as having a fairly strong resemblance to his half-brother Ellison, though Ellison was ten or fifteen years younger.

The bedroom's furniture remained, perhaps because it was so massive, grandly antique. But the picture hangers on the walls were all empty now, and faint marks in a light layer of dust on some shelves showed where other objects had lately been removed; Ellison must be already scavenging. Any material object that might have helped Thorn to grasp the late owner's personality had, it seemed, already been removed. And this personality seemed harder to grasp than that of the dead girl. About all that was left was a little dust, some large impersonal furnishings, and shadows.

Thorn passed down the upstairs hall again, rather like a shadow himself, and silently entered the bedroom of Ellison Seabright. It was a guest room, really, but Ellison had made it his own. A snoring mound of body, clothed in an eastern garment of silken decadence, floated quite alone in a vast waterbed. Thorn did not gaze long upon this spectacle, but turned promptly to a door that connected this bedroom with another. With an anticipatory quickening of the pulse he entered the chamber he had been saving until last.

Stephanie Seabright's rumpled bed was empty. She

sat nude in a soft chair before a softly lighted triple mirror, looking at her multiple images in the glass, and for a moment Thorn thought that she understood, had sensed his presence, and was waiting for him. Almost, he began to resume man-form. But he delayed a little, watching; and presently he understood that her attention was focused wholly on herself.

A luxurious robe was crumpled on the white carpet at Stephanie's feet. A small glass that smelled like pure vodka stood on the dressing table before her, bottle at hand to match.

Stephanie stood up suddenly, chair toppling behind her, and Thorn saw that what gripped her was fear. Not of him. She still had no awareness, consciously at least, that he was there. It was not a sudden fear, but one that had been growing, and still grew. Her attention was still on her own reflections.

Age was the terror.

Age, abetted by too much sun in some careless summer not too many summers past, was beginning to make the skin wrinkle. Here at the armpit when the arm was down, there at the corners of the eyes. Time soon to consider cosmetic surgery and all its implications. The shape of the breasts, even though they were small, hinted at sagging, the flesh on the thighs was no longer of perfect smoothness, but had begun to be slightly mottled with subcutaneous fat . . .

He could have appeared to her, a dim male figure standing or sitting in a pose devoid of menace, an apparition so gentle that she would not scream. He knew exactly how he might have done it. Experience rather than pride assured him that the seduction would be easy, and he could foresee its every move. Within an hour he would be able to taste her blood . . . she would perhaps begin to understand the centuries of youth that he could offer her . . . and she would tell him all she knew about the painting . . .

Which, unfortunately, would probably not be much.

Did his unknown opponent know him? Had it been calculated by that invisible but unavoidable foe that tonight Prince Dracula would seduce Stephanie Seabright?

The man now calling himself Thorn could perceive, not far ahead of him in time and space, some blunder he must not make, a tripwire he must never touch. A life of half a thousand years well stocked with perils had taught his inner senses a great deal about danger, and had also taught his conscious mind to trust such inner warnings when they came. He must be careful, very careful now. He could be no more concrete about it than that. But the danger was vital. A trap, whether consciously set for him or not, lay there, not far ahead, and he had to identify it, move around it somehow, before he could advance. The phantom tripwire held him back, prevented his approaching Stephanie, prevented also his returning to the adjoining room and bluntly, brutally interrogating Seabright about the missing painting.

He waited long minutes in Stephanie's room, invisible, watching, waiting for a sign. Until weariness and vodka overcame her, and she clothed herself again in the rich robe that lay on the floor, and fell back, weeping, into her solitary bed.

Now, in his own solitary room at the hotel, Thorn played and replayed in memory the singularly unrewarding visit. Thoughts came and went, all of them discouragingly impractical. He had watched and listened to the news, and there was no word yet on the missing plane. A massive search was underway but everyone knew success was doubtful.

The tripwire was still there, he could feel it. Immunity to personal fear often made personal danger stand out with precise cold clarity when it came. And danger there was, in the near future, though just where and when he would encounter it he did not know.

Or could the instincts of half a thousand years be wrong for once, and he was confronting nothing but shadows? If a painted image could wring tears out of his eyes . . .

When the phone rang at last, Thorn roused from reverie with a quite human start. Outside the high windows the fires of day had dimmed considerably. Looking at his watch, he saw that hours had passed.

He lifted the instrument. "Thorn here."

Joe Keogh's voice said: "I found out from the archdiocese that Mary Rogers did work here in Chicago as you described. She's never had anything in the way of a criminal record in this state or any other. We'd know if she did, because she was so heavily investigated after the Phoenix killings. Everyone connected with that affair was. And you asked about Idaho; she did live out there in a convent for a couple of months, about two years ago. That's all I've been able to find out."

"I see. Thank you. And Mr. O'Grandison?"

"Well, he's something else, not exactly what you'd call a winner. He does have a record here in Illinois: marijuana user, cocaine user, no evidence that he's ever done any dealing. He's twenty-one now, according to our records; been in and out of juvenile homes and mental hospitals since he was twelve. No connection with illegal porn is shown; doesn't mean there couldn't be one, of course. Six months ago he was charged with contributing to delinquency—girl about fifteen years old who gave the name of Annie Chapman. But this girl disappeared from a detention home somehow before the case came to court, so it had to be dropped."

"Annie Chapman."

"You know her?"

"I do not think so, Joe." *A girl named Annie, just*

a runaway. She didn't count. "Pray continue." The
tone of Joe's voice had suggested to Thorn that news
of importance was still to come.

"All right. I've talked to an officer on the force here
who remembers O'Grandison. And he says
O'Grandison was in the right time and place to have
met Helen Seabright when she was here on her
runaway. No evidence that he actually did, but he was
on the scene or very near it."

"Annie Chapman too?"

"We don't know where she came from, what she
might have been involved in, or where she went.
There was some mixup at that juvenile home, evidently; they just let her walk out."

"Joe, you are sounding interested. Almost excited."

"That's a very big case out there, the Seabright
thing, and now the missing treasure. I hope you
meant it about giving me a tip when you can."

"Hmm. And where is Patrick O'Grandison now?"

Caution returned. "Why do you want to talk to
him?"

"Joe, Joe, I have said that I mean him no harm."
Thorn smiled, very slightly. "Have I ever told you a
lie?"

"Yes, goddam it, you have. Don't treat me like a
kid."

The smile went away. "Have I ever lied, after
pledging my solemn word?"

There was a sigh in the distance. "No, I'll give you
that. Also I know you saved my life once, and
Kate's . . . all right. My informant said he thought little
Pat was still in town here. Are you coming after him?"

"Perhaps later, Joe; not immediately. Consider my
word pledged on that much, if you like. I am busy
with other matters."

"Listen." Joe's voice had altered. "Kate's told me
that Judy's out there in the Southwest, for a summer
school or camp or whatever they call it, near Santa

Fe. Mountains, horseback, opera under the stars, and so on. I mention the fact only because I assume you know all about it already. I don't suppose there's any use my trying to talk to you about Judy, how young she is."

She had, as a matter of fact, recently turned eighteen; Thorn had sent a discreet birthday gift. (Ah, Mina, you must understand. He could do no less, seeing the family resemblance over four generations, seeing so much of you in her.)

"You are a truly moral man, Joseph." Thorn called him Joseph only rarely. "Thank you, you have been most helpful."

He hung up the phone. What Joe, like many other breathing people, failed to appreciate was how young all breathing women were—those utterly enticing creatures!—when seen from the viewpoint of an age of five hundred plus. Certainly differences exist between eighteen, say, and thirty-six, and again between thirty-six and seventy-two. But they are not really such great differences as breathing males seem to think. Delightfully subtle dissimilarities, rather, with the elder blood having its own bouquet, the blood of full womanhood its own of course, and of course in the young the sweet elixir of youth itself . . .

Still, Thorn thought dutifully, looking out the window into the burgeoning night, eighteen *is* rather young in these modern times, and actually Joe is right. He tried to make himself think solemnly about the problem.

Sometimes he thought that he would never live long enough to bring his own life under a proper measure of control.

TEN

Coming downstairs from the attic of the *Palazzo* Boccalini, Helen walked in front of me. Her hands were behind her back, her wrists looped with the thin chain, whose free end rested lightly in my grip. Her torn shift perforce gaped shamelessly. She looked as if she might be on her way to execution.

On the second flight of stairs we met the fat cousin, Allessandro, on his way up, candle in hand. He stopped at once, eyeing us inquisitively; evidently he had been impelled upstairs by curiosity as to just what games I might be playing with my gift.

"I have thought of a sport that needs some room," I told him, answering his quizzical look.

"In the courtyard," he suggested.

"Not room enough." It was not the Medici palace. "We will need the street."

Allessandro looked doubtful at that, but said nothing as he followed me down again. When we reached the ground floor I hailed the first male servant who came in view and gave bold orders for the front door to be opened. The masters of the house were already beginning to gather round, and looked at one another doubtfully. Watching them, the servant hesitated. But Helen was right on cue, displaying alarm at the prospect of being taken outside—the tall foreigner must at least have hinted to her, upstairs, what this new sport was to be like—and my adoptive cousins immediately warmed to the idea.

"Come on!" I roared. "Bugger the watch and the curfew. You don't mean to let them cheat you of some fun?"

Once I had put it in those terms, there was only one reply red-blooded youth could give. So far, at least, everything had been almost too easy. The night outside in the street was dark as tar, except for one feeble torch in a servant's unenthusiastic hand. "More lights!" I demanded, wishing for a distraction, and for some delay to let whatever Medici agents might be watching get themselves ready for action.

A manservant went back into the house for lights, reducing the odds minimally. I did not wait for his return; as soon as I had Helen facing the dark street in the direction I wanted, where there should be running room at least, if no active help, I gave two quick tugs on her chain. In a moment she had slipped her hands free of its loops and was off at top speed, running in desperate silence.

Watching the startled faces of the men around me, I tarried for a quick count of three and still got off in pursuit ahead of any of the others. My intent was to appear to be chasing Helen, at least until it became necessary to do more.

Helen ran with better speed than I had counted on, her white figure staying a little ahead of me in the darkness, maintaining a lead my long legs did not overcome. My drawn sword in my hand slowed me a little. I had taken off belt and all on entering the house, as a twentieth-century visitor might have doffed his hat, but then had routinely buckled the weapon on again as I came out.

Before I had run ten strides, shouts shattered the
night behind me. A great alarm was going up,
drunken voices, in which merriment was still the
dominant tone, bawling for more torches. But not
everyone, unfortunately, insisted on waiting for more
light. Two pairs of feet were pounding after us, and
one of these pursuers was already getting uncomfortably close. Meanwhile, ahead of me, Helen's first burst
of speed was faltering. Fear indeed lends wings, but
chaining and hunger are not the best of training
regimens.

No use trying to delay what must now be done.
I stopped and turned abruptly and cut at the nearest sportsman, aiming low for the legs. My blade bit
bone, and with a loud cry he went sprawling. My
second pursuer was drawn and ready for me when
he came running up. He was evidently an armed
professional retainer of some kind, and managed to
delay me in masterly style, our swords conversing
almost invisibly in the near darkness, whilst he bawled
for help. But his allies behind him still dawdled,
clamoring for their precious torches.

At last I got him with a thrust to the midsection,
and was able to turn and run away again. Behind me
the cries of my latest victim went up alarmingly,
mingled with a new uproar from dogs safe behind
stone walls. There was no hope now of avoiding a
pursuit in deadly earnest. But of course I very soon
had to slow my flight, begin to grope my way slowly,
meanwhile calling the girl's name loudly as I dared.
I added in her own language such assurances as I
could think of, and prayed that she had had the wit
and nerve to stop and wait for me, or else that some
of the Medici men had come to her aid.

There were actually, as I later learned, no Medici
men on hand. Their sole spy on the scene had stayed
prudently where he could keep a good watch on the
Boccalini. But fortune and the saints smiled upon us

anyway. Helen's voice, a ghost-whisper of softness, replied at last to one of my more urgent hisses, and presently her small hand came reaching out of darkness to touch mine. I sheathed my sword and took it. "Can you find the way," I whispered, "to the workshop of the artist called Verrocchio?"

"Yes." She paused as if surprised. "Yes, I think so." A moment more to get her bearings, and she tugged at my hand and we were off. Helen had been in the city longer than I had, had walked in it much more, and so had greater knowledge of its streets. More dogs awoke behind the walls surrounding us; but behind us the enemy was still organizing, perhaps suspecting some trap, at any rate not ready to dash recklessly off into the dark.

We turned corners; the sounds of their preparations fell behind us and disappeared. I began to breathe a little easier.

"Why are we going to Verrocchio?" The king's sister was not shy of asking questions.

"They know us there, and are friendly. It has been arranged."

Helen said nothing more at the time, but led me through alleys and narrow ways, until we emerged upon a broader street almost at the painter's door, having met no one en route. It took a minute of rapping with my dagger hilt to get any answer at all from within the studio, and somewhat longer than that to get the master of the house roused and brought to the door. Then, however, it was opened for us promptly enough. Verrocchio, candlestick in hand, alarm showing in his heavy features, his gross body wrapped in a fine robe, motioned us hastily in; we were already past him. After one last fearful glance into the darkness, he closed the portal quickly behind us.

"Send word at once that we are here," I ordered him, thinking it unnecessary to specify to whom word should be sent. Then turning to the gaping servants and apprentices, I demanded: "Bring decent garments for this girl at once." The help all stumbled away hastily under my glare, wrapped in whatever oddments of bedcovers and clothing they had grabbed when the alarms began, the younger apprentice tugging the bearded one by the arm to get him moving. Leonardo, who slept at home, was of course not in the group. Helen meanwhile stood quietly at my side, waiting for whatever might happen next.

"What happened?" Verrocchio blurted to me, then looked as if he did not really want to know. He turned his head and called after his retreating staff: "Perugino, there is a message you must carry!"

I took the candle from the master's shaking hand, and set it on a table, and seated myself there. I did not bother to answer his question. Helen, at my gesture, seated herself next to me.

The bearded apprentice was back in a few moments, fully clothed. As he was unbarring the front door again, ready to go out, I detained him with some words of caution. If he should have the bad luck to be collared by the watch for breaking curfew, he was to say that he carried an urgent business message for the Medici, and demand to be escorted to their house; and if it should become necessary to tell the watchmen any more than that, he could add that the message concerned a painting of the Magdalen. He gave me a look of fear and desperation mingled, and hurried out as soon as I released his sleeve.

Verrocchio and I barred up the door again. When I turned back to the table, Helen was gone—into a back room to change her dress, an old woman servant assured me. I sat down again to wait. In a minute or two Helen was back, and as she re-emerged into the light of the candle on the table I rose unconsciously to my feet. What they had given her to put on was the very gown of the painting.

"It's all we have that really fits her, sir," muttered the old woman, a little perturbed by my reaction.

"Never mind . . . it is all right . . . it is beautiful. Now, bring us something to eat and drink. Biscuits, wine, whatever."

Again Helen, my unknowing bride-to-be, sat down with me at table. The dress that had appeared glorious in dim candleglow at the far side of the room was not as glorious seen close up. Faded, somewhat worn, a little dirty here and there, tired with the flesh of many models.

Paintings, stacked in racks along the far walls of the room, regarded us with dim eyes. Verrocchio, still nervous, joined us at the table when I gestured. He was still wrapped in his fine robe. Biscuits and spiced and watered wine were brought, in fine dishes and crystal goblets that were doubtless used ordinarily only as artists' props. I sipped wine, but after all did not feel much like eating. Helen, after days of hunger, was not going to let any opportunity pass. Noting her appetite, I counseled myself that tomorrow I should begin to limit her intake; I had no wish for a fat wife.

Only after my drowsy thoughts had reached this banal conclusion did I realize that I had decided a matter of considerable importance, without ever giving it full conscious thought.

"Why are we waiting here?" Helen asked me, between measured mouthfuls of her second biscuit.

"For some friends to join us." I wondered how much more to say, and sighed. She was going to have to be told at some point, and the telling really could not be put off much longer. "Including one who is a priest."

At that Helen looked bewildered. I glanced meaningfully at Verrocchio, who with apparent relief stood up and left the table and the room. The girl and I were alone with the dim-eyed paintings.

I met her darkly puzzled gaze. "The priest is coming here to marry us," I informed her.

Comprehension grew by degrees in Helen's eyes. Never shall I forget how she looked on that first night we were together, sitting at that rude table. (Mina, my beloved, you will understand.) The model's gown, begrimed by use like all the women who had worn it, yet held some glory in its rich brocade. Her hard, small fingers, crumbling a biscuit. Her beaten, hunted, haunted face, so young. Her bare feet worn with the stones of Florence, with the hard roads of half of Europe. Her wild and filthy hair. Leonardo should have been on hand *that* night, and so should Goya.

As understanding grew in Helen's eyes they shifted from mine, to go staring past me at the wall. She raised a dirty hand and bit its thumbnail. Looking for the moment even younger than her years, she slowly began to weep, tears streaking down her cheeks.

Now this was a reaction that I could scarcely take as complimentary. But it was obviously no calculated insult either, and somewhat to my own surprise I was not angry. I had understanding enough to realize that she wept for her whole ruined life, in which my portion was so far quite a minor one. So I only waited, silently, till she should be ready to talk to me again.

At last the tears stopped, and in a little while the silent sobs. Helen's eyes came back to me, and when she spoke again her voice was under good control. "Matthias allows me no alternative." Though stated flatly, it was really a question.

I shrugged. "Of course it is nearly always possible to kill oneself. But I think that if that path held any attraction for you, you would have taken it ere now." My first wife had in fact traveled the route under discussion, in a fit of madness two years earlier, her point of departure being my castle roof. I thought that I had learned to recognize the signs; I saw them not in Helen.

My blunt comment had made her look at me in a new way again. Now, you must understand that it was not my intention to be cruel. Cruelty I understood; I was, alas, already expert in inflicting pain, as well as undergoing it, and I could have been much more fiendish than that if I had tried. No, my apparent callousness was really intended to be helpful; and I still think it helped her more than if I had tried or pretended to be kind. For Helen I was a hard rock rearing up suddenly out of the treacherous bog of life, a rock that was not going to be put aside for her own purposes. But, on the other hand, this stony intrusion offered firmness and support; she could cling to it, for long enough to catch her breath at least, without fear that it was going to sink. Nor was it going to attack her treacherously; it would never turn harder and crueler than it looked.

Helen's eyes fell to the table, to the bread and wine that had come to her through me. She looked up at the rustic but sturdy roof-poles of the shelter that I had brought her to. She rubbed the chain-sores on her ankle, and pulled the worn and gaudy gown a little more closely round her body. "What has the king promised you, in return for marrying me?"

"Nothing specific. That I will have an honorable position somewhere is implied, understood between us." At least I hoped that the king agreed with my understanding on that point.

"And what about me? Am I to be put back into the convent as soon as we are wed? Or what is the arrangement?"

"No convent. And there is no arrangement, except that you are to be my wife." I looked her over thoughtfully. "The ceremony will be here. Directly afterwards we will proceed, with some kind of protective escort, to a gracious house not far away. There you will have a bath." (Bathing, contrary to popular belief in the twentieth century, was as well thought of in that day as in this, at least among the well-to-do.) "And I expect we will remain in that house for a day or two, being hospitably entertained, if I know anything of our hosts."

Helen was looking at me with a measure of disbelief. I went on: "After that—well, what comes after that has yet to be decided. But I can promise that as my wife you will be treated with respect. And I think I can promise that from now on you will be well fed." There were a few more things, of great importance, that I meant to say to Helen; but I judged that the saying of them could wait till after the ceremony was over.

It was my turn to be judged by her; a king's daughter and a king's sister looked through the grime. "You are of good birth, then. Yes, I might have known that my brother would not marry me to a churl, whatever else . . . well, my lord Wladislaus the Romanian, or whatever I should name you . . . but that is not a Romanian name, is it? I hope you gain the reward that you are counting on for all these efforts and sacrifices to please my brother."

Her manner implied her doubt that I would gain much. And the king's sister looked long and boldly into my eyes, trying to puzzle me out. I continued to study her, with the same object. For whatever reason, the feeling grew in me that my decision had been correct. When at last Verrocchio peeked into the room again, I signed to him that we no longer required privacy, and he hesitantly rejoined us.

But before he could cough up any of the questions that must have been troubling him, horses were stamping in the street just outside his door. Presently another dagger-hilt came rapping on the wood. This time I answered the knock myself, and a moment later was joyfully letting in Lorenzo. Helen had been in

Florence long enough to recognize the young tycoon
on sight, and her eyes widened.

Immediately young Lorenzo, smiling, fresh, and
good-natured at an hour that would now be called
three in the morning, took me aside and heard from
me privately the full story of our escapade. He did
not trouble to hide his glee when I came to describe
the street fighting; that several of his rivals in business had been pricked with sharp weapons did not
grieve him in the least. As soon as this brief confidential talk between the two of us was over, he went
back to the street door and opened it again. In a
moment we were joined by a sleepy friar, just dismounted and scratching his backside. Ten or a dozen
horses were gathered outside the door, and I could
hear the low voices of other men; Lorenzo would
never have come on such a mission in the dead of
night without a good escort.

The friar asked few questions and showed no
surprise, being evidently experienced in matters of
intrigue. As evidence of Medicean forethought he had
come armed with all necessary holy dispensations, civil
permits, writs, blessings and the like, enough spiritual and bureaucratic armament to have wed two
Barbary apes on short notice had such a union
appeared desirable. Only on one point was he in the
least anxious, and I hastened to assure him that the
formalities of my own conversion from the Eastern
to the Roman Rite had been accomplished ere I left
Hungary.

The bearded apprentice had managed, somehow,
somewhere, to gather an armful of flowers in the
middle of the night, and came to present them to
Helen. She appeared quite touched. The younger lad
had at last found her a pair of respectable shoes that
almost fit, for which I thanked him. Verrocchio did
not seem to know quite what he ought to do about
a wedding gift; if he would keep his mouth shut

afterwards, I thought, that would be quite enough. In the end he gave each of us a gold ring, making sure Lorenzo saw the gesture. And so finally my bride and I were standing before the friar, the menials all dismissed, a worried Verrocchio as one witness, and Lorenzo-the-Magnificent-to-be, nodding benignly, as the other.

Helen was taking it all quite well, I noted with cautiously increasing optimism. At least she spoke the required words in a firm, clear voice: "I, Helen Hunyadi, of the household and family of Matthias, King of Hungary—"

Then it was my turn. "I, Vlad, son of Vlad Drakulya and of his household, Prince of Wallachia—"

I had surprised Helen one more time. Without taking my gaze from the priest I saw her face turn up to me.

ELEVEN

"It's nice of you to help out," said Mary Rogers, her blue eyes looking up trustfully at Thorn as he unlocked and opened for her the right-side door of his rented Blazer. Her strong legs in worn blue jeans swung her athletically up into the vehicle. "Robby had to take the Ford," she added, when Thorn had gone round to his own doorway on the driver's side and was climbing in.

"I understand." Thorn first secured his seat belt properly—his sometimes ferocious conflicts with machinery were never *his* fault—and then put the key into the ignition. Presently he was driving down the swooping ramp from the hotel garage, squinting through sunglasses as he pulled into the city street awash with the molten daylight of late afternoon. The sun itself, he had made sure, was safely behind some buildings. It would not be getting any higher today. Robinson Miller, whose more-or-less gainful employment was with the local Public Defender's office, was working late this evening, visiting on his own time with clients said to be in great need. And a couple of hours ago Mary had received a phone call from

343

the Seabright house. A woman on the staff there, a Mrs. Dorlan, who Mary had apparently got to know during her residence at the mansion, had told her that her remaining belongings were ready to be picked up.

"She sounded sort of in a hurry. Why they're all of a sudden in such a hurry to get rid of the stuff, I don't know. Cleaning house, I guess. But I feel more comfortable going over there if I have someone with me. And you did volunteer earlier."

"I assuredly did." That of course had been before his first visit to the mansion, when he was still looking for an invitation of some kind, any kind, to let him cross the Seabright threshold. But now he welcomed any good reason to be alone with Mary.

She said: "I suppose they'll just have the stuff piled out on the porch. There isn't very much."

Thorn snarled faintly at an errant Volkswagen. "I take it you have not yet told Helen's mother of that strange telephone call?"

"Stephanie's not much of a mother. A nasty thing to say but it's true. Anyway I don't think she'd talk to me. I could write her a note about the call but she'd never believe it."

Thorn did not argue that. "Then I suppose you have not informed the police, either."

Mary was studying him. "No, we haven't. You said something about an official connection that you have. I'd like to know what you found out through that."

"Not much. Confirmation of things you had already told me. No hint that Helen might be still alive." The last sentence seemed to echo in his mind when he had spoken it. But he had settled that.

"Damn." She was obviously disappointed. And worried. "Well. Whoever it was, she didn't sound like she was in any immediate danger. So if it was Helen, I guess she can call home for herself any time she wants to. If it wasn't . . . I can't imagine who it might have been. Or why they'd want to play such a trick."

The rest of the ride out to the wealthy suburbs passed for the most part in silence. This evening no one was manning the mansion's great iron gates. But still the gates were locked.

"I don't understand. They knew I was coming out tonight."

Half a minute of intermittent horn-blowing at last produced a smallish man, in yardworker's clothes, hurrying over the lawns from the direction of the tree-screened house.

"Oh," Mary said. "It's Dorlan." She waved to him through the gate.

The little man, peering from inside, seemed to know Mary too, though he offered no real greeting. "Didn't recognize the car," he mumbled, and set about unlocking the gate and rolling it open by hand.

"Mr. Dorlan, this is Mr. Thorn, a friend of mine. He just came along to give me a hand with the things."

Dorlan, who had not been visible on either of Thorn's previous visits, nodded grudgingly. "I'll just ride up to the house with you and let you in."

"Let us in?" Mary echoed in an uncertain voice.

"They've all moved out," replied Dorlan. There was a kind of grim shyness in his manner, and he did not look directly at either of his visitors. He left them momentarily to shut and lock the gate again, after Thorn had driven the Blazer in.

"Moved out?" Mary asked him blankly when he came back.

"Me and the Missus are the only ones left. We're leaving in the morning. The rest of the staff all got paid off. Mr. and Mrs. Seabright are gone to Santa Fe."

Thorn made a faint hissing noise, almost a sigh. Otherwise he made no comment. The Blazer rolled along the graveled drive with Dorlan perched in the

small rear seat. Mary looked vacantly at the house
as it appeared from behind the screens of palms and
citrus. The portico was empty. "My things?"

"Still inside, up in your old room. They told me
to get 'em out on the porch before you come, but I
ain't had time."

Thorn stopped near the front of the house. Sunset was still lingering in the second floor's west windows. "The move is permanent?" he asked.

"Far as I know. They want all their mail forwarded.
This place is being closed up. Though I hear Ellison's
the owner now."

Mary opened the door and hopped out briskly.
"Well, I'm just as glad. I don't want to look at him
again. At any of them."

Thorn got out too, followed by Dorlan, who was
now looking intently at the taller man, as if fascinated
despite himself. Dorlan yawned suddenly. "Damn
tired," he complained. "Worked all day. No friggin'
air conditioning this afternoon. Power's off in the main
house already."

"Very tiring," agreed Thorn. "You will be glad to
get to sleep." He extended a hand, palm up, while
Mary watched in growing puzzlement.

"I'll say," Dorlan fumbled a set of keys loose from
a chain at his belt, and handed them over. He yawned
again, and tottered to the portico, where he leaned
against one of its imitation Doric columns. A moment
later he sat down. His eyes had closed.

"*Oh* dear," said Mary, and fell silent, forgetting
whatever comment she had been about to make. A
large mastiff had just appeared at the corner of the
house. From her days in residence she remembered
the beast as an unpleasant and dangerous watchdog.
It was staring at them intently and a low vibration
of warning issued from its throat.

"Quiet," said Thorn softly. Mary had no doubt that
he was talking to her, but instantly the dog's growling

trailed off. It leaned forward, as if about to charge, or topple, in their direction. Then somehow there was a change of plan. The great head, ears askew, turned away from them. The dog sniffed the gathering dusk. Then it turned round twice in place, scratched at an ear, and lay down peacefully.

A faint snore arose from Dorlan, who sat leaning against his post. Mary looked from one phenomenon to the other, and seemed to be trying to think of some suitable comment. She was evidently unable.

Keys jingled briskly in Thorn's fingers. "Come. I should like to see the room you occupied." He unlocked the great front door and pushed it open, and like some old courtier bowed Mary in ahead of him. She found herself accepting the bow as something perfectly natural.

The house was filled with what felt like an unnatural heat—it was only the day's heat that had crept in through fallen defenses, Mary realized, but it felt strange in rooms where she had never known anything but cool comfort. Out of habit she flicked a light switch in the cavernous great hall—nothing happened, of course. But enough daylight remained to see that a start had been made at covering up furniture, getting the place ready for some extended period of inoccupancy.

With Thorn at her side Mary crossed the great, silent hall, heading away from the study and the elevator, toward the foot of the broad main stairway. But when she reached the stair she stopped. "I haven't been back here since—that night. Oh, I came back once with the police, re-enacting what I could remember for them. But . . ."

"But it all comes back to you much more strongly now."

"Yes, you're right, it does." She shivered.

"Good. Very good. Shall we go up?"

Mary wanted to protest that it was not very good

at all, that she was growing frightened. But she would
not be a coward. She would get her property that she
had come here for, and then she would leave, if
possible before the darkness thickened any further.
She started up the shadowed stair. Thorn's feet, closely
following, were inaudibly light.

> *As I was going up the stair*
> *I met a man who wasn't there . . .*

How did it go? Something like that, anyway.
Actually she was quite glad for his tall, silent presence. It was not this man she feared. She hadn't
realized, or had lately forgotten, that when she lived
here she had felt real fear of certain other people
in the house. In her imagination she could see Ellison
Seabright now at the head of the stairs, as he had
been standing on that night, looking down at
her . . . and behind Ellison, another and truly terri-
fying figure that came and went before Mary knew
who it was, and maybe she didn't want to
know . . . even only in her imagination . . .

She half-stumbled near the top of the stairs, and
Thorn's hand came to her support her elbow neatly.
"Thank you," Mary murmured. "God, yes, you were
right. How it all comes back . . ."

"Your bedroom," said Thorn, interrupting a silent
pause, "must have been down this corridor, on the right."

"Yes. But how did you know?"

Thorn was pacing slowly away, not answering. He
reached a door and pushed it open, and stood in the
hallway inspecting the dim interior thoughtfully.

"That wasn't mine."

"Delaunay's."

"How could you have known?" She came up beside
Thorn; the room he was gazing into was so dark it
was impossible to see anything. "Oh, of course, some
of the magazines published plans of the whole layout,

didn't they? There was so much publicity. I'm glad that's finally beginning to be over."

"What was Delaunay like?" Thorn was looking into the room as if to read its very shadows.

"Oh . . . big. Not quite as big as Ellison, and five years older, but there was a fairly strong resemblance. Physically, I mean, of course, that's all. Del was a kind old man, shy of publicity. He was always kind to me, anyway. He came here from Australia when he was very young. He still had something Aussie, as he called it, in his speech at times. He and Ellison had the same father, different mothers."

"How was the family wealth amassed?"

"I'm not really sure. Somewhere a couple of generations back, I guess. Del built up the fortune even more during his lifetime. He never seemed to me to be the tycoon type, you know, mean, agressive, a go-getter. But I guess things could have been different when he was young." Mary seemed about to add something but then decided against it. Thorn thought that for once her mouth closed prematurely.

"What?" he prompted.

"I . . . well, I shouldn't say it. But sometimes I wondered about him."

"Oh? In what way?"

"Well . . . just that I didn't think he could have been as nice to everyone as he was to me. He was just a little bit too good. Oh, that's a rotten thing for me to say after he was so generous to me and all. But you know what I mean?"

Thorn nodded encouragingly. "Perhaps I do."

Once over the hump, Mary plunged on. "Look, I've known one or two people, in religious orders, who I thought were really saintly. It's not all that common there, believe me. But there were one or two who I wouldn't be surprised if they were canonized someday. They were really good. They had a, a kind of joy about them. Well, I never felt like that about

Del. He went through all the motions of being very good, with me at least, playing the role of this extremely nice old man. But . . ." Mary, with a helpless gesture, despaired of saying it just right.

"But," supplied Thorn, "he could have been acting."

Mary sighed and moved away from Del's room, going down the corridor, her steps picking up briskness as she went. "It's wrong of me to talk like that. He really gave me that Verrocchio."

"Did he, indeed? Then where is it?"

But Mary had been distracted. Halfway to her old room, walking the thickly padded, silent carpet, her steps moved irregularly to one side, as if in some involuntary reaction.

Thorn took her again by the elbow, gently stopping her forward progress. "Where did you find the murdered girl?"

Mary had backed up against the wall and was staring at the floor just in front of her feet. Now her voice was a mere whisper. "Her legs were stretched out in this direction. Like she had been running, and then was shot from behind, and just fell forward, you know? But she must have been turning her head to look behind her just as she was shot, because her face caught it. The whole front part of her head was . . . I couldn't have identified her face, no one could. But otherwise it looked like Helen. She had on a white robe of Helen's, and there weren't any other young girls around. At least not as far as I knew."

"Annie Chapman?"

Mary tried to read Thorn's eyes; he had taken off his sunglasses at last, but the dim light made it hard. She said: "That's the name that . . . the girl on the phone mentioned. I swear to you I never heard of any Annie Chapman, not until we got that crazy call. I've been racking my brain trying to remember, and the name means nothing. But since then I've been thinking . . ."

"Yes?"

"Well, maybe Delaunay wasn't as good, as perfect, as he let on to me. And I know he was involved with trying to help runaways; or he told me he wanted to get involved with it anyway—"

"What are you trying to say, Mary?"

"Well. Maybe—ordinarily he'd have told me, or Helen would have told me, if they were giving shelter to some other kid. But maybe, well, maybe he—just had a girl in his room for the night."

"I suppose it would not be terribly surprising." Thorn sounded faintly, fondly amused. "Men of good repute have done even stranger and more wicked things than that."

"I know," Mary agreed uncertainly. She was looking down at the carpet again. "She—the girl, whoever it was—was lying right about here. Somehow they've cleaned up all the bloodstains. The white robe she was wearing had fallen open, and I could see she didn't have anything underneath it. Helen told me once that she had taken to sleeping that way, in the raw, ever since she'd been on the road."

"Mary, I would like to hear your story of that night from the beginning. According to the news accounts— were they at all accurate?"

"Pretty much, I guess." Mary's brashness had been fading steadily. Her voice was now almost a child's.

"According to them you heard noise, ran from your room, and came upon the dead girl. What happened next?"

"I—it's hard for me—"

"Go back and start again, Mary. You were asleep."

The pattern in the carpet before her eyes was being melted by the onrush of night outside the windows, disappearing into darkness. She didn't want the fixed pattern to go. She held onto it desperately, resisting the voice of Thorn.

"I want you to go back and start again, Mary. Go back—"

In sudden fear, Mary turned toward him. Her hands folded themselves like the hands of a woman praying, or diving into deep water, and in a moment she had completed a soft lunging motion that brought her face into secure hiding against his chest. "Hold me," she murmured.

His hands held her, and they were warm. But his voice was inexorable. "Go back. You were asleep."

I can't do it. Her protest was silent, but vehement as any shout, and she knew that it was heard.

"I will help you. You are under my protection now. I would not ask it if it were not important. Will you not help me to find out the truth about Helen?"

Mary dared not open her eyes. If she looked up her eyes might meet his.

"Go through it all. Once more, with my help, through it all, and that will make an end to it. An end to the bad dreams that now plague you almost every night."

Surprise tricked Mary into looking up. "How did you know that?"

His eyes were hard to see. But it was hard to look away from them again.

"No," Mary said once more. But she knew that the force of her protest was failing.

Mary was sleeping, something she still did most comfortably and deeply in her old nun-pajamas. And even as she slept it seemed to her (though with some fitfully active portion of her mind she simultaneously knew better) that Thorn was unreal, that his talk in the dark mansion with her was nothing but a fading dream. A dream from which she would presently awake, to find herself in her own sun-lit room, the bedroom next to Helen's. When Mary awoke it would be cheerful morning, and she would be surrounded and defended by all the safe wealth of the Seabright house . . .

. . . and into her sleep there tore a fist of shot-gun noise. The roar slammed against her bedroom door from the outside, jarring Mary instantly awake. Her eyes flew open to register dark midnight, only accented by the pale dial of the bedside clock.

Whatever that slam of sound had been, it must mean that something was terribly wrong. Adrenalin propelled Mary out of bed, grabbing in reflex for the red robe that lay as usual over a nearby chair. One arm in a sleeve of the robe, struggling to sleeve the other, she flung open her bedroom door and ran out into the hallway. Here the darkness was less intense; as usual some muted illumination was coming in through the hall windows from the security lights that ringed the exterior of the house. Somewhere out there now the mastiff, and another watchdog, were raging futilely.

A few steps down the hall, a white bundle lay on the floor. Mary ran to it, and stopped when one of her bare toes touched warm stickiness on the carpet.

Vaguely she was aware of sniffing the unfamiliar stink of burnt explosive. She could see the white thing on the floor quite plainly now, but in a state of new shock she was still trying to make sense of the world in which this white murdered thing could have existence. There were urgent human voices, not far away, saying—Mary could not quite make out what. She hardly raised her eyes. She still had not moved when vague figures walking the darkness, two coming from her right, one from her left, closed in to bracket her. A ski-masked man standing at her left was pointing a long-barreled firearm of some kind right at her midsection. Mary's belly shrank toward her backbone.

Delaunay Seabright, also in robe over pajamas, slippers on his feet, was standing at Mary's right.

Another ski-masked man was holding the muzzle of another, shorter weapon against the back of Delaunay's head.

"Mary," Delaunay said. There was only a small tremor in his voice, which was basically calm and careful. "Mary? Do what they say."

"Oh. Uh."

"Mary. Listen to me. Keep control of yourself."

To this at last she gave some kind of an assent.

As if he had been waiting to see what her reaction would be, the masked man holding his gun at Del's uncombed gray head now spoke for the first time: "Move along."

The other gunman gestured and prodded Mary ahead of him, toward the descending stairs. Turning briefly, a few steps down, Mary saw that Ellison and Stephanie had come out of their rooms and were watching. They had stopped as if the first sight of the gunmen had petrified them in their tracks. One of the masked men had turned round too, and was motioning silently for Ellison and Stephanie to follow—keeping them, Mary thought, in sight, away from telephones.

As Ellison obeyed, advancing slowly, he moved into a patch of security light from one of the hall windows and Mary got a look at his face. It was a good look.

She was prodded again, and turned, proceeding down the stairs.

At the foot of the stairs, on the floor of the great hall, some of the household staff were assembled, as for a called meeting. Not pausing in his slow descent, the man who was pointing a gun at Mary raised his voice, including them all as he recited a small speech.

"You'll be hearing from us about Delaunay Seabright. Getting him back is gonna cost you a lot of money. But this woman here"—a gun barrel poked Mary's back—"is just insurance. Now get this

clear. I don't want to see police cars following us—
we'll leave her brains on the pavement for them to
run over. I don't want to see or hear no choppers
overhead—they'll see us put her out of the car doing
eighty. We got high explosives out there in our truck
too—if worst comes to worst we'll go that way, and
take both these people with us. We got all the cards.
That girl on the floor upstairs is there because she
ran, she panicked, and to show that we mean
business.

"Got all that? Remember? Don't forget to explain
it all to the pigs when you call 'em in."

Mary had turned her head slightly again. Ellison
Seabright understood, all right. All too well, as Mary
saw. Oh, Ellison's face was controlled, but Ellison's
face *knew*. He was frightened, perhaps, but neither
surprised nor terrorized. When one of the masked
gunmen looked at him, he nodded, twice, and that
was the only objective sign of his complicity in the
plot that Mary had been able to name to the police
later. Other people probably nodded, too. But as she
watched him there grew in Mary the incommunicable
certainty of his guilt. He had known all along that
his brother was going to be kidnapped tonight, and
Ellison was very glad beneath his fright.

Mary and Delaunay went helplessly the rest of the
way down the stairs, passing among the motionless,
helpless servants to the great front door. Now in an
alcove at the far side of the great hall one man of
the household staff was observed in the act of trying to pick up a phone.

"Put it down, you, put it down! Or we kill her right
here, and take one of you in her place."

The butler put it down.

Then Mary, Delaunay, and the two kidnappers had
passed through the front door and were outside. The
great dogs were still savaging the air with their noise,
fenced away (by sheer accident, it was later testified)

where they could not get at the marauders. The night
was a warm one for so early in the spring. On the
gravel drive there waited in darkness a late model
pickup truck with an elongated cab containing a rear
seat. The vehicle was tall as a Blazer, with high road
clearance, standing on grotesquely rugged all-terrain
tires. Mary was prodded up into the back seat, then
pushed down into a crouching position on the floor
between the front seat and the back. Her whole body
was forced into the narrow space where people riding
in the rear seat would ordinarily have some trouble
fitting in their legs and feet. The cab was broad, the
front seat evidently had plenty of room for three, big
Del included. A burlap cloth, under the circumstances
an effective blind, was thrown over Mary. Doors
slammed. Then one of the abductors, leaning back
from the front seat in what must have been a strained
position, dug a gunbarrel joylessly into her elevated
rump.

"No jokes, Seabright. You understand that? I'll blow
her ass right off."

"I understand."

The truck's engine roared. Gravel flew up from the
drive to bang the fenders. In moments they were on
paved road, having passed through a front gate that
was obviously being held open somehow. Almost from
the very start of the ride, Mary lost track of where
they were. Different types of pavement roared under
the rough, speeding tires, but she could not think
coherently to tell what the changes signified. Now
they must be on some main highway, for speed was
constant. The heavy-duty shock absorbers in this off-
road vehicle made even the highway ride a relatively
rough one, kept death's obscene metal organ jiggling
against her body. From time to time there was a little
talk of some kind among the three men; Mary could
hear murmuring but in the roar of rough tires and
racing engine she could not understand a word.

With heartfelt fervor she recited prayers, and fragments of prayers, that yesterday she would not have been able to remember. The ride remained continuously fast; there was little traffic to contend with in these lost hours of the morning, and as far as Mary could tell there were no pursuers either.

In Mary's original experience the ride had been mercilessly long, containing lifetimes of terror. But duration in this reliving was somehow modified, her time in the back seat cut short. Moving cautiously in her cramped, aching position, she registered the fact that at some recent time the gunbarrel had been removed from her flank. She tilted her head under the burlap, enough to see that dawn had begun to filter into the cab. By now the truck had slowed somewhat from its headlong highway rush. It seemed to be jouncing at thirty miles an hour or so over an unpaved road.

The vehicle, without slowing, turned rather sharply. It slowed down, then, and turned again, with a shifting of gears. The men in front had been silent now for a long time. Now Mary felt a perceptible tilting. The road must be climbing rather steeply. Turning, climbing, shifting, went on for another unmeasurable time. Mary was taken completely by surprise when brakes brought the vehicle to a halt and the engine was turned off.

She didn't try to move immediately; she wasn't sure she would be able. The door behind her opened, and cold air rushed into the cab along with the new day's light. Now her burlap cover was pulled off. Groaning, she tried to rise on her numbed arms and legs.

She was alone in the truck. The men had got out already and were standing together just outside. Del's head was bowed, his gray hair disheveled. The vehicle had been parked on a steep slope, so it looked almost in danger of tipping sideways. It stood on a segment of primitive road, whose ruts were cut so deeply as

to be impassable to an ordinary car. On all sides grew
tall trees, the vague shade of their needled branches
dimming the predawn whiteness of the sky. One of
the masked men, standing just outside the downhill
door, reached to take Mary by the arm as soon as
she had risen halfway on her deadened limbs. He
half-helped, half-pulled her out.

The other gunman stood patiently pointing his
long-barreled weapon right at the midsection of
Delaunay Seabright, whose hands, Mary now saw, had
been bound behind him. Del had raised his head and
was looking at Mary. Across some tremendous gulf,
as it seemed to her. The man who held her arm
dragged her away from the truck. Her legs were
barely functional. They crossed a space of thin tree
growth that could hardly be called a clearing, and
approached a small, weathered cabin that Mary did
not see until it was only twenty feet away.

"Mary," Del called after her in a hollow voice.
"Chin up. You'll get out of this."

She glanced back at him, but could think of nothing to call out in return. One of her bare feet trod
on a patch of hard-frozen snow. They were somewhere high in the mountains, toward Flagstaff. The
cabin was almost invisible under the tall pines and
fir. Its door squeaked loudly in the still mountain air
as the man with Mary yanked it open. Darkness still
ruled inside, and when the door shut again behind
her, full night had returned. There seemed to be no
windows in the rude shack, no openings at all besides
the single door. She stumbled ahead across an earthen
floor, trying to make her legs start working properly,
rubbing her arms. Near one wall her feet found stones
suggesting the remnants of a hearth. She bent, groping, to discover a fireplace of sorts, a chimney. The
aperture was much to small for her too think of trying
to force herself inside.

Suddenly the door behind her was opened again,

letting in some light. One of the masked men, wearing a holstered pistol and carrying a hunting knife along with some lengths of cord, came in. He said nothing. Repressing an urge to struggle, to scream pointlessly, Mary let him tie her hands behind her back, her ankles firmly together.

When the job of binding her was done, tightly, the man went out again and vanished from sight somewhere, leaving the door open. Standing in the middle of the cabin floor, she could see just the rear end of the truck, protruding from behind a thick double tree-trunk. Delaunay was standing near the large tree. His robe was open in front, so he must be cold in his pajamas. His hands were still behind his back, and his ankles had been tied now too, so that when he turned toward Mary and the cabin the movement was an awkward shuffle. The second masked demon was still looking over Del's shoulder from behind.

"Mary?" Del called again. "Are you all right?" The real concern in his voice was plain.

"So far," Mary managed to get out. It seemed that under present conditions such trivia as wrenched joints, numbed limbs, chills, and nervous exhaustion did not deserve notice.

The man standing behind Del poked him with something, making him sway forward. Then he inched a little closer to the cabin in his bound-ankle shuffle. He cleared his throat. "Mary, they tell me the plan is this. You are to be left here, tied up but unharmed. They'll phone the police and tell them where you can be found. Returning you safely in this way is meant to show that I'll be safely returned, too, as soon as the ransom's paid. Details about the ransom will be passed along soon. Right?" Del turned his head to ask the question; the mask behind him nodded.

Del went on: "Neither you nor I have seen these

men's faces, Mary. We've hardly heard them speak. Neither of us will be able to identity them. So, I believe them when they say they'll let me go as soon as they're paid. Now I want you to emphasize that, to everyone, when you're set free. Will you do that?"

Set free. Set free. Mary could hardly hear or understand another word beyond those two. Del was staring at her strangely. With a great effort she finally managed to make her brain function, and her tongue. "Tell everyone you believe you will be released. If the ransom's paid. Yes, yes, I will."

"Please do, Mary. They also say they'll kill me if the ransom isn't paid, and I believe them about that, too. Is that all?" The two masked men were both standing with Del now; he looked at them, one after the other, and received a single nod.

Del nodded toward Mary. "You're going to have to do something to protect her from the cold. It'll be hours."

One of the men moved away, toward the half-visible truck. A truck door opened and closed. He came back, bearing an armload of blankets; rough, brown, army-surplus-looking things. He draped them wordlessly round Mary's shoulders, front and back. As long as she did not move much, they should remain. Then he went out of the cabin again and with his companion took hold of Del.

They dragged him off among the concealing trees, out of sight toward the truck. The last words that she heard from Del were: "It'll be warmer, Mary, when the sun gets up. Hang on. Help will come."

Could it be that she had never said goodbye to Del at all? Had never given any last words of encouragement to that old man who had done so much for her. She had heard the truck doors opening and closing, once again. And then, moments later, the totally unexpected blast.

✧   ✧   ✧

Mary had collapsed onto the earth floor, groaning, at the explosion. Something terrible was happening again, though she could not at first grasp what. The brief thudding of debris upon the cabin roof kept her crouched down. One piece hit so hard that dust and fine fragments fell from the inside of the crude roof. She huddled there for an endless time, in a dazed state approaching madness.

Light grew slowly outside the cabin door, which had been blocked open with a piece of branch. Day had come officially. Birds started to sing at last. Mary could smell the burning, and she could hear the faint crackle if she listened. The woods were wet, almost dripping, branches decked with late spring snow, or else they might have gone right up. Gas burned, rubber burned, other things burned and she could smell them when the breeze blew some of the smoke toward the cabin.

When finally she began to try to look out of the cabin door, she could no longer see the pickup anywhere as an integral object. Only debris, unidentifiable pieces of this and that, lay within Mary's field of vision outside the cabin.

After a time she painfully dragged herself, losing some blankets in the process, over to the door. From there she could see more. There lay a fender. One of the truck's wheels had come to a stop against the cabin wall.

After another time she raised her eyes. On the other side of the semi-clearing. Del's robe was draped between two high branches of a Ponderosa pine. The robe sagged like a laden hammock. There was no sign of Del's head or hands or feet, but the robe was certainly not empty . . .

. . . and the scene of the cabin and the wreckage began to vanish. This vanishment was a process as intermittent as the disappearance of the lights of a house passed on the road at night behind a long screen of trees.

On the road at night. Driving a lonely road while slowly and surely things seen passed away.

Driving, riding, along a desert road, with her head slumped on a shoulder that gave her, oh, such a marvelous feeling of security...

She was back in the jouncing truck again, but no it was not the truck this time thank God it was the Blazer, and Mary was upright in the right front seat. Ahead of her the headlights speared continuously along a curve of high desert road, narrow unpaved road with bear grass and cactus along its sides. There were no other lights to be seen, in all the midnight land about.

She had gone to the Seabright house, to pick up her things, with Thorn...

Thorn.

He was driving, and he glanced sideways at her for a moment, mildly, as the weight of her head came fully up off his shoulder.

She drew a hard breath.

"Softly, Mary. Gently! It is all right. You were remembering some unpleasant things."

"I was ... I was right there ..."

"No, you were not there tonight. I had started to drive in the direction of the cabin, the place where the explosion happened. But it proved unnecessary to take you there. Everything worked, you were able to tell me all en route. So we are now heading back toward Phoenix—that pleasant glow in the sky ahead is from the city's lights. We shall be there in a couple of hours."

A couple of hours. She yearned for the lovely city. She felt weak inside, as though recovering from an illness. Loneliness and night and disorientation overcame her. She had never felt so far from home in all her life. She had never understood before how runaways must really feel.

Weakness turned her back toward childhood. She

was a bad girl, and she wept now, for all the sins of her past life. For infatuation and sex in Idaho. For broken promises. For living with Robby, endangering his immortal soul. Was it really his idea or hers that they should not get married?

Thorn glanced at her again. "Ah. You are experiencing a common reaction to the experience you have just been through. It will pass. Presently you will feel much better."

"What experience have I been through? What have you done to me?" The words came out in a snuffle.

"What have I done? Very little. Ah, here we are. I must obtain some petrol."

In half a minute the deep invisibility of the night gave forth a small, almost abandoned looking gas station into the headlights. Thorn could hardly have seen the place before the headlights picked it out; he must, thought Mary, vaguely be familiar with this road. Anyway, the place was certainly closed, utterly dark and still.

Thorn pulled in, though, and up to the gas pumps, and turned off his engine as confidently as if he had seen some of those television-commercial attendants cartwheeling out to give him service. When the headlights went out, Mary saw that a thick crescent of desert moon had risen, to make the setting a ghostly stage.

"I shall be only a moment," Thorn said from just outside the vehicle, and slammed the door carelessly behind him.

Mary was not going to offer any comments on the practicality of trying to get gas here tonight; not now, and not to Thorn. With great relief, though, she found some of her mental strength returning. All right, she had done some things in her life that were wrong, but nothing all that terrible. Even when she closed her eyes again, Thorn's face seemed to hang before them. It wasn't his fault that she felt lousy. He understood. And he didn't want her to cry, to suffer.

For some reason, what Thorn wanted had suddenly become important to her. Even more important than—than—was it really love that she knew with Robby, after all?

She opened her eyes again, just in time to see her companion vanish beside the silent station. Yes, vanish was the right word, though the building was near, and the moonlight fairly bright, it seemed that he had just disappeared.

Mary waited quietly, wondering if the owner perhaps lived somewhere in back, and had heard the car door slam—

And Thorn was back again, even as he had gone, standing now beside the gas pumps with keys jingling in his hand. He was rattling them impatiently against a pump, with a muttering of what sounded like Latin oaths.

Mary said, through her partially rolled-down window: "You hypnotized me, didn't you? We were at the house . . ."

"Your property that we went to retrieve is all in the rear seat. This damnable device will not . . . ah."

Very faintly, there came the sound of small motors, electricity.

Mary turned to look into the rear seat of the Blazer even as the dim figure outside began to pump gas into its tank. There were here familiar string-tied boxes, one of them unopened since Chicago. There was the small, battered spare suitcase that she had all but forgotten. Things she evidently didn't really need. All her essential stuff was now at Robby's house.

"Thank you," she called out softly, turning back to the window.

"It is I who should thank you. You have been of considerable help."

"How?"

He didn't answer. The desert here was high enough so that the night had grown quite cool. Mary breathed deeply of its coolness, meanwhile listening to a distant owl. Her thoughts were ready to go with the bird, fly through the night. Sadness was rapidly being replaced by a fierce though quiet elation.

When Thorn had finished filling the tank, he came like a conscientious attendant to treat the windshield with a squeegee no one had bothered to lock away. That task complete, he vanished again in the direction of the building. This time Mary made a more intense effort to watch closely. But this time too Thorn simply disappeared.

Then abruptly he was standing at the driver's door again, opening it to get in. I don't believe this, Mary thought, feeling delighted, as by some stage magician's cleverness.

"You had to go back in to return the keys," she remarked cheerfully.

"And to leave payment." His voice seemed to chide her gently for having omitted anything so important. "Not, of course, at the outrageous rates listed on these signs."

"Oh, of course not." Was this really her, so eager to be agreeable?

He was now seated beside her, with the door closed. Looking at her. But for the moment he made no move to start the engine.

Something in the way he looked at her made Mary sigh faintly and lean back in her seat. "You were right," she said. "It was hard to go through that, but now somehow I feel sure those dreams aren't going to bother me any more."

"I trust that they will not."

The moonlight was silver and strange. Mary had the feeling that she had never really looked at moonlight closely before.

Again she was the one to break the silence. "I have

the feeling," she announced, "that when you kiss me I'm going to enjoy it very much."

One of his eyebrows went up. "Then I must seem churlish indeed to delay. But I would like to find a better place than this."

Thorn turned the key in the ignition. He was immune to personal fear, but not to horror. And he supped full on horror in the next moment, when he heard the strange reaction, and sensed the hellish fire of the bomb blast, blowing backward and upward at him from the engine.

TWELVE

Our wedding night, or wedding morning rather, was spent at Careggi, the beautiful Medici villa which lay only a few miles outside the walls of Florence. Lorenzo praised that country retreat to me extravagantly as we rode out through the silently opened city gates before dawn, and told me that much of his childhood had been spent there. I was on my own stallion, Helen at my side on a docile young white palfrey that Lorenzo had begged her to accept as his own wedding gift.

We reached Careggi just as the sun brightened the Tuscan countryside. Piero, gout and all, was waiting for us on the grounds, seated on the rim of one of the great stone fountains near the main house. The head of the Medici family rose to offer us greetings and congratulations, then led us to what would now be called a debriefing session, in the guise of a wedding breakfast at which the men and women of course sat down separately. The questioning was very polite and very smooth, and accompanied with intervals of real celebration; but in the course of an hour my hosts had managed to extract from me more information than I had been aware of carrying regarding the Boccalini and their affairs. When I was finally milked dry and yawning, Piero made flowery apologies for the delay, presented me with a jeweled collar and a warhorse as my own wedding gifts, and released me to join my bride. The sun was fully up by now, the day already growing warm.

The women had finished their own breakfast somewhat earlier. Helen had been bathed and perfumed under the direction of the ladies of the household, and was already installed in a second floor room that in years past had served, so I was told, as a bridal chamber for members of the family. I was now, amid some merriment, conducted thence myself.

Closing the door of this room behind me with a weary sigh, I turned to the great bed to discover my new wife fast asleep. I hardly needed a second look to make sure that this was no coy bridal ruse, but only the natural result of great exhaustion. I did not intend to wake her; I myself had had almost no sleep during the past two days, and at the moment rest felt more attractive than any other sensual delight. Yet when I had undressed and turned back the covers, I paused to look. Nightclothes of any kind were still the rare exception rather than the rule, and my bride's whole inventory of physical charms was available for inspection. The wholesale removal of rags and grime had left visible a number of bruises I had not been able to see before, along with a few half-healed scabs. But it was a young body, basically healthy and of a trimly attractive shape. It seemed likely that it would give me considerable pleasure, and might bear me strong, healthy sons as well.

Pulling a cover over us both, I let my head fall back in weariness upon a pillow. But the finely woven bed canopy above was bright with morning, my mind was full of a hundred concerns, and sleep refused to come at once.

That there should be an unfamiliar, girlish breathing at my side in bed was in itself no strange phenomenon. But it was strange, very strange, to reflect that this particular sound would not only grow familiar, but it could nevermore be lightly put away.

At least she did not snore.

It was approximately mid-day when I awoke, with my right shoulder gently going numb under the steady pressure of a smallish head covered with brown curls. I needed a moment to identify the head with certainty. The hair looked much different since it had been washed, and there was also a delightful difference in the smell; my slowly awakening senses discovered some essence of the flowers of the Tuscan countryside.

The girl was still in a deep sleep. She was not clinging to me, exactly, though she lay with one arm across my chest—again I got the impression rather that I was the rocky protuberance upon which she had been cast ashore by the storms of life.

Gently I eased free my deadening arm, drew open the bed curtains, and looked around the room. Someone had been in while we slept—bedroom privacy was not valued then as much as now, and anyway the curtained bed provided it. Fresh clothing of fine cloth and the latest cut had been laid out for us both, upon a pair of great wooden chests that served both to decorate the room and provide storage.

Atop a third such chest leaned paneled Magdalen, her back propped against the wall. I considered her presence, and understood from it that all my few possessions must already have been brought here from the Medici house in town. From this in turn I understood that my wife and I would be expected to avoid the city, at least while the affair at the Boccalini house was still fresh. Which seemed to make obvious sense.

Shortly after being dislodged from my shoulder, Helen had moved voluntarily in her sleep, turning on her back and pulling the cover up close under her chin. She lay with pretty pink lips parted to reveal surprisingly good teeth. Reclining with my head propped up on one hand, I studied her. I found myself turning my gaze from her flesh to the Magdalen's freshly painted face, and back again. As I have mentioned, the painting was still unfinished, but the work remaining to be done consisted of details of the woman's dress and of the background. As far as I could see, the modeled face was nothing short of absolute perfection. It was Helen, and yet was not—it seemed rather that the living face beside me had somehow failed to reach its own ideal.

That I, Vlad Drakulya, now had possession of both breathing flesh and painted image, was a fact; and the more I considered this fact the more momentous it grew, the more pregnant with a significance whose nature I could not grasp at once. Like other men of the fifteenth century, I was usually more than half ready to see omens, hidden meanings, wonders spiritual and supernatural. Even in the warm sunlight of midday.

Helen, this girl of hardly more than half my size or age, stirred in her sleep beside me. Then she turned on her side away from me, and a moment later snuggled backward till her soft flank touched me under the light cover. I forgot the painting, and moved to accomplish the one thing still necessary to seal our marriage completely in the eyes of God and man. Helen, only half awake at first, resisted me mechanically—but then, as she awoke fully, she relaxed, and even gave some evidence of enjoyment.

As soon as the first dance was over, I pulled some pillows into better position for both of us, and we lay there side by side, regarding each other and the world from a nest of greater physical comfort than either of us had lately been accustomed to.

"My bride," I meditated aloud. There was a grave expression in those dark young eyes now fixed on mine, and I was trying to fathom what might be going on behind them.

"Yes." The one-word answer somehow conveyed, I thought, her willingness to accept brideship as a starting point and to see where it might lead. And I was cheered by the fact that she did not seem to be a heavy talker. Reticence by day and lack of snoring by night would count for much.

A light warm breeze was stirring the fine gauze curtains at our open window. I could hear gardeners at work not far outside. They were digging, snipping branches, scraping at the earth. A good male voice rose lightly in Italian song. We were a floor above ground level, secure against casual observation from outside, but from where we lay much greenery was visible. The grounds at Careggi were quite as impressive as the house. When I sat up fully in our bed and pulled its curtains farther open I could glimpse graveled walks, distant lawns being smoothed by grazing sheep, and beds of massed flowers. There was a fountain, studded with statuary and rimmed by concentric rings of masterly stonework. All shimmered in late summer's warmth.

"Ah," said Helen, in a new tone. I looked and saw that she had just discovered the painting. Next moment, without pretense of modesty, she had slipped out of bed and gone to inspect it at close range.

"I wish my face was truly so," she said at last.

"But I think the artist has accurately caught your beauty." I was an experienced husband, you will recall.

"But no, this is really a marvel. I never had the chance to take such a good look at it before—I was always on the other side of it, you know, when I was posing."

"I agree, a marvel. Too bad it is unfinished."

Without turning, Helen gently waved one hand in my direction, dismissing that objection; and, certainly, the painting was essentially complete. "I think," she said in Italian, "that boy has been touched by the good God."

But my mind was turning elsewhere. The two of us had important matters to talk about, and I judged the time had come. "Helen."

A hand on one bare hip like Donatello's *David*, she turned her head at the new sound in my voice, and probed me with her eyes. Then slowly she returned to stand beside our bed. She took the hand that I extended to her, then paused, fingering its ring. The circlet was then still fat with gold. Helen looked at it, and at the untanned groove worn by it into my finger underneath. "You have been married before, my lord," she said.

"It will please me for my wife to call me Vlad. Particularly on such private occasions as this. Yes, I have been married. My first wife is now two years dead."

"I will pray for her soul."

"Thank you." Sooner or later, I supposed, I would be called on by Helen for some explanation of her predecessor's leap from the parapet; she would learn something of that tragedy from others even if I never brought it up. But right now I was not going to mention it.

"And you have children?"

"They are staying with relatives at present." I sighed; another subject that could wait. But Helen's question had brought back to me my grief for the son I had loved most. He was a love-child indeed, born to a favorite concubine. He had been riding with me, before my saddle, when I began that last ill-fated retreat from the Turks, the withdrawal that had degenerated into a desperate flight, and had ended for me only with my personal surrender to Matthias. During that fiasco my son had been lost, and when I spoke to Helen on that morning at Careggi, I thought him dead.

"Helen. There is a matter between us that I wish to dispose of now. I intend to speak of it this once, and then never again. Nay, let me put it this way—in future I will not even have this subject mentioned in my presence."

Of course she knew what I was bringing up; she must have known that it was coming sooner or later. Her eyes were withdrawing from me as I spoke, though they still looked in my direction. Her royal chin was lifting.

I went on in a businesslike tone: "I mean of course these shameful escapades of yours during the past few years, since you broke off your betrothal to the Sforza. The whoring and debauchery."

"You say whoring?" Some sparks flared up; she pulled her hand free with a jerk.

I let her break my grip. "If 'whoring' is the wrong word," I answered coldly, "then pray instruct me, what should the right one be?"

With that I expected for a moment that she might try to strike me. But then her body sagged in weariness, and she sat down on the edge of the bed, not touching me. Curls of dark hair hid her face.

Finally she spoke. "Men, as you know, have taken me by force. And, yes, at times I have sold myself, for food, for survival. And yes, I have known lust for men." Helen paused, still looking away from me. "That is all I care to say."

"It is enough. More than enough, indeed. Understand that I demand no apologies, confessions, explanations, for anything that you have done up to now. All that is over, finished, wiped away completely, and I shall never reproach you with it." I drew breath. "What I *do* demand concerns your conduct from this moment forward. It must be that of a model wife of exalted birth: virtuous, modest, obedient. In every detail beyond reproach."

Helen had lifted her face enough for me to see her eyes under the dark hair; but I could not read them. She gave me an inspection that went on for what seemed a long time, and still I could not guess what she was thinking. When she spoke it was only to ask a question that seemed to me insultingly irrelevant. "How long do you mean for us to stay here, in this house?"

My hand seized her wrist; if she had not been Matthias's sister, it would have taken her by the throat. "Have you been listening to me, woman? I want to know that what I say is understood." My voice was still not loud; I have never been one for shouting much.

Helen gasped and leaned forward, easing the pressure on her forearm. "Yes, my lord Vlad—I have heard and will obey. I meant my wedding vows— every bit as seriously as you meant yours." When I released her arm she sighed, and closed her eyes, and rubbed it gently.

"Then I will gladly proceed to answer your question. I believe our hosts will be happy to entertain us here for a day or two. Meanwhile some other arrangements will doubtless be made. It will be suggested that we might like to travel, leaving the region of Florence, at least for a time, lest our presence here become known and be an embarrassment. The news of our wedding is doubtless already on its way to your royal brother—our royal brother, now. Perhaps we will go to Pisa, or Genoa, and wait there for a while to know his pleasure."

"But I thought . . . you mean it is possible that we will not soon go back to Hungary?"

"It would please you to remain in Italy?"

She hesitated. "Yes. Yes, it would."

"I would say that it is more than possible." And Helen appeared relieved to hear this news.

As I had predicted, the two of us spent the remainder of that day and all the next as honored guests at the Medici villa. We rested, and did what newlyweds in all times and places are supposed to do. Our hosts called upon me to demonstrate some tricks of fencing, for which they offered appreciative applause. We joined them in conversation, the skill of which I believe I first began to appreciate when in that household; and in games, and music, and in listening to the poetry of Lorenzo and others. On our first evening at Careggi I had the pleasure of meeting the beautiful Lucrezia, Piero's devoted and intelligent wife, who looked much too young to be the mother of grim-faced, beardstubbled Lorenzo. You can see her beauty still, in the face of Ghirlandajo's *St. Elizabeth*.

I remember Lucrezia talking alone with Helen, at great length, while I was telling Lorenzo as much as I could about King Matthias's artistic patronage. In particular Lorenzo wanted to hear more of the royal book collection. Later that night I could see that Helen had been weeping; but I chose not to question her about it. Experienced husband or not, perhaps I made a great mistake.

On the morning of our third day at Careggi, as I had more or less expected, my bride and I were cordially invited by our hosts to visit a house they owned in Pisa. Pisa was a small city at no very great distance from Florence, and at the time under Florentine—and therefore Medici—political domination. We were loaded with more presents, and furnished with an escort for the journey.

The house, when we reached it, proved to be no more than a comfortable cottage; no doubt it looked smaller than it was because we came to it from the opulence of a palace. Yet I was content with its modest comforts, considering it only a way station on

the road to power and glory; and it seemed to me
that Helen was content also. She had recovered from
whatever had made her weep, and was playing the
role of devoted wife to my fullest satisfaction.

A few weeks later, when autumn was well under
way—it was an extremely lovely autumn in Italy, as
I recall—a message at last reached me from King
Matthias. The royal blessing was pronounced upon
our union—rather perfunctorily, I thought, at no great
length and with no special warmth. Then to business.
I was to join the king and his army in Bosnia as soon
as I could possibly do so, and that was that. Reading between the lines of this missive, I felt sure that
the campaign was not going as well as had been
hoped. In fact it seemed likely to me that a military
disaster of some magnitude might have been in the
making when the king wrote; fine considerations of
peace and harmony in the officer corps no longer
prevented his using another good field commander.

Well, I was ready. A honeymoon idyll in flowered
idleness now and again was enjoyable, but I was
basically a soldier. I made immediate plans for my
departure for the distant front on the morning after
the letter arrived; and, following a terse hint in the
king's message, for Helen's departure from Pisa on
the same day as mine. She would go back to Florence,
where she would remain under Medici care. Eventually she would be sent under escort with some
traders to Buda, there to remain till I should be free
to join her.

On what was to have been the morning when this
planned temporary separation began, I was awakened
by a servant crying that something was amiss. Helen
was already gone, though not with any Medici escort.
On the pillow beside mine, my own bare dagger had
been laid, its point aimed at my head.

THIRTEEN

Thorn in his timeless mode of horror had no choice but to watch the centimeter-by-centimeter progress of the wavefront of the blast as it rose toward him along the steering column. The shockwave of it was so intense that it distorted vision like thick glass. He could watch it coming, but he could not get away in time; not even he could move that fast. Nor were his extranormal powers able to dissolve his solid flesh to mist quickly enough to allow him to avoid the onrushing pain and shock. He could think, and, thinking, doubted that the blast was going to end his life; it was too artificial a thing to be able to do that. He would survive, though with what injuries he did not know. Yes, he would survive.

As for Mary . . . if he could not save himself, it was even more hopeless that in these first microseconds of the expanding bomb blast he should be able to do anything for her. He had not even time to move his eyes for a last look at her, much less reach out an arm in even the feeblest gesture of protection.

The only thing that he could do, he did: willed himself to change into a form intangible. He did this with all possible speed, yet the change did not even begin until his feet and the lower portions of his legs had already been engulfed by the blast-wave. A fraction of a microsecond after his eyes reported the immersion of his feet, his vampire's nerves already had brought the pain of the fire and force enveloping them to eat at his brain like acid.

The dissolution of his solid shape began to ease the pain, though not before it had risen as far as his lower torso. Something hard and mechanical, yes, the steering column itself, came spearing, raping its way right through his melting abdomen, reaching for his fading spine. His last clear sight of the blast through solid human eyes showed him the walnut-grained instrument panel exploding with an awful velocity toward his face. *If it is not real wood,* he had the time to think. *It cannot kill me even if I am not fast enough to get away.* But he was gone before the panel struck.

Ten yards outside the vehicle, the blast-wave already past, and the first surge of secondary flame beginning, Thorn gathered his mist-shape back into that of man. He reformed his body as quickly as he could, despite the renewed pain brought by the re-created nerves, and the consciousness of real injury done to his feet and legs. In solid shape he could see more clearly, and act with greater force.

When his vision cleared, the roof of the Blazer was completely gone, as was the hood, with new fire blooming where they had been. Some portion of the explosion directed downward had lifted the front of the heavy vehicle clear of the ground, and it was now in the process of falling back. Debris still sang like shrapnel through the air around Thorn's ears.

Before the blasted wreck had fallen back again on its four burning tires, Thorn leaped toward it. His motion began on two feet and ended on four, beside the wreck; instantly a second bound on wolf-fast legs

bore him, armoured in thick fur, straight through the
flames where doors and windows had once been.

Mary was no longer there. Her mortal/form, or
what was left of it, had been blown clear of the
vehicle on its far side.

A wolf's teeth closed on her hair, and on what was
left of the collar of her shirt. She was dragged away
from the fire, to a distance where its flames were no
longer hot enough to burn.

One of Mary's arms was gone, off at the shoulder.
Both of her legs were twisted, lying at wrong angles
like those of some great discarded doll. Still her eyes
were open, and alive. They were blankly blue, familiar
eyes in a blasted face from which most of the lower
jaw had been ripped away. In man-form again now,
Thorn crouched over her. He must have looked half-
dead himself, with his clothing blown to rags and his
skin covered with the black residue of the explosion.
But though his nervous system still rang with pain
he could tell now that his own injuries were minor,
a result of organic matter in his own clothing impact-
ing his body under the force of the blast: the leather
in his shoes, the cotton in some of his clothing. His
wounds would quickly heal.

But Mary.

It was obvious from the first look at her that she
was not going to survive.

Unless . . . there was one desperate chance to take.

Thorn closed his eyes, and willed the double fang-
growth in his own upper jaw. Then he crouched lower
over the girl, bending till his lips touched her charred
flesh. In a moment he had tasted of her living blood.
Then, kneeling erect again, he ripped open the burnt
remnants of his own garments at the chest, and with
one taloned fingernail nicked his own blackened skin.
Then he lifted the girl like a nursling babe toward
his wound.

He tried, tried desperately, to give Mary his own

vampire's blood to drink. With her jaw gone, her own blood drowning her, it was impossible.

She never drank the blood that might have given her a chance for a transformed life. Yet still it took long minutes for her death to be complete.

"Who's it from, Bill?" Judy Southerland followed the back of Bill Bird's blue shirt through the sunlight of highland New Mexico, along the pine-needle path that led from her cabin, past the schoolroom-studio where Bill taught and worked at sculpture, to the lodge that housed the school director's office.

Bill turned his head back briefly. He wasn't handsome, not by Judy's standards anyway, but very nice. "He said he was your brother-in-law. But then he said to be sure not to scare you, that the family's all okay."

"I see. Thanks." But Judy was sure she would have felt it had there been something serious wrong with Mom or Dad or Kate or Johnny; she felt things like that, even at a distance, and always had. There had been a bad dream last night, she suddenly remembered. She frowned, but the content of the dream escaped her now.

Brown-haired, sturdy, never in her young life a runaway, she walked wearing jeans and plaid shirt into the director's office. The outer room was otherwise unoccupied at the moment, maybe so she could take what sounded like an important call in privacy. The walls here, as in most of the other camp buildings, were of thick logs, the interior surfaces cut flat, heavily and neatly chinked. After that the walls had been sealed with a glossy finish through which the wood shone yellow. With walls like these it was possible for life indoors to be as civilized, as cultured, as anyone might wish, even amid mountains verging on wilderness. The fanciest interior furnishings did not look out of place. Fritz Scholder prints hung here in the office, along with the obligatory Navajo rugs.

Judy picked up the phone, meanwhile smiling reassuringly at Bill, who had remained hovering just in the doorway. "Hello," she said. Outside the screened window, open on this warm late spring afternoon, tall pines waved in a breeze.

"Judy? This is Joe. Kate and everybody here are all okay, it's nothing like that."

"So Bill said."

"But there's something I still thought I ought to talk to you about."

Judy glanced at her watch. Mid-afternoon in Chicago, one time zone away. Joe must be calling during his duty hours at the station; for him to do that, it must be something important indeed. She knew now who it was about; the feeling, though not the manifest content, of last night's nightmare came back in full force. She felt no surprise; as if, on some interior level, she had already known. "I didn't think it was the family, Joe."

"You see," said Joe's voice through the long-distance buzz, "I got a call just a little while ago from the Phoenix police. A vehicle was blown up with a bomb out there in the desert last night, and at least one person killed."

He can't be dead, I would have known at once if he were dead. "I follow you."

"They were trying to trace the man who had rented this vehicle. He had also occupied a certain hotel room out there, from which room a long-distance call was made to me here in Chicago. Judy, I think you know which man I'm talking about."

"Suppose I do." Bill was still hanging in the doorway; no doubt courtesy was urging him to leave, but something he saw in Judy's face was evidently compelling him to hang around. As soon as the call was over he would offer to try to be of help.

"Don't be defensive, Judy, I'm trying to help."

"I know you are, Joe."

"Have you seen him, since you've been out there? Have you heard anything from him? It could be very important."

It certainly could, to me. "Why? Are the Phoenix police after him?"

"Not in that sense. At least I don't know that they are. They're naturally trying to find out where he is, after his car blew up, and a young woman who must have been sitting in it was killed. There could be some possible connection with that Seabright murder and kidnapping case out there a few months ago. You've heard of that."

"I've heard of that. And about What's-his-name Seabright's missing painting just the other day. They haven't found the aircraft yet. But I haven't heard from the man you're talking about."

"Good. I didn't have any reason to think you might have, just a hunch. For your sake, Judy, I just don't want you to get involved in any way."

"I see." *Why was she so angry? Joe meant well.*

"Now if he *does* contact you, for any reason, will you please for God's sake just give me a call?"

"I suppose I could do that." She could hear her own voice still chilly and upset. She was really angry with herself, Judy supposed, because she had almost missed completely being aware of how much trouble *he* was in. Might he be badly hurt? She couldn't tell. Once before when he was hurt, to the point of death, she had been able to help. Now . . . the contact between them had evidently faded, without her being aware of it.

Phoenix. But at the moment she had no feeling for where he was.

Bill still fidgeted in the doorway, watching her. Good. Maybe she would need some help from someone. She smiled at him.

Joe's voice said: "I didn't tell Kate I was going to call you on this. And of course I didn't tell your folks."

"Of course." Judy's parents and brother had no idea of the truth shared by Joe and Kate—that vampires existed, and that Judy had had one as a lover.

"I just thought it was my duty to make sure that you don't get involved in this. You being out there in the same part of the country and all."

"Oh, damn it, Joe!" Judy never swore. "Are you sure you wouldn't like me to drive a stake through his heart if I get the chance?" Only after the words were out did she remember Bill listening. But Bill would take them as metaphor of some kind; odd, how easy it was for some kinds of truth to remain hidden.

"Judy, Goddam, Judy." Joe on the other hand tended to swear a fair amount. The phone now made his anger tiny. "I'm just trying to look out for your own best—"

"It seems to me that *he* once let himself get involved in some pretty serious trouble that *we* were having."

For a few moments the long-distance buzz had the line to itself. Joe's voice when it came back was decently troubled. "I know, we owe him a lot. After what he did for Kate and me, I'll stick my neck out. But how do we know what he's involved in? I'm just trying to get *you* to stay clear, kid, for your own good. This other young lady who was blown up and killed in his car was probably on good terms with him too, and—"

"Thank you." Judy got the two words out in an acceptable voice, and then quickly hung up the phone. She hoped Joe heard them and really appreciated that she understood and was grateful for his desire to help. Joe really did mean well. It was just that right now Judy was too mad to talk to him any longer.

Bill was still in the doorway, with concern for Judy's troubles written all over him. She smiled at him again. She didn't want to involve anyone else in anything dangerous. But she would, if necessary.

Her hand still on the cradled phone, Judy closed her eyes. Feeling guilt, and love, she tried for contact. As soon as she really tried, it came. The man called Thorn was still alive, she was completely sure of that. Somewhere to the west and south of her, at some considerable distance.

She thought that he was now asleep. But even in the sunny log room she trembled. She was frightened at her perception of his pain and rage.

FOURTEEN

The servant whose howls had wakened me was a weepy old woman, her past scarred, as I now suppose, with tragedy of one kind or another that must have driven her half mad. She was diligent about the house, but given at times to supernatural fantasies. Her cries continued in the middle distance as I sat there in my bed. I know not for how long, looking at that dagger on the pillow and fatalistically pondering its meaning. I did not require the noise of the ancient seeress to convince me of disaster.

The only logical conclusion I was able to reach regarding the dagger was that Helen had considered killing me with it before she fled—already, somehow, I had no doubt that she was gone—but had then for whatever reason decided against my murder. Still, she wished me to realize that the topic had been under consideration, and she had left the dagger so aimed to symbolize the fact.

Besides this vaguely humiliating and cryptic communication, no message from my departing wife could be discovered. As matters turned out, the old woman was screaming for no more occult reason than having been told of her mistress's defection by one of the grooms. This unusually unintelligent lad, while about his morning chores an hour or two earlier, had chanced to see Helen leaving. He reported belatedly how she had ridden off into the predawn mists on her white palfrey, a thin roll of clothing with a few other belongings tied up behind her sidesaddle, and accompanied by a cloaked male figure astride another horse.

The lackwit groom stuttered and stammered this story again to me, adding that it had never occurred to him to raise an alarm when he saw this. It meant nothing to him, he asserted, that his mistress should have decided to go for an early morning ride. Herein he was mistaken; it meant in fact that I paused to slit his nose for him before I took to the road myself in a frantic effort to pick up my lady's trail.

It turned out that there was no trail, at least none that I could find. In a state of rage that grew ever colder and more pure, I rode at a good speed for an hour along the road that led in the opposite direction from Florence, but caught no sight of the one I sought. Nor would any of the folk I questioned in passing admit to having seen Helen ride that way with her secret lover, with that faceless, unidentifiable figure in the groom's stammered story, a man who would be glad to settle for losing part of his nose when I caught up with him.

As for what I mean to do to Helen ... I do not remember making any specific plan of vengeance then. But it was well for her that morning that I could not find her.

Of course I might well be pursuing in the wrong direction, and after an hour I turned round. It then naturally took me another hour to get back to our Pisan cottage. I had sent some of the servants I considered most trustworthy to scour the neighborhood in other directions, and these were back before

me. They trembled when they announced that they
had nothing helpful to report. Their fear was wasted,
for when I looked at them I believed that they had
really tried.

What was I to do? Missing spouse or not, honor
and wisdom alike forbade me to postpone by so much
as half a day the start of my long trek to Bosnia. The
king's orders had been explicit, and the urgency of
his need apparent in them.

I did what little packing I had to do, and concluded
the business of closing down the small household. In
all this I was surrounded by servants who moved in a
desperate, counterproductive hurry. My servants in my
homeland had sometimes tended to be that way also.
Whenever I glanced at these folk or spoke to them
they dropped what they were carrying, or shook so that
their fingers could not tie a knot. Matters were not
helped by the gurgling moans, drifting in from the
stables, of the groom with the runny nose. Once or
twice I was on the point of going out to quiet him.

A quick inventory disclosed that Helen had left
behind the greater part of her new wardrobe, including items I had bought to please her, as well as the
lavish gifts of the Medici. I directed that the servants
should share these out among themselves, which acted
as a tonic to their morale. As far as I was able to
determine, my fugitive wife had taken with her no
money, or very little; and no jewelry or gold of any
particular value. There was no telling, of course, what
contribution of wealth her mysterious escort might
have brought to the escape.

At last my eye, searching the vacated rooms for
any bits of important business left unfinished, fell
again upon the painting. My first impulse at that
moment was to draw my bloodied dagger and hack
the thin panel into splinters. But a moment's cool
thought held me back from any such rash demonstration. Not for a moment had I considered permanently

giving up the search for Helen. When eventually I should be free again to look for the woman who had so basely used me (as I then saw the case) and then deserted me when her fortunes had improved, such a close likeness could very well, I thought, prove invaluable.

So, I delayed the start of my own long journey enough to send the painting back to Piero in Florence. Along with it I dispatched a brief written explanation of what had happened, and a request that he should keep the picture for me until I either returned or sent for it. To this I added a plea that the Medici use all their powers to try to find the woman for me whilst I was away at war; and that, should they succeed, Helen be held in some secure convent against my return. To some degree I shared my king's misgivings about convents; but given the society we dwelt in, no better alternative was apparent. Also it galled me, as it always has, to have to ask anyone a favor—but again I could see no better course available.

All this was quickly done. Before midday, a few scant hours after my wife's desertion, I was on the high road out of Pisa, in the company of a few mercenaries I had recruited locally, still growling oaths into my mustache as I rode.

My plan was to go overland, passing the Alps before snow flew. I wanted to avoid the uncertainties of taking ship upon the Adriatic at that season. And besides, if it must be admitted, I had then and have now no particular liking for the sea. Unfortunately for my plans, the first snow of the season reached the high passes simultaneously with myself and my small escort; it cost us a slow and dangerous struggle to get through.

What with one delay and another, I did not reach the scene of the summer's and autumn's fighting until almost midwinter, by which time military operations were nearly at a standstill, King Matthias had withdrawn himself and much of his army to Buda. On the whole, the campaign had gone better than I had expected for the Christian cause. Mohammed II, in personal command of sizable forces, had invested the fortified town of Yaytsa early in the fighting season, but the timely arrival of the Black Army with the King of Hungary at its head had soon broken the seige. Historians, if there be any quick ones in the present audience, may wish to note that the generally unreasonable preference shown by European rulers for mercenary troops during the following few decades can be traced back to this victory by Matthias's well-trained hirelings.

I had missed all the glories of this warm-weather campaign, such as they might have been. But I was not too late, while carrying out a mounted reconnaissance, to take part in a snowy skirmish of more than ordinary stupidity against a Turkish patrol similarly occupied. From this brawl I escaped with my honor and my life, my horse and my sword, the dagger which had once been left on a pillow aimed at my head—and a slow-healing thigh wound that temporarily made any further martial activities on my part out of the question.

I rested in camp until I felt able to sit a horse again, then set out for Buda, progressing by slow stages through a landscape that grew more familiar as I went. I had not been invited to present myself before the king; but then I had not been forbidden to do so, either. Indeed, I had heard nothing at all from Matthias since my leaving Pisa. So I judged that some kind of a personal report was necessary, though I did not look forward to delivering it.

It was already the early spring of 1465 when at last, still hardly able to stand, I appeared before His Majesty in his palace. Matthias looked older; kingship and the Turks were aging him rapidly. He received me in private as before, but with a lack of warmth that was immediately noticeable.

"Where is she, Drakulya? Word reached me months ago that you had lost her."

It was I who had sent him that word, of course. "I do not know where she is, sire." I tried to explain the circumstances as best I could.

He cut me off with a gesture. "I see you have a wound there that prevents your fighting. But you can travel, or you would not be here. So take yourself to Italy again, and find her. It would have been wiser for you to have stayed there last year and seen to the matter. She is your wife now, and I hold you responsible."

Such are the ways of kings, and the difficulties of trying as loyally as possible to serve them. We dissolve now to a shot of me galloping madly right-to-left over the Alps. No, of course in actuality it was not that quickly done. This time the king was not so eager to provide me with letters and with gold. But eventually he had to admit that if I were to go, it were best that I succeed; and if he wanted me to succeed he had better give me all the help he could; and by the time he was convinced of this my leg was better, well enough to try the mountains.

Officially, you understand, I was all this time still imprisoned in the Tower of Solomon. And in truth there were a few moments during this epoch when I might have been tempted to settle for a return to my comfortable cell. But in fact, by the early summer of 1465, I was again on my way south to Italy. This time I was traveling as an officially nameless member of a delegation from Matthias to the new Pope, Paul II. Leader of the delegation was Janus Pannonius, who was what is now called a humanist, and also a poet, of about my own age. Pannonius and his uncle Janus Vitez had long been on good terms with their ruling kinsmen, the Hunyadi family. In a

few years both Januses were to be entranced by an
ill-starred conspirator into a revolutionary intrigue, and
Matthias was going to have them killed; but in 1465
their prospects were still bright.

By the summer of that year, Matthias had somewhat revised his earlier thinking on the subject of
papal crusades. If he, the King of Hungary, was going
to have to make a career out of fighting the Turks
anyway, then he might as well have all the help he
could scrape up, well organized or not. Pannonius and
his delegation were in fact going to Rome to plead
for a new Crusade.

Having gone to school in Italy as a youth,
Pannonius spoke the language well, and with his help
I brushed up on my own Italian during the journey.
En route our leader entertained the rest of the party
with songs of his own devising, verses about the
difficulties of politics, the perils of dealing with the
infernal Turks, and the pains of life's personal tragedies. When he warbled about a cuckolded husband,
he seemed oblivious to the fact that I gave him close
attention, and so I wisely restrained my reactions,
judging that my own history was not known amongst
my companions. All in all, Pannonius blended show
business and politics in a way you might have thought
startlingly modern, could you have heard and understood his yodelings. For my part, at the time I was
little in sympathy with either art. And my mind was
filled with affairs more personally important. When
at last our little party reached Florence, I quietly
dropped out.

Piero had grown a little goutier since I had seen
him last, and a little older under the burden of his
new responsibilities as head of Medici Enterprises.
Still he welcomed me more warmly than my own liege
lord had at Buda. I think it was during this second
trip that I first began to fall in love with Italy. And

the merchant chief listened sympathetically to my problems. Yes, he had been instructing his people to keep their eyes and ears open everywhere they went. But unfortunately he still had nothing to report of Helen's whereabouts. She had perhaps, he thought, gone very far away this time.

I had to agree, though in the past she had demonstrated an affinity for Italy. And perhaps, I thought to myself, this time the Medici were really not so very interested in trying to help me find her. Well, they could scarcely be blamed. They had done much for me already, and they certainly had plenty of other projects to keep them busy, for example trying to make a living, and keeping a complex city-state going in a difficult world. It must have been plain to them that my marriage was a lost cause, even if my bride could be found again; and that Matthias was unlikely to be pleased however the situation turned out now.

As he strolled beside me through the cavernous rooms of the *palazzo* Medici, Piero gripped my sleeve in a friendly way and gave it a little shake. "Have you spoken to Morsino yet, friend Ladislao? It may be that he has heard something that we have not."

"I doubt it. But I will talk to him. And one thing more, Signore Piero, if I may try your patience. Remember the painting that I had sent to you from Pisa? Would it be possible to have some of your people look at it before they depart on trading missions." I said this partly, I suppose, to impress Piero with my unflagging determination.

He nodded vigorously, as if pleased to be bothered with still one more request. Probably he had little intention of honoring it anyway. "The painting is very beautiful, and I thank you for its loan. I have kept it where my eyes can fall on it every day." And with a little beckoning gesture he led me into another room and showed me the Magdalen above a fireplace. We both regarded it for a few moments in silence.

Then Piero went on: "I will have it moved to your room, if you like . . . of course you are going to stay with us, while you are in Florence."

"Thank you, Signore Piero. Your hospitality and generosity are more than a poor soldier like myself deserves." I was about to add that I had no wish to find the painting gazing at me each morning when I awoke, when a new idea struck me, what I considered to be a really clever thought. "And yes, I would like it in my room. Though I trust that my stay will not be long."

To implement my new brainstorm, I paid a visit that very day to Verrocchio's studio. This time I went alone—Lorenzo, I should perhaps explain, was out of town on business at the time.

The studio had been transformed in the year since I had seen it last. There were at least half a dozen apprentices in sight, all of them busy shoveling sand, mixing and grinding pigments, hammering boards together into a platform, sweating and sending up a haze of dust from all the drudgery that lies behind serene fine art in metal and stone and paint. None of these youths recognized me, nor I them. But one went promptly to inform the master of my arrival, and returned in a moment to lead me to another room.

The very structure of the building had been changed considerably during the last twelve-month. A neighbor's stable had been taken over, and built into the growing complex. Raw timber walled some rooms completely new. But though the place was much enlarged, it was still crowded by its new production; business was booming tremendously.

I was conducted to where Verrocchio was at work, in one of the newly added rooms. The master, who had not changed noticeably, was not really glad to see me, though he made me welcome with effusive words. *Here comes trouble,* the expression on his fleshy face proclaimed. He was at work sculpting a

clay figure, about half life-size, whose model, a sturdy
lad wearing only a leather apron and some token bits
of ancient-looking armor, stood on a small stage under
the usual skylight. At a second glance I recognized
this youth, altered by a year's fast growth, as the very
one that I had come to see.

"Messer Verrocchio," I began, "I suppose you have
seen or heard nothing of the Hungarian woman since
the last time I was here?"

"Nothing. Well, that is, only that she . . ."
Verrocchio broke off, looking embarrassed.

"You mean you have heard of my marital difficulties
with her, and that she has run away again."

He nodded.

"Be sure and let me know if you hear more. You
know where I can be reached. But it is really a
painting that I have come to see you about today—
a painting, and this young fellow who did it."

Verrocchio proved willing enough for me to hire
away his apprentice and model for what I said would
probably be a few days' work. He probably thought
that his powerful patrons were still more interested
in helping me than they really were, and I did not
trouble to enlighten him. And so that very afternoon
I was standing with Leonardo before the Magdalen
in my small guest room at the *palazzo* Medici.

"It is only the face that I really want, you see. As
many copies as you can make, drawing well, in the
time that you can work for me. Here is the painting. And you must still have the woman's face in your
mind's eye, as she spent a long time posing for you."

The boy was handsome, but there was something
inhuman, almost, about his eyes. If I had met him
armed in the field, I should have expected him to
be extremely dangerous, for reasons having nothing
to do with size or training.

He said only: "Tracings could be made, if we had
thin paper."

"I can get you paper, or give you money to buy some. What I must have are good likenesses of this woman. I want a man who has never seen her to be able to recognize her when he does, once he has studied one of your sketches."

Leonardo was pinning up a small sheet of paper on the small easel he had brought with him. "Yes, I think I can do that, provided the man who looks has good eyes to see."

He began to draw. I, having learned how sometimes good artisans were bothered by close observation, moved away to look out of the window into the courtyard.

"Have you ever seen the woman again in the flesh?" I asked, as casually as possible. I had not forgotten that only this young artisan's tip had enabled me to locate Helen the first time around.

"No, *signore,*" the boy answered. But there was something in his voice that made me turn back to look at him. I found him regarding me in that calculating, almost robotic way of his. Then he added: "But I have seen Perugino since then."

"Perugino." It took me a few moments to recall where I had heard that name before. Yes, Verrocchio had spoken it, at some point during at least one of my visits to his place of business a year ago. "Perugino was the bearded apprentice, in your master's studio last summer?"

"He had shaved, the last time I saw him."

"And where was that? And when?"

"I saw him here in Florence. About six months ago. But since then I have heard that he has gone to Rome, to paint some murals in a church there. Which church I do not know." Leonardo looked at me for a moment longer, then turned back to his work.

I turned back to the window again. I found one hand, knuckles white, wrist shaking, clutching my dagger's hilt. Dolt that I was! not to have known. But still I could not believe that a king's sister could have left me for a mere artist . . .

Before my eyes in imagination, I brought the face of the bearded one, clear as my memory could focus it. Now I could remember how that countenance had looked when I first brought the rescued Helen into the studio—the very place where *he* had first brought her to be a model. Confused, stunned, displaying a strange mixture of emotions. Somehow I had got the impression that Perugino had first met her in some Florentine tavern. But what had Morsino said? . . . *an attractive girl, of diminutive stature, recently arrived . . . in the company of a troop of traveling players, or an itinerant artist, or something of that kind . . .*

And Matthias, earlier. Something about an artisan. How his sister had actually run off with one. If she could do such a thing when a Sforza wedding was in prospect, then why not as the bride of a Drakulya?

. . . and again, just after the wedding ceremony, Perugino handing her an amful of flowers. How had he looked, then? Could I trust my memory to tell me? And she . . .

It was still almost impossible to believe. I turned away from the window again. "Leonardo," I called softly. In my greatest angers I maintain full control of myself and my behavior. "Be plain. You are telling me that she ran off with this Perugino."

"It is nothing to me, *signore*. I do not wish to become involved. But yes, I think that is what happened."

"I see. And has this matter been discussed at the studio?"

He hesitated. "Not really. Not much. I think we all guessed, last year, what had happened. Perugino quit the studio a little while after you left for Pisa. But you were gone. There was no way to tell you anything. Signore Lorenzo did not come round again to the studio for a long time."

"I see." No one wanted to get involved, really. I supposed that that was natural enough.

Now I thought that the youngster was suddenly afraid of me, perhaps wishing that he had kept quiet. Still his hand sketched steadily enough. He unpinned one paper from his easel and put up another. He was working quickly, already there appeared to be several finished preliminary sketches.

I was about to speak, when I glanced down at them. To study the topmost paper better, I picked it up. It showed the essential lines of the Magdalen's face, angellically done, the key to the face captured, just as I had wished.

Again I was about to speak when the corner of another drawing, at the very bottom of the small pile, caught my eye. I pulled it out. It was every bit as well drawn, but a grotesque.

It was a male countenance, set in an expression, almost a mask, of insane rage. I needed a moment to realize that I was holding a caricature of my own face.

FIFTEEN

Rage augments strength, and sometimes cunning and the will as well. If one can harness it properly, and take the time to seek out tools, and improvise means, then eventually if one has eyes that see in virtual darkness, in a matter of only a few hours perhaps, the door of even a heavy wall safe can be seen swung back, with its great lock reduced to hanging wreckage. Success had been greatly aided by the ability to work on both sides of the door alternately. And now the cans of films and containers of tapes could be brought out. It was something to do, somewhere to start; and it had become necessary now to make a start at once.

Electric power to the Seabright mansion had recently been shut off, a difficulty overcome by some attention to the main. Dorlan and his wife had also departed by the morning after the bombing, which was a help.

The laboratory tucked away in the mansion's lowest level was equipped with projection devices of all kinds, and these when sworn at properly in medieval tongues were at last persuaded to function properly.

The private show, sans titles, soundtrack, or any other frills, began.

At first glance the star of the show, an enormous fat man who cavorted naked with adolescents of both sexes, as in some gross parody of more conventional porn, appeared to be Ellison Seabright himself. At a second look it did not appear to be him. The monumental man in the film looked as big as Ellison and resembled him facially but was even older, with a fringe of white hair round his massive head. Now and then he could be seen casting a look toward the hidden camera that must have done the filming through one of the concealed ports in the playroom wall. It was recognizably the playroom-lounge of this very house where the action was going on. The huge old man knew without a doubt that the camera was there. He was intending to watch himself in action later, evidently thus doubling his enjoyment of these acts. Here we did not have your common garden variety of senior citizen. Mr. Thorn, no stereotype of the golden years himself, had no doubt at all that he was beholding the image of Delaunay Seabright.

The broken safe had yielded up perhaps a dozen cans of film in all, with an equal number of video-tape cartridges. A sampling of three, four, five, six of these containers showed no essential variation in content, though the supporting cast appeared to be always different. With one exception. Several times the same lean, dark man of thirty or thereabouts appeared—otherwise the players were all quite young and interchangeable, coming and going like seasonal flowers in a vase.

After the sixth sample, Thorn turned off the projector and sat in darkness trying to think. He could feel that sunny daylight had come, aboveground, but that did not concern him here. His course of breaking into the safe, despite its first feeling of instinctive rightness, was proving to be of no apparent help. The sad secrets of the safe seemed to have nothing to do at all with Mary Rogers or her death. Nor did they explain why Seabright or anyone else would have any reason to want to eliminate Thorn. Nothing here to tell Thorn who was guilty, where to start a search . . .

A faint sound, aboveground, out of doors but near the house. A car had stopped.

Someone else was coming to the mansion.

There was no hurry on this job, no need to be furtive. As former butler-bodyguard in the house, the man called Brandreth still had a set of keys. If the police or the FBI or reporters should be watching the place this morning, he could tell them he had been sent by Ellison Seabright to check on things, and Ellison Seabright would back him up.

Brandreth eased his car to a stop outside the iron gates, and got out to unlock them. Even before he stopped, he had noticed the other car, parked a little distance away on the other side of the road. Whoever was watching the place from over there wasn't trying to be very subtle about it. Brandreth of course would go on in, the perfectly respectable servant doing a job. Only when he was in the house and sure, very sure, that he was alone, would he get on with his real job and go to open the small hidden safe that Gliddon had told him of . . .

A couple of hours earlier, about dawn, Brandreth had met Gliddon in a small town in northern Arizona, to get keys and instructions. Brandreth had been at the door of the dingy hotel room, leaving, when Gliddon called him back. "And, listen, if you ever get any ideas about seeing what's on those tapes and films and putting them to use yourself—"

"Not me, boss. Not me."

"—then you can go right ahead and try. They're not *worth* a cent, get me? I'd go and take care of them myself if that was the case, even if I am supposed to be missing. They're just something that could mean trouble for whoever is found in possession of them, and Seabright tells me he wants 'em out of the house. So get 'em and dispose of 'em, and I mean thoroughly."

"I will. I—"

"How are you going to do it?"

Brandreth, with an inward sigh, leaned his large body against the doorframe. Gliddon's stare always unnerved him and he tried to take a relaxed pose in order not to show it. "Want me to bring 'em here?"

"All the way up here? No. I won't be here anyway, I have to disappear again. Just tear them up, burn them, scatter the ashes. Then stay in Phoenix, where I can get hold of you by phone. I may have another job for you soon."

Brandreth looked a question.

"No, I don't think it'll involve wasting anybody, this time. Never can tell, though."

"I did all right on that Blazer, huh?"

"I guess." Gliddon looked meditative. "It just bothers me that the guy we were supposed to get wasn't in it after all. Maybe we shouldn't have been so cute, using delayed timers and all."

"That was your—"

"I know, my idea." Gliddon spoke very patiently and reasonably. "I just didn't want your thing going off in the hotel garage, injuring innocent bystanders and all. Too much heat gets generated that way. It's bad publicity. Well, it looks like maybe we got rid of Thorn anyway; he may still be running. And I don't think our employer's really unhappy either that we blew up that bothersome broad. Teach her to go out with strangers." And Gliddon had smiled.

Brandreth, watching, felt something like a shudder, purely internal. Even if Gliddon was not as big, and a queer besides, Brandreth was afraid of him.

❖   ❖   ❖

Now, several hours later, Brandreth going calmly about his butler's business had just got the iron gate unlocked when he heard a car door from across the road. He looked up and saw that a lone man had just got out of the vehicle, an ancient sort of wreck, that was parked over there. The man was walking across the road toward Brandreth, approaching tiredly, almost reluctantly. Not a cop, probably not a reporter either, although there was nothing specific about him to rule out either possibility. He had long brown hair and an unkempt beard, and looked as if he hadn't slept all night.

When the man got close he said: "I was just watching, wondering if anyone was home over here."

"The house is vacant now, sir." Brandreth was wary, but confident. He had several inches and about thirty pounds on the other man, not taking into account the pistol in his belt under his jacket, if this turned out to be a game of some kind. "I'm one of the staff. I just come round periodically to check if everything's all right."

"Oh." The other considered this, with vacant sadness. He put his hands in his pockets and brought out a big-bowled pipe and put it away again. "I'm Robinson Miller. Mary Rogers was . . . was a good friend of mine. She used to live here once. Maybe you knew her."

"Sir?"

"Mary Rogers. The girl who was blown up with a bomb last night. I've been at the morgue, looking at her, trying to find out something from the police. You ever look at anyone in a morgue? Who's been all torn to pieces by a bomb?"

Brandreth had to bite the inside of his cheek to keep from smiling. Talk about coincidence, this was good. Gliddon would get a chuckle out of this one when Brandreth told him—or would he? "I'm sorry to hear that, sir. There was something on the radio about someone being blown up in a car."

"She was out here, at this house, last night, you see. With a man named Thorn, the one the car was rented by. Did you know that?"

"No, sir, I had no idea she was here last night." Brandreth found the impulse to smile completely gone. He was watching this dazed man very carefully and at the same time trying to think. "Dorlan, he's the regular caretaker, would have been here then."

Robinson Miller wasn't really listening. "You see, I talked to the police at the morgue, but I didn't really say anything important. I wanted to think things over, first. Like I might have an idea of who was behind the bombing. It was these people here, this Seabright bunch, who killed her, one way or another. Oh, I don't blame you, you just work here. There was a man named Gliddon who worked here too, and he's supposed to be dead now but he's not."

"He's not?" Brandreth had no trouble at all in sounding surprised.

"No he isn't. Thorn told us that and they killed him, or tried to. Mary knew it, and they killed her."

This sounded like it might be too serious to let it get by without taking action. "Sir? You really don't look well. Would you like to come into the house for a moment? I can get you a cup of coffee, or a drink, or something."

Miller sighed. He rotated his head, and rubbed the back of his neck in weariness. "That's good of you. Maybe I will, if you're sure they're all gone. I wouldn't want to face them just now. I don't know what I might do."

"They're all gone, I'm sure. Listen, there might be a thing or two I could tell you about the Seabrights, if you're interested. I don't want to get involved, though."

Miller suddenly looked somewhat more awake. "A thing or two? Like what?"

"Oh, not about bombings. Nothing like that. But . . . look, sir, why don't you just drive your car in through the gate, and park near the house? There's been some problem lately with vandalism in the neighborhood."

"With my car, it doesn't matter," Miller said. But then when Brandreth looked anxious he trudged back across the road and started up his engine. With the gate standing open, they drove both cars in; then Miller waited in his while Brandreth locked up the gate again. Then he followed Brandreth's car up to the house, where neither car would be visible from outside the gate.

As he led the way up to the main door, Brandreth looked the place over carefully. The house looked tightly closed up, all right. But as soon as he had unlocked and opened the front door, he stopped; an overhead light just inside was burning, and he had thought that the electricity was supposed to be already turned off. Well, things might go a little easier on this visit if it wasn't. Like a good butler Brandreth switched the overhead light off now, then gestured deferentially. "The bar's downstairs, sir. If you'd like a drink." Downstairs was more certainly private, if things should happen to take a turn for which privacy appeared desirable, as Brandreth was beginning to feel sure they would.

"It's morning, but—hell yes. I want a drink."

Since the power was still on, Brandreth led the way toward the elevator. Once he had his guest down in the rec room at the bar, he filled an order for Scotch on the rocks, and then tried to reach Dorlan on the intercom that communicated with the Caretaker's quarters. No one answered. Evidently the man and his wife were gone, and the dogs with them, as Gliddon had said they would be. All satisfactory, the place would be lonely as a tomb.

Brandreth flipped off the intercom and gazed across the bar at Miller, who already looked like a lonely drunk. Half the Scotch was gone. Brandreth asked: "Did I understand you correctly, sir? That you have some reason to think Mr. Gliddon is still alive?"

Miller looked up, though not as if he really saw Brandreth, or heard him. He chewed his brown mustache. "You know, she just wouldn't leave it alone. She wouldn't. She kept harassing Seabright, and threw that stuff on him, and then she went off with Thorn to cook up something more. I don't know what, but . . . I guess she never really understood how dangerous the world can be."

"Sir, I can make you another one of those if you'd like."

Robinson Miller looked down at his glass for a fairly long time. "I don't know," he said at last.

"Excuse me, sir, I just want to check on something in here." While Brandreth was waiting for his man to get drunk and/or talk some more spontaneously, he thought he might as well do the job that he had come here for in the first place. Switching on more lights as he went, he walked off into the white tunnel and through it to the laboratory area just off the museum. Here a white panel in the wall came loose, just as Gliddon had said it would, and the small safe hidden behind it opened properly for Brandreth when he used the combination Gliddon had provided. He closed up the safe again and started to walk back to the lounge. All the valuable art had already been taken out, of course, and everything looked—

What was that wrecking bar doing, lying beside the inner laboratory door? Brandreth detoured a few steps and stood looking down at the tool. He thought he recognized it as one that was customarily kept in a shed near the caretaker's lodging.

He had broken into houses himself in his time, and he had a feel for when something was going on along

that line. The lab door was locked, but it took
Brandreth only a moment to find the right key in his
bunch. With gun in hand he opened the locked door,
to behold ruin—a big wall safe, one Gliddon hadn't
even mentioned, yawning open. The door of it had
somehow been cracked, with parts dangling from their
steel roots in the concrete-reinforced wall.

Someone was behind him, and Brandreth spun,
brandishing the gun. Miller had doubtless been
approaching innocently, for he was carrying his drink
in hand. At the sight of Brandreth's face and weapon
he recoiled, and seemed to come fully awake for the
first time.

Miller started to say: "You've got to be in on—"
before he caught himself. Then he tried again, lamely:
"There's been a robbery."

"Brilliant, cocksucker," said Brandreth, and raised
the gun. He had been surprised and upset at a moment
when he thought himself in control of the situation,
and when that happened he sometimes tended to lose
his head. Miller turned, cowering away, trying to protect his head. Brandreth brought the gunbarrel down,
cracking on a forearm, bringing a yelp of pain. Then
he laid the second blow alongside Miller's hairy head,
not too hard. Miller pitched forward on his face, and
lay there groaning, trying to move.

"Now, son of a bitch," said Brandreth. "You're
gonna tell me—"

He reached down, meaning to yank the smaller
man to his feet. But something that felt like a gorilla's
paw closed on Brandreth's own left shoulder. His
reaching arm was stopped. Then his whole body was
yanked into the air, as it hadn't been since he was
pint-sized and in the orphanage. Now he was being
thrown. The room spun round him with his flight,
and smashed him with its far wall, almost hard enough
to knock him out.

He wasn't that easy to take out, though. Gun still

in his right hand, he got himself up on one knee, ready to use it on—

—on one thin man in dark, burned-looking clothes. A man with a pale, half-familiar face, calm now as an utter lunatic. Thorn, God yes, it was Thorn. Brandreth, when playing butler, had one day answered the front door of this very house to let him in. He must be a black belt in judo, to throw a man of Brandreth's weight like that . . . but Brandreth held the top card in his own hand now. As his head cleared, he smiled, even though his left shoulder still wasn't working, and was going to begin to hurt like a bastard in a minute.

The situation, and Thorn's burned clothes, made Brandreth smile again. "Holy shit," he remarked. "You must have been standing right beside the car." Then he made a preemptory motion with his gun. "Who else is in here?"

"No one," the singed man said calmly. "We three are quite alone."

"You blew that safe? I guess you're pretty good in the trade yourself." Brandreth could see, in the far corner of the room, Robinson Miller getting slowly up to his hands and knees. A drop of blood dripped from Miller's head to the carpet. But this time it wasn't going to be Brandreth's job to clean up anything.

Thorn inquired: "In the trade?"

"You know. Making things go bang. I'm pretty good at that myself."

At last there came a change in Thorn's madly cool expression—a relief for Brandreth, it had begun to make him nervous to have someone look back at him like that from the wrong end of a gun.

"Then it was you," said Thorn, "who planted the bomb . . . ?" He had no need to finish. He could read his answer in Brandreth's face. "How fortunate," he added in a softer tone, and came walking forward.

"You're better off dead, you lunatic," said Brandreth, and fired. Twice.

And somehow missed, both times. How could he have missed? And fired again, and—

The grip this time came on the arm that held the gun. Brandreth screamed, feeling the bones go.

When he came out of it, or at least out of it enough to know where he was, he wished he hadn't. He was sitting propped up in one of the chairs inside the laboratory, which was almost dark. In front of him a projection screen had been rolled open, and Thorn stood nearby, fussing with a projector. Beyond Thorn the door was open to the small room with the cot, and Brandreth could see that Robinson Miller was lying in there. Miller's face looked pale in the dim light but he was only sleeping, for his chest rose and fell.

Thorn lifted his head from what he was doing, enough to glance at Brandreth from the corner of an eye. He inquired softly: "What is on this film that you were carrying?"

"Honest to God . . . I don't know."

"We shall soon see, in any event. Why did you come to this house today?"

"I—I was the butler here. Just checking up—"

Thorn put out a hand and touched him on the arm. "That is a half-truth, and not acceptable. Ah, if screaming will relieve your feelings, pray continue. I feel sure that those who scream down here are never heard outside."

The next time Brandreth's senses cleared, Thorn was bending over him again, but only speaking very gently, pointing to a frozen image on the screen. "That is the face of Delaunay Seabright, is it not?"

"I . . ." Brandreth tried his best to see the screen clearly. He was still slumped in his chair, groggy with shock, bathed in a cold sweat. His left arm wouldn't work and his right felt as if the bones might be about to poke out through his coat sleeve. He didn't want to know if they really were. "I dunno." His voice was pitiful. "I never saw Delaunay. Honest to God. Ellison's the one who hired me."

"And Gliddon?"

"Gliddon was already working for the Seabrights. I take orders from Gliddon. He passes on what . . . Ellison wants." Brandreth drew a deep, shuddering breath. Once he had been seriously afraid of Gliddon. But now he understood more fully what it could mean to be afraid. "Gliddon's supposed to be dead now. But he's not."

"To be sure," Thorn said soothingly. "And it was Gliddon who sent you here to get this film?"

Brandreth nodded. He could feel another faint coming on now, and tried to fight it back. He knew that if he fainted now he was going to be revived. But he didn't know how.

"And what were you to do with it?"

"Destroy it. The film and tape both. Just the ones in the little, hidden safe. Gliddon said there were more in a big wall safe somewhere, the one you blew I guess. But he didn't care about those. Why these are so important I don't know. Something big is going on here that I don't know about . . . I don't ask questions. I need help with this arm. Or I'm gonna pass out."

"Who helped you with the bombing?"

"I . . . do all that on my own. Gliddon just told me to do it."

"Not Ellison Seabright?"

"It was supposed to be what he wanted done. I dunno. I hardly ever talk to Ellison. He's supposed to be in Santa Fe now. As far as I know, he is."

Thorn turned away, to the projector. Brandreth let out a sighing groan. In the next room, Robinson Miller mumbled something but did not wake up. Now the screen darkened, then brightened again with a closeup of Delaunay's face, talking.

"This will be Session Thirteen," Delaunay's bass voice said, addressing the camera. He was filmed sitting in the laboratory. He was wearing a turtleneck sweater under an expensive sport coat, and looked vastly more competent, somehow, than his half-brother ever did. "Session Thirteen, on the fourth of April. I think we made real progress yesterday, and I hope for more today."

Darkness again, and when the scene came back there were two people sitting in the lab. In a soft reclining chair facing Delaunay and what was probably a hidden camera sat a teenaged girl with brown hair, small and slight, demurely dressed. Delaunay was also fully clothed, and it was soon apparent that both participants were likely to remain that way.

The girl was gazing, dreamily, at a small instrument on Delaunay's desk that sent a rhythmic, gentle, flashing light into her eyes.

"—sleep," Del was intoning gently as the scene started. "Deep sleep. And you will not wake up until I tell you. You will be able to hear me perfectly, and follow my instructions, but you will not awaken until I tell you . . . Helen? Are you asleep?"

"Yes," the girl answered in a calm, remote voice. Her eyes were now closed.

Delaunay brought his hand out from under his desk, where it had perhaps been on a hidden control that served to turn hidden recording devices off and on.

In Brandreth's ear Thorn whispered: "Who is the girl?"

"It must be Helen Seabright. The one who was killed. It looks like her pictures. I never saw her."

Thorn stood up straight, emitting a faint sigh.

"The last time we talked, Helen," Seabright was now saying, in the voice of a chatty psychiatrist, "you told me that next time you'd tell me why that painting fascinates you so."

"I don't want to talk about that, Uncle Del." It was a prim, calm voice, the voice of a young lady who knew her mind.

"But next time is now, Helen," Seabright prodded gently. When he got no response he tried again. "I'll make a bargain with you, if you like. How's this? I'll leave the painting where you can come and look at it anytime. And in return—what, Helen?" The girl had said something, very low.

"I said, it was really Annie who liked the painting anyway."

"Oh yes, of course. But you can like it too."

"And Annie's dead now."

"No more Annie. That's quite right. And do you miss her?"

Helen frowned.

Seabright said softly and with great certainty: "Annie was always running away. She had no home, no family, no love. Always and forever on the run. Don't you think it's really better that she's dead?"

"I don't miss her, really. She's really better off . . . but sometimes . . ."

"Yes. All right. Now, as I started to say, Helen, I'll leave the painting out somewhere, where you can look at it. And in return you, now don't frown, you don't have to talk about the painting at all if you don't want to. Only about some other things, that happened to you when you were . . . much younger than you are now. How does that kind of bargain sound?"

The girl was troubled. Frowning, she shook her head, and mumbled something.

"We don't necessarily have to go back very far in the things we talk about. Not right away. Suppose we began with that night when, how shall I describe it, that night when Annie was here for the first time? Would it bother you—I see it would. All right. All right. You needn't do anything that you don't want to do. Not at all. Not for Uncle Del. Would you rather talk to me about the painting, then? It's a nice, fascinating old thing, isn't it?"

"Yes. Oh yes, it is." And Helen's agitation, that had been growing, eased somewhat.

"Who painted it, my dear? Who do you think did?"

Brandreth, somewhat surprised at himself that he still hadn't passed out again, heard a small, strange sound from somewhere nearby. From Thorn.

Delaunay Seabright's image explained: "You see, my dear, some people think it may have been done, long years ago, by a famous painter called Verrocchio. Have you heard of him?"

"Yes."

"Now don't say you have, don't say anything just to please me. You really did hear of Verrocchio, before I mentioned him?"

"Yes."

Seabright paused, as if hopeful that the girl might say more. When she did not, he went on: "Others, on the other hand, think it barely possible that a certain young boy did that painting. A boy who became quite famous in later life. Most authorities believe the boy was too young when this was painted, that he hadn't yet started to work in Mr. Verrocchio's studio. Now I wasn't there myself and I don't know. But I'd like very much to find out. If—"

The girl was toppling forward in her chair. Seabright moved quickly for all his bulk, to catch her, ease her tenderly back into a sitting position. Her face had gone completely pale, drained-looking. "All right, Helen. All right, that's it for today. You are feeling fine. You are going to wake up soon, when I tell you, as from a deep, refreshing sleep." It took another minute of careful coaxing and urging to bring the girl back into what appeared to be her original hypnotic state.

"I'm going to wake you up soon, Helen. First, though, would you like to give Uncle Del his big hug for the day?"

The girl's eyes opened for a moment, then closed again. She arose, dutifully, and walked to the man's chair to bend over him and hug him, gently, almost formally, like some shy distant niece. The huge man patted her back with one hand. His other hand went to the hidden control beneath his desk. The screen went dark.

The ringing phone jarred Chicago police lieutenant Joe Keogh out of sleep. He was lying in his and Kate's bedroom in their condominium apartment on the North Side, just off Lake Shore Drive. This was not one of the supremely expensive towers down close to Michigan Boulevard, but an older building of modest height, somewhat farther north. The place had large rooms, from the days when they built them that way, and hardwood floors and a fireplace. Joe would have been hard pressed to make the mortgage payments on his pay unaided, let alone trying to furnish and decorate the place the way Kate had. He found it really pleasant to have married into money.

He rolled his spare, muscular body over in the wide waterbed, establishing waves, and lifted the phone. "Hello, who's this?" At home he used a more guarded answering technique than the efficient response that was his habit at the office.

"Joseph, I have some information for you."

Joe was fully awake in an instant. He switched on the bedside lamp, and at the same time glanced over his shoulder toward Kate, as if for reassurance that she still slept at his side. He could see, between a mounded blue blanket and a white pillow, a familiar mass of honey-blond hair and the curve of one naked shoulder. For a man with his job, middle-of-the-night phone calls were nothing out of the ordinary, and in six months of marriage Kate had already schooled herself to sleep through most of them.

Joe was sitting up straight now, running a hand

through his sandy hair. The waterbed was no scene for serious drama; it wobbled gelatinously, gently rocking his body and his wife's. "Are you hurt?" he asked the phone.

"No, Joseph, not seriously. I appreciate your concern." The voice sounded much as it had on the comparatively few occassions when Joe had heard it before: precise, slightly accented in a vaguely middle-European way. Good-humored. Still good-humored, after a bombing, oh my God.

Joe found himself sweating slightly, and turned back the covers a little. "Go ahead, then."

"First of all I would like to confirm what I have heard about how it could have been done; how the bomb could possibly have been planted where it was."

"Yeah, the bomb. I heard about that. They called me about it. Were you near the car when it blew up?"

"I was in it."

"Oh." Good God. "And you're . . . who do you think planted the bomb?"

"On that I believe I now have information that is accurate, if incomplete. The technician was a man named Brandreth, acting on orders from a man called Gliddon. The very same, I believe, whose aircraft was supposedly lost not long ago."

"Ah. That business about the painting. And where are Brandreth and Gliddon now? And how do you spell Brandreth?"

"Gliddon is probably somewhere in Arizona or New Mexico; I have no precise information. And Brandreth can be found in the Seabright mansion in Phoenix. The place is otherwise unoccupied."

"He's in—"

"You need make no hurried calls, nor be concerned to write down his name. He will be there."

"Oh."

"Now about the bomb. By the way, Joseph, is your home telephone secure?"

"I guess. Internal Investigation doesn't tap it any more, if that's what you mean. Since you were here in Chicago they've given up. They don't want to know what's going on with me."

"Then let us discuss the bomb. No one, I think, could have planted it in that vehicle between the last proper functioning of the starter and the explosion."

"Okay, I have a couple of ideas. Sometimes I talk shop with a friend of mine who's on the Bomb Squad. It's possible to use a detonator that doesn't function until the second or third time the starter's used. Or to use a timer. A timer could be set for a specific time, or else not to start running until the engine did."

"I see. Yes, that confirms what I have been told. Thank you."

Joe glanced again at Kate. She hadn't moved, and he thought it probable that she was still asleep. He said: "The Phoenix police told me on the phone that it looked like a real professional job. See, your hotel there had a record of a call from your room to my number at the station here in Chicago. So naturally one of the first things Phoenix did in their investigation was to call me."

"Naturally. I suppose they named no suspects? Did the name of Ellison Seabright arise at all in your conversation?"

"No it didn't. I wouldn't have expected them to name me suspects even if they had some. You think he was involved too?"

"Gliddon works for the Seabright family. Or he did. Much is still obscure to me. And there are matters involved that I find personally troubling. I want to be certain about Ellison before I move against him."

"Please do."

"And what," the distant voice inquired, with casual brightness, "did you say to the Phoenix police about me?"

Kate had moved. She was facing Joe now, and at least one of her baby-blue eyes was open, regarding him over a mound of pillow as she waited calmly to find out what was going on. Maybe she had already heard enough to know, or guess, who he was talking to.

Still watching Kate, Joe cleared his throat. "I told them that a man calling himself Thorn sometimes phones me and gives me information. That I had no idea of this Thorn's real name or where he lives or where he calls me from. That's not as crazy as it might sound. There actually are informants who behave like that, and sometimes they give useful information."

When the other end of the line remained silent, Joe went on: "Of course the next thing they asked was what you had been calling me about from Phoenix." He paused again here, thinking carefully. If ever it should come to a choice between getting himself into legal trouble, police trouble, and making an enemy out of the man now on the phone, he knew which choice he'd have to make. Kate's family could afford the best in legal help, but a lot of good that would do him if—"I said you'd talked to me about a possible lead on the missing painting that's been in the news, but that you hadn't given me anything definite on it at all. Is that all right?"

"Yes, Joe, that is quite all right." A soothing tone.

"Of course they quickly discovered that there isn't any Oak Tree, Illinois. And since your home address was a fake they'll probably assume that the name Thorn's a fake too. So most likely they're stuck as to where to look for you next. Since your body wasn't found with the car, they'll assume you weren't in it. Maybe they think you planted the bomb yourself. By the way, there were parts of a pair of men's shoes, pretty well destroyed, found in the wreckage."

"I am not surprised to hear it. Brandreth's shoes fit me tolerably well."

"They thought the woman's body was lying on the wrong side of the vehicle for her to have been in the driver's seat. It was the Mary Rogers you were asking about, I assume you know that. Say, was she a friend of yours? If so, I'm sorry."

The long-distance hum of equipment. "We had not grown to know each other well," Thorn replied at last. "Still, I think a certain rapport was beginning to grow between us. We might have become good friends. One has few good friends even in a long life, and one loses even them. Yes, her death grieves me."

Kate reached out to touch Joe's arm with one finger. When he looked at her, her lips formed a silent, one-word question: Judy?

Joe shook his head minimally. He had no reason to think as yet that Judy had come into it at all. Then he asked the telephone: "What about that O'Grandison you were asking about, is he connected with this in any way? None of my contacts here seem to know where he is. They say they haven't seen him for a while. Have you reached him yet?"

"I have not. I know no more about him now than when I spoke with you last."

"Okay. Do you want me to tell Phoenix that I've heard from you again? That you blame the bombing on Gliddon and this Brandreth or whoever he is?"

Thorn took a moment before answering. "If in return, when you hear anything about the whereabouts of Gliddon, you are willing to tell me—then yes, you may tell them that."

"On second thought I guess I won't have to mention Brandreth. But I'll tell them that you called again, and that you claim Gliddon's still alive. How's that?"

"That will be fine. . . . Joseph."

"What?"

"Do not worry, about me. I mean that I am an old friend of Kate's family, which is now yours. I know that you are my friend, and mean well. And I am not all that greatly concerned about what you tell or do not tell the police in Phoenix or anywhere else. Trouble with the law does not mean much to me, ultimately. Take care of Kate, and of yourself."

And with a distant click the line went dead. Joe had the vague sensation that his ears were burning. As if he had been caught out in cowardice.

Slowly he hung up the phone, and looked at Kate. He said: "I was going to tell you. I did call your little sister, earlier, trying to warn her not to get involved in this. She got a little angry at me, but I think she knows I'm right."

Kate looked doubtful at first. Then she looked worse than doubtful. "I don't know, Joe. You say you made her angry? Were you issuing orders?"

"Come on, give me credit for a little more sense than that."

"Still, I don't know. She's quite grown up now. Maybe even suggesting what she ought to do was a mistake."

"I figured she must have heard in the news about the bombing. I don't know if she knows that now he's calling himself Thorn. I don't have any idea when they've seen each other last, to tell the truth."

"I don't know either." Kate sighed. "Maybe it's all over. And her school *is* at least five hundred miles away from Phoenix."

"I don't think it's all over for her. She got angry. But as far as I could tell she wasn't really planning to do anything, like go to Arizona. She's anything but a wild kid, usually." Then Joe paused, listening to his own words, what he was saying about a girl who had had an affair with a vampire, however brief.

Husband and wife lay looking at each other,

exchanging hopeful and supportive thoughts. At least Joe was trying to make the exchange hopeful, and he could see that Kate was doing the same.

"Well," Joe added at last, "we could call her again in the morning, and tell her that we know for sure now that he's still alive."

"She must know that much at least," Kate said positively. "There's still at least that much contact between them, if there's any relationship left at all."

"Yeah, I suppose. That's spooky." Joe knew that Kate knew more about the subject than he did.

"Give me a hug, Joey."

Joe rolled away from Kate to turn the light off. Then he rolled back again. Kate hugged his face against her bare breasts.

The telephone rang again.

For a moment, as he floundered his way back over the quaking mattress to pick up the receiver, Joe's imagination flickered with a truly horrible suggestion. Suppose, just suppose, that Thorn had been deranged somehow by the bomb's concussion, and turned into a crank phone caller. To imagine *him* gone mad, driven out of the state that with him passed for normality . . .

"Hello, who is this?"

In the next moment; puzzlement and fear had a new tangent. It was a woman's voice on the phone, one that Joe had never heard before. It sounded young, and, of all things, vaguely British. "Yes. Am I speaking to Mr. Joseph Keogh?"

"Lieutenant Keogh. Yes. Who is this?" It didn't sound like long distance this time.

"Sorry, lieutenant, of course, of the police department. I don't suppose you would recognize my name. I should like to communicate with Mr. Jonathan Thorn. Have you any idea at what number I could reach him quickly?"

SIXTEEN

Pat O'Grandison was heading west again. From northern Indiana he thumbed his way through Chicago and right on, following Route 66, or Interstate 55 as they called it now. His intention was to find Annie, the girl he really liked.

He had missed Annie, he had to admit it to himself, more than he could remember ever missing anyone before. They had met—well, never mind where they had first met, but they had spent days together in Chicago some months back. Then Annie had dropped out of sight and Pat had just assumed that she was gone for good, like everything else good that had ever happened to him. Then bang, gosh, one night in Calumet City, Indiana, she had shown up again out of nowhere. At least Pat was almost sure she had. Not really *absolutely* sure, because next morning he had been having a bad time with his mind again, and the morning after that he woke up in the looney bin again.

He stayed in the mental hospital for a few weeks and was then discharged, with all the usual bullshit about commitment to a sheltered care program and a case worker and so on, and on that same day he sniffed the air and decided that the warm weather was far enough advanced to hit the road. And headed west.

Damn, but he missed her. Annie was the only girl, the only female, practically the only person of any kind that Pat could remember feeling anything like this about. Almost the only person he could remember ever really liking. And what made it even stranger, was that as a rule he could get along okay with girls and women but he didn't usually seek them out, or care for them as close associates. For a companion, a partner in bed or on the road, he generally felt better with another male. Preferably a bigger and stronger male whose presence could afford at least the illusion of protection; as almost any boy, by the time he was half grown, was bigger and stronger than Pat, that particular condition was not too hard to fulfill.

But now he just kept on thinking about Annie, the girl he really liked. She had told him once, just before they took her off to the juvenile home in Chicago and got ready to put Pat on trial, that her last name was Chapman. A lot of the people that Pat met had changed or were changing their names for one reason or another, so he tended not to take names very seriously—he wasn't always completely sure what his own real name ought to be, if it came to that. But he was sure that he liked Annie, whether Annie Chapman was her real name or not, and he needed her as much as he had ever needed anyone. She was all girl, nothing dyke about her, and yet she still had an air about her of being able to offer protection. Small as she was, no bigger than Pat himself, there was this hard core in her that he sensed he could lean on. And even if the protection she offered was not physical—well, maybe there were kinds of protection even more important.

In bed she did some kinky things, at least as far
out as anyone else he'd ever known. And he had
known a few. And the coupling of his body with hers
had given him more than he'd ever got before, with
man or woman or girl or boy. And maybe, Pat thought
in a corner of his mind now that he was on the road
again, maybe he had better convince himself that it
was just the good sex with Annie that was making him
look for her now. Because, if he thought about it, he
was almost sure that there was more to it than that;
and somehow it bothered him deeply that there
should be more.

It could be that one of the things that had him
out on the road again looking for her was the simple
fact that Annie *liked* him. She had talked with Pat,
stayed with him when she could have chosen to go
off with someone else, had gone out of her way
sometimes to do little things that she knew would
make him happy. Very few people ever did that. Most
people of whatever age or sexual orientation did not
like Pat for long, once things between them had got
beyond the elementary first stage in which they simply
admired his more-than-half-childish good looks.

So here he was, hitchhiking southwest on the
interstate out of Chicago. And how many times had
he come this way before? He didn't really know. More
than a couple. He wasn't at all sure how many. One
of the problems with being periodically insane was
that things in the past always tended to get blurred.

But, on the other hand, what you might have
thought would be a difficult problem, that of locating Annie, didn't really bother Pat at all. Because he
now had a strong feeling for where Annie ought to
be. Where she had to be, in fact. He couldn't name
the place but he could tell where it was. Roughly
southwest of Chicago, and at some distance considerably more than a day's drive.

This was another thing that could be scary if he

stopped and let himself think about it much. He knew it wasn't normal to have this kind of a strong hunch for where another person was. But then there were a lot of things about himself that were abnormal, as he had known for a long time. A number of doctors and other experts had found different words to tell him so. If you looked at it in that light, one more abnormality didn't seem all that worrisome. Besides, he had figured out that his hunch could have a logical explanation. Annie might have mentioned to him sometime that she intended to head for some certain place in the Southwest, and maybe Pat had been stoned or drunk or half asleep or a little crazy, or all of the above, and what Annie said hadn't registered properly with his conscious mind. But on some deeper level he had heard, and remembered.

On the first day of this present trip, going southwest through Illinois and then Missouri, Pat told the people who gave him rides that he was headed for California. Each time, as soon as he had told someone where he was going, they wanted to know where he was coming from, and each time he said that he had just left home. To questioners who tried to pin him down more closely, he answered that home was in Chicago—it was a big city, as good a place to be from as any other. He never mentioned his just-concluded stint in the Indiana mental hospital, or any of his previous stints in similar institutions elsewhere. Pat knew he was crazy, but he had never been crazy enough to tell a benefactor that.

As evening approached at the end of his first day's travel, Pat hiked himself down off the main highway. Spring was far enough advanced so that he wasn't going to freeze to death overnight no matter where he slept, but he hoped to somehow get inside. He thought he would be able to manage that. Enough trips on the road, and you developed a feeling for such things, when things were likely to be easy, and when hard. Here the crickets were out as darkness fell, and it was almost like summer. Pat liked deep summer best.

On the outskirts of Joplin, Missouri, he found himself hiking past a deserted-looking house. No other houses were very near. A look around and another quick sniff of the air decided him that he was not likely to find a better prospect. He went to a side window and checked out the house. No furniture. It was not only deserted but seemed to have been standing vacant for some time. Pat broke a window in the back and climbed inside.

He put his knapsack on the floor for a pillow and covered himself with his light jacket, the best he could do toward keeping warm. As for food, the last people to give him a ride had bought him a sandwich, too, out of pity, and that would have to do for food until tomorrow. Pat was used to not eating a lot. Though it was still early in the evening he fell asleep almost at once, stretched out on the bare floor.

At first he knew that he was asleep, and shivering a little. Then he began to dream of Annie. In Pat's dream, *she* was asleep, stretched out also upon boards, but her boards looked like the floor of an attic somewhere. She was wearing a nondescript pullover shirt and jeans. Then Annie in the dream opened her eyes and looked at Pat, and smiled at him, and he knew beyond any doubt that in a moment she would reach out her arms to him and they would make love. Instead all that happened was that he woke up, uncomfortable on the boards after having got used to a hospital bed again, and shaking a little more with cold than he had been before. Well, life was usually like that.

Late next morning, when he had got as far as Oklahoma, Pat began to have serious doubts about California as his real destination, though he continued to use it as an answer whenever he was asked.

Everyone more or less expected that a young drifter would be headed for the Coast. Whereas if he had said that he was bound for somewhere in Arizona or New Mexico, that would be an interesting answer; people would wonder why he was going there, and ask more questions, and think about him some more. Or so it seemed to Pat. As a general rule, the less other people wondered and thought and talked about him, the happier he was.

As the day went on a little, he began also to have a feeling that he didn't want to go to Arizona. He wasn't sure why. But he certainly hoped it would turn out that Annie wasn't there.

A few of the people who gave him rides asked him what he meant to do when he reached California. He answered that he meant to get a job there making films. Whenever he said this, his questioner looked at him again, and chuckled to himself or herself in one tone or another, and immediately became patronizing. Because they could see he wasn't joking. But in fact his answer was quite sane and realistic. He would have got a job making films if he had been going to California. Not Hollywood movies, no, which the people assumed he meant. But there were a number of people in other towns out there making a lot of other movies of one kind and another, and during the past few years Pat had already been connected with several of them. In matters having anything to do with movie-making he was an authentic genius, though totally unpublicized, usually unemployed, and practically unpaid.

Sometimes the people who gave him rides asked him how old he was. They were beginning to have plans for him, at least tentative plans, of one kind or another, when they asked that. Pat's answer would vary, depending. If he thought the tentative plan was to hand over poor young Pat to the juvenile authorities somewhere, for his own good, he could answer with the truth. To the best of his own belief he was actually twenty-two, though he had to overcome a certain inner reluctance to admit to himself that he was that old. And he could document that age with a driver's license that bore his photograph, if the discussion ever got that far.

In cases where the plan did not involve turning him over to the cops, he often varied his answer downward. No one as far back as he could remember had ever doubted him if he said he was sixteen. If he said he was seventeen, they sometimes still doubted, believing him to be certainly younger than that.

To the truck driver he was riding with when he reached Albuquerque, Pat had said he was sixteen. The truck driver had then responded with: "First time away from home, huh?"

"Yeah."

"I got a long drive ahead. We'll keep going all night," said the driver, and squeezed Pat's thigh, and smiled.

It was still early afternoon. Pat smiled back and made no protest about the hand on his leg. The driver was surprised and chagrined when just a little later, at a truck stop near the junction of Interstates 40 and 25 Pat announced that he was getting out, for good.

"Hey. What the hell. I thought ya wanted to go to California."

Still smiling, Pat slid down from the cab to stand on the sunstroked pavement. He stretched. Mountains whose name he had never learned, though he had come through this way going east or west so many times, rose barrenly a few miles to the east. He had chosen a good place for his announcement; a truck stop surrounded by a city, with a fair number of people about. The jilted trucker was not going to be able to do anything, or even to argue very much.

"Hey. Kid."

Pat did not even turn, but simply walked away. His feeling for Annie had altered suddenly. West was no longer the right direction. Now she had to be somewhere to his right, somewhere to the north of here. He could tell that she was out of walking distance still, but now she was no longer anything like a full day's drive away.

Interstate 25 going north out of Albuquerque was a new route to Pat. But one highway was not all that different from another; he was really at home on them all. Hiking the shoulder now, going up an entry ramp toward the northward traffic flow, Pat felt a certain relief. Not only at leaving that particular trucker behind—sadistic tendencies there, experienced instinct whispered—but at not having to go on to Arizona, which was the next state west.

There had been a bad scene out there in Phoenix, once. Real bad. Pat couldn't remember it consciously. But the stink of it still came up to conscious memory, like something dead and too shallowly buried. A warning: Don't dig here.

Pat topped the entrance ramp and kept on moving, hiking, looking over his left shoulder at a burst of speeding cars that passed him. Like an accomplished athlete or an old actor going into an old routine, he only needed to use half his attention in trying to flag a ride. Meanwhile he could use the other half on the question of what he ought to do when he reached Annie.

He could tell where she was, in a general way that seemed to get more particular the closer he got to her. But he couldn't tell what she was doing. For all he knew, she might be home, reconciled with her parents; or maybe in some other situation that she wouldn't be anxious to leave, just to hit the road again with Pat. So he ought to have some kind of hopeful proposition ready for her, something really attractive to suggest.

He would talk about—what else?—getting her into movies of some kind. Every girl liked that idea, and Annie was quite good-looking enough to make it credible. In fact, now that he thought of it . . .

Now that he thought about it, making movies with Annie was suddenly the one thing Pat wanted desperately to do.

Sure. Of course. There would be some way. Why not? Almost forgetting to work at picking up a ride, Pat hiked excitedly along the shoulder. The mountains to his right were forgotten, as was the intermittent roar of traffic at his left elbow. He would find Annie, and they would go off somewhere and make films, and everything in his whole screwed-up life might fall into the right place for once.

He remembered now how he had been talking with her in Chicago once, and she had been fascinated by some of the stories of movie-making that he'd had to tell. She seemed to understand that he was telling her the truth . . . or maybe it wasn't in Chicago. Somewhere. She *had* been with him somewhere else, before Chicago, now that he came to think of it. Or was it after?

Somewhere else. A place he didn't want to think about right now. But she had liked him, and it had been so good, that special way that they'd made love . . .

A movie with Annie in it was certainly a great idea, and if he wasn't crazy he would have thought of it before now. Could he really do it? Could he really at last straighten out his own life that much? The idea, when put in those terms, scared him a little.

He knew he could handle the movie itself, if he ever got the chance. He would pick up Annie, and they would go somewhere where he could get a job with some filmmaker. Maybe even right here in New Mexico. There were bound to be people here somewhere making films, and some of them had probably heard about Pat from people out on the Coast. When you were good, word got around.

Porn was by far the easiest kind of work to find, for Pat at least. Particularly when they found out that he was ready, willing, and able to double as an actor. He did well in front of the camera as well as behind it, though acting or performing of any kind wasn't really what he liked to do. His androgynous good looks were in demand, for straight, gay, or free-style porn. There was only one kind of thing he'd never touched, and never would. So he took part in the filmed sex smiling like the madman he sometimes was, faking the sex as much as possible, meanwhile continuing to keep himself happy by thinking how he would do the lights and the camera work and time everything differently if he were put in charge. Of course there was a dreary sameness in all porn, or almost all. But there were an infinite number of ways to disguise the sameness, if you knew what you were doing. Pat never doubted that he did.

But very rarely had he ever been allowed to take charge, to show what he could really do, though sometimes his suggestions on specific points were taken, by filmmakers who were always gratified with the results. The equipment and the space had always belonged to someone else. Nowhere, as far as he knew, was there a complete film of any kind that he had made. Once he had been allowed to take complete charge, at some real madman's house in Mexico. And once, another time, in this mansion with giant roof beams they had been going to let him take over, but . . .

. . . something had happened. And now here he was, hiking north on Interstate 25 and trying once more not to think about Phoenix. Today for some reason was a day for struggling with that problem. Maybe just because this was the first time he had returned to the Southwest since . . .

. . . someone had brought him into that rich guy's mansion out there, someone promising what they called a party. And Pat had thought he understood what that entailed . . .

His thought recoiled now, twisting, from a half-vision of blood. The memory faded, like a dying dream, almost as quickly as it had come. It left behind it no new knowledge, only a wash of sick fear. What he couldn't stand was the fear that that time he had been maneuvered into working on a snuff film.

Real torture on film, and real death. That would be for Pat an ultimate profanation, a blasphemy. He would have no part in it at all, though what exactly was being profaned, he could not have said . . .

His inner thoughts had become a burden, and it was a great relief when a car stopped for him at last. A new yellow Pinto, stopping cautiously, well ahead. Pat hitched his small backpack higher on his back, and trotted. The face peering back at him from the window on the driver's side was that of a middle-aged man with steel-rimmed spectacles, alone in the car. A fatherly type, it would appear. Perhaps genuinely so. As soon as they were underway, the man would begin to wonder aloud just why a young kid like Pat was hitchhiking alone; didn't he realize it could be dangerous?

"Hi, young feller, you going up to Santa Fe?"

Something about the name sounded reasonable. "Yeah," said Pat, and climbed in on the right. Santa Fe was one of those towns whose name everyone had heard, but he had never seen the place before. Right now, though, it sounded congruent with Annie.

The car was rolling, easing cautiously off the shoulder onto pavement, picking up speed. The man asked: "You got some family up there?"

Pat not-answered, as he often did. Looking out the window, he pretended that he hadn't heard. The man cleared his throat but did not repeat the question.

Later on he would. A small roadside sign announced that they were entering an Indian reservation. God, what could even Indians do on land as barren as this? Raise sheep? But there were none in sight.

You could make movies, of course, you could do that just about anywhere. Pat visualized a line of Indian dancers a thousand strong, their line stretching away over the yellow-brown plain. Make it ten thousand, the line would still look small. A camera in a low-flying aircraft, skimming just above their heads . . . tell them to show no expression on their faces . . .

The Pinto sped in scanty traffic. They kept topping long brown hills, one after another. Annie was getting close. In the distance, on every side now, more mountains reared. Somehow the highway had shrunk, it seemed too narrow here to be called an Interstate. Pat hadn't been watching the signs. The man, after his first attempt to talk, was unexpectedly going to be silent. Who knew what went on inside people's heads? No one did. No one. It was all right, silence was okay with Pat.

After they had driven for the better part of an hour through virtual nothingness they topped a final long hill. Now, miles ahead, some kind of a town or city came into view, looking as if it had been dropped at the foot of the tallest-looking mountains around. Their peaks still showed white that Pat supposed was snow.

The man cleared his throat again. "Whereabouts can I let you off?"

Pat brought his gaze back into the car, shifted his position in the seat. Annie was near. "Somewhere around the center of town is fine. If you're going that way."

"The Plaza?"

Pat didn't know what The Plaza meant. "That's fine. Anywhere around there is fine."

The man stopped the Pinto twenty minutes later

to let Pat out in the midst of a minor traffic jam in narrow streets. Slanting afternoon sunlight warmed low buildings covered with what Pat would have called beige stucco; they put him vaguely in mind of pictures that he had seen of Indian cliff dwellings. And here were some Indians, real-by-God Indians, with their blankets spread on a roofed sidewalk to display pots and jewelry for sale. Above their heads the rough ends of unfinished logs stuck out of the edge of the building's roof.

"Thanks for the ride." Pat flashed a merry smile as he got out. He always liked to do that, no matter what. Maybe he hoped that the people would remember him.

The man huffily not-answered as he drove away.

Annie was somewhere around here. That way. Within walking distance now, or almost, Pat started walking.

On the rear patio of his huge house near the northern edge of Santa Fe, Ellison Seabright was trying to get his wife posed properly to paint before the light changed any more. They were out on the rear patio, overlooking a spectacular scene of what was almost wilderness. Only a few other houses were visible, around the edges. Ellison had given Stephanie a supposedly genuine seventeenth-century Spanish shawl to put around her while she perched on the low stone balustrade that rimmed the patio. Just behind his subject, a slope of sandy earth and sparse wild grass, punctuated with dwarfish juniper, fell unfenced and almost untrodden for a hundred yards to end in the bottom of a sinuous ravine. Somewhere down there was an unmarked line where Seabright land ended and national forest land began.

Beginning right with the steep opposing slope of the wild ravine, the Sangre de Cristos mounted to the north and east, claiming the sky in one great rounded step above another. The highest and most distant shoulder of the mountain, blue-clad in distant fir and pine, hid behind it the bald snowcapped peaks projecting upward beyond timberline. Almost all the land in view was government land, unsettled and unpeopled. The mountains went up a mile or more in altitude above the seven thousand feet or so of the patio; a thousand years, Ellison thought, or maybe more than a thousand, back in time.

Ellison vaguely enjoyed thinking about the mountains, and liked knowing that they were there as a subject for his own painting, whenever he got around to it. He seemed to be chronically pressed for time, and rarely felt he could take time out from business to pick up a brush himself. But today, at last, he had Stephanie at home with him. And a few hours without people or business to interfere.

Stephanie, sitting on the balustrade, had at last got the shawl arranged to Ellison's satisfaction. She smiled into the lowering sun, as if she enjoyed its warmth.

"You're in a cheerful mood today," Ellison commented, getting some paints out of the box.

"Why shouldn't I be?" Her voice was lighter and easier than he had heard it in some time.

"No reason. You're basically a lucky lady." Except for Helen, of course, a few months back—but if Stephanie could start to forget that now, Ellison wasn't going to remind her. "But last week in Phoenix you were worried about the sun, how it aged the skin and brought on wrinkles. You said you weren't going to pose for me any more, out in the sun."

"The sun here isn't as hot."

"And you've stopped imagining you have wrinkles, I hope."

"I don't intend to get them. I know you divorce your wives when that happens, and look for someone younger. You've done it twice before."

Ellison looked at her. She gave him back a smile, enigmatic, Mona Lisa. "Shall I cross my legs?"

"No," he said, pretending patience, wondering what was going on. "We have the pose all settled. Let's just concentrate on keeping it." A change in his wife lately, sure enough; he had thought it was only Helen's death, but it was more. Ellison squinted about the huge patio, all winey sunlight and bluish shadow, with more furniture than a small house. He was looking for his tube of titanium dioxide white. "Do you realize," he asked, "that it's now been almost four years since you have posed for me?"

"Really? That long?"

"Since shortly after we were married."

"Surely it hasn't been that long."

"Oh, yes. I remember that Helen was hardly more than a little girl. She kept sneaking around to see what we were up to. In those days I generally had you posing in the nude."

The mention of Helen seemed to have had no effect. Something else was certainly on her mind.

"I wish you would have posed nude again today. Out here, against the mountains. I gave all the help the day off, you know."

"I know. But it's too cold today. Maybe next time."

"There. That's just the smile I want. Hold it for me, if you can. Just like that."

Ellison found that he was a little nervous about the painting. God, it was a long time, it must be a couple of years now, since he had really tried to paint anything at all. Would he really be able to do it now?

He suddenly spotted the tube of paint he had been looking for. It was on a small stone ledge not an arm's length from where he had set up his easel; now he recalled setting it down there. He picked up the tube and fidgeted with it and dropped it back into the paintbox. Then holding a stick of charcoal he looked at his model, and then beyond her to the mountains, where the changing sunlight made blue folds slowly appear and disappear. The light changing like that, and it was so long now since he had really tried. It was going to be hopeless.

"Are we going to talk about Del, sometime?" Stephanie asked him suddenly.

"What's there to talk about?"

"We both know that he's still alive. You don't have to be so cagey with me."

"Yes," said Ellison. He was not going to try to get the background in at all today. Only Stephanie. "Yes, well, don't you think it's wiser not to talk too much about the fact?"

"No one can overhear us. I just wondered how much you knew about the—details. I know you're handling business deals for him. Do you think anyone else knows he isn't dead?"

"I say it's wiser not to talk, even out here. There could be someone up there, behind any of those rocks, listening. Directional microphones have amazing capabilities these days."

Stephanie glanced behind her, at the hillside, then resumed her pose without appearing to be convinced. "Someone? Who?"

"My dear, you must have some idea of how much that painting is worth. Whenever such amounts of money are concerned, a lot of people take an interest."

"Ellison, our phone might be tapped, but no one's hiding up on that mountain twenty-four hours a day watching our house."

"How do you know that?"

The sound of the doorchime came drifting coolly out through the open patio doors, from inside the cool caverns of the house. Ellison sighed, put down the charcoal stick, wiped his hands, and went to answer. Having all the help gone was not necessarily a boon.

He supposed this would turn out to be some neighbor brat with Girl Scout cookies to sell.

The boy standing at the front door was undersized and shabby. He was a total stranger to Ellison, yet at first glance Ellison knew he was not selling cookies. Nor was his presence here merely some routine mistake. The young face waiting had something extraordinary about it; and not only extraordinary but wrong. This unusual wrongness Ellison accepted as a sign that the visitor knew what door he stood at.

"What is it?" Ellison demanded. In annoyance he used the lordliest tone he could produce, even though he was already sure that there would be no getting rid of this lad that easily.

The young eyes, cloudy blue, looked back at Ellison. Most people would have seen in them a probability of innocence. But Ellison saw more, and worse.

"I want to see Annie," the apparition announced, in a voice whose boyish appeal seemed to have been practiced.

The name meant nothing to Ellison. He only looked at the intruder, willing without much hope that he should go away.

"Annie knows me. My name is Pat O'Grandison, I'm a good friend of hers. I know she lives here."

"No one named Annie lives in this house. Or ever has."

"You her father?" the youth asked doubtfully. "Maybe she's not here right now, but if not she'll be back soon. Has she run away from home, or something like that? If that's it, she'll soon be back."

Ellison heard a soft sound behind him, and turned to see Stephanie approaching. She came looking like a great Spanish lady, with the old shawl still round her shoulders. Her face was troubled as she stared at the visitor.

Ellison spoke to his wife while nodding toward the

boy. "One of Del's old crowd, perhaps?" he mused. "But he never brought any of them here, to my knowledge. I thought all that went on out in Arizona, not here under my roof."

Stephanie only shook her head slightly in reply. Eyeing the visitor up and down, she asked him: "Who are you? Why are you here?"

The boy put out a frail arm to lean his weight tiredly against real adobe bricks. He scratched at one with a black-rimmed fingernail, as if he wondered what it was. "Can I come in and get a drink of water, please? It's all right, I really know Annie." Then he focused on Ellison suddenly; as if, Ellison thought uncomfortably, he might be trying to recall where he had seen the big graying man before.

"I think we'd better let him in," advised Stephanie. "He looks a little sick to me."

"*On* something, more likely."

"What's the difference?"

"Oh all right, let him in."

The boy came in and like someone near exhaustion dropped himself into the first handy chair. He was blond and undersized, dressed in travel-worn jeans with white road dust on them, and a plain T-shirt, once white. A small knapsack of fabric dull as camouflage lay on the floor beside his chair, one of its straps still resting limply in his slack right hand. His snub nose and beardless cheeks made him look no more than fifteen or so. But Ellison was sure that he was older.

Several components of Ellison's mind, one of them artistic, considered that young face with growing fascination. Here was one of Del's people, certainly. The face was beautiful. And, leaving aside whatever might be due to present tiredness, there was that inward something that was very wrong, that had told Ellison at first glance that the boy was here for some real purpose. His coming meant trouble, maybe, but there was nothing accidental about it. Ellison wondered: Did Del send him here?

He asked: "Have you been here before?"

"No." A hesitation. "Though I got the feeling that maybe I seen you someplace."

Ellison looked at him.

"I guess I'm mistaken. Hey, if Annie's not here, how about Helen? It just occurred to me, maybe it's possible that you and I know this girl by different names? I mean, sometimes when people run away they'll use a different name?"

The blue eyes shifted from Ellison to Stephanie and back again. It was impossible to read just how much was truth in them, and how much guile.

Ellison looked at his wife, trying to get some cue from her, but he couldn't. She kept regarding the visitor very thoughtfully. At last Ellison said: "There was a girl named Helen in this family once, living in this house. She's dead."

The boy considered that. He had slumped down in his chair until his head rested on its padded back. The strap of the backpack had fallen free of his limp fingers.

Stephanie crouched down gracefully beside the chair. "Helen was my daughter. If we're really talking about the same Helen. It's true, she did run away from home once. And she is dead—there was a lot of publicity about it at the time. You must have read some of that? Seen it on television?"

The visitor opened his mouth, then closed it again, evidently reconsidering whatever he had been going to say. "I didn't know she was dead. Sorry."

"Where," asked Ellison, "did you think that you had seen me before?"

"I dunno. Maybe I was wrong about that, too. Sometimes my ideas get all, all screwed up."

Stephanie straightened up. She was smiling briskly, almost like a nurse, as she touched the youth on the shoulder. "You must be hungry and thirsty," she said in bright inviting tones. "Come along with me to the kitchen, and we'll see what we can find. What's your name?"

"Pat." And Pat got up out of his chair quickly, following Stephanie like a puppy entranced by a first kind gesture.

A few moments later, Ellison followed them both, keeping a little distance. Peering into the breakfast room, he could see the youth seated at the table there, his back to Ellison, already chewing on something. Stephanie was pouring milk into a plastic tumbler for him. Beyond, in the kitchen, the sink was modestly stacked with dirty dishes from lunch. It would be tomorrow morning before any of the help came back.

Once the wanderer in his dirty T-shirt had been launched on a meal, Stephanie rejoined Ellison for a conference. "What do you make of this?" she whispered.

Ellison tugged her a little further from the kitchen, into the next room. "I don't like it," he answered in his own almost rumbling whisper. Then with a gesture he retreated further still, to where the boy had left his pack. Ellison bent and opened it. A dirty, lightweight jacket came to view, along with a few other items of spare clothing. In the bottom were some granola bars, their wrappers worn with a long time of jostling in the pack.

Ellison stood, grunting. "And I don't know what it's about. But I'm going to take whatever steps are necessary to find out."

SEVENTEEN

Oh, I could regale you now with all the sights and sounds and smells of fifteenth-century Rome. But it would be misleading, insofar as my story is concerned. The truth is, that at the time of my first visit to Rome I was scarcely aware of my surroundings except as they affected my search for Helen. I was beginning truly to wonder whether I might be the victim of some enchantment, so obsessively had this woman's image, in paint and sketch and memory, come to dominate my thought. Of course I wanted revenge on her, and on her lover—but gradually I was coming to realize that I wanted something more as well. More than mere vengeance, however ferocious, would be needed to give me satisfaction. What exactly the other thing might be, I did not know. But I hoped I would know, in the first moment when I looked on her again.

From Roman church to Roman church I plodded like a pilgrim, searching for the artist Perugino. I had not imagined there would be quite so many Roman churches. At my waist was the dagger that had once been left on a pillow, aimed at my head. Folded into my purse was a small bundle of sketches by Leonardo da Vinci, likenesses of the sister of the King of Hungary. I was having trouble finding any places to dispose of these pictures where I might reasonably expect them to be helpful.

On the third day of my Roman search I found a small church where, one of its priests told me, an artisan named Perugino had been painting some murals a few months past. But the painter was certainly gone from the neighborhood now, gone completely away from Rome the priest thought, and his mistress with him if he had had one. The priest had never noticed any woman at all in Perugino's company, let alone one speaking Hungarian and bearing a resemblance to my sketches.

I thanked him, and took my search for Helen to one of the nearby taverns. There some local men said they thought they might have seen her—said it with an exchange of winks. They were sophisticated city-dwelling jokers, metropolitan wits who jested at the expense of the lovelorn barbarian on his fool's quest. Somehow it was not plain to them that I was seeking vengeance and not love. I left one dead, two wounded, and had to take my searching elsewhere. My best talents are not in diplomacy, nor in the craft of the detective either.

After I had spent another day in fruitless prowling about Rome I visited the precincts of the Vatican. There I located my former traveling companions, the Hungarian delegation come to ask for a Crusade; while waiting to see His Holiness they had taken lodgings near the old St. Peter's. In Florence, where I had dropped out, they had been joined by my old acquaintance Morsino. Now Morsino greeted me in friendly style; he looked grave, though, when I told him of my recent brawl, and he counseled me to make no further requests or demands for official help in any Italian city. King Matthias, Morsino thought,

was no longer fully committed to the search. As long
as Helen continued to remain out of sight, commit-
ting no more public scandals, that seemed to be
enough for the king; and Morsino thought perhaps
it ought to be enough for me as well. The idea
seemed to be to let sleeping Helens lie where and
with whom they would.

My own views, I promptly explained, were different. The king had sent me here with orders to search
for Helen, and search for her I would, for my own
honor as well as that of royalty. If he, Morsino,
thought that he could organize the hunt in Rome
more discreetly and effectively than I, well, he was
welcome to take a hand. And this invitation the
worried envoy at last reluctantly accepted.

I hung around St. Peter's environs for another two
weeks, undergoing fits of restlessness that alternated
with periods of almost immobile depression. Then
Morsino's efforts at last bore fruit. An agent hired by
him brought me a witness, a poor woman who swore
she had once lodged near an artist and a Hungarian
woman who had been living together in the neighborhood of the church where Perugino had done his
painting. Shortly before their disappearance some
months past my witness had heard the couple talking about moving on to Venice.

I am not going to write much in these pages about
the next twenty months of my life. It was a period
in which I did things that I am not proud of, and
which there is now very little purpose in remembering. My leg was fully healed by this time, and I could
ride and fight effectively. Good fighting men, and,
even more, capable military leaders, were at this time
very much in demand in Italy because of the ceaseless
squabbling of the city-states and petty principalities,
not yet forged into a nation. I had not been many
days in Venice before I signed a soldier's contract with

the eminent mercenary Bartolomeo Colleoni. My
funds were running low; and I expected to retain
enough time to myself, and freedom of movement,
to allow me to continue the search for Helen.

Colleoni had then been for ten years the General
in Chief of all the Venetian armed forces. But, like
most of the other successful *condottieri* of the time,
he had as his ultimate goal the carving out of his own
personal domain. Some of his colleagues, like the
founder of the Sforza dynasty in Milan, succeeded
admirably in this enterprise. Many others failed
miserably; but, like Sforza and Colleoni, most had had
but little to lose when they began.

My new employer was famed for his vigor, both
marital and martial, at an advanced age; for his ferocity (which was somewhat remarkable even for the
time); his collection of rare books (when all books
were rare); and for his pioneering efforts in the
development of what would now be called field artillery. Whereas if he is remembered at all today outside of a few history books, I suppose it is only
because of Verrocchio's titanic equestrian statue of
him, still standing in a square in Venice . . . but I
digress.

When Colleoni heard from me that I had lived in
Florence recently, he took it for granted that I had
served there as *condottiere* also. What else would he
expect a foreign soldier to be doing? He promptly
began to pump me for all the information I could
give about the state of Florentine military prepared-
ness: How many in the militia? How well were the
fortified walls maintained? I told him what I could,
which was not much, and he evidently took my reticence as evidence of praiseworthy loyalty to a former
employer. I did not trouble to disabuse him of this
idea.

So it was that in the winter of 1466–67 I found
myself serving as a company commander in Colleoni's

nominally Venetian forces. I had under me about a hundred men—or, as the reckoning was usually kept then, thirty lances. In very early 1467 my troops and I were engaged in the investigation of the assassination of a Colleoni agent, the mayor of a village whose name I must admit I have forgotten but which could hardly mean anything to you now in any case.

The investigation was soon proceeding according to the standards of the time, which is to say that my men had taken a score of hostages, and we were on the point of beginning to hang some of them unless someone who knew something about the assassination should come forward. In fairness to myself I ought perhaps to be allowed to interject that the mayor had evidently been a good man, for his time; a good politician for any time, perhaps; and that I still think the assassins would fairly have deserved hanging if we had ever caught them.

Snow was in the village air, and misery was rife as usual among the populace. I found myself seated one morning at a writing table that might have belonged to some scholar, to judge by all the papers on it, in a house that was mine so long as I and my armed men chose to occupy it. I had sat down at the table to write out a report for Colleoni on the affair, and I suppose that those of my men who from time to time looked in at door or window assumed that the black frown upon my brow was due to the difficulty of wielding a pen in such a wise as to leave an intelligible message upon paper. Alas, no. I was even then something of a writer—I could at least set down my letters large and clear. What was troubling me were things more fundamental. I was grappling with matters of Conscience and the Law.

Contemplating the last year's work of my own hands, I found that it was not good. Oh, my activities had been legal, of course, or could be argued such, according to the contracts, the agreements, that

I had with Colleoni, and he in turn with Venice. And there were the customs, traditions, treaties, oaths, and whatnot that established Venetian dominance over these poor sheeplike villagers I was oppressing.

All legal. Everything I did. And yet in the end it came down to my setting the edge of a blade, or the loop of a rope, against the throat of some poor wretch. Then whatever I said was law; and whatever he said meant nothing, if it were not agreement.

As if I—I, Drakulya!—were no better than a highwayman.

At home in Wallachia I had been Prince, and there too my word had been law. But there I myself had been the anointed ruler, which justified much—did it not?

The front door of my borrowed house creaked open, and there came in white light from the snowy day outside, and then a blurred human shadow thrown across my papers. Glad of any interruption, I looked up.

To behold Helen.

EIGHTEEN

Eighteen-year-old Judy Southerland didn't know where she was going tonight. She knew only that the man who had been her lover appeared to be in desperate need, and that she had to try to give him what help she could.

Dressed in casual hiking clothes, which would fit in just about anywhere that she had to go in the Santa Fe area, she stood looking at herself in the mirror of the pine dresser in her one-room private cabin—Astoria was a very expensive school. She was wondering if the clamor of her lover's need, so strong in her mind, showed in her face; she decided that she couldn't tell if it did or not. Nor could she tell if she was thinking straight in her effort to do something about that need.

She wasn't even sure if the man she felt so bound to help was still her lover.

Judy had encountered him for the first time in Chicago, last December. The affair between them had begun then, and another episode had been added to it when she had visited Europe with her family in January. And then, after making love with a vampire, she had come home to live with her unsuspecting parents in a Chicago suburb, where somewhat to her own surprise she had resumed a life at least outwardly quite normal for a girl her age. Dating young men who never would have dreamed of drinking blood from her neck, and who, if she had ever tried to tell them the truth about it, would have thought that Judy was utterly—

And there had been some doubting moments, earlier this spring, when Judy had wondered that herself. Was it after all possible that she had imagined the whole affair? Or dreamed it, somehow, to go along with the bizarre problems that the whole family had been having then? But when she began to doubt, a word to Kate or Joe was enough to assure her that it had all been real. Judy could understand, now, why people who had had experience with vampires were never heard from on the subject.

The contact-at-a-distance with her vampire lover had been established at the beginning of the affair. At first it had been quite strong; anytime she felt like tuning in on him, and on several occasions when she didn't, there would come through a strong sense of his environment, and of whatever he happened to be feeling at the moment. With the contact she had had no trouble at all in locating him in Europe, nor he in finding her. But after the European episode, as the days of separation grew painlessly into weeks, Judy had begun to suspect that the goodbye he had murmured so lightly there had after all been meant as permanent. Come to think of it, no arrangements for another meeting had been definitely established, and a fading of the subconscious contact had set in. The fading had been imperceptible at first, and then there had been whole days, and then whole strings of days, in which the contact was not only absent but forgotten. It would come back, with a dream's vague aura of unreality about it. And then it would go again—

—and then the savage explosion, many miles away, had sent shockwaves of reality through a midnight dream to wake her. She knew at once that *he* had been hurt. Not so badly hurt this time as once before, when she had come to him and saved his life. But again he was alone and injured. He was beset by injuries, half-mad with wanting revenge for them, and driven wild by the theft of some *object* that he craved so much there had to be more to it than mere wealth, however great.

He apparently had no idea where this object had been taken. But Judy, who had a special kind of sensitivity of location, a sensitivity much heightened by her experiences, could see it a little when she tried. It was a painting, an old painting, and Judy thought its subject was a woman. The painting had been wrapped in rough cloth now, and it was leaning against a rough wall, somewhere in darkness . . . somewhere . . . she thought it was not far from Santa Fe.

If she went to it herself, then the contact that *he* must still have with *her* would show him where the painting was. Words never came through the contact, nor did conscious thoughts, and try as she might she could think of no other way to help him, and to ease the pain that his need had inflicted upon her.

Her image in the mirror looked perfectly solid. The pale surface of her sturdy throat was no longer marked by even the faintest remnant of the puncture-scars. Those scars had always been tiny and inconspicuous, and she was surprised to realize that she did not know herself on what day they had completely disappeared.

There had been times, last winter, when Judy had felt sure that the affair must go on to the conclusion that *he* had once or twice spoken of in warning. Becoming a vampire was not as quick or as simple as the foolish motion picture stories had it; but let them exchange blood enough, and Judy would be changed, and permanently. But he had never gone into detail about the change, and Judy had been left free to fill in the particulars with her own imagination. Would her mirror-image give warning days in advance, as it slowly went transparent? Or flick out like a switched-off light? And afterwards, would her shadow still be visible in reflection, adding one more complication to the mockery of science? Judy was unable to remember ever seeing *his* shadow in a mirror. . . she did remember his saying once that there could be photographs, at least those made with cameras that did not employ interior reflective surfaces to position image upon film. There could be photographs of him, but he didn't like the idea and so as a practical matter there were none.

Judy's eyes dropped to the note that she was leaving on her dresser, propped up against the mirror. If all went well she would be back here in a few hours, safely, before anyone else had come into the cabin and read it. But she had to admit to herself there was a pretty good chance that things were not going to go *that* well.

To Whom It May Concern:

Something very important to me personally has come up, and I am going to have to be away from school for a short time. It may be for only a few hours, or for a couple of days. I am leaving this note here on Tuesday evening.

I intend to call in to the school office within about 48 hours if I'm not back by then, and say that I'm all right. Please do not start any wide search for me before then, as I should be perfectly all right. If I should fail to call in within about two days, then you can search. But I don't think there'll be any problem.

Sorry, but I don't see any better way to do this. If it is felt absolutely necessary to call someone about my being gone, please call my sister, Ms. Kate Keogh, and not my parents. Her number is on file in the office.

This is nothing terrible but it's necessary.

Judy Southerland

The salutation at the start, now that Judy read it over, looked somewhat grim to her, like the opening of a suicide note or something. But she wasn't about to take the time now to do it over. The sense of urgency, of need, grew ever more pressing, and she couldn't afford to let it go untended until she had to run around and scream or something.

She thought the message looked okay otherwise. If she wasn't back before the staff started looking for her they would come into her cabin and find it, and then it would probably be read over the phone almost immediately to Kate and/or Joe. That was all right; they would be able to guess something of what was going on, and when the police were called in, Joe could . . . well, it was too bad, but right now Judy had to leave.

She had money, a couple of hundred bucks, in her pockets, and credit cards. What else did she need? It was hard to say, since she didn't really know where she was going. But money in some form was all you really needed, as a rule.

Judy slipped into her windbreaker, turned out the lights, and went out into the spring night. After a moment's internal debate she left her cabin door unlocked; somehow that seemed to make her departure less serious, more temporary.

The next step, of course, was to arrange a ride of some kind into town. Once she got there . . . well, she

would just have to see then where she was
go.

Walking toward the cabin that served Bill Bird
combination studio and living quarters, Judy saw with
a mixture of guilt and relief that the lights were on
inside. Bill looked first pleased and then somewhat
wary when he saw who was tapping so discreetly at
his door.

"Judy. What can I do for you?"

"Something's come up, Bill. I absolutely need to
get into town right away, and I wonder if you could
give me a lift."

A hesitation. "Oh. Did you check at the office?"
There was a prescribed system of signing out, and
also one of pooling rides.

"Can I come in a minute?" And once inside the
one-room cabin, much like her own, Judy pulled shut
the door behind her. A crude female nude, about half
life-size, stood under lights. The clay looked wet, and
Bill was wiping his hands on a rag. It seemed he must
have been working from memory; anyway there was
no model in sight. "I'm going to level with you, Bill.
There are reasons why I didn't want to do that."

"Oh? Something private?"

"Yes. And the truth is I don't know when I'll be
able to get back. I want to—meet someone, in town
or near town."

"Oh."

She wished he would stop saying *oh*. "No, it isn't
anything like that. Just someone who desperately
needs help. And there's nothing illegal or wrong about
it, but at the same time it's very private."

Bill opened his mouth, but failed to utter the
anticipated word. Now Judy could almost see the
wheels turning over in his head. Abortion appoint-
ment? Drug rendezvous? Or a friend of Judy's on
a bad trip with some drug, or in some trouble with
the law? Or simply running away from home? Bill

are you supposed to meet this

to explain. I'm sorry. Look, can you
ride into town? If you don't want to,
and I'll figure out some other way of
I appreciate that there's some chance
of your getting into trouble here if you break the
rules." *Is this really me,* Judy wondered, *willing to
use someone in this way?* She thought that for the
first time she could begin to understand how alco-
holics, addicts, could be as ruthless as they sometimes
were. The craving—dominated.

Bill was looking at her carefully. "It's all right, Judy.
I'll give you a ride."

"Thanks, Bill. I mean it. I really do appreciate it,
I can't tell you how much."

Waiting for Bill to take care of a few things and
grab his coat, getting ready to go out, Judy leaned
against the doorframe, groping mentally.

He, the man she sought, had been very recently
in a great desert basin which contained a large city
and a mass of warm air, almost hot air, fairly heavily
polluted air. Names of course never came through the
contact, but Judy had no trouble recognizing Phoenix. But Thorn, she perceived now, was there no
longer.

. . . he was coming closer, moving almost straight
toward her from the southwest. His feet were running, racing at a terrible pace . . . four feet running,
and all of them were his . . . this was a mode that she
had never experienced before.

"What's wrong, Jude?"

She opened her eyes and pushed away from the
doorframe, making herself stand up straight and smile.
"Nothing . . . maybe a little headache."

Bill looked doubtful. But he was holding the door
open for Judy now, and she went on out. Her own
feet trod again the springy needle carpet of the forest

path. Two human feet, hers were, in shoes, not like . . . the landscape around *him* had been momentarily clear to Judy. It had seemed to be bright moonlight there, though from here her merely human eyes could see that tonight's moon was only a dim crescent.

Those distant, running feet were coming closer quickly, loping almost directly toward Santa Fe. It would be hours yet before Judy could meet them. How many hours she could not guess.

They were in Bill's car now, a small Buick several years old, and he was starting the engine. As he turned the key Judy at the last moment knew irrational panic that a great bomb under the hood was going to go off and turn them both to jelly. So strong was the sensation that she had to bite her tongue to keep from crying out. Nothing happened, of course, and now he was driving over the rutted gravel of the parking lot toward the gate, which as usual this early in the evening was standing open. He asked Judy casually: "Where exactly are we going?"

Her conscience would not lie down quietly. "Bill, I don't want to get you into any trouble for doing this. Maybe you'd better not."

"Oh, just driving you to town isn't all that bad. Bending the rules a little, maybe, but . . . oh, hell, look, Judy. *You're* already in real trouble of some kind. I'd have to be blind not to see that. I don't know if it really has to do with some friend, or if the friend in trouble is you—anyway I can see that you need help. So why don't you just tell me where you have to go? And on the way, tell me what it's all about."

"Oh, Bill. You're beautiful." Suddenly near tears, Judy reached to squeeze his bicep, which felt surprisingly large and hard. "Bill, the trouble is, I don't *know* anything exactly yet. Just that I have to be there . . . maybe when I get into town, things will be clearer."

"How is that going to help?"

"It's difficult to explain." Or maybe impossible. Once when her brother Johnny had been in the hands of kidnappers, Judy had been able to see, to locate perfectly, the house where Johnny was being held. Of course that time she had been hypnotized, by . . . maybe the trouble was that this time she wasn't hypnotized.

"No, I don't think I want to drop you just anywhere." They were driving the camp road now at a brisk pace, traversing a midnight aisle of trees. "Tell me, Judy. Are you really intending to cut out from school altogether? Or do you really mean to come back tonight?"

"I *hope* to be able to get back tonight, Bill. I've left a note in my cabin, just in case . . . but oh God, I hope I can get back there before anybody reads it."

Bill turned his eyes from the night road long enough to look at her. He whistled softly. "All right, this is very serious, I can see that. Is it all right if I ask what the note says?"

"It says . . . it's just meant to be reassuring. I'm trying to keep my parents from finding out . . . Bill, don't mind me if I act a little crazy tonight. I know I'm acting like I'm crazy but I'm really not. Do you know anything about the psychic?"

"Psychic . . . well, not really, I guess. But I like to think I have an open mind."

NINETEEN

Helen was garbed in much poorer clothing than the elegant garments in which she had departed our Pisan cottage. She was shivering with cold, and her rags, like those of the traveling poor of any century, were marked with the dust of the road. Her face looked thinner than I remembered it, and her hair had returned to the condition in which I had first seen it. Otherwise her appearance had changed very little in the two years since her desertion. She was leaning one hand on the wooden doorframe now, and the knuckles of the hand were white, as if she felt it necessary to grip something to keep from turning and trying to run away again.

I remember that as I looked at her my first reaction was only a curious numbness: all right, she is here. I looked past her then, and nodded a dismissal to the soldier who had brought her to the house. He went out behind her, and closed the door.

"Come in," I said. But of course she was in already.

My wife and I considered each other in silence. I saw now that she had rags wrapped around her feet in place of shoes. Her shivering arms folded now beneath her breasts, she stood there waiting. I thought I could see in her face something of the same numbness that I felt myself.

"So." That was my next attempt to start. The truth was that in recent months I had no longer spent much time dreaming of revenge. I think now as I look back, I really think, that the first feeling I began to have was a simple, uncomplicated relief—that I could now settle the thing between us, somehow, and after that I would no longer have to stay near Venice and work for Colleoni.

Helen asked: "Have I your permission to sit down?" She was almost swaying on her feet, I saw. Certainly she sounded tired, or rather as if she had just been beaten, though I could see no bruises. Her voice had changed more than her appearance.

I gestured, and she sank into a chair, hands covering her eyes. "I am giving myself up into your hands," she said.

"I can see that."

"Because I am too tired to run any longer. Too tired even to try to bargain with you. Just giving up, that's all."

"I see." But really I did not, and I puzzled over the matter for a few moments in silence. "But what is there to bargain about? And why come to me at all? You are still young, still attractive. Surely you could find some protector who would take you in."

Helen at first slumped in her chair. Then she straightened, raising reddened eyes. "All right, Vlad. Maybe you really do not know. But I am too exhausted for any . . . so I am going to tell you. Perugino is one of the hostages your men have taken here. Now maybe I have damned both myself and him to hell by coming to you. I don't know. I can't tell any longer what I should be doing. I'm too tired and weak and hungry to know anything. I'm giving up."

"Ah. Perugino." I leaned back in my chair. The name had a strange sound on my lips; it had been a long time since I had spoken it. Actually I had never really looked at the hostages, only glimpsed the huddled gray mass of them from a distance. I suppose I had not wanted to look at them closely. My men had informed me how they were being held, under close guard in an otherwise empty barn just across the road from my borrowed house. There were a lot of empty barns in the country now. And now I wondered if I would have recognized Perugino had I seen him. My memory could no longer give me a clear image of what he had looked like, and anyway he might well have changed.

Helen spoke again, in the dead voice that was now hers. "We have been on the move almost constantly. We have run from the soldiers, yours and others, and we have looked for work. Artisan's work, peasant's work, anything. From Rome to Venice, even to Milan. There I saw Sforza once, by accident. We were quite close, but he looked right through me without seeing, as if I were a ghost. Then we moved back to Venice again. Then out here. We have been living in the next village down the road." Suddenly she put out a hand to grip my writing table's edge; she looked pale, as if she might be about to topple from her chair.

"You will need some food," I said. And instead of calling in a servant, whose presence I did not want just then, I got up and began to look around for some myself.

"Yes, some food please. I need some. It was not easy for me to come here, Vlad. Vlad? I ask you to let him go."

In a rucksack I found some bread, and brought it to her. It was dark bread, and stale as I recall, having been for some time left in the pack forgotten. We soldiers had enough. Helen took a couple of bites with animal hunger. Evidently her teeth were still good. I sat down again and watched her eat. Whatever vengeance I decided to pronounce upon her and her lover, it would have been foolish to try to gloat over her with it as she lay on my floor in a dead faint.

Chewing, she asked: "The hostages are all going to be hanged, aren't they?"

"So it would seem. No one has yet come to us with the names of those who killed the mayor."

"Is that why the hostages were taken? We did not even know."

"Bah. You really expect me to believe that?"

"We in the next village, I mean. That is where Perugino and I have been living. The soldiers just came through, rounding up all the men that they could catch."

I looked at Helen closely, decided that she was telling me the truth, and made a small sound of disgust. The village I was in, now that I thought about it, did look small to have provided so many hostage bodies. I was going to have to take some disciplinary action, hoping to instill in my squad leaders some glimmerings of intelligence.

Helen went on: "There is always hanging, butchery of some kind, going on in these villages. I wonder that the people manage to grow any food at all." When I did not answer, she was emboldened, and pressed on: "You could let him go. It will not matter to you, will it, if there are twenty bodies hanging, or only nineteen?"

I thought to myself that it was hardly going to matter if there were twenty or none at all. Except of course to the twenty themselves, and to their families. And to leave the men alive might work a benefit to the land at large. But my words through some bitter perversity followed a different path than my thoughts.

"Maybe," I said, "I will be doing them all a favor

by hanging them now. If I let them go, they will have a few more years of suffering in this Godforsaken country and then die anyway. Will Perugino be better off or worse off if I let him go?"

"I don't know, Vlad." And I believed that she did not. But then she began to weep, sobbing so that she had to stop chewing on her bread. "I don't know. But let him go. Please, please, let him go on living."

"You still ask me not to hang him."

"If you put it that way—then you are going to do something to him even more horrible. Oh, I knew it, I should never have come to you." Yet hunger made her try to bite the bread again; she choked on it and went off into a fit of coughing. I got up from my chair again, to dipper some water for her from a pail.

"And suppose—just suppose—that I should let him go, entirely free? What would *you* do then? Assuming that for some reason you were given a choice."

Helen drank, and choked again, and drank a little more, and put off answering. Later she was to tell me that at this point in our interview she felt sure that I was only playing with her, mocking her, that at any moment the horrors would be announced, that I would call out for the torturers to enter. But I was not playing. I was much less certain than she was of what was going to happen next.

It occurred to me that what I really ought to do was hang Perugino, who was demonstrably guilty of something, and let the nineteen innocent clods go free. But then the guilty man's troubles would perhaps be over—a church-painter like him would be sure to make his peace with God before he reached the gallows—whereas the nineteen would be doomed to who knew how many more years of suffering. Well, that was the kind of mood that I was in.

The reader doubts, perhaps. I have and had a bloody reputation. How is it possible to prove today that I did not torture a certain wretch to death in 1467? Well, can the reader himself prove himself innocent of all crimes committed in that or any other given year? But, the reader protests, in 1467 he was not yet born. Let him prove that, too, say I. If I can live so long, then why not he or she?

Forgive me, gracious Mina. I am overwrought, with reliving things that have more power over me than I guessed they would, when I sat down to write.

Let me put it this way. Though it was claimed even then that I had ruled too harshly in my own land, I had never gone so far as to hang nineteen men who were not even suspected of any crime. And if, in the time when I was Prince, some officer of my realm had reported to me that he was carrying on an investigation in such wise, depopulating my land of healthy industrious peasants to no purpose, his own carcass might soon have been observed in a position higher and more uncomfortable than that afforded by any ordinary scaffold.

Something in my face must have inspired Helen to new hope. "Vlad," she burst out suddenly, "I know that I have already made wedding vows with you, and broken them. But they were forced and I did not consider that they bound me. I will make them again, if you would have me still. The position you hoped to gain can still be yours—you will be the brother-in-law of a powerful king—if you will let Perugino go free. I will never see him again. I will, I swear it to you by whatever you like, be a faithful wife to you, whatever you choose to do to me."

Now it seemed to be an effort to think about her at all. I rubbed my face, and suddenly felt tired, and angry—an anger on the level of irritation, as if my wife had been nagging me for days. "Quiet," I said, and as if to demonstrate her new talent for obedience, Helen broke off some renewed plea before its first word was fairly out. I sat there looking at the

papers on the table as if I were eager to get back
to them, as if Helen's coming had interrupted some
delightful task.

"Where did you first meet Perugino?" I asked her.
"I have often wondered about that."

Helen was silent for a few moments, trying to
compose herself. Then she said: "It was when I was
in the convent—the first time, I mean, the convent
near Milan. I was staying there while the final
arrangements were being concluded by my brother,
for me to marry the Sforza. Perugino was working
in the convent chapel. He had been hired to make
paintings on the walls."

"Which Sforza were you to marry?"

"Galleazzo Maria himself. The negotiations were
all secret. Matthias badly wanted an alliance with
Milan."

"Ah. Small wonder His Majesty was so angry at you
when you thwarted him. Tell me more. I suppose the
bridegroom-to-be was perturbed also?" If Galleazzo
Maria Sforza's reputation has now fallen behind
mine—I should say remained above it—it was not
always so.

"There was a delay in the final arrangements. The
Sforza was away on some business or other, I was
never told what. So of course there I was, waiting
in the convent, as the only proper place for me to
stay. And in the chapel a young painter was at work.
I was consumed with quiet anger at my brother, at
what he was doing with my life for the sake of politics. As if I were only a soldier, to be used up in battle
at the commander's will."

"That is the way of battles. And of life."

"I tell you I . . . not of my life. Or so I thought.
It began, with Perugino, as a way of getting back at
Matthias. But Perugino was the first man I had ever
had, and it became . . . great love. The two of us ran
away together. And we have been together ever since,

as much as we could be. We thought we would be quickly caught, so at first we lived with a kind of . . . raging joy. Do you understand? To do just as we liked, to fear nothing. I wanted to leave scandal wherever we went, to get back at my brother and at the world. For what they had tried to do to me.

"Then later, it was . . . later it began to be no good. I have sold myself, to get food when we were starving. Again to get shelter, when Perugino was ill. When I was sick, he . . . I don't know what he did, but he stayed with me. Now to save his life I will do anything you like."

"Why did you leave that dagger on my pillow?" Helen did not seem to know at first what I was talking about. I drew it from the sheath at my belt and held it up by the tip of the blade. The steel was still lightly notched where I had used it once to cut through a small chain. "This very dagger, here."

At last she remembered. "That? It was meant to show you that I did not hate you, you were not my enemy. Otherwise I would have killed you before I ran away."

"I see." I looked at the weapon, and restored it to its sheath. "And where have you been living? Just now?"

"As I said. In the next village down the road."

I had one more question. "Does Perugino know that you have come to me now?"

Helen took thought, then shook her head. "I don't see how he could."

"I want to talk to him, before I decide anything." Helen wanted to speak, but I put up a hand and she was silent. "I am going to have him brought over here now. I want you to step into the other room, and listen from there. As you value his life, keep hidden and silent, no matter what you hear, until I tell you to come out."

❖   ❖   ❖

Perugino's beard, if he had ever in fact shaved it as Leonardo had once informed me, had long since grown back to greater length. There was gray in it now; though he was still in his twenties, probably a decade younger than I, his face was already becoming that of an old man. Still, I was quite sure that I would have known him, had I ever gone to look closely at the hostages.

"I recognize you, Perugino," I announced, when the soldiers who had brought him had gone out of the house again, leaving the two of us together. "Do you know me?"

I honestly do not believe that he did know me, at first. He was shivering worse than Helen had been, and I believe a good part of his shivering was due to fear.

"Come. In your position you have nothing to lose by admitting it. You know that we met at Verrocchio's studio."

Gradually it dawned on him. He almost met my eyes, and then would not. His hands were bound behind him, which made it hard for him to find the least refuge in a pose, or in gestures.

"Well, speak up, man. Answer."

"Yes, *signore,* I think I do know you. I'm sure of it, in fact." Perugino's voice was so low that I could scarcely hear it. There seemed to be no resistance of any kind left in him; there had been some in Helen, despite her continued claims that she was giving up.

"Good," I said cheerfully. "Good, I am glad. Then the chances are that you remember my wife as well."

Despite the cold, Perugino stank of sweat. Old sweat, fear-sweat. The stink grew now a little fresher. His face sicklied over with an attempted smile. He shook his head a trifle, not knowing what I wanted of him, how much I knew, or what if anything he ought to try to say.

I tried to imagine him impaled on a high stake. He would stink even worse that way. The image brought me nothing but disgust. I sighed. It was hard to imagine that this creature before me had at one time been truly young, and good-looking, and brave enough to play at games with the betrothed of Galleazzo Maria Sforza inside high convent walls.

I said: "I am in no mood to play games with you, man. I know that you and she have been together. The thing is this. We have taken some women hostages, too, at the next village. And it happens that Helen was among them."

Perugino's expression hardly changed. Perhaps he had no extremes of reaction still unused. It was at this point that I finally decided what I was going to do.

"Now, are you listening to me, artist? I have orders from Colleoni to hang thirty people here, to make an example of this place. But I find that some of my soldiers cannot count too well. The total of hostages, men and women included, is now thirty-one. Are you following me?" The lies came to me quite easily as I went along, and they were of a kind to be readily believable to any inhabitant of that region. As for Perugino, I think I could have told him that the key to the pearly gates was in my pocket, and he would only have nodded agreement with that same sickly, insanely hopeful smile.

"Listen to me further, wall-painter. I tell you that I have sworn a great oath—never mind why—that my vengeance shall not fall upon both of you, but on one only. Therefore I am compelled to set one of you free. I will then hang the other—after some preliminary punishment. Now the question is, which is it to be? The guilty wife, or her seducer? Which goes free, and which one suffers?"

I think, looking back, that I was wasting my inventive powers. I think that of it all he heard and understood almost nothing but those two words, "goes free." The moment I was silent, he fell on his knees in supplication.

"You will set me free? Lord, sire, you are a great lord, a blessed man. My aged mother will bless you. Her prayers and mine will go with you from this day forward, to the hour of your death . . . I swear that I will never bother anything of yours again. My gratitude will be eternal . . ."

I do not remember now the whole catalogue of these absurdities he babbled. But it went on and on, perfectly disgusting. I cut it short: "What of the woman's fate? Does that mean nothing to you at all?"

"The woman. Ah. You will know best about that, sire. I swear to you that I am never going to look at her again. I swear . . ."

I was as good as my word to Perugino. A few minutes later he was walking out the front door of my borrowed house, his hands cut free of their bonds by my notched dagger. His pass with my signature on it was in his hand, and one of my soldiers was with him to escort him to the edge of town.

Now I can hear the gentle reader murmuring again. What would the infamous Dracula have done, had the man proved as self-sacrificing as the woman? Well, it is my theory that Helen in coming to me was really not all that altruistic—she was tired, as she said, and took what she saw as the best chance, obeying an almost suicidal impulse—to get out of an intolerable situation even if it should mean death. On the other hand, if Perugino had proven himself ready to sacrifice himself for her—I did not think he would, but if he had—well, I should probably have taken him up on the offer.

As matters actually went, I walked into the room as soon as Perugino was gone. I stood there silently confronting Helen, who had sat down on my bed.

"But he is no longer a brave man," she murmured,

staring at my boots. "If he ever was. So much has happened . . . what did you expect?" Then her eyes lifted. "Tell me, are you going to have him killed now after all? Stabbed to death somewhere down the road? Tell me now if it is so."

I had considered some such plan, but had decided against it. I half-expected that the fog of war was likely to carry out the postponed execution without any active effort on my part, local conditions being what they were. This was a faulty expectation, as we now know; Perugino's lifeless paintings done after 1467 are still to be seen covering a great deal of wall space in a number of Italian churches.

"It is not so," I assured her. "I do not mean to have him killed—unless he should come near you again. Then I will kill him, but only as an annoyance, not as a matter of honor. Do you understand?"

Helen tried to look agreeable, but I could see that she did not understand. She could not, perhaps, or she did not care.

So I explained it to her, once. "That man is already dead."

TWENTY

Pat O'Grandison was dreaming again, and again the dream was of Annie, and in this dream she was naked. She and Pat were in bed together, and the sheets were satin. There were paintings and statues all about, watching. Pat was enormously aroused, but even more important was the secret that Annie was about to whisper into his ear.

Before he could hear a word of it, he awoke with a small start. It was dusk, and he could not immediately remember whose great house this was or how he came to be in it. He was lying on his back on a sofa in an unknown, luxuriously furnished room. His shoes were off, and his knapsack was under his head where he had put it to make a pillow against the sofa's wooden arm. He was beginning to remember now.

A brown-haired, slightly built girl was sitting at the foot of the sofa, looking at Pat. She wore jeans and a loose pullover shirt.

"Annie?" Pat was fully awake in an instant, and his body jerked up into a straight sitting position. At first glance he was sure this girl was her. The sense of Annie's presence was very strong. But as soon as he got a good look he could see this wasn't Annie's face, though this too was a face he ought to know. He had been asleep, and there was certainly a resemblance, and the lights in the room had not been turned on as yet.

"I'm Helen, Pat," she said, in a voice that was certainly not Annie's either. "Annie's friend. You saw a lot of me in Chicago. Don't you remember?"

"Oh, yeah. Sure. Gosh." *Gosh* popped out in Pat's speech fairly often, part of a general plan, never deliberately thought out as such, to remain as young or at least as young-seeming as he possibly could. Sometimes this plan worried him and he wondered at its purpose.

The girl took hold of his foot in its dirty sock, squeezing it absently, as if she were petting a small child. Her fingers were strong. "Pat? You know Ellison has just been on the phone, talking to someone about you. He was very guarded in what he said, but I'm sure you were the real subject of what they were talking about."

"Ellison?"

"My stepfather. He owns this house. The big fat man who looks a lot like Del."

"Del?"

The girl sighed faintly. "Del is his older brother. You don't remember anything about that night in Phoenix, do you, when you and I first met? That was at Del's house."

Pat pulled his feet free from her near-caress and swung them to the floor, where he started fumbling them into his shoes.

Helen told him: "I wouldn't be a bit surprised if Ellison is making plans to get rid of you tonight. I don't know why else he would have let you sack out in his house like this. He doesn't like boys the way Del does sometimes. He just wanted to check with Del first, or with Gliddon, about what they want to do with you. Maybe they'll want to find out how much you know."

"Oh my God. I'm gonna split." Somehow Pat doubted that the girl was making any of this up, just for fun or just to get him out of the house. There was something about that huge old dude, her stepfather, that made Pat believe he could be capable of murder. Anyway, even if Helen was making it up, it wasn't a situation Pat wanted to prolong.

But even now he couldn't just leave without trying once more. "Helen? Tell me where Annie is. I know she's right around here somewhere."

Helen shook her head, and appeared to be annoyed. But then she reached over and with cool fingers touched Pat on the cheek. It was almost like the way that Annie had used to reach and touch him sometimes. "Pat, I know you liked her, and she liked you." Helen paused there, looking at him with strange eyes in the dusk. "She was there on that night in Phoenix, too. She met you the same time I did. A lot of things got started on that night."

"I don't really give a shit about that night in Phoenix any more." Pat was jerking on his shoelaces to get them tied. One lace broke, and he just let it go. He stood up. "Where is she now?"

"I was trying to tell you." Helen, sounding irritated, stood up too. Pat could see now that she was barefooted; still she stood a little taller than Annie. "The bad news about her. She was just a runaway from somewhere, and she didn't count for much. Anyway, you see there was another real bad night at the house in Phoenix, a few months after you were there. I mean the night when Del was supposedly kidnapped. Something went wrong with the scheme and Annie was killed. Almost everyone thought that I was the girl who died. Just as they thought that Del was dead—he wants everyone to think that, of course. But really he had another body ready, the body of a fat old man, that would look enough like Del after it had been blown up in the truck. And he even faked dental records and everything, just in case. You can do a lot, when you have as much money as Del has. And—"

"I don't wanna know about all that, I wasn't there. I'm gonna leave."

"Sure. You'd better get out of here now. But what are you going to do, just walk the roads? You'll be picked up, that way."

Something in the way she said it made it a special warning. "Picked up?"

"I don't mean just by the law. Look, Pat, I'll give you a ride somewhere, okay? I know Annie would want me to look out for you if I could. She thought you were something special, you know. She talked about you quite a lot."

"She did?"

Helen didn't answer, but moved away. His back-pack dangling from one hand, Pat followed her on tiptoe through several darkening rooms. They came to a heavily grilled back door, where Helen bent to do something to the lock.

"Where are your folks now?" Pat whispered near her ear.

"Sometimes they don't seem much like my folks," she whispered back. "They're around. Be quiet. Here now, I've got to hold this—you go on out."

The door swung open to a small patio. Pat had been in mansions before, enough to know something about alarm systems. He went out quietly. Helen delayed behind him, doing something to a mechanism attached to the heavy door, then closing it carefully behind her when she was out too.

After that she led Pat along the side of the house, over a brick walk, to an outside entrance to the garage. Again there was a brief delay, while she used keys and stealth for a tricky opening. They were inside the garage then, where it was very dark. Helen led

Pat past two cars to a third smaller one and unlocked
the right door for him. When the dome light came
on he could see he was getting into a Subaru, one
of the small station wagon models that he thought
usually came with four-wheel drive.

Helen walked around and got in on the driver's
side. It was cold in the garage. The engine purred,
headlights came on, a garage door rolled itself up
ahead of them, and now somewhere an alarm bell was
ringing stridently.

"Now they're going to wonder what's going on,"
Helen said, a certain satisfaction in her voice. The
Subaru leaped into the night.

She drove Pat in a direction that must have taken
them away from the center of town, for the roads
remained up-and-down-hill gravel. You might have
thought you were already way out in the remote
countryside, except there were so many mailboxes
along the road, and gravel driveways curving away
from the road uphill and down. There must be a fair
number of houses tucked just out of sight. In the dark
it was hard to tell.

Gradually the driveways and mailboxes thinned out,
then finally ceased to appear at all. They were really
getting out into the boondocks now.

"Where we going?" Pat asked, beginning to get
curious.

Helen didn't answer right away. "There's something
I think I want to show you," she said at last.

A lot of road was going by in the lonely headlights. Traffic, that had never been heavy, had
thinned out now to nothing. Pat wondered, and
couldn't tell for sure, whether or not they might be
driving in some great circle, and it was all a hoax,
a joke on him.

"Sometimes," he said, to be making talk, "I feel
like I been on the road a hundred years."

"Don't talk like that. I feel that way too much myself."

"You?" He sighed. "Actually you've just tried it once, right? With Annie to Chicago? And now you're home again."

Helen turned on the car radio. Rock music came in. But then almost at once the music began to fade, as if they were far and getting farther from the station. At last she said: "Yeah. Just that once."

"And that's where I met you. Right?"

"No." Now her voice was remote, and there was something in it that frightened Pat. "I told you where we met. It's no good just trying to forget what has happened, Pat. You can't change things that way. You met Annie and me both that first night in Phoenix. Uncle Del was giving a party—that's what he liked to call it, anyway. You were invited. I mean Gliddon brought you in, along with a few other road-kids that he collected somewhere. He's good at collecting. And he likes that kind of party too."

"Helen? Maybe you could just take me back somewhere near the center of town, and let me off. I'll do okay getting a ride from there."

"But you got stoned so early you probably really don't remember anything. Dear Uncle Del and his parties. And that one was especially bad because someone got killed. And did you know, we were all in a movie that night? You're such a movie freak, I bet you remember that much anyway if you tried hard."

Pat had an inward feeling, terrible and indescribable, that he got usually when a bout of mental illness was about to strike. But he knew what was going on. No way he was going to be lucky enough to get out of that.

"Or most of us were in a movie, anyway," Helen amended, turning off suddenly onto an almost invisible side road. "On some of us it wouldn't take," she added obscurely. The car jounced violently. The road, or track, was badly rutted here and obviously little used. A branch dragged across the windshield. Then the bottom of the car scraped hard on a rock or graveled hump projecting up between the ruts. Helen drove on as if she hadn't noticed the noise. Apparently no serious damage had been inflicted.

"Was Annie in the movie?"

Helen didn't answer.

"Come on, Helen, tell me. Annie isn't really dead, I know that much. I got this feeling about her, you know?"

"She's dead!" Helen snapped at him, in a new and abrupt voice. She turned her eyes from the road to look at Pat, long enough so he wished she'd turn back and watch where they were going. Again low branches of some kind clawed at the windshield, and the car rocked in and out of ruts. So far the four-wheel-drive was pulling it through. Helen had to turn back to watch her steering. Angrily she said: "How can I help you when you keep on saying crazy things like that?"

"Sorry, I . . ."

A sign came unexpectedly into the headlights. It had been crudely improvised long ago, long enough that the wood and the white paint were weather-worn, the message barely legible. It said, simply enough: BRIDGE OUT.

"Helen, you sure you know where we're going?"

Helen rounded one more curve, and then slowed down some more. Not for a sign, though. The headlights had now fallen upon what at first appeared to be a wreck—an old car slewed diagonally across what was left of the road, as if it had stalled in some attempt to back out or turn around. Standing near it and squinting back into the Subaru's headlights were a pair of young people, a dark-bearded man and a brown-haired girl. Pat knew another moment of spurious recognition; but this girl was obviously too big and sturdy to be Annie. The man with her was bigger still; both were dressed casually but well.

"Shall we stop?" Helen asked abstractedly, as if she were conversing with herself. Actually there hardly seemed to be a choice, given the blocked and narrow road. A moment later they had come to a halt, a few feet from the stalled car. The man on foot, trying to shade his eyes with one hand, approached the Subaru warily on the driver's side. But before he reached it the girl, her eyes now freed of the headlights' glare, was looking in through the window that Pat had just rolled down. She looked at Pat, and at the young girl driving, and relaxed.

Helen was saying nothing, so Pat spoke. "Can we give you guys a lift somewhere?"

"Sure," said the girl. "I'm Judy Southerland, this is Bill Bird. We got stuck."

The young man, also somewhat relaxed now, was looking in at Helen, who had finally rolled her window down. "We'd really appreciate it," he said with feeling. "I guess it was kind of crazy, our trying to get through here, especially at night. Where are you guys headed?"

"Just riding." Helen sounded cool and remote. "I'm Helen, this is Pat. Actually there was something I wanted to show him, out this way. You want to come along?"

The young man called Bill was silent, as if he didn't quite understand. Pat could hear a nightbird somewhere. The thin moon was down by now. He could see about a million stars, but not a man-made light in sight other than the one pair of headlights.

"Sure we will," said the girl called Judy. "Or I will, anyway." She looked over the top of the car at Bill, and something passed between them.

He shrugged. "Okay." And he moved to open the Subaru's back door.

"No," said Helen, surprising them all. "From here we walk."

"Walk?" All three of them said it.

"It isn't far. Come on." And she turned off the car's lights and engine and got out. She seemed to Pat to be perfectly calm and serious. She moved to the uphill side of the road and paused, evidently waiting for the others to follow.

Pat and the others exchanged puzzled looks, as well as they could by starlight, then he moved to Helen and the other two followed. In single file they began to climb.

The ground was rough and pathless, but Helen moved as if she knew her way. Pat looked down at her feet and realized with a chill that they were still bare. She *had* to be crazy . . . he didn't know whether he should appeal to the newcomers for support, demand they call a halt, or what. He himself was crazy, that much he knew already. As if there were no other choice, he kept quiet and let himself be led.

The hill at least wasn't high. Soon they were going down its other side, now completely out of sight of cars and road. Then partway up another hill, and along its twisting flank.

Judy wondered aloud: "Does anyone think we'll be able to find our way back? Where are we going, anyway?"

"*You* don't know?" asked Bill.

Helen paused calmly and turned back. "There's a sort of settlement where we're going. They have a phone there. I know you can't see it from here. But it's just over this next hill." Her voice sounded completely reasonable.

"Oh," said Judy. They went on. Pat had lost track of how far or in which direction they had come. He kept on, following Helen's soundless feet. He hadn't thought, on first seeing her this evening, that she was high on anything—Pat could almost invariably tell—

or that her head was screwed on wrong. But now he was dead sure that something wasn't anywhere near right.

Once he paused, turned back, almost determined to call a halt.

The girl, Judy, walking close behind him, shook her head minimally and pushed him gently on. Her eyes were focused past Pat, on the darkness ahead where a low mass of shadow now seemed to indicate trees. She knew, on some level, what she was doing.

He turned again, and walked, one foot loose in its shoe with the broken lace.

"Here," said Helen quietly, turning long enough to utter the one word, then pushing on. And the way began to slope down, the ground underfoot smooth enough to indicate a path. The sound of running water drifted upward, very faint at first. There was at least a respectable trickle.

They came in among the first trees, and darkness deepened. Judy asked: "What is this place, anyway?" Pat could now see buildings of some kind, faintly visible in tree-shaded starlight.

"There used to be a mission here," said Helen. She came slowly to a halt, looking ahead into blackness.

"But you said there was a phone. Didn't you?"

"There is. It's a radiophone of some kind. I guess some special, secret kind."

"What?"

'We'll ask Gliddon if we can use it.' Helen's voice was still dream-calm.

"What? Who?"

A new voice, harshly male, said: "Don't move. All four of you freeze, right where you are." And light sprang at them, a blinding beam of it from each side. Pat, as soon as he could begin to see again, made out the ski-masks and the shotguns; and he devoutly wished that he could immediately go mad.

TWENTY-ONE

I rode with Helen, across a countryside infected with war as with a plague. Before we had ridden two hours toward Florence, a small band of brigands appraised us, then let us pass by, though we two were quite alone. Colleoni's soldiers were behind us in the village, where before leaving I had ordered all of the remaining hostages released; I hoped that some of those peasants at least would have wit enough to abandon their homes and flee with their families before whoever was appointed my successor took control and rounded them all up again.

To have thus breached my signed contract with Colleoni did weigh somewhat on my conscience. I was not one to break any solemn agreement lightly, though it was common for mercenaries of the time to do so and change sides. But my conscience found relief in an excellent argument, namely that my loyalty to King Matthias must take precedence over any such temporary pact made for money; and so, by extension, must my duty regarding the king's sister and my wife, now that I had located her again. As to exactly where my duty with regard to Helen lay, I had not yet made up my mind. Certainly, I told myself, it was not the kind of problem I wanted to deal with offhandedly, whilst I was distracted with carrying out some lunatic persecution of the poor.

Helen, mounted on a spare horse that I had commandeered, rode beside me and just a little to the rear. The storage chests of the scholar's house had yielded up enough women's clothing to afford her an air of respectability, though the garments showed as ridiculously too large when she dismounted. She said little as we rode, but watched me almost continuously. I knew she could not believe that I was not plotting some utterly fiendish revenge. Tonight, or tomorrow, she was thinking, I would contrive somehow to serve her Perugino's faithless heart baked in a pie. And as soon as she had partaken thereof I would, with a maniac's cackling, tell her so; and then I would spring upon her, and get on with whatever torments I meant to use to end her life . . .

Oh yes, I admit, I did play in the back of my mind with some shadowy plans along such lines. But somehow my heart was not in them and they never took on substance. Where Helen was concerned I had no will for tricks like that. On the other hand my honor would certainly seem to demand that I inflict some serious punishment upon her for running off with another man. But what was the punishment to be? I could not decide.

Meanwhile I counseled myself that while I was making up my mind I ought to lead her into trusting me, by pretending that all had been forgiven. I would play the model husband, that when the hour for vengeance struck at last, it would be all the sweeter and more exquisite. And the delay would give me time to plan and prepare revenge carefully . . . eventually, I told myself, I was bound to hit upon a plan for which I could feel some enthusiasm.

Our road wound among silvery-green olive groves, past cypress that looked dead with winter and war. Snow lay scattered on the Tuscan earth that summer would once again make lush with greenery. Still, after only a day's ride, the land was starting to look less like one of Goya's later portraits of war. Peasants and some other natural creatures of the earth were once more to be seen, behaving normally.

"This is the road to Florence, my lord." At last, it seemed, I was to have some conversation.

"And is there any reason why we should not take the road to Florence?"

"None. Oh, none. I am willing to go wherever my lord wills."

Though I offered no explanation then, I had decided to go to Florence because in all that turbulent land there was no other place where I could be so sure of a welcome; I brought with me detailed news about a powerful enemy's plans against that city, as well as a strong sword-arm to help oppose those plans.

The journey took us several days. There were no haystacks to sleep in, but plenty of abandoned buildings. My lady appeared to welcome my husbandly attentions inside these, as once she had inside a palace. On our last day of travel, when we were almost at our goal, we passed that very place, Careggi. I rode to the gate and gained admittance. But the great country house of the Medici proved to be unoccupied in winter except for a caretaker staff. Some of these goggled at my companion, making me suspect that news of our coming would precede us to the city, even though we headed directly on to Florence after only a brief pause for refreshment.

The palace on the Via Larga was even busier than I had seen it before. Yet again the leading men of the Medici family welcomed me, and greeted Helen, almost without twitching an eyebrow. They were used to wonders, in that house. And yet again their welcome had a different tone. The first one, more than a year ago, had been strongly tinged with curiosity; the second, last summer, polite. This third reception had in it the wholehearted enthusiasm of men who were being given needed reinforcement on the brink of war. I quickly discovered that Colleoni's plans of conquest were already known here in broad outline, though the details I could provide might well prove invaluable.

Lorenzo listened appreciatively to the version I gave him of events since I had seen him last—according to which Helen and I had merely gone through a lovers' quarrel, and she had been living with me almost continuously since our separate departures. Doubtless he did not believe it, but understood that it was to be taken as official. By then Piero had rounded up his military advisers, and closeted himself and me with them, to study greedily the lists of material and drawings that I was able to set down pertaining to the Venetian war machine. Interest in Colleoni's new model firearms was intense. While we were relaxing a little later, both men amused me with the account of how Lorenzo had saved his father from assassination in 1466, outwitting ambushers hired by the rival Pitti family. I found out later that the Medici vengeance for that attempt had been prompt, precise, bloody, and discreet.

Helen and I were domiciled in one of the visitors' rooms. There the painting was again brought in to stay with us, as if it were some antique Roman household god. On the first full day of our stay, the Duke of Urbino arrived at the palace. The Florentine Council, who governed the city generally under instructions from Piero, had found the Duke available and currently an enemy of Venice, and had placed him in charge of preparations against Colleoni's expected onslaught.

I respected the Duke's military reputation, and

found him an impressive figure. He was already dressed in light armor, though by most calculations combat was still some months in the future. Listening as he chatted with our hosts, I was surprised to realize that he too was a serious book collector, or at least aspired to be one, in the same league as the Medici and King Matthias. I thought to myself that the world seemed to be changing drastically. No longer, it appeared, would fighting, praying, and the maintenance of honor be all that were required of a successful man. Very well, I thought, I am going to have to learn to think as well. I have always been able to manage great changes in my lifestyle when necessary.

One day in the palace, with a group of officers pondering Colleoni's field artillery, I was sketching the weapons from memory as best I could, when some man entered the room where we were gathered but then immediately withdrew. This made me glance up, just in time to recognize the retreating back of one of the Boccalini.

"There will be trouble, Lorenzo," I said to my young friend a little later.

Lorenzo had been in the room also, and had noticed the near-encounter. "Perhaps not," he soothed me now. "We will try to prevent it. There are others, too, who, shall we say, do not work well together. Yet Florence must be defended. If the Boccalini and the Pitti can work with us, they can tolerate you as well."

"Even when we meet face to face?"

Lorenzo furrowed his swarthy brow, considering. Already he looked forty. "I suppose that you, my friend, are going to take an active part in the fighting, and will be going out into the field shortly?"

"Yes. The Duke has already asked my help in training and organizing new troops."

"That is good, because the Boccalmi will be staying

in town. Meanwhile I advise you, not that you need
any such advice, to guard yourself."

Shortly thereafter, whether because of the Boccalini
or for some other reason, it was delicately suggested
that Helen and I might want to move out to Careggi,
which was now beginning to be occupied by other
military guests of rank; and yes, the painting came
with us once again. From Careggi I presently
departed for an advanced camp in the field. Helen
appeared to be concerned as she bade me farewell.
My own feelings about leaving my wife behind were
fatalistic; I did not ask the Medici to put her into a
convent, or to set a watch upon her whilst I was gone.
What would be, would be. Somehow I had never got
around to deciding upon a suitable vengeance for her
earlier transgressions, and now . . . now other decisions
were more demanding.

In the spring, under the direct leadership of the
Duke, we mercenaries and the more valiant citizens
of Florence met the more numerous forces of
Colleoni at the town called Molinella, roughly halfway between Florence and Venice. The land there
was marshy, and horses tripped and fell in mud, and
some of the wounded drowned. What we fought was
certainly not a great battle, by the standards of those
combats that have changed the world. But for some
hours we fought in earnest, which was not always
the case when one mercenary opposed another. The
fight began near midday, and went on, with pauses,
until after dark, and the dead totalled six or seven
hundred on both sides. Colleoni's new cannon served
his cause well, until I managed to lead a squadron
of cavalry into his rear, where we overtook a pack
train carrying his reserve of gunpowder. After the
ensuing fireworks he was unable to make headway.
By nightfall the Florentine forces had been worn
down, but so had the Venetian; still, it would have
been senseless for Colleoni to advance against our

fortified city walls, whilst our army still remained in the field against him.

Successful *condottieri* were nothing if not practical, and did not care to squander today lives that could still be useful to them tomorrow. With much practiced torch-waving, and shouting back and forth, a preliminary truce was worked out, though night had already fallen, making communication difficult. Then by torchlight the Duke and Colleoni embraced each other, exchanging congratulations on their personal survival.

I was suspicious of treachery, but those with more experience in these parochial wars laughed at the idea; and in the morning both armies indeed retreated, as had been agreed.

A few days later, I returned to Careggi. As I approached the villa, I found it difficult to maintain my fatalistic attitude on the subject of my wife. If she should be gone again—I had difficulty in trying to think beyond that point. But I recognized in myself the signs of inward rage.

To my surprise Helen came running to meet me, in the yard near the stables, having evidently observed my approach from the window of our upstairs room— this time we had not been granted the bridal chamber.

Before I had dismounted, she was at my stirrup. "You are alive," she said. Her eyes had a look I could not remember seeing in them before.

"It pleases you to see me so, madam?"

"Pleases me? Pleases me?" Helen sounded the words. Evidently she would not have thought of putting her feelings just that way. "But you are all I have."

TWENTY-TWO

The half-ruined building into which Judy and her three companions were urged at gunpoint was evidently very old. The door was shielded on the inside with a blackout curtain, in the form of a sheet of dark plastic; once that barrier had been passed, Judy, Bill, Pat and Helen emerged blinking in the white glare of a Coleman lantern set on a rough table. They were standing in a large room, walled with old brick in bad repair. Judy could recognize the soft-looking light brown that she had recently learned to identify as real adobe. Three temporary cots had been set up along one wall. More sheeted plastic was suspended overhead, to protect the beds and other contents of the room from the effects of what must be a leaky roof.

"Sit down. Here," ordered one armed man, pointing to the open space in the middle of the hard-packed earthen floor. "Hands behind you when you sit. Then nobody move."

The four of them sat down. And nobody moved, or spoke. One man passed behind them, tying wrists. He was quick about it. It was as if he had had cords ready for some job like this, and had been practicing.

Hasty glances to right and left assured Judy that her companions were looking pretty sick. She herself was not quite as scared as they appeared to be; she had an inner certainty that help of a most effective kind was on its way. Judy was sure that *he* now was aware, at least dimly, of her presence here, near the very thing that had already drawn him so powerfully, and he was coming, at great speed.

The trouble was that Judy could not be at all sure of how far he had yet to travel, or how long it would be until he got here.

As soon as four pairs of hands had been tied, the tallest of the masked men, the one who gave the orders, got the prisoners to stand up again and then went along the line going briskly and impersonally through all their pockets, and dumping out Pat's knapsack as well. Judy could see from the corner of her eye that the searcher took no money from Bill's wallet. He appeared to be chiefly interested in ID's, which he looked at and then put back. But Bill's car keys did disappear into the tall man's pocket.

This quick search completed, their chief captor stood in front of them, looking at them for a moment. "Ralph," he said abruptly then, "better get the Jeep out." And he tossed one of his henchmen the two sets of car keys he had confiscated. "It'll take some towing to get both their vehicles around the hill and under cover, but we'll have to do it, now we've come this far. Ike, you go along and give him a hand. Cover up the tire tracks. I can manage here."

The other two men went out of the room by a side door that led into some sort of hallway. A minute later Judy could hear an engine starting, as if the Jeep the men had been told to use were parked in some attached garage or shed, with no closed doors between. Gradually the sound of the engine moved away.

"Sit down," said the ski-masked man who still

remained. The four sat, a movement made awkward
by bound hands. The Coleman on the table emitted
a faint hissing noise, and sent out its glare. The masked
man set down his shotgun, where he could reach it
easily and at a careful distance from the others, leaning
against a stack of crates that appeared to hold food-
stuffs. Then he said: "Well, people. We've got some
things to talk about, before I can let you go."

He certainly has no intention of doing that,
thought Judy to herself. Whatever was going on
here . . . had something to do with that painting. The
painting, the old painting showing some woman . . . it
was still wrapped in rough cloth. And now Judy
could tell there was clear plastic around it too. And
it still leaned against a rough adobe wall in darkness—within a few feet of where she was sitting at
this very moment.

Judy opened her eyes with a start. But the sound
she had heard was only the wind, scraping a pine
branch lightly along the building's ancient roof.

The standing man had turned his head toward her
at her motion. Now slowly he turned back to the girl
who had introduced herself as Helen. She was the
one getting most of his attention.

The man said: "A little bird tells me your name
is Helen Seabright. How come you're carrying car
keys but no license, no money, nothing else?"

Helen shook her head. She didn't look especially
frightened now, Judy realized. Dazed, but almost
eager, as if she would like to hear the answer to that
question herself.

"I know you too," Helen answered. "You're
Gliddon. I don't think anyone ever told me your first
name."

"You called me by that name outside. I'd like to
know why. Also, I want to know just what the *fuck*
you're doing up here at midnight, talking about a
radiophone."

Helen was unperturbed. "I know you have one, in this building. Back in the other room where the stove is. I've seen it."

Gliddon whistled softly under his mask. He said no more. He stood there looking at them all until the other two men came back from their task of moving and hiding vehicles. It took them the best part of an hour.

Galvanized when his household alarm shrieked that a locked door somewhere had been opened, Ellison Seabright jumped to his feet and hurried at once toward his bedroom to check the master security console and to arm himself with a Luger that he kept there. Stephanie, with whom he had been arguing in the breakfast room, for once caused no interference, but fell silent and came along. She had to step lively to keep up with him. He could still move quickly, Ellison told himself, when there was good reason to do so.

Puffing, he entered his bedroom and switched on the light over the security console—the sun had gone down a little while ago and the house was full of gathering dimness. From a table drawer beside the bed he grabbed his weapon. Gun in hand, he saw the console's indication that the intrusion had been in the garage.

He grunted at Stephanie and started out of the room. She followed. They both understood that there could be no question of calling the police.

When Ellison poked his head into the garage, one of the doors was still standing open to the thickening night, and the inside lights were on. The Subaru was gone.

Ellison looked around, then closed the door to the outside and turned off the lights. He glared at his wife. "You—" he began, sure that whatever had happened was going to be her fault. Then he led the way at a quick walk back to the room where they had left the boy asleep. The young visitor, or intruder, was gone.

Ellison switched on another light. "He's taken our car," he said. His wife did not answer, and he glared at her. "Well, hasn't he?"

Stephanie gave him back a strange look. "I don't know. It may not have been him who did it."

"No?" Ellison was suddenly aware of the gun still in his hand, though it was hanging motionless with muzzle pointing down at the carpet. "There was no one else in the house." At that she looked more peculiar than ever. "Was there? Was there? Stef, why did you do it?"

His wife only sighed, a sound blending weariness and impatience. "Oh Ellison. Do what?" For some reason she had never adopted any diminutive or nickname for him. Sometimes in the past he had wished secretly that she would do so.

The gun like a great weight seemed to pull his arm down toward the floor. "Don't pretend to be stupid. You guided him out of the house for some reason—"

"I was with you when the alarm went off."

"—and you arranged somehow to give him the keys to the car. You may have done a lot of damage to important plans, plans that you don't begin to understand."

"*I* don't begin to understand?"

"Did it worry you so much, that I might decide to have him killed? Your own daughter was killed and you got through that." Then Ellison thought to himself: I shouldn't have said that.

"Ellison. I didn't help him. I didn't know he was going to leave. I didn't want him to leave until it could be decided what to do about him. If he had any help it came from someone else. And you don't have to be so secretive, about your plans to sell the

painting secretly and make a fortune, you and Del.
Del's told me about that. Or your own bombing
scheme. Del wasn't too happy about that one." She
paused, sniffing. "Oh my God," she said.

"What?"

"Don't you smell it?"

"What?"

"Very faint, but it's there. The perfume Helen used
to like to use."

"Stef, this is very stupid. You're trying to distract
me. There was no one else in this house, and someone helped that boy to get away and steal my car.
He couldn't have done it without help. Even if he'd
found the keys, how could he have avoided the other
alarms?"

"I'm not trying to distract you, Ellison, I'm trying
to explain something. But I suppose I ought to leave
it to Del. Oh God, don't you know anything of what's
going on?"

That stopped even Ellison, for a moment. "Now
just what in hell is that supposed to mean?"

"I wish you'd put that gun away. There are no
burglars. It'll be better if Del explains to you himself. When was the last time you talked to him?"

"I haven't seen him since the kidnapping setup, and
the last time he called was days ago. It bothers me
when he calls, though he keeps assuring me that the
phone here isn't tapped by anyone. How can he know
that?"

"Oh." Abruptly Stephanie was almost smiling. "He
now has ways of telling, about things like that."

"That's exactly what he said. I don't understand
what it means, and I don't like it. He's taking too
many chances."

"He *did* tell you that he means to come here
tonight?"

Ellison was astonished. "Of course, he told me. I
didn't know he'd let you in on it too. He talks too

much. And that's another thing, his coming here. When I asked him how he knew the house wasn't being watched, he just laughed. He wouldn't even discuss it."

"If Del says it's all right, then it's all right, Ellison. Believe me."

"*Why?* Will you answer that simple question for me?"

"Del," said Stephanie, in a new voice. Ellison spent a moment trying to make sense of this as an answer, and then realized that it had been a greeting instead. She was looking over his shoulder.

Beyond a doorway, in the dimness of the next room, towered a figure as tall as Ellison himself, almost as broad. It certainly looked like Del, though Ellison could not at first make out the face in the dim light. It looked like Del, but something had been changed—but it was Del, it was so like him to stand there like that, listening, not saying a word until he was discovered.

Ellison cleared his throat. "I didn't hear you come in. How did you get here? How do you know the house isn't being watched? What if—"

The figure came toward them, moving with Del's walk into the light. Del's face, undoubtedly. But vastly changed, young, lean, no longer sagging in cheek and jowl, under a full head of crisp brown hair.

Del looked at least thirty years younger than when Ellison had seen him last. How? Plastic surgery? More than that. But what?

"Del. You're . . . you're . . ."

"Ellison. You're you're you're." Del's rejuvenated voice mocked him, while Del's young face smiled. "You're you're you're. Still as much of an idiot as ever."

Then the smile, changing as it moved, was turned on Stephanie. "All this ringing on the radiophone would seem to indicate something serious. I was coming anyway, so I thought I'd just come over instead of answering." Del's manner was supremely confident. "What's it all about?"

Stephanie took a step closer to Del, reaching for his hand. "I'm so glad you did. There was a boy here. Ellison thinks maybe he was one of the kids you . . . who was at the house in Phoenix once. The boy kept asking for Annie. Said he knew that Annie was here, and he didn't want to go away. Now he's gone, and so is one of the cars."

Del's forehead creased in a mild frown. He glanced up quickly at the ceiling. "Did you—?"

"No, I haven't been up there. I don't know if she's there now or not. And I haven't talked to Ellison about her being there. I've been waiting for you to do that."

"A wise decision," said Del.

Ellison raised his voice. "Will someone kindly inform me what is going on here, under my roof?"

"Close under your roof, old man," said Del. His young face looked so strange, so strange. It wasn't, it couldn't be, simply makeup or anything like that. It brought back authentic memories. This was really the way Del had looked, thirty, forty years in the past.

Del asked Stephanie: "Did this boy give a name? What did he look like?"

"Short, blond hair, very young." Ellison couldn't remember the name, but Stephanie did. "He said his name was Pat O'Grandison, something like that."

"Ah," said Del. "Yes. *She* talked about him, before she decided she was going to be Helen. I suppose she's gone with him. But I'll go up and take a look."

And with the last word, Del disappeared. Just like that, from the middle of a lighted room. Ellison found that he had raised his own arms, and like a sleep-walker was groping through the empty air where a moment earlier his rejuvenated brother had been standing.

And was standing again. Del's powerful young hand, materializing in mid-air, casually warded Ellison's groping arm out of the way.

"She's not in the attic now," said Del to Stephanie. "The earth and everything looks undisturbed." His light frown had solidified but did not seem to dent his confidence. "So the two of them apparently took off together. They're both crazy so I'm going to have to check up on what they're doing."

Stephanie said: "She was wearing Helen's perfume again."

"Oh, she's completely settled in as Helen now, in her own mind. I don't know how she justifies to herself sleeping in the attic all day, and occasionally flying out through the wall at night and enjoying a drink of blood. Not the way Helen should act, certainly not in Annie's dream of the home-sheltered adolescent. She may be five hundred years old, I don't know, but inside she's still a little girl wanting to be loved."

Ellison groped his way to a chair and sat in it. He looked at the gun still in his own hand and wondered for a moment what it was doing there. He tried to frame questions that he could ask and that would do him some good, but got nowhere in the attempt. The crafty suspicion suddenly sprang to life: his wife and his half-brother were conspiring to drive him mad.

The spark of suspicion had no sooner been ignited than it sprang up in a roaring blaze.

He looked up, keeping his face calm. Understanding seemed to grow. "You're not really Del," he announced his sudden insight. No one could shed, really shed, thirty or forty years. Stephanie had murdered Del, after all, and had found this young man who looked like him. Could Del have had a son who looked this much like him?

Del's young face looked at him, and away again, contemptuously. "I'll see you in a little while, then," the youth said to Stephanie. "Can you manage things here?"

Stephanie was clinging to him impulsively. "Don't go yet. Del, change me now, tonight. You said you would, as soon as you were changed yourself. Now you're all set. I don't want to go on like this, with him, another day. Not another hour if I can help it. You can't imagine what it's like. Take my blood once more. Change me."

"Oh, I can imagine. But, as I say, I'm going to be busy for a while. If she heads for the painting again tonight there could be problems. Gliddon's out there, and his men, and they don't imagine that there are any such things as vampires. I'm not quite ready to be rid of them all just yet."

To Ellison, listening, the whole conversation had become utterly insane, incomprehensible. Yet it was perfectly plain to him from looking at the two of them just what was going on. What had happened between his wife, *his wife,* and the giant young demon-figure that somehow looked like a young Del.

Now Ellison watched as the young man who looked like Del took Stephanie by both arms, and kissed her softly on the forehead. He said, in his perfect imitation of Del's young voice: "I will. I'll change you. You'll be young forever too. But you have to understand that when that happens, it will make a difference between us. No more lovemaking. It doesn't work between two vampires, you understand. Then we'll just be—friends. So I don't want to rush things. I love you just as you are."

Stephanie gave a wild cry. "You don't want me any more. I can see it. You're through with me now. And, my God, I gave you my daughter for your games. You've had both of us and used us up. Helen's dead, and I'm—now you want to leave me with this, this obscene old lump of fat—"

Ellison was not conscious of getting to his feet, or

of saying anything, though he could hear his voice. And the gun in his right hand rose levelly and seemed to go off by itself. He had at last got Stephanie's full attention. She stood up very straight, and gazed at Ellison with wild and unbelieving eyes. Then her hand caught at the seventeenth-century Spanish shawl and at her breast beneath. And then she fell.

Ellison held the gun up higher now, and shifted his aim. And now he was looking straight down the long Luger barrel, at Del's eyes, excited but unfrightened, that gazed straight back at him.

"You haven't learned a thing, have you old man?" said Del. Ellison fired, but somehow Del was not falling, though he winced as if with pain. Anger and triumph were in his face and he was moving rapidly toward Ellison, reaching out for Ellison with young powerful hands. The Luger fired and fired again, and Del came on unharmed.

TWENTY-THREE

Fade in on violence.

If you have seen one tournament of jousting, you have seen them all. But then, unless you are after all, in tune with my jests, almost as old as I am, you have never seen even one, have you? Never mind.

There were church bells in my ears, when I knew that no bells rang. Angels swam round me in an alarming swarm; not, as modern legend has it, looking for the point of a pin to sit on, but rather to cluster before my eyes inside my steel helm, good and evil disputing for my soul.

I understood vaguely that my helm was being lifted off, by gentle hands, but the knowledge made things no clearer. I saw the *totentantz;* and I saw, as on a stage, tableaux from the old French story in which three living men meet their three doppelgangers all wrapped in shrouds.

"Is he dead, then, at last?" It was the voice of my dear wife Helen, and she was despairing almost utterly. "He is dead. I know that he is dead."

Someone else muttered something. If this was death, at least I did not fear it. The Angel of the Lord

...ped near to me, dispersing the fog of lesser ...erubs who were swarming in my eyes, and spoke to me. What the angel said to me then I may not yet reveal.

"He is not dead," said another, non-angelic voice.

I was lying on my back inside a jousting pavilion of fine white cloth, lit gloriously from above by bright sunlight. My armor had all been stripped away, and my body, wrapped now in white linen almost like a shroud, was a mass of many hurts. I hurt no more, though, than was seemly for one who had been knocked off a horse by the brutal impact of a long, sharp-ended pole, and had probably been trampled on by horses' hooves thereafter. Meanwhile the Angel of the Lord transformed himself into Helen, who sat at my side dabbing with cool perfumed water at a certain abominable lump upon my head.

Presently I understood that this wretched lump was coextensive with my head itself.

"I feared for you, oh my lord." And Helen was weeping softly. Dab, dab, oh so gently. Her perfumed kerchief of fine Florentine cloth was mottled red.

"That I was dead?"

"Yes. Oh, Vlad, your face was pale and still."

"Know then that I am alive." I raised an aching arm to catch Helen's hand, whose dabbing ministrations had become more irritant than help; and, to provide a sweeter reason for the catch, I squeezed what I had caught, and brought it to my lips. "And, even if I had been dead, to have such an angel ministering to me would make me rise again."

A non-angelic face in the background coughed and grimaced at this remark. It was, I realized now, a friar standing by there. Doubtless he had come to anoint the dying.

"I would not have you jest about such things," said Helen. But I think what really bothered her was her perception that I was not jesting. This was in early

1469. By then we had been five years married, and had lived long enough as man and wife to begin to know each other well.

"Your good wife speaks wisely, my son," the friar chided me. "You have been near death today, but today it is God's will that you live. You should consider that one day He must will otherwise. Death will come to us all, or soon or late."

I considered the friar's long face, and liked it not. "Nay, father. Does it not say somewhere in the Scriptures, 'we shall not all die, but we shall all be changed'?"

The friar's face said emphatically that mine was not a proper attitude; but what could one expect from these foreign soldiers who were the bane of Italy? "It saith also, that the devil may quote Scripture when he likes." After that, sensing himself no longer quite welcome, the priest bowed out through the tent flap and took himself away.

"Vlad, do not sit up yet. Rest yet a while, and I will tend to you."

"I will sit up." For the moment, though, it was quite enough just to get my elbows under me and raise my shoulders. "And shortly I will rise, and walk. I want to see the progress of the tournament." There was a large roar, of many excited voices, not far outside. The pavilions had been set up in rows quite near the stands and the lists. Now there came groans, and loud prayers of alarm; again some shrewd blow had been dealt. "Who unhorsed me? Who dealt me such a devil's blow? I don't remember."

"I do not think I saw who it was."

"Nay, Helen, it is only a game, is it not? Do you think I am going to go looking for revenge?"

The great misbegotten lump that was my skull ached all the more mercilessly when I sat up. But evidently, despite all my interesting visions, I had not been unconscious for very long. The brightness and warmth

of the sun shining through the pavilion top told me
that the time was still near midday, and the crowd's
voice sounded as fresh and enthusiastic as ever.

Again shouts of encouragement and triumph,
mingled with those of disappointment, drifted in.

"Who is winning?" I wondered aloud. And without
letting myself think about the problems of movement, I got to my feet and began to dress myself.

Helen sighed and let me have my way. "I do not
know. They say the grand prize will be awarded to
Lorenzo himself, whatever happens in the jousts. It
is his wedding we are celebrating, after all, even if
he is no warrior."

I grumbled reflexively at that. Not that I wished
for myself the fame of winning. I did not want to be
prominent in the public eye; I was still Signore
Ladislao in Italy, because I was still theoretically,
officially, imprisoned in Hungary by my brother-in-
law, and would be for another seven years. His
Majesty King Matthias was still wary, still uncertain
of what reception I might be accorded were I to
appear in a place of honor at his court; and he was,
for somewhat different reasons, also unsure of what
Helen's reception would be there. Meanwhile I had
been occupied with other things. Some of these were
tasks undertaken for Matthias, and none of them have
any proper place in this history. But I was on better terms than ever with the Medici, who ruled more
firmly than ever in Florence; and they would not take
no for an answer to their invitation to this tournament and wedding.

It was a celebration, a festive occasion, the like of
which had perhaps not been seen in those parts since
the days of ancient Rome. Arm in arm with my wife
(She was, I must admit, helping me to keep steady on
my feet, though she managed to make it look as if I
were the one supporting and assisting her) I presently
walked out of my pavilion, which stood surrounded by

a multicolored mushroom forest of other tents like
itself. I was at once congratulated upon my quick
recovery, by smiling gentlefolk nearby. Only a few yards
away, the temporary stands held cheering thousands.
In the middle distance the *Palazzo* Medici was strung
with flowers from every doorway, window, and cornice,
as were many of the other buildings in this quarter of
the city, and even some of the many church spires in
the distance. The land where the tournament was
being held had been, only a few months ago, a waste-
land of abandoned buildings, emptied decades ago by
plague. At Piero's direction, all had been leveled and
made smooth for a jousting ground to help in the
celebration of the wedding of his eldest son to the
lovely Clarice Orsini. Now, as I strolled with my wife,
the prize seats of the grandstand came into our view,
and I could see some of the Orsini delegation there
now, the future in-laws of Lorenzo, ready to weld their
elder dynasty to his.

"Shall we go and watch the fighting, Vlad?"

"No, I have changed my mind. I think I have seen
enough of combat for one day." And I guided Helen
in the opposite direction from the lists. "I prefer to
seek more soothing entertainment."

Through increasing crowds, lively with celebration,
we moved toward the palace. There was something
strange about the crowd, and it puzzled me until I
realized there were few hawkers; food and drink were
instead being given to the masses free during these
proclaimed days of joy. Musicians played on a small
green, and some gentlefolk were in sport performing for the crowd, treading the stately old French
basse danse. It reminded me for a moment of the old
French story in my dream, or vision.

Helen must have seen me smile. For whenever I
displayed good humor she was wont to bring up some
topic she had been saving till I should be in a good
mood.

"Vlad, you have been fighting so much these last few years. In these little wars, and tournaments. Do you mean to keep on fighting always, until one day when I think that you are dead it turns out I am right? Is it not time to let the younger men do their share?"

"Oh, am I old?"

"You are—mature. And there should be more to life than giving and receiving blows. And—Vlad, I tell you truly—on the day that I do see you lying dead, I think I shall go mad." She said it simply and without emphasis.

"I am a soldier."

"My husband, with your agreement, I am going to write a letter to my brother. He could end this farce of your supposed imprisonment at any time, and then we could go home. I think that by now I have demonstrated that I can be well-behaved. And you—you could be Prince again, in Wallachia. Matthias could install you there if he wanted to."

"I can see political reasons why he would not want to. Not now, at least. I think he will not agree to your proposal."

"Then I should wait for a time, and write again. You would like to go home? Such a change would please you?"

I looked around me. I had, as I have written, fallen in love with Italy. Yet it was not home. Then I looked intently at Helen. "It would please me very much," I said, "to rule in Wallachia again, this time with you beside me. Though you must realize that things there are not *always* perfectly peaceful. There have been moments, one or two in history, of unrest, invasion, murderous intrigue and treachery—a few upsets of that sort." I had to smile. "By St. Peter's beard, you worry about me in tournaments, and yet wish to see me on that throne again?"

Helen was distressed, but determined also. "Oh yes,

I know there would be dangers at home, too. But there—how can I put it?—the dangers would have meaning. You would be defending our own homeland. That is what a sword ought to be for, and a cannon too."

"I think you have a woman's view of swords and cannons and war."

"Well, and if I do? A woman can be right. And if death came, in some great, just cause, then in death too there would be meaning. If you were to die so, perhaps I would not go mad to have you taken from me."

I did not know quite what to say, or think. "I have told you, wife. I mean never to submit to death without a struggle. The old scyther will have from me such a fight as he has not known in a long time."

Arm in arm we walked on, through celebrating crowds toward the palace. I had heard that Leonardo was to be there this afternoon, discoursing of his art to those folk who loved such things more than tournaments.

TWENTY-FOUR

It was after midnight when Gliddon finally heard Ike and Ralph returning the Jeep to its shed. Shortly after that the two of them came into the room where he was still standing over his prisoners. They described to Gliddon the Subaru wagon and the old Buick, and told him how they had searched through both without finding anything of interest. Both vehicles were now covered with old tarps, in a ravine where no one was likely to look. Ike said they had done a good job in getting rid of tracks.

Gliddon listened, and nodded, and presently gave more orders. He wanted his four captives disposed in four separate rooms for their interrogations. There were plenty of rooms, otherwise unused, in the old place, and Gliddon preferred to have four separate stories to sift through for the truth instead of one. He didn't anticipate any great trouble in getting at the truth, or at least the part of it that these four unlucky kids could tell him. But he could see that even when they'd told him all they could, plenty of problems were going to remain.

In his days of hiding out here Gliddon had

wondered sometimes whether the many little rooms in the sprawling old building might have been monks' cells in the old days. Many of the rooms still had doors, though few had ever had windows. When Gliddon looked into the little earth-floored chamber where Helen had been put to wait for him, he saw that what had been a tiny window must have been blocked up earlier by Ike or Ralph, with chunks of wood and wads of plastic, as part of the general effort they had made to keep out some of the cold and to keep their lights from being visible. Anyway, Gliddon thought it a damn good thing that one way or another they weren't going to have to camp out here much longer. The deal for the undercover sale of the painting ought to be concluded any day now, according to what Gliddon had heard from Del Seabright on the phone.

Keeping his small battery-powered lantern aimed at the girl, Gliddon set it down on the floor. The old door of the room sagged half-closed behind him, and he let it stay that way. It was cold in here, even colder than out in the big room, and Gliddon in his heavy jacket was no more than comfortable. But the girl sitting on the floor was barefoot and without a coat; still she wasn't even shivering. Or very much frightened, either; the expression on her face as she looked back at Gliddon was half dazed, half arrogant.

She's on something, all right, Gliddon thought, staring back at her through the eyeholes in his mask. She's got to be. He could only hope that she was not too far out of it to do a little useful talking. Del's niece. Well, that was just too bad. Del might make a fuss, but Gliddon couldn't see any way to avoid wasting this girl, and the three who had come with her as well, now things had gone this far. Helping Del sell the painting his way had been an okay idea, but it wasn't necessarily the only way for Gliddon to go. He himself was no art expert; but experts could be hired when they were needed, as Gliddon himself had been hired, often enough, for his own specialty. Now he had the painting, and he had an airplane, and he knew one or two people down in Mexico who would be glad enough to welcome him there with his treasure any time he wanted to drop in. He understood he wouldn't be getting anything like full value for the painting that way, but still he ought to be able to turn a nice profit. And tonight things were looking more and more like that was the route that he was going to have to take.

He stood there looking down at Helen for a while, and her expression didn't change. That was a bad sign. "Well, girly. You and your friends have sure got yourselves into a bunch of trouble here. I mean a real bunch. Can you understand that? Am I getting through to you at all?"

Evidently he wasn't, for Helen still sounded almost cheerful. "My Uncle Del is going to be angry with you for this. He's going to be out looking for me. He loves me a lot, you know, just like I was his own daughter."

"Yeah, I bet he does. And in several other ways as well. I think I see how that goes, kid. But there's one thing I definitely *don't* get. You see, I really thought that you were dead. Just like everybody else, I thought so. Now it turns out you're not dead, and you've been hiding out with Uncle Del, and Mommy and Stepdaddy too, I suppose; so okay. But *I* should have been told that you were still alive. I mean, I was in on that snatch operation from the start, all the way, and *I* thought for sure that you were the one who was gunned down in that upstairs hall. We sure as hell shotgunned someone."

Gliddon paused, with a faint sigh. The sappy look on the kid's face didn't hold out much hope that he was going to learn much from her tonight. Could he believe anything she said, anyway? But it was

important that he try—something was going on here
that he wasn't in on. Something even deeper than the
faked kidnapping and killing, and the faked loss of
the painting. Something very important, no doubt
about that. And he hadn't been told by the Seabrights.

But wait. At last, as the kid considered what he
had just told her, her eyes were beginning to look
shocked. "That was my girlfriend Annie who was
killed," she whispered. "Did you do that?"

"You know, Helen, I think you've changed a little
since that night. Stand up for a minute, let me take
a look."

Obediently the girl stood up on her bare feet. She
managed the move quickly and without difficulty
despite having her hands fastened behind her back.

"I think you're a little taller now, Helen, than when
I saw you last. I can recognize you, but . . . you've
changed. How old are you, anyway?"

Helen tossed back well-cared-for brown hair from
her face. "When was that? When did you see me
before?"

"Look, kid, you've seen *me* before, right? You were
pretty sure about my name."

"That's . . . different."

"Yeah, sure. You know when we saw each other,"
Gliddon assured her softly, "if you can get your brain
working. It was at your dear Uncle Del's house in
Phoenix. One night he had a special kind of party
there, he used to have them regularly, and I suppose
the old fart still does. This time he wanted you to
play along, and your mommy wanted to make him
happy and she said you could. Either he didn't invite
your mommy that time or else she didn't want to
come. But I remember I was wishing she had,
because she looked like a real good piece still."
Gliddon paused. He was remembering what he had
done with this very kid on that very night. But that
had nothing to do with anything now, and the look

on her face assured him that she wasn't remembering much of anything at all.

He went on. "Anyway, where we met doesn't matter all that much. The point is that I know you, and that I'm going to find out why you came out here tonight. How'd you know that I was here, and had a radiophone, and so on?"

The girl brightened; she understood now what he was talking about. "Your phone has some kind of a scrambler thing on it. So if someone else listens in when you talk to Uncle Del or Mommy or Daddy, they can't understand a thing."

"Uncle Del and Mommy and Daddy Ellison really tell you a whole bunch, don't they? I wonder why."

"Uncle Del does. I don't see Mommy much any more. Because I sleep in the attic a lot now. And Daddy thinks I'm dead. But he doesn't really care. He's only my step-daddy anyway." Helen giggled prankishly.

"I get it. Or maybe I don't. So I suppose you brought your friends out here tonight to show them the radiophone."

"Pat is the only friend I brought. I don't know the others, we just ran into them by accident. And what I wanted to show Pat was the painting."

Gliddon sighed. At this stage, he wasn't really surprised. "You can sit down again if you want to, Helen. Who told you about the painting being here? Uncle Del? Or was it your mother?"

Accommodatingly she sat down. "Uncle Del. He's always wanting to talk to me about it."

Well, people could get their kicks in an infinite variety of ways; Gliddon had understood that for a long time. Still there was something going on here that he knew he didn't yet understand. "Now look, Helen, what I'm going to ask you now is very important. You want to get out of all this trouble that you're in, don't you? How many other people have you talked to about there being a painting out here, and a radiophone, and all?"

"Nobody." And now at last, delayed, the sniffles started. "Just the kids who are here."

"Nobody else at all? You're sure? You're very sure?"

"Yeeesss." The word trailed off into a great sour violin-note of a sob.

Gliddon felt like slapping her, like killing her. But for the moment he wasn't rough. He was very seldom rough without calculation, and right now it wasn't called for by the situation. He found himself tending to believe the kid. If what he heard from the other three captives tended to confirm her story, then these four but only these four would have to go. Then maybe the operation of selling the painting as Delaunay planned could still go on.

He patted Helen gently on the head. "Just take it easy, kid. We're going to get this all straightened out, but it's going to take a little time. I'm going to have to keep your hands tied up for a while yet, okay?"

She was sobbing and didn't answer. Maybe he ought to talk to her again, Gliddon told himself, when she'd had a little time to come out of it. He picked up his lantern and went out through the sagging door, which almost fell off when he moved it. Ike, still skimasked, was sitting at the end of the corridor like a guard in a prison, in a position to keep an eye on all the cells. Gliddon nodded to him, then turned away and went into the cell where they had put the boy he also remembered from Phoenix. Another Uncle Del special.

This one was obviously scared shitless. He sat on the floor in the corner as Helen had been sitting, but he had twisted to hide his face in the corner of the wall. He looked around with eyes squinted almost shut when Gliddon entered with the lantern.

Gliddon put the lantern down casually on the floor, and then took a relaxed pose, leaning with his back against the wall. "Kid, we got ourselves a real serious problem here. But I have hopes that we can straighten it out without anyone getting hurt. Does that sound to you like the way we ought to go?"

The boy nodded quickly. "Oh yeah. Gosh." Obviously he wanted desperately to believe what Gliddon had just said, about no one being hurt—but maybe he couldn't quite believe it. He made a little choking noise in his throat.

"On your driver's license it says your name is Pat O'Grandison." Gliddon's mind had had a little time to work on the name by now, and it sounded right to him, like he had heard it before and it really belonged to this punk he recalled from Phoenix.

"Yeah, that's right. We didn't mean any harm by walking around here, we just got lost. The bridge was out down there, and one of the cars was stuck. The girl said she knew where there was a phone, back this way."

"The girl?"

"The one I was riding with. She was just giving me a ride. I didn't want to bust in on anything up here."

"When you say the girl, you mean Helen Seabright?"

"Yeah. That's her. That's who she told me she was."

"Well then *say* Helen Seabright. I want to be filled in on all the details, so tell me everything you can. What happens to you from here on is going to depend a lot on what you tell me." Gliddon worked a cigarette and a match out of his shirt pocket and lit up. "Here, want a drag?"

"Sure. Thanks."

Gliddon held the smoke, let the kid inhale deeply. "Now, you say that Helen Seabright was just giving you a ride. You mean she just picked you up along the highway?"

The kid hesitated. Gliddon could see him

wavering, and then apparently deciding to tell the truth. Yippee. "No, we started from her place in Santa Fe. Her parents' place, I guess. Great big house. Gosh."

"And her Uncle Del was there with you, and you were all having a sort of party before you decided to take a ride."

"Party? No. I just came to the house looking for another girl."

"You like girls?" The boy was silent, and Gliddon went on: "Never mind. Who was this one you say that you were looking for?"

"Annie Chapman, her name was. Still is, I guess."

Annie Chapman. One name Gliddon was never likely to forget. Not after that one party night in Phoenix, and what had happened afterward. Del's big secret, whatever it was, that Gliddon wasn't in on—it would have something to do with her. "All right. Then what?"

"Then . . . I kind of conked out on a sofa for a while. When I woke up this girl, Helen, was sitting there and she started talking to me. Also there was a woman in the house, and a man, an old guy, real huge. I don't know if he was her Uncle Del that you mentioned, or her father, or who."

"You never saw him before, huh?" He peeled off his mask. "How about me?"

The kid was immediately struck blank and hopeless. "I don't know. I don't think so. I don't always remember things too good."

"That's fine. Outta sight. Some things you're not supposed to remember. But when I ask you to remember something, you make a special effort, huh?"

"Sure. Anything you say."

"Now do you know who that big old man was?"

"No. I don't. Really."

"Okay. And the girl you started out looking for was Annie Chapman."

"Yeah, but they all swore she wasn't there and they didn't know her. You know her? She looks quite a bit like Helen."

Yeah, there had been a good resemblance. Gliddon pondered. Sisters, somehow? Nothing seemed to quite make sense. And this kid didn't seem to recall that orgy night at Phoenix at all. Gliddon himself had picked up both Pat and Annie on that night, one at a bus station, one on the road—recruiting for parties had been part of his job for Delaunay. Another part had been joining in—Del liked to have a physically able and trusted employee on hand in case things got rowdy, as they often did. That night the group had included Helen, Pat, Annie Chapman— and what's-his-name, that muscular young drifter who had followed Annie when she danced off into the museum room, and had been killed by her there. Gliddon could see it yet: the strong, naked young male swinging the silver artifact, some kind of model ship, right for Annie's head; and Annie dodging and reaching up somehow out of her crouch, grabbing her assailant by wrist and ankle, and—and just *flipping* him somehow, so that his long-haired head smashed on a marble base, and blood sprayed on the white carpet. Gliddon had seen a few fights in his time, but never before a stunt like that.

And from that moment, Del had made Annie his special project; he had wanted something special from her, obviously. And Gliddon, looking back, couldn't be sure that the special something had really had anything to do with sex. Gliddon had seen very little of her from that night on . . .

And then, on the night of the engineered kidnapping, it must have been Annie Chapman, running in panic through the upstairs hall of the same mansion, who wouldn't stop when she was yelled at and so had caught a charge of buckshot in the head. Del must have known who the dead girl was; but he had said nothing to Gliddon; and the family had identified the dead girl as Helen, and had cremated her.

Why?

Something to do with inheritance, with wills, with who gets what. Gliddon didn't understand all the legal angles of what happened when someone as wealthy as Del died or supposedly died. Del wanted to be thought dead, to disappear, while in fact retaining control over most of his own great riches. Gliddon could understand that; he was trying to do something like it himself. But he was more and more convinced that something else important was being planned by Del, and Gliddon hadn't been dealt in. Except, maybe, in some way, he was going to be set up to take a fall.

Damn the whole Seabright crew, anyway. They were trying something that Gliddon wasn't going to like when he found out about it. The way things were looking, more and more, they pretty well had to be.

The boy still sat on the floor, looking up at Gliddon, growing more and more frightened; he looked sick. "Listen," he pleaded now, "I gotta go to the toilet. Please."

"Okay," said Gliddon. He turned away and stuck his head out of the door of the cell. Suddenly he found himself feeling and thinking like a jailor, and it was amusing. "Ike? You got a client here. Take him for a walk and bring him back. I want to talk to him some more, later."

Judy could hear, down at the other end of the strange little hallway, the voices murmuring, sometimes rising a little in anger or in fear. The implacable man who had made them all prisoners, whose name apparently was Gliddon as the girl called Helen had said, seemed to be making his rounds like a doctor in a busy clinic, going from one treatment room to the next.

At least none of the patients were screaming. Yet.

Judy, to control her own fear, concentrated as much as possible on something else—on that hurrying approach that only she could sense. *He* was coming, in an onrush that seemed utterly tireless. The difficulty remained, though, that Judy could not tell how far he had yet to come. With a great effort she tried to communicate her own fear and need to the one approaching, and after a while it seemed to Judy that his speed had become greater still. But no words, no plans could be exchanged, and she could not be sure. The landscape around him was still all wild and empty, she could perceive that much . . . but where were his running feet? Abruptly Judy realized that he was now wingborne.

A bright light against her closed lids startled her. She squinted open her eyes to see Gliddon, now without his mask, looking down at her over a small lantern. His face was more ordinary than she had imagined it. In one hand he carried a casual, half-smoked cigarette.

His voice was not unkindly. It might even fit the doctor she had imagined. "Let's see, your name is Judy Southerland, as I recall from your ID."

"That's right." Her own voice came out pleasingly strong. "I think you'd better untie my hands."

"Now just try to have a little patience, Judy. I didn't ask you to come here, you know. What are you people doing here, anyway?"

"I . . . any answer I give to that is going to sound pretty silly."

"Try the true one on me. That'll save time and trouble."

"I—no, I don't have to tell you anything at all. Except that you'd better let me go. Help is going to be coming for me."

The man set down his lantern carefully on the floor. Then without changing expression he drew back his arm and hit Judy open-handed across the face. Never in her whole life before had she been struck like that. Now she understood what was meant by the old expression about seeing stars. A moment later she tasted blood. And her tongue had become an odd, paralyzed lump that in a moment was going to hurt badly. It started to hurt.

She tried moving her jaw, and was a little surprised to find that it still worked. Then, speaking carefully around her tongue, she said: "You're going to be sorry you did that. Oh God are you ever going to be sorry."

Perhaps her sincerity made a momentary impression on the man, for he seemed to hesitate. Then he took a puff on his cigarette, and reached out to grab Judy by the hair. She saw what was coming, and uttered a little shriek. "All right! All right, I'll tell you the truth, if that's what you want. Don't blame me if it sounds completely crazy."

Her hair was released. "I'm listening."

"I just talked Bill into giving me a ride. Then we ran into these other two by accident. I have no idea what they were doing out this way. But our car was already stuck down there when they came along."

"I see. It was your idea for Bill to drive you out here."

"Yes."

"Why? You just like to take rides in the middle of the night? On roads like that one? If you just want a peaceful place to screw, you don't have to drive out of town this far."

Judy was silent. A hand rested on her head, and here came the cigarette again, toward her face. She yelped.

"Wait! I'm going to the Astoria School, you see. Up in the hills on the other side of Santa Fe."

The approaching fire paused. "That's nice, tell me more." July could feel in the man's hand on her head that he was enjoying this.

"It has a bearing. Wait. Well . . . one of the girls there was saying that her brother had been out this way recently, deer hunting, and there were some people living here in the old buildings." Judy stalled there. Invention had flagged, because of the way Gliddon was looking at her.

This time the cigarette came all the way. And it didn't withdraw until she had screamed, twice.

"Deer hunting in the spring," the man said then. He let her go, and leaned back against the wall, looking at her thoughtfully while she sobbed.

"You know what I think I'm going to do?" he said at last. "That young guy who gave you the ride, as you say. I haven't talked to him yet. I think I'll bring him in here and talk to him. As soon as either one of you tells me another funny story, I'll pop out one of his eyes. I have a way of doing it with my thumb, just like this." Gliddon demonstrated in mid-air. "Then we can talk some more about deer hunting in the spring, and I'll take out the other. I'll use him up a little at a time—"

"All right, all right! We know about the painting. I mean I know about it. Bill doesn't know a thing."

Her interrogator sighed. It was an angry sound, but Judy realized, slowly and with fearful relief, that the anger this time was not at her. Gliddon stared at the adobe wall for a time, as if he were looking into the distance. Then his attention came back to her. "You were all at one of Del's parties tonight, right?"

Judy nodded agreement. She had no real idea of what she was agreeing to, only that agreement was the expected answer, the believable answer, the answer that would at least postpone more pain.

"I thought so. At Ellison's house in Santa Fe?"

Judy read the question as well as she could, and nodded her head again.

"Yeah, I thought so. And for once the old asshole

got stoned himself and talked too much. One time when I wasn't there to look out for him. How many other people were there, besides you four that I've got?"

Judy paused. Thought, hoped, prayed. "No one."

"You know what I think? I think you're lying to me again."

"No. No I'm not. No."

Gliddon sighed faintly. Basically he believed Judy. Hurting girls was something that he enjoyed very much, but right now he had one more person to talk to. First, though, he meant to take a short break and grab something to eat.

For Pat, being left alone with his imagination under present circumstances was almost as bad as being worked over. Almost. He had been worked over seriously a time or two in his life, and he understood how lucky he had been to survive those occasions without permanent damage. He feared that this time he was not going to survive at all. When the man called Ike had taken him out of his cell, Pat had feared that he was going to be killed at once. Then when that hadn't happened, he considered trying to seduce Ike. But in Pat's experience in rough situations such efforts only tended to make things worse.

Back in his cell, crouched shivering again in his adobe corner, he could imagine the worst of everything that was going to happen to him. He almost welcomed the shivering that shook him and made his teeth chatter. Maybe if he was lucky he would freeze to death before Gliddon got around to him again.

To Pat it seemed now that he had always known that he was going to end something like this. There had never been any use in hoping for some other outcome. Life as he had known it had been basically like this all along. A few bright intervals here and there. But he seemed to have spent an awfully high percentage of his lifetime alone in the dark.

But this time be wasn't left alone in the dark for long.

After the glare of first Gliddon's lantern and then Ike's, it was hard to see anything in the dim cell. But as soon as Pat's eyes became accustomed to the gloom again he could see, or thought he could see, someone standing just inside his door.

He could have sworn the door hadn't been opened again, but . . . and then he saw that it was Helen. Her hands were free, and she was looking at Pat gleefully, like some small girl triumphant in a game of hide and seek. Pat knew a relief so great that it made him feel for a moment as if he were going to faint.

Helen put a finger to her lips—as if Pat might need any warning to keep silent. Then with an impish smile she stepped close to him and squatted down. "I fooled them," she whispered. "They thought I was sad because I was crying."

Pat wanted her to get to work at once on his bound hands. But she just squatted there. She added: "They're going to be mad—I already set Bill loose." She continued to look at Pat fondly, as Annie had used to do sometimes. But Helen was doing nothing helpful.

"Helen," Pat pleaded at last, in quiet desperation. "Help me get loose."

"In a little while. I want to kiss you, first."

"Not now, not—"

She was leaning toward him, and now her lips stopped his. Her lips—Helen's lips?—felt cool. In another moment Pat had recognized their touch, even before they left his mouth and moved down toward his throat.

"*Annie.*" His own whisper was still very soft. But it carried the astonishment of a shout.

"Hush, lover, hush," the girl murmured against Pat's neck. Her brown hair brushed his face. Only Annie had ever really bitten him in making love. And now he felt her teeth again.

It wasn't pain. But as he had known it with Annie a dozen times before, it had the intensity of great pain. Never, with anyone else, anything like this . . . it went beyond, unimaginably beyond, anything that he had known of sex.

Pat moaned. He couldn't help it if the sound was loud. He forgot his bound hands and even the threat of death. He couldn't tell how long it went on. He never could. He knew only that at last it ended, and that the moment Annie took her mouth from his throat and let him go the shivering came back, even stronger than before. Pat felt he wasn't going to be able to go on living in this condition. Something was going to have to happen soon to end it, one way or another. He felt so weak now that he wondered if he was dying. But the idea conveyed no fear.

He was miserable, colder than ever, very weak, but no longer afraid as he slumped back again in the angle of the wall. The adobe behind his back felt soft and crumbly. "Annie, don't leave me." As long as she stayed with him, he wasn't even going to worry about how she had managed for a time to look so much like Helen.

"*You* can call me Annie," her soft voice answered. "For you to is all right." She was standing up straight again, in the middle of the little cell, and despite the darkness Pat could see her a little better than before. "Poor Pat. You don't look good. But it's going to be all right, Annie knows what to do for you."

"Annie."

"Or you could call me Helen. I was Helen once before . . . a long time ago."

With crossed arms she grasped her loose pullover shirt at the waist. In a quick motion she slid it up and off over her head. Her upper body, completely uncovered, was slender and pale in the darkness.

"Annie . . . help me . . . get me out of here."

"Don't faint now, Pat. Don't, my lover. Here." And what the pale girl in the darkness was doing now seemed very strange; even Annie had never done anything quite like this before. With her left hand she cupped and lifted one of her small breasts, and with the nail of her right forefinger she drew a line just underneath. A short dark line appeared on the pale skin. Annie was bending over Pat, bringing the dark line closer and closer to his face. "Here, lover. This'll help. This'll help a lot."

He understood now what was expected of him. In a moment it no longer seemed strange at all, and his lips parted, hungrily.

A little later, when the shotgun fired at the other end of the building, Pat didn't hear a sound.

TWENTY-FIVE

Gunfire and uproar brought Gliddon running, cursing through the fragments of sandwich that he spat out of his mouth, grabbing up his shotgun from where he had left it leaning against the stacked crates of food. At the far end of the building, Ralph reported to him that the prisoner as yet unquestioned, Bill Bird, had somehow got loose. Ike had seen him, with unbound hands, sneaking out a door and then making a break for it. Ike had fired at him, evidently missing completely; and then Ike had gone in hot pursuit.

"Get him!" Gliddon snarled, shoving Ralph toward the door also.

"He could maybe try something like doubling back, to get the Jeep—"

"I hope to hell he does. Get him!" And Ralph ran.

Gliddon drew a deep breath, let it out. Well, all right. He had pretty well made up his mind anyway that he was going to have to cut out alone, and probably tonight, sometime before dawn. So anything that got Ike and Ralph out of the way, kept them from raising any objections, might well turn out at this stage to be an actual advantage.

He trotted toward the shed where the aircraft was kept, at the other end of the building from the Jeep. Should he stop on the way and finish off the people left in the cells? No, first things first; it looked like there was a good chance of one witness getting away anyway. First make sure of the painting and the plane.

He reached the aircraft shed, which was attached to the north end of the building. He, Ike and Ralph had built it carefully out of old lumber so it wouldn't look strange from the air. Now at once Gliddon dragged open the wide doors. In the moonless night the section of abandoned road which served as runway was vaguely visible. Lantern still in hand—now was no time to worry about showing a little light— Gliddon then turned back toward the deep end of the hangar-shed, where he had stashed the packaged painting in the middle of a stack of rotted lumber, studded here and there with rusty nails.

And as soon as he had turned, he stopped. In the beam of his lantern stood the slim young girl, Helen, bending over the pile of old boards and timbers. Her hands were free, and now she was down to wearing nothing but her jeans.

"God," said Gliddon, speaking aloud but to himself. "They're all loose." And any one of them could finger him for kidnapping, at least.

"Don't you point that gun at me," the girl said, straightening up and turning, a hand on one hip. She put her other hand on a flimsy table that Gliddon had brought into the shed when they were doing some maintenance on the aircraft engine, as a place to set down tools and parts.

And Gliddon paused for a moment, struck by her face. It was suddenly different. And her voice . . . maybe he was starting to go crazy himself, he spent so much of his life around nuts of one kind or another.

She was starting to say, again, "Don't you—" just

as Gliddon fired. And at the same moment, somehow, the table she had been holding came flipping
up into the air toward him. As if the girl had tossed
it, though no little girl could possibly—and the charge
hit the table in midair and blew the middle of the
table into fragments. The legs and various splintered
parts of the top went flying everywhere. The thin
wooden tabletop was not enough to save the girl, of
course, not at close range like this. She went down
at once. Gliddon shone the lantern briefly on the
bloody mess, then set it down so he could rub his
right forearm. One-handed wasn't a good way to fire
a twelve-gauge, even if you did have a powerful grip.
Anyway, he hadn't broken any fingers, though one had
been torn slightly by the trigger guard in the recoil.

He set the weapon down too. Then it took him a
minute to dig through the lumber pile and get the
painting out, bulky and heavy inside its special protective crate and wrappings. Grunting, he wrestled
the package over to the Cessna, got the cargo compartment open and worked the package inside. A tight
fit; carefully planned by the Seabrights, probably, even
as far back as when they bought the aircraft; give
them credit for being planners. That was one reason
Gliddon didn't want to ride with their plan to the very
end, not once it had become obvious that they were
keeping important secrets from him.

He reloaded his shotgun—he liked a simple
double-barrel for reliability, two shots were enough
if you knew when to use them and could put them
where you wanted. Then he headed back into the
building to finish off the two live witnesses he could
still reach. In passing he glanced down once more
at the dead girl. He thought she had moved amid the
blood. Even so, there didn't appear to be any need
to waste another shell on her, but he would check
again on his way back.

Tonight everything was one surprise after another.

Looking into the room where he had left the punk
called Pat, he saw that the kid appeared to be dead
already. Pat lay still, on his back, bound hands underneath, with open, unblinking eyes and some kind of
bloody mess around his parted lips. Beside him lay
the sweatshirt Helen had been wearing. Well, whatever, the kid looked dead. Making sure, Gliddon knelt
down, felt a forehead that was already cold. No
heartbeat under the shirt. He flicked an eyeball with
a fingertip and got no reflex blink. No need to waste
a shell here, either.

With a growing sense that speed was necessary,
Gliddon turned away. He had to make sure that the
last prisoner, the girl called Judy, was still where she
was supposed to be.

Indeed she was, though she was working to get the
door of her cell open when Gliddon got there. She
was alive and still hand-tied, and satisfyingly terrified.
It was reassuring to find at least one person behaving as they ought.

Gliddon would have loved to play with her for a
while, but there just wasn't time. He set down his
lantern and raised his gun and grinned. "Sleep tight,"
he said.

And whirled round, on nerves that had become
hair-trigger, at the ghost of a small sound just a few
steps behind his back.

The small brown-haired girl with the bloody torso
stood there, seemingly ignoring her great red wound.
In the reflected lantern-light the wound now looked
more like scar tissue than like hamburger. Gliddon's
eyes must have played him tricks a minute ago, the
flimsy wooden tabletop must after all have saved her
life. Temporarily.

"Gliddon, Gliddon." She didn't even sound hurt.
Her little-girl voice held a tone of soft reproach, and
it appeared that she was smiling at him.

Gliddon's nerve might have held up, would have

held up, if she had been yelling, or attacking him, or crying out in pain for mercy. But he couldn't take this kind of a reality just now. He fired both barrels right in her face. The girl's hair blew back in the wind of the blast, but her face remained untouched. The wall behind her cratered widely and shallowly, and a choking cloud of brown adobe powder burst into the air. The girl stood there with her lovely, smiling face untouched.

Gliddon dropped the emptied shotgun, grabbed up the lantern again, and at the same time drew his pistol. The lantern's beam shining through the cloud of settling dust showed him Helen's dazed and gentle smile. The great red scar along her ribs and belly looked almost superficial, like an old, half-healed burn or scrape.

"Gliddon, no, you shouldn't. Uncle Del's going to be awfully angry with you. He loves me, I'm his niece. I'm just like his very own little girl, he says."

Gliddon couldn't think any longer. He triggered his revolver at the figure, and behind it wood and adobe shuddered and burst, gave up flying fragments to the air.

There was something else in the air, at Gliddon's elbow. He sensed another presence, saw another human figure starting, trying, to take shape. He turned and ran, fleeing by instinct to the aircraft shed.

Judy, gazing at the new apparition, almost broke down in her near-hysterical relief. "You're here, you're here, thank God. I was . . ."

Her voice trailed off. The figure of the vampire taking shape before her eyes was not that of the man she had been expecting. She stared as the form solidified. It was that of a huge man, massively built. He looked quite young—she knew how deceptive that could be—and Judy was sure that she had never seen him before.

He was looking at Judy oddly. In a bass voice he asked her: "Who did you think I was?"

Before she could answer, another man's voice screamed outside in the night, a hundred yards or more away: "Ike! Gliddon! Help!"

Judy slumped, knowing behind closed eyelids a sudden vision: white teeth quenched in red blood. The help that she had waited for had come.

In the aircraft shed, Gliddon hurled himself into the Cessna's cabin. The engine would be cold, but he had kept everything as ready as possible. He was going to make it now. Mexico, here we come.

He grabbed for the electric starter. The engine caught on the first try . . . then coughed, and died. He tried again. The pale figure of the girl was following him. Here she came, walking toward the aircraft through the dim shed, and in the restored silence when the engine died again he could hear her softly calling.

Any moment now he was going to wake up. But no, this time the engine caught and held. He released brakes and grabbed the throttle, and now he was rolling for the doors . . .

The slender blue-and-white figure of the girl in jeans came sleepwalking right into the path of the rolling aircraft. Gliddon could see the disaster coming but it was too late for him to do anything about it. Just at the moment of catastrophe everything seemed to be happening at once, and he had not even time to perceive it all; but he had the distinct impression that at that very moment there was yet another person in the shed. A dark-clad man with a pale face, standing near the girl and in the act of reaching for her with one outstretched arm . . .

. . . Gliddon's right hand had hit the switches, and was reaching for the throttle, but too late. The sound of the blow had elemental power, and Gliddon knew the wooden prop must have been sprung if not completely shattered. The aircraft shuddered with the impact, the engine dying finally in a great cough. Gliddon had a door open and jumped out of the cabin again almost before the Cessna had stopped rolling. Something lay on the floor, but he was not going to stop to decide what it was. If there had really been two people in front of the propeller, quite likely it had hashed them both.

Moving in desperate haste he wrenched open the cargo compartment again, pulled out the awkward package and ran with it, stumbling, arm muscles quivering, out of the shed and through the passage that led to the other shed where the Jeep ought to be parked. The Jeep was there.

Gliddon wedged the encased painting into the back seat, then sprang into the driver's seat and started the engine with a roar.

The Jeep bounced out of the shed and away into darkness, following a route that twisted among dimly visible boulders and over tiny hills. Next Gliddon headed down into a breakneck ravine that took long minutes to work through, at walking speed, even with the four-wheel drive. At the bottom end of this ravine a small stream murmured almost invisibly. Otherwise the night had grown quiet; so far, there was no pursuit. Tires splashed, and then the Jeep was working its way uphill again. Gliddon drove out of the rough at last on the old road, not far from the point where the punks' cars had been stalled. Only a few more miles and he'd be on highway. Then he'd head south. He had in mind a place or two where it ought to be possible to steal another plane.

He felt it was safe to use the headlights now. As soon as they came on they showed him a solitary figure ahead, walking along the primitive road in the same direction he was driving. This figure too was small and slight, but it had on a shirt, and its hair was light in color. As the Jeep slowly overtook it from the rear, it turned. The pale eyes did not squint in the headlights. Numbly Gliddon recognized Pat O'Grandison's dazed, childish face and bloody mouth.

But Gliddon had begun by now to regain his nerve. He was able to believe again that the world was manageable. If tonight's events hadn't beaten him yet, there was no way they were going to.

It wouldn't really be practical to try to finish someone quickly by running over them, on this twisting, humpy, low-speed road. Especially not on a night like this, when people who had looked finished kept coming back.

Calmly watching the Jeep approach, the kid stuck out his thumb, hitchhiking. Well, why not? Gliddon saw that somehow, and it was against all sense, the kid had even managed to pick up and repack the knapsack that Gliddon had emptied onto the earthen floor during the search.

Gliddon slowed the Jeep, meanwhile feeling with one hand for his pistol. It was gone. He must have dropped it somewhere. Never mind, there were plenty of other ways. But he'd rather not delay for a killing until he'd got a few more miles on his way.

He stopped the Jeep beside the waiting boy. "Want a ride, kid? Get in."

The kid didn't even appear to recognize Gliddon. "Thanks," he acknowledged, and got in quite calmly, just as if this were afternoon on the Interstate somewhere. He slipped out of his knapsack and dropped it on the floor, after noting that the back seat was pretty well filled with a huge package. "I'm headed for California."

"Me too," said Gliddon, and eased the vehicle ahead, tires gripping the edges of an old rut, scraping around a rock. Maybe, just maybe, his luck was starting to turn a little for the good.

❖   ❖   ❖

In the weeks since he had succeeded in inducing the girl to transform him into a vampire, Delaunay Seabright had reveled in the new keenness of his senses, among other things; and he had discovered that they remained most usefully acute when he retained the form of man. Thus it was that he was walking on two human feet when he moved stealthily into the aircraft shed. In the shed there was much more light than his eyes now needed, an electric glare streaked with shadow, spilling from a battery lantern that someone had dropped and left on the dirt floor.

The Cessna was almost at the opened doors. It looked wrecked, with its cargo compartment door standing open and one blade of its wooden propellor broken to half its length. But Seabright gave that little attention. Directly in front of the plane, the figure of a lean man dressed in black, turned in profile to Seabright, was down on one knee. The man, head bent, was giving his full attention to something on the earthen floor. Seabright could not see his face at first, only his white and bony hands, sifting the dry dust.

Even though Seabright continued to advance into the shed, one step and then another, the kneeling man did not look up. Surely anyone of even moderate alertness would have by now sensed his presence . . . then with a quiet shock the realization came that the kneeling man knew Seabright had entered the shed, but simply did not care.

Seabright advanced yet another step. He now had, or thought he had, an understanding now of what his dark-garbed visitor was, if not of who. For some time now Seabright had known it was practically inevitable that sooner or later he must encounter one or more of the Old Ones—that was how he had thought of them, when in private thought he had made his plans. It had taken him years of research into the ancient and the arcane to convince himself of the reality of vampires, and to be able to recognize, however belatedly, that the girl called Annie was what some of the old books called *nosferatu*. He was not at all sure what the others, when and if he met them, would be like. Surely they were not all mad, as the girl had been. In his heart Seabright expected that they would prove to be not all that essentially different from breathing people—manageable, for the most part, by someone like himself, once he had grasped what really made them tick.

He would not submit to being ignored, and now he moved forward yet another step. First he would make sure that his own credentials were established, and then . . .

The kneeling figure in dark clothing at last raised its face. And Seabright, who in recent weeks had imagined himself totally immune to fear, found himself stepping involuntarily backward. The face was pale and thin, and on the surface it held nothing terrible, though it was marked with wooden splinters from what must have been the propellor's terrible impact against another body that was now nowhere to be seen. From one splinter in the forehead a trickle of dark blood ran down into one eye and out of it again like tears. Yet Seabright retreated another step, and yet another, until the adobe wall came against his back. One of the Old Ones. But he had never dreamed it could be so hard simply to confront one of them.

The figure straightened slowly until it stood erect. It was actually not as tall as Seabright, but from several yards away he got the impression that it was towering over him.

"I was a second too late," the man in dark clothing said softly, in precise and only faintly accented English. "A second too late, and she is dead. Already nothing but dust. That is how we old ones go."

With a great effort Seabright made himself push

away from the wall, and speak out boldly. "Who's dead? Who do you mean?"

"You are Delaunay Seabright," the man said. "And you used her."

"You're Thorn," said Seabright, suddenly understanding a little more. "No wonder you . . . I heard about that bombing. No wonder you were able to escape alive." Trying hard, he made himself look closely at the other's face, and was astounded. Were tears mixed with the blood on those almost emaciated cheeks?

"She is dead," said Thorn.

"Look, I'm really sorry about that. Very sorry. She and I were lovers, you know. But she was more than a little bit crazy, and it's not my fault she—"

An invisible giant's fist closed down on Seabright. He was picked from his feet and spun through the air back against the earthen wall, with a violence that tore his clothing and his skin. Imposed force choked his outcries in his throat. Desperately he tried to change his shape, to melt his flesh to mist or nothingness for escape. But his own powers, that he had thought almost perfected, were infantile against the potency that held him now.

Delaunay Seabright sought to strike back at the dark man. But he could no longer even see where his opponent was. The vise-grip blinded his eyes, even as it crushed his ribs. Now he could feel the bones of his elbows, pinned to his sides, shattering in their sockets, and he could not even scream. Then, still capsuled in solid form, he felt himself being propelled helplessly through the air again, driven by what felt like the energy of a locomotive. His eyes were allowed to open, in time to see the ancient wooden beams of the building hurtling toward him.

Nothing prevented Judy Southerland from screaming, and scream she did. She knew that her long-hoped-for rescuer was now somewhere near at hand. But he had not come to her. And she could feel that something had happened, something terrible, something to drive him mad, though she had no idea what it was. Violence as shocking as a bomb was bursting, just on the other side of the building, while Judy, her hands still bound, could not get out of her cell, could not do anything to help herself.

Then, abruptly, came help in a surprising form. A woman Judy had never seen before, a young-looking woman wearing some kind of high-necked granny dress, was bending over her. There came sharp snapping sounds and the tough cord fell from Judy's wrists.

"And you must be Judy," the young-looking woman said. She strongly resembled someone Judy knew—yes indeed, she actually resembled the image that Judy still saw daily in the mirror. In the middle distance there rose a great cry, as of some huge predator in torment. "There now, he's making a great lot of noise over there, isn't he? And I must go to him, but I wanted first to have just a quick word with you. You see, you can't understand what has happened to him tonight—I understand it, a little bit, and I must go, and you must stay here quietly and not try to talk to him just now."

"Gliddon!" That was another voice now, a man's voice shrieking from not far away. "Gliddon, it's got me, for God's sake helllp—"

Judy stuttered: "I . . . he's . . ."

"He's been your lover, yes, Judy, I know. He was my lover in the same way, but that was many years ago . . . my name is Mina, by the way. We shall meet again, someday, perhaps—but then perhaps not. In either case I wish you well. I must go now, to do what I can. He can be very dangerous like this."

The woman, or the vision of a woman, was gone. No, it had been more than a vision, for Judy's hands were free, the cords that had bound them lay snapped away like thread. And the door of her cell, that she had been trying vainly to force, now stood slightly ajar. Judy pushed weakly against it, then stopped, her eyes closed. Her contact with her once-beloved, strained by the burden of things that Judy had never imagined it might hold, had broken and was gone.

Or had it been deliberately cut, as by some seamstress' scissors?

For the moment she did not care. Freed hands, freed mind—for the moment it was enough, it was all that she could ask for, to enjoy both.

Then Judy's eyes opened, and she cried out again. Great wing-beats of throbbing sound were buffeting the roof above her head. For a moment she cringed from monsters. Then there was a glare of harsh electric light outside, and her own good sense came to her rescue. The light bobbed and probed with the throbbing roar, seeking a good place for helicopters to come down.

Gliddon had at last maneuvered his Jeep as far as the highway. It was a dirt road, smoothly graded and two lanes wide, that could pass for a state highway in this part of the boondocks. Gliddon looked both ways into darkness, at zero traffic. He considered, then suddenly reversed the Jeep. A few yards back he had noticed a branching road, and now he found this again and backed into it for a few more yards, until he had reached a place that he was sure would be out of sight of the highway by day.

He stopped the Jeep there, and grinned over at his young companion. "Afraid this is as far as you go, kid."

"I'm going to California," the boy repeated vaguely. He rubbed at the dried mess around his lips, looked at his fingers, then touched one with his tongue. He appeared to be trying to remember something.

"Sure. This is Hollywood and Vine. Hop out. I'm gonna fix you up with a job in the movies."

"I'm going to get a job out there making films. My home's in Chicago." But the kid got out on his side, obediently enough.

As Gliddon stepped out of the Jeep on his own side, he remembered something else. "Hey, kid, you were pretty good that night in Phoenix. Better than any of the girls. I wish we could have finished good friends, the way we started." He walked through the beams of the headlights and put a hand on Pat's shoulder. "I wish we could get a little fun in right now. But I'm in a hurry." And Gliddon, remembering the wounded finger on his own right hand, drew back his left arm and with a practiced, lethal snap sent the blade of his hand with full power against the youngster's neck.

And Gliddon shouted, blinded by the pain and shock. It felt like he had struck a thick wooden pole.

Before he could begin to think of what to do next, the kid had taken him by the right arm. And somehow Gliddon, try as he might, could not pull free.

"Your finger is bleeding, gosh," the boy said. There was something in his voice that was not sympathy, and was certainly not fear either. Whatever it was, it made Gliddon look closely at the kid's face, and then try to pull away again. When Gliddon saw those dried stains around the childish mouth. And how Pat's teeth had changed. When the boy displayed them in a merry smile.

EPILOGUE

They had flown Joe Keogh out to Albuquerque, where the FBI people looking into the matter of the missing painting had set up their headquarters. They wanted to talk to Joe about Thorn, and to try to understand some things. He happened to be talking to them—they were working late hours at the time—when the report came in about a crazy-talking young man named William Bird, who said that he and Judy Southerland had been ambushed that very night by masked gunmen up in the hills.

Fortunately some helicopters were available, and Joe didn't have to talk about Thorn—or try to avoid talking about him—any more that night.

After a late night and early morning of doing what he could to sort things out, and a few hours' sleep in a hotel, he flew back to Chicago the next evening. Judy came with him.

Judy, who had the window seat, was dozing. Joe sat next to her in the middle seat, and the aisle seat at his right was empty, as were the seats on the far side of the aisle. The scattering of passengers elsewhere in the cabin were pretty effectively walled off from Joe's view by high seat-backs, shadows, and the pervasive quiet appropriate to the late hour.

And then all at once the seat at Joe's right hand was empty no longer. For a moment he wondered if he had dozed off, and so given the young lady a chance to sit down unnoticed. But then he understood.

The brown-haired girl in the high-necked gown was smiling at Joe. She was quite attractive, and he at once caught the strong family resemblance to Judy. Glancing back at Judy briefly now, Joe saw that she was deeply asleep.

He turned back. He wasn't exactly used to this sort of an experience yet, but similar things had happened to him before and he could handle them. He returned the smile. "I think," he said, "that I spoke to you on the telephone once, Miss."

"It's Mrs. Harker, actually." Her voice was soft and charming, slightly British. "But please call me Mina. Vlad has told me a good deal about you, and I really feel we are already friends. And since we are sharing a ride tonight I wanted to say hello. And to reassure you, perhaps, on one or two points in connection with these recent—events, that have been so distressing."

A stewardess, passing in the aisle, looked vaguely unsettled by the sight of an unremembered passenger. But the stewardess naturally had plenty of other things to worry about already—there was no problem, really, with a pleasant-looking, undemanding young woman who simply sat chatting with a man. No need to concern oneself; and Joe's understanding grew of how the whole vampire business could remain a secret even while it went on and on and on.

"Well," said Joe, "I'm glad you say 'reassure.' The one kid, Pat O'Grandison, is still missing, and the painting also. And Mr. Thorn, of course. Otherwise there are just bodies all over hell, in mansions, in Jeeps, in garages and old adobe ruins."

"Yes," Mina agreed with a sigh. "It has been a terrible business. Just terrible." She looked at her nails, as any young lady might. They were neatly manicured, Joe noted, and not very long. Certainly nothing at all talonish, not at the moment anyway. She added: "And I don't think they are going to have any success in looking for the painting."

"Oh no?"

"It is my feeling that the real owner might by now have put it away safely somewhere."

"Oh." Joe turned his head to glance once more at Judy, who had not moved. "According to Judy, he was rather crazy, there at the end. She says it was very lucky that you showed up when you did. I was wondering . . ."

Mina smiled again. "Vlad's going to talk to you himself," she said. "Say hello to Kate for me. If you think it wise." She leaned back, and was gone. But the seat remained empty only for a moment.

Joe flinched, just slightly. He couldn't help himself.

If Thorn noticed that infinitesimal recoil, he gave no indication. He smiled lightly at Joe and patted him on the arm. "Thank you, Joe, for your support."

Joe tried to make his arm relax on the seat divider. "You're welcome. Er . . . ah . . . Mina told me there's no use our looking for that painting any longer?"

"Your sense of justice, Joe, may be soothed to know that for the first time in centuries, it is now in the hands of its true owner."

Joe didn't have to ask who that might be. He wondered suddenly if the painting, disguised somehow, could be cargo on this very plane. He wasn't about to try to find out.

"There is one more point, Joseph, on which I wished to speak to you. I mean the young man, Pat O'Grandison, who has disappeared."

"Oh. You're not through hunting yet."

"I detect a certain disapproval." Then in a sort of parenthetical action Thorn leaned forward in his seat and slowly reached past Joe toward Judy. With one finger he very gently touched the burn on her cheek, and her puffy lip. She was sleeping deeply, and did not stir. Thorn sat back. "Actually this particular hunt is one that I should think you might want me to conduct. The youth has not wronged me; I am not seeking revenge."

"Sorry. What, then?"

"He is . . . a runaway. In years, not a child any longer. But not a responsible adult. In fact he is intermittently mad."

"As I understand it, he's been like that most of his life. So are a hundred thousand others running around loose. So what's—"

"Joseph, you do not understand. Remember how the body of the man Gliddon was found."

Joe had heard about that. The state police had said it looked like Gliddon had been half eaten by some animal. "Oh. I thought that was . . . not that I would have blamed you, after . . ."

"Oh, I would have killed him, certainly. But his blood would have been carrion to me. Not to that boy though. That boy is *nosferatu*, now; or rather in a grotesque halfway state that may persist indefinitely. And he is out there somewhere, hitchhiking. If I were greatly concerned for the welfare of the breathing populace of this great nation, I would be anxious that he be found; I would concern myself about him. Of course, as you say, there are thousands of others—"

"What?"

"Oh, not insane vampires, not all of them, but just as dangerous sometimes. To themselves, if not . . ." Thorn's voice trailed off.

Joe stared into the pale face, and could see torture there.

"As *she* was," Thorn went on at last, whispering. "For centuries, it would appear. Since the day, perhaps, when she saw me fall to traitors' swords and thought that I was dead. Wandering the earth. Seeking to have a home again, and human contact. . . in, as I say, some kind of halfway state. Able to eat the food of breathing humans, to face the sun without distress, to find a kind of sleep anywhere on earth. But able to find real rest nowhere at all. They are mad, and they are outcasts from both worlds, and I do not know how many of them there are who wander the earth tonight. Too much happens to them in their breathing lives, and madness supervenes. Too much happened to me, but I was—very strong. Yes, very strong."

Impulsively Joe put a hand on the arm of the man, the human being, who rode in the seat beside him.

Thorn looked at him. "It was she, though." He paused. "I am almost sure."

Got questions? We've got answers at
BAEN'S BAR!

Here's what some of our members have to say:

"Ever wanted to get involved in a newsgroup but were frightened off by rude know-it-alls? Stop by Baen's Bar. Our know-it-alls are the friendly, helpful type—and some write the hottest SF around."
> —**Melody L** *melodyl@ccnmail.com*

"Baen's Bar . . . where you just might find people who understand what you are talking about!"
> —**Tom Perry** *perry@airswitch.net*

"Lots of gentle teasing and numerous puns, mixed with various recipes for food and fun."
> —**Ginger Tansey** *makautz@prodigy.net*

"Join the fun at Baen's Bar, where you can discuss the latest in books, Treecat Sign Language, ramifications of cloning, how military uniforms have changed, help an author do research, fuss about differences between American and European measurements—and top it off with being able to talk to the people who write and publish what you love."
> —**Sun Shadow** *sun2shadow@hotmail.com*

"Thanks for a lovely first year at the Bar, where the only thing that's been intoxicating is conversation."
> —**Al Jorgensen** *awjorgen@wolf.co.net*

 Join BAEN'S BAR at
WWW.BAEN.COM
"Bring your brain!"